TONY
THE CHAPTE
AT THE START
CHANGE IT.
READ CHAPTER 2 FIRST THEN 3 THEN 1
THEN CARRY ON AS NORMAL FROM 4.

16

# A Funny Few Days

by

Andrew Clive Johnson

SO READ IT,
2, 3, 1, 4 THEN CARRY ON AS
NORMAL FROM 5.
HOPE YOU ENJOY IT!
ANDREW JOHNSON
MAY 2020.

First published 2020

This novel is a work of fiction. Names, characters, places and incidents are used fictiously or are products of the author's imagination. Any resemblance to actual events or persons, living or dead, is unintentional on the author's part. I thank you.

ISBN 9 7986 1896 2742

This is for my wife Aileen and my two sons Matthew and Richard. Thank you for putting up with me!

# Chapters

Hit and Run

Honey is sweeter than beef dripping

Plenty more fish in the sea

Stepping on snakes looking for ladders

A draught or fresh air?

Live and let live

Bustle in the hedgerow

What goes around comes around

Better late than never

Whatever trouble there is will eventually blow over

# Chapter One

## It is an ill wind that blows no good

Sam wasn't one of his exceptional countrymen. He was never going to see clearly how a gorge could be crossed by a bridge or have the bravery to risk blowing himself up mixing different compounds or risk all that he owned and his reputation starting a factory. That was for an exceptional individual to do. Sam wasn't an exceptional individual. He was an ordinary middle-aged bookkeeper who lived in London.

It was early morning and he was asleep in his chair in his study. It had been another late night and the small climb to his bedroom had been put off by the effort of it all. How much effort he routinely put in could be gauged by a large canvas he'd commissioned on the wall above his desk. A stern man's face unflinchingly stared out over him with an accusatory finger pointing out. Below the finger in large letters was written:

DO NOT LET THE PENNY DROP!

The noise of his maid's footsteps coming up the wooden stairs outside the door woke him. She knocked for permission to enter. He rubbed his eyes and slapped his lips to remove the dryness in his mouth.

"Come in," he said rather hoarsely.

The door opened and in stepped a stupendously shapen maid in her early twenties. Her hair was hidden beneath a brown bonnet which made her eyes which were the colour of forget-me-not flowers seem too large for her head. But the bigger the better. They were beautiful and so was she. The drab cloth of her dress wrapped around her was as pleasing to the eye as silk hung from a lesser woman. She held a tray which had upon it a bowl of steaming soup and some crusty slices of bread. "Good morning sir. Your soup is ready."

She put down the tray at a small eating table. Sam wouldn't eat at his desk as soup and ledgers had proved to be an unhappy mix in the past. She turned and gave him a smile that could probably melt ice from a January windowpane. She was obviously devoted to her employer.

"Thank you Natalie. Did you and Cook sleep well? It was hot last night." He was friendly but not familiar.

"Yes thank you sir. We took it in turns to hold the window open through the night. We'll have the last laugh on that thievin' chippie yet!"

"That's the spirit girl!" replied Sam proudly. "I don't spend my time chasing every last waif and stray down dark alleys and scary places only to have some chippie attempt to use softwood when the price quoted had clearly indicated hardwood would be used!"

"Well that's why you have a reputation as one of the best bookkeepers in London sir!"

Sam gave a little "nonsense girl" shake of the head but you could tell he agreed. "You don't think of me as a bully then?" he asked smiling.

Natalie abruptly straightened stung by such a thing. "You leave the waifs alone then they become pickpockets, then burglars, then highwaymen, then bank robbers and then even the crown jewels aren't safe and neither is the realm! No you chase them all down and you put them in their proper place!"

"Oh sweet kind innocent Natalie. You'd make an excellent bookkeeper if ever society became stupid enough to allow such a thing."

"No fear sir!" said Natalie shaking her pretty head at such an absurdity. "You enjoy your soup whilst I scrub the bedroom floors."

"Oh that's a noisy job I don't like," tutted Sam looking up at the ceiling as she turned to leave.

Then as though she had been dying to do it all along she hitched up her simple brown dress to reveal cloth pads strapped to her knees. "So they won't knock on the floorboards!"

Such a beautiful sight first thing in the morning would have pleased most men but Sam clapped his hands for a different reason. He recognised the material. It had been a decrepit cushion that he had reluctantly thrown out last week. He had no doubt that his resourceful maid could probably find something useful to do with his toe clippings.

"Oh Natalie what would I do without you?" he said happily.

She was beaming as she left the room.

It was far truer than his beautiful maid realised. He was in no doubt that his maid Natalie had become indispensable to him. It wasn't the tiny detail of blowing on his soup – he could do that, it wasn't the bigger thing of keeping his house spotless with all the noise of a shadow – there were lots of good maids in London, it wasn't the unquestioning loyalty that couldn't be bought – his mother could still provide that. What Natalie had was something he had never encountered before: he had an excellent memory but it was merely a duck pond compared to the lake Natalie rowed upon. A pebble thrown into its deep waters didn't disappear but surfaced around the shoreline and in her little boat any time she wished she could find it. He couldn't be sure how he'd first noticed or indeed when he first started making use of it but now he knew he couldn't function at the level he did without her. Not that she knew this. She wouldn't have guessed and Sam had no need to tell her.

He leant over the bowl to take in a deep sniff as this would tell him what day of the week it was. That he had been called "Structured Sam" (amongst other things) had been remarkably perceptive of his classmates at school. It was carrot so that meant it was Wednesday. He knew what he had to do this Wednesday but would summon Natalie to make sure after finishing his soup. But as he began wheeling over his chair to the eating table something very queer happened. A pane of glass in the window violently vomited up a small round object that skittered across his study floor trying to avoid the mess it had caused until it came to rest perfectly at his feet. Process driven by nature it would have to be something momentous to visibly shock him. Calmly he looked to the window and then slowly to the object giving it a good stare. It appeared to be a piece of paper wrapped around a stone. It shouldn't be there but there it was. He scooped it up with the spoon and tipped it into his hand.

"Well I'm sure this isn't meant for the soup," he said putting down the spoon.

Sudden thunderous footsteps on the stairs outside were quickly followed by an urgent knock at the door. "Sir! Sir! Are you alright?" demanded Natalie.

He was about to call her in when he stopped himself. This could either be the chippie being a prat or something best kept secret for the moment. The possibility of being messed about by a bloody chippie suddenly irritated him. "On with your chores Natalie!" he ordered. "Do not disturb me again unless I call you!"

There was a very reluctant "yes sir" from the other side of the door then Natalie's more composed steps down the stairs. Sam unfurled the note:

Is that you Sam? Come to the window!

Sam rubbed his chin thoughtfully whilst he looked at the note. It couldn't be the chippie. He doubted that berk could write at all let alone so neatly. He didn't believe he had any enemies - he had upset quite a few people by forcing them to act correctly in the past - but he didn't believe he had upset any one enough to wish him harm. So was it likely someone wanted him at the window to take a pop at him? The answer was no. But recently with the assistance of Natalie he had been able to venture out into deeper water where the bigger fish swam. It had been more lucrative waters but he was aware it was where you were more likely to find sharks. Fish that very often took a bite first and asked questions later. But they were also the first to smell the blood of a whalekill. Did they keep it to themselves by communicating with each other in such a way? He looked down at the note questioningly and then at the hole it had made in his window. He smiled as the thought occurred to him he was literally looking at his window of opportunity. He had been recently introduced to an important man that would probably behave like this. My God the man had even had the black eyes of a shark! Sam knew he was dangerous but life changing opportunities for him had been alluded to. Was this the day he took up or walked away from his big opportunity? A man's big opportunity was never going to be clearly labelled and there was always the risk of a fool's errand. Was he brave enough to swim further out in the company of a known shark?

He rose slowly out of his chair not sure what he would do. He would either skulk out of his study or make the few steps across to his window and stand there with his hands proudly on his hips – which is what he found himself doing.

Rather disappointingly he was greeted by a drowsy Buckingham Street yawning up at him. Nothing appeared to move and there was definitely no golden archer about to release a golden arrow in his direction. There was the wife of that new couple brushing her hair in an upstairs window. She didn't appear to have any clothes on but she had struck Sam as dreadfully vulgar when they had moved in and he wasn't surprised it was the sort of thing she would do. Her husband seemed even worse. It wouldn't surprise Sam to learn he had made a fortune selling steak and kidney pies with no kidney but a breed of South American fly substituted instead. Employing a slave army of Peruvian girls pulling the legs off the damned things boiling them up and sending them over to his bakery as kidneys. Sam was considering how much gravy it might take in each pie to get away with such a thing when the husband suddenly appeared next to his wife. Regarding him Sam had no doubt he was capable of it. He had the wild hairy face that had obviously seen more moonlight than sunlight. "I'm glad you're over there," thought Sam giving him a neighbourly wave before looking away disinterested.

After some time his arms fell involuntarily to his sides. With more shadow than light in the street below he was forced to return to his desk none the wiser as to whom sort his presence. Had he been too slow in getting up? But no sooner had the material of his breeches touched the leather of his chair than there was another shattering of glass. This time he bounded to the window.

"If this *is* the chippie being a prat!" he cursed at Buckingham Street's indifferent acquiescence.

He looked around for a second ball of paper and found it in almost exactly the same place the first had come to rest. He took out the stone and smoothed out the note:

*Do not waste time gawping out of the window! My master wants a word NOT a pair of curtains! Be prepared for a very important message shortly!*

Sam's chair was expensive. It was a sound investment. He spent many hours in it. It had useful features like the ability to swivel which he used now to face the window. It also had the ability to recline which much to his surprise at the length of his wait he found using. It also had a little pocket at the side in which he kept the current book he was reading. He touched the spine then pulled his fingers away as though it were hot. It wouldn't do to get distracted. Then as he got bored waiting he had removed it but not opened it then put it back. Finally, at such a protracted wait he took it out and opened it asking the window, "who's wasting bloody time now?"

The pitiful window was still sulking at having two of its teeth knocked out and refused to answer.

"This is stupid!" said Sam immediately snapping the book shut and getting out of his chair. "I've got real work to do!" He decided to "gawp" out of the window in spite of what he'd been told.

He had barely got there when his world was stopped by a terrific pain, a blinding flash of red mist and a cold, clammy blanket seeming irresistible under its vile weight trying to bundle him into darkness.

"IT IS the bloody chippie!" he cursed through gritted teeth as he stumbled clutching at his forehead which even through the painful mist felt frighteningly wet. He was just able to stagger back and fall heavily into his chair. For a few seconds he thought he could push the blanket back but then some nanny from hell entered the room tucking him in leaving him in no doubt that it was to be "night night little Sammie."

On the floor lay the head of a garden gnome still smiling despite being removed from its body, roughly wrapped in a note and hurled at its owner as soon as he had appeared at the window. The note lay slowly unfurling next to gnome's head. Within a few seconds most of it could be read:

Throwing notes through windows seems a bit daft to me but if that's how you do it around here so be it. Next time I find a visitor of yours skulking outside my front door I won't just ask him to leave at the point of a gun I will actually blow his head off! I may be a doctor but I'm not actually known for my patience! Furthermore my wife prefers to get ready in the morning without some pervert from across the street watching her do it! Understand you

# CHAPTER 2

## The Devil makes work for idle hands

Anyone who understands what a joy it is to behold something made well would weep to see what had been done in the drawing room of Lord Ecin's country estate. A beautiful mahogany dining table had been buried beneath a ton of dirt and lots of broccoli to resemble a "realistic battlefield". To stop all this mess falling off planks of roughly sawn wood had been nailed around all the edges except in one corner. Here there was a large grandfather clock filling the gap where they'd run out of planking. It looked out of place and they hadn't been happy with it until Lord Tig had smashed the case glass filled it with rocks and told the other two it was now the "escarpment." The other two being Lord Ecin and Lord Dratsab.

The three Lords were too old to be getting up to such mischief but they were all bachelors. It appeared that even the prospect of becoming a Lady had not been enough for a sensible woman to put up with any of them yet. Not that they seemed to care in the slightest. Lord Ecin was positively jiggling with anticipated glee at one corner of the table holding out a wooden box. Lord Dratsab and Lord Tig held out similar boxes at their own corners. Only the sorry looking grandfather clock in the fourth corner looked unhappy.

Looking way too smug Lord Dratsab shouted out, "Three two one!"

The three of them eagerly tipped out the contents of their boxes onto the "battlefield". Out spilled from each box about twenty or so what had been white mice. I say had been because they had all been dipped in paint. Lord Ecin's in red, Lord Tig's in blue and Lord Dratsab's in black. But clearly Lord Ecin had done it too early. Most of his mice fell out stiff unable to move in a thick coat of dry crusty red paint. Much to Lord Tig's and Lord Dratsab's amusement.

After they had finished laughing at Lord Ecin's poor start Lord Dratsab shouted across the table, "I bet you two have fed yours!"

"Of course," replied Lord Ecin looking down at his army wondering if he could rub the paint off with his fingers but not wanting to touch them when they looked like that.

"I haven't fed mine for a week!" said Lord Dratsab looking down proudly at his black warriors.

"Oh I see," said Lord Tig understanding now, "so when you said I should dip mine in olive oil and roll them in sugar for an armour coating that was for your benefit not mine?"

Lord Dratsab clapped his hands laughing deliciously, "Did you?"

Lord Tig widened his eyes. "No! For the last week mine have been on a strict diet of mice painted black!"

Lord Dratsab no longer looked smug.

But he needn't have worried. To their surprise and disappointment the mice that could actually move (all of them had used far too much paint) seemed more interested in exploring the perimeter of the table or munching on the broccoli rather than ripping each other apart.

After a few minutes of nothing much Lord Tig shook his head, "I told you it wouldn't work."

"Come on Tiggy. It's not that bad. So we've ruined Ecin's table – but you don't mind do you Ecin?"

"And his clock!" said Lord Tig pointing at it.

Lord Dratsab gave a little harrumph walking away, "well that was nothing to do with me."

Lord Tig shook his head at Lord Dratsab but turned to Lord Ecin. "I'll let you have a clock of mine for a good price."

"Well it was worth a try," said Lord Ecin looking terribly disappointed. "I'll ask a maid to bring in some cats. They can tidy this mess up."

"That's a good idea!" said Lord Tig. "Either of you fancy a little wager on which colour they'll eat first?"

"I'm not doing it now," said Lord Ecin coming away from the table.

"You interested Dratsabby?" asked Lord Tig.

Lord Dratsab was already sitting at one of the three large comfortable leather chairs by the fire pouring himself a drink. "Sit down gentlemen. I've something to ask you both."

Lord Ecin and Lord Tig came over and sat down as instructed.

"How many people do you have working for you Tiggy?" asked Lord Dratsab

"In service or at the mines?"

"In service."

"Oh I don't know. About four hundred. Why?"

"And you Ecin. How many do you have?"

Lord Ecin looked warily at Lord Dratsab and then at Lord Tig almost asking if it would be wise to answer. Lord Tig gave him a very discrete little nod. "I don't know exactly. Six hundred at a guess."

"This is a big estate Ecin but if it's taking you six hundred people to run it you need to look at your management," said Lord Tig reaching for the decanter.

"Oh I don't know. Four hundred then?" suggested Lord Ecin.

"Four hundred?" said Lord Tig sitting back with his drink. "You only said that because I did!"

Lord Ecin ignored him looking at Lord Dratsab. "If it's important I can find out exactly but why would you want to know?"

"Because my dear boy I have three hundred. So why are we messing about with painted mice when we easily have over a thousand people to play with?"

"You can't play war with your servants!" laughed Lord Tig nervously.

"Why not?" demanded Lord Dratsab.

"How would any work get done?" asked Lord Tig.

"I'm not saying all the time just now and again."

Lord Ecin looked concerned. "People would get killed. We can't play soldiers with real people.".

"Politicians do it all the time," replied Lord Dratsab coolly.

Lord Ecin now looked distinctly uncomfortable as well.

"Ecin is right," said Lord Tig putting a hand on Lord Dratsab's knee, "I can see where you're coming from but if war hasn't been declared then there's a word for getting men killed – and that word is – MURDER!"

"Does seem a strange concept doesn't it - one day taking a man's life is legal and the next it's not just because some men decide if we're at war or not?" said Lord Ecin looking into the flames of the fire.

Lord Dratsab and Lord Tig totally ignored him.

"Obviously I'm not suggesting anybody should really snuff it!" said Lord Dratsab moving his leg so Lord Tig had to remove his hand.

"We'll just have to go back to playing with the toy ones," said Lord Tig shrugging his shoulders.

"But we got so bored with that!" spat Lord Dratsab. "There's just got to be a way!"

There was an uncomfortable silence which Lord Ecin didn't like so decided to break, "I'd like a drink too please Tig."

"You don't drink at this time. It's only -"

"That's it!" said Lord Dratsab jumping out of his chair. "What if we made it a drinking contest?"

"What?" asked Lord Tig looking up at him incredulously.

But Lord Ecin had jumped up too clasping his arms firmly around Lord Dratsab. "We could have an army each! And the idea is to get the other army drunk before they get yours drunk! There could be tactics! We could develop new drink weapons! Choose how and when to deploy them! If we run out of time there could be a headcount of those still standing to decide the winner. No one could get hurt!"

"Yes!Yes!Yes!" Lord Dratsab was nodding then he stopped as something amazing occurred to him - "We could have night battles! Day battles! River battles with real boats! And we could dress the buggers up in uniforms or keep it simple with a coloured hat!"

"No real uniforms! Real uniforms! I'll pay!" said Lord Ecin unclasping himself and throwing his hands in the air with excitement.

"There would have to be some ground rules," said Lord Tig deciding now to calmly join in. "If someone collapsed but then vomited and recovered. Would they be allowed back in for instance?"

"Yes," said Lord Dratsab eagerly nodding, "we'll do it properly with proper rules!"

"Ah," said Lord Tig suddenly tutting, "what about the women? Do we use the women? Two thirds of our service staff must be women.

I'm sure most of mine can drink more than the men but we don't want it getting bawdy."

Lord Ecin sat down suddenly stung. "I don't think it would be nice to use the women. They don't go to real war."

"They might if the worst thing that could happen to them was a bad hangover the next day!" said Lord Dratsab almost jumping on him with excitement. "We'll have a think about it! Promise! Now send for some paper and pens! We've got a lot of planning to do today! And just imagine – not one of us has a wife to stop us doing this!"

They spent the rest of the day deciding on rules and eagerly planning for the first time. Or as the event soon became known: Operation Legless.

Operation Legless took place a few weeks later. So none of their estates would grind to a complete halt they had decided to leave the women out of it. They might add them in the future it all depended on how today went. All in all they had about six hundred gardeners, stablelads, grooms, chimney sweeps, window cleaners, manservants, and general dog's bodies to play with. The three armies (the three Lords thought this a stroke of genius on their part) would each defend a flag. A flag could only be removed when there was no-one left sober to defend it. Absolutely no force was allowed. If there was anyone at the flag still conscious even if they were slurring then they had to be made completely incapable **BY DRINK ONLY** before the flag could be taken.

Lord Dratsab's army were defending a red flag by the lake and wore red berets. Lord Tig's men were bedded in a coppice behind the main house defending a blue flag and wore blue berets. Lord Ecin's men because it was his estate they were using were in the large courtyard of the main house. For such a defensive advantage the other two lords had insisted he defend a white flag and his men wear pink berets. Lord Ecin didn't mind because he had no idea what a white flag symbolised and thought the pink berets rather "jolly". In reality it was Lord Dratsab and Lord Tig being petty when Lord Ecin refused to pay for the uniforms as he'd said he would. In his defence the other two lords had escalated the uniform requirements to the point that every man was to be issued with an imitation firearm made out of solid silver. The fact all said firearms were to be handed over to the winning Lord as "mementos" finally ringing alarm bells in Lord Ecin's mind.

Unusually for a battle the three "Field Marshalls" were allowed to wander freely amongst enemy camps. This was for verification that the rules (rudimentary as they were at this stage) were being followed and to lead a charge. Only three charges each were allowed in the whole game so getting them right was important. There were several independent adjudicators whose word would be considered in any disputes. Lord Dratsab and Lord Tig had wanted to call them spies but Lord Ecin said that just sounded nasty so they agreed to call them barmaids because that's what they were from Lord Ecin's local pub: The White Hart. Who better to recognise when a man was drunk than a barmaid? Lord Dratsab and Lord Tig knew it wouldn't have occurred to Lord Ecin to bribe them like they would have done so they let him have them.

It was a lovely day for Operation Legless and all over the estate could be heard the sound of men whistling happily in their work.

Lord Dratsab's red army were setting up their trestle tables by the lake and heaving onto them large wooden barrels. Some had **BEER** burnt into the wood in black lettering, others **CIDER**, and then some smaller barrels labelled **KABOOM**. This was a concoction Lord Dratsab and his Vintner had developed very quickly. The staff that had proven the most resistant when exposed to **KABOOM** formed the special forces of his army. He reckoned he had about fifty such men whom he considered his Whisky Men (Whisky was the principal ingredient of **KABOOM** but that was a secret) and they had a large **W** embroidered on their hats. They hadn't been told why because Lord Dratsab didn't want them feeling special or important. That wasn't how he managed his staff. It proved unfortunate when the battle was raging when their own comrades as well as enemy soldiers became very vociferous in what they thought the **W** stood for. There was a definite consensus but nobody thought it stood for whisky!

The same barrels of beer and cider (standard issue) were in the other two camps but no secret weapon from either of the other two lords. Lord Tig had put his faith in copious bottles of Scotch glinting like long golden hand grenades in the low light of the coppice. Lord Ecin was relying on sheer weight of numbers. There were now more bottles of wine in his courtyard than in his cellar! But he wanted his men to enjoy it as much as he hoped to. Soon everyone was ready and waiting expectantly for the noon start.

Just before noon the three lords assembled on the roof of the west tower. Lord Ecin had a surprise for them - a real cannon! They had intended to blow a hunting horn but this was much better! Until Lord Dratsab found out there was no ball in it just powder. When the other two weren't looking he poured a bottle of gin down the muzzle for good luck.

At noon Lord Ecin took position behind the cannon with his hand shaking with excitement holding the smouldering lighter.

Lord Tig turned to see Lord Dratsab cowering so asked him, "what are you doing?"

"The wind's bloody changed! Get down!"

It was how the two of them avoided the worst of the fireball that engulfed the roof of the west tower when Lord Ecin lit the cannon.

"Flying Frog Swarm! How much powder did you put in there?" demanded Lord Dratsab when the smoke had cleared.

Lord Ecin's blackened smouldering hair stood on end, his face and hands were all sooty, his jacket had been blown off, and his shirt and trousers were all ripped. BUT - his teeth looked amazing!

"That was BRILLIANT!" he gasped.

"Well he who smokes with a farty dog on his lap gets what he deserves! Come on Tiggy we've got armies to muster!"

They both scuttled off down the stone staircase.

Lord Ecin feeling more alive than he could ever remember stayed to watch the activity by the lake. Lord Dratsab's men formed orderly queues at the trestle tables each holding an empty glass. The idea was the first man in line filled his glass and walked off towards a large blackboard with a barmaid standing next to it. When he had drunk his drink to her satisfaction she would make a cross on the blackboard and he could join the back of a queue for another. Lord Ecin watched them quickly get the hang of it. There was a blackboard for each camp and it was the same for all of them – each army had to consume a minimum of one thousand pints of beer or cider in their own camp before a charge could be made. That was five pints each on average. Whether this was too small or too large an amount to begin with only time would tell.

Lord Ecin watched the red army fascinated. Way too long before it occurred to him he should check on his own men in the courtyard below.

"Take it steady! Slow and steady wins the race! Keep those berets on straight! Big Beryl how many crosses?" he shouted down.

"Over three hundred me Lord!" Big Beryl the barmaid shouted up.

As she had he inhaled a bit of burnt hair making him cough and he had not heard her clearly.

"Three's a bit disappointing," he said quietly to himself. "Three in as many minutes! That's wonderful! Slow and steady wins the day! Keep it up men!" he shouted down.

Next to the barmaid stood Lord Ecin's wise old butler. He thought the whole thing preposterous and the result of the bad influence upon his master exerted by Lord Dratsab and Lord Tig. "He's so excited he doesn't realise it's been half an hour already and he thinks you said three not three hundred which is far too much at this stage," he said to her. But she was too busy chalking crosses on her blackboard to reply to him.

Lord Ecin watched as Lord Dratsab moved  amongst his men waving his arms in the air chanting, "Quoff! Quoff! Quoff!" His barmaid was struggling to keep up. The fool was rushing it! At this rate his raggedy lines of men had more chance of falling in the lake than making their first charge. He decided he could afford to pay a visit to Lord Tig's camp but was suddenly dumbfounded by the sight of about forty ginger-haired men charging the red army's right flank. His astonishment that Lord Tig had been able to mount a charge so soon was quickly replaced with aghast. The men were not wearing their blue berets or anything else for that matter! Everything was jiggling about in a horrible ginger way. And most of them seemed hell bent on tossing forward small trees they'd grubbed up from his coppice! It was no wonder most of Lord Dratsab's men were backing off. This looked too much like force! He was going out there to remind everyone of the rules!

Down below when he reached his confused and noisy courtyard he called for his horse only to be informed, amongst much giggling derision, that none of his stable lads were capable of doing it. All eight of them were lightweights and were now unconscious in the hay barn.

"Well how could they get so drunk on three beers?" he wanted to know.

His wise old butler stepped forward to point him in the direction of the blackboard. It was festooned with so many crosses it was no longer a blackboard but a whiteboard. Next to it Big Beryl was laughing holding a large glass of wine enjoying the amorous advances of one of the window cleaners called Tim the Tickler.

"May I please take charge my Lordship?" begged his wise old butler. "Look at you. Look around you. Surely this isn't what you wanted."

"War is hell!" snapped Lord Ecin at his butler. "All of you berets on straight! Do what you can until I get back!"

Those that heard him raised their glasses happily. Many of them patting him on the back as he passed through which would have been unthinkable behaviour under normal circumstances.

When he finally made it to the lake he was in for a great shock. The naked men were strewn around like an explosion in a sausage factory.

He wondered through the carnage of white, ginger and vomit. Only one of them seemed conscious. The pale naked ginger haired top and middle man lay on his back muttering to the sky. "Bloody stuped...eek! It wu' on tha bloody label Hen...eek! Kaboom! And ye still drank it...eek!"

He suddenly focussed at the blackened man with the spiky hair and clothes in shreds standing over him, "Tel' me tha' truth Hen. De I luk asba' as yu?"

Lord Ecin didn't have the opportunity to answer him as he suddenly stiffened then slipped away...snoring loudly like the others.

"Tiggy will have to do better than that!" It was Lord Dratsab emerging from his men.

"Where are they from?" asked Lord Ecin looking around horrified.

"Tiggy's plantation in the West Indies! Where do you think? It's his place in Dumfries. I thought he might. Silly sods thought it was the Kaboom. But it's when you mix it with the sherry chocolate biscuits it does the real damage." Lord Dratsab picked up an empty tray and tossed it at Lord Ecin's feet. "Scots have got a sweet tooth. I'm telling you Ecin - I've thought of everything! Give it up now!"

Lord Ecin didn't know what to say or do just then but he wasn't going to give up.

"Booby Betty how many crosses on my board?" asked Lord Dratsab swaggeringly.

"Fifteen hundred and twenty two King Optic!" replied the most attractive of the White Hart's barmaids.

"King Optic?" asked Lord Ecin suddenly wanting to laugh but stifling it.

"I also see everything! Now my wonderful red army gather up the barrels of Kaboom and sherry chocolate biscuits because we're going for a stroll in the woods!" A great cheer went up from his men. "Ecin! That's your cue to get out of my way!"

"I've been having second thoughts about some of the rules," said Lord Ecin.

"What? Can't hear you! Come on you stout red beret men of incapable inebriation! Cheer louder! King Optic can taste victory!"

Lord Ecin knew it was useless to protest. They had all agreed to see it through until the end. Nightfall or a fatality were the only stoppers. He turned towards the house hoping the delay in his men's drinking would strengthen them for later when Lord Dratsab made his charge. He had no doubt Lord Tig had shot his bolt and it was the red army whom he had to prepare for.

Lord Ecin's grandfather who'd instigated the family fortune had built at great expense a water feature in the centre of the rose garden as a 60th birthday present for his wife. It had given much pleasure and pride to the family ever since. It was a sign of how much they had loved each other and was easily as beautiful as some of the ones found in Rome. All of the most precious of Lord Ecin's childhood memories of his grandfather involved the rose garden and the water feature. His grandfather always seemed eager to pass on what he had learned about life when they had strolled hand in hand through the roses or dipped their feet in the cool water on summer evenings. His grandfather always began with, "now the men are alone we can talk," which always made him feel very grown-up and important. He missed his grandfather in a way he never missed his father and the water feature in the rose garden was always the place his feet took him when his mind didn't know where to turn.

"So Lord Dratsab and his men have finally ordained to join us," said Lord Tig opening his arms.

"That's confident talk considering your best men are lying unconscious by the lake," replied Lord Dratsab.

"Best men? *Really?* - Busty Beatrice how many crosses are on my blackboard?"

"Hold on Tiggy - why are all these beer dispensers from the White Hart incredibly chesty?"

"Answer our adversary first Busty Beatrice then my question if you please."

"No girl's gotta a right to work unless she's got somehat' up top to give! - Thousand crosses General."

Lord Tig sneered haughtily. "I think the beer and the food is rubbish but you will get a right eyeful. However, more importantly - how many of those are my *brave bonnie lads* responsible for?"

"All of them General."

"All of them!" repeated Lord Dratsab unable to hide his surprise.

"So you can confirm none of my men here have touched a drop?"

"Barmaid's honour," said Busty Beatrice crossing her ample chest, "that's the truth or you can shove it up -"

"Yes thank you Busty Beatrice!" shouted Lord Tig grimacing.

"Well my men have won fifteen hundred and twenty two crosses," said Lord Dratsab looking behind him by way of introducing them.

"Five hundred and twenty two more than they needed to. I wonder if you will come to regret that *King Optic*," taunted Lord Tig.

There was a titter at his title amongst Tiggy's men which Lord Dratsab didn't like. "King Optic sees all of your demise!" he said defiantly. "Now hand over your flag or piss off!"

Lord Tig looked with pride along the front line of his men standing shoulder to shoulder behind him with their blue berets all straight and correct. He turned defiantly to face Lord Dratsab. "Piss Off!"

It was the proper manner in which to begin and a great cheer went up from both sides.

Ten of Lord Tig's men stepped forward with three tables which they put in line to form one long one. Then they lined up behind it and took out from their pockets a bottle of scotch each and two tumblers. Acting in unison it was obvious they had been drilling. Lord Dratsab picked ten men without a W on their berets and ordered them to stand at the table opposite Lord Tig's men.

When all seemed ready Lord Tig issued the order, "Fire!"

His ten men in perfect unison opened their bottle, filled the two tumblers, pushed one forwards, took up the other, raised it in salute and then downed the contents in one go. Its precision seemed quite sinister and unnerving.

"Return Fire!" ordered Lord Dratsab.

His men picked up their tumblers and downed the contents. Two immediately doubled over coughing and spluttering.

"Stand firm!" ordered Lord Dratsab. They straightened themselves with some difficulty.

"Fire!" ordered Lord Tig. His ten men cheered on by their comrades went through their drill again perfectly. It may have been water to them for all the effect it had.

"Return Fire!" ordered Lord Dratsab. His men picked up their tumblers and swallowed the contents but this time the two coughers couldn't control it.

"Hats Off! Hats Off! Hats Off!" chanted Lord Tig's men.

Lord Dratsab strode over to the table and tore the berets off the unfortunate pair. A great cheer rose from Lord Tig's men. They two skulked off still coughing to be replaced by two others. Lord Dratsab was disappointed but not too concerned because at this stage he was merely testing the defences and using expendable forces.

"Fire!" ordered Lord Tig. None of his men faltered.

"Return Fire!" ordered Lord Dratsab. This time two of his men fell forward across the table. Their berets were unceremoniously torn off and they were dragged away to be replaced.

"Fire!" ordered Lord Tig. This time one of his men dropped to the ground as though his spine had suddenly been removed. Lord Tig was swiftly over to tear off his beret and everyone heard what he spat at the man. "Call yourself a Geordie? You're being replaced with a Scotsman!"

An unhappy murmur went through Lord Tig's men and Lord Dratsab saw his chance.

"Fall back! W Men Kaboom and Sherry Chocolate Biscuits!"

His men staggered away from the table to be replaced by ten with W's on their berets each plonking down a barrel of Kaboom and a big tray of sherry chocolate biscuits. They couldn't just launch straight into the Kaboom because Lord Tig's men had finished their tumblers and Lord Dratsab's previous men hadn't.

"Defuse!" ordered Lord Dratsab. His W men heartily gulped down the tumblers and now it was his turn to feel pride in his men and to know he had now struck discourse into the enemy. The line of Tiggy's men were positively itching to get their hands on those sherry chocolate biscuits.

"Fire!" ordered Lord Dratsab

His W men filled the enemy's tumblers with Kaboom then pushed forward a tray. Every one of Lord Tig's men greedily gorged themselves on the sherry chocolate biscuits before touching the tumblers of Kaboom. But when they did the effect was almost instantaneous. Down six of the men went just like those by the lake.

"Hey what's going on?" demanded Lord Tig. "Nobody said anything about nibbles!"

"They don't have to eat them! Now replace six of your men and get on with it!" shouted Lord Dratsab.

Lord Tig wasn't happy but had the six men replaced.

"Do not eat the biscuits!" he ordered when they were all ready.

His men ignored him professing they were "starving" even having seen what would happen. Greedily and noisily cramming in the sherry chocolate biscuits as Lord Dratsab's men casually sipped their tumblers of Kaboom. Then they drank the tumblers of Kaboom and it was goodnight more or less straightaway for most of them. Those that survived it first time couldn't resist a second helping of biscuits. And they couldn't survive that.

But Lord Dratsab ran out of sherry chocolate biscuits! How he cursed at the news. Why hadn't they brought more trays of them? Why hadn't anybody thought to make more? Without the biscuit accompaniment Kaboom was far less effective against Tiggy's men. Sure it was still a good contest. Some really amazing drinking and some fine banter going on but not the breakthrough he required.

Then suddenly Lord Tig shouted, "Release Mons Meg!"

A huge ginger bear of a man wearing a kilt the size of a tent strode out of the trees. How they had kept something so big hidden seemed impossible. As a man caught sight of him he stopped whatever he was doing and just stared. Mons Meg yanked the blue flag out of the ground and tucked it into his enormous jacket so the material fluttered above his great head. Then he strode across to the line of tables and the current skirmish. He put a great paw on the closest of Lord Dratsab's men and easily spun him around. Then with both hands he lifted his kilt as high as he could for all to see what he had underneath. Bottle upon bottle of scotch tied around his waist like a great bunch of golden glass grapes. He reached in and pulled one out letting his kilt fall. He proffered the bottle in a great wide arc then abruptly bit off the top and poured the contents into the great ginger hedgerow covering his face. Finally, tossing the empty bottle aside he burped more loudly than the cannon had been.

"Too far Tiggy!" condemned Lord Dratsab. "That's definitely too far!"

"I thought you might be here my Lordship."

"Well you know me better than anyone - now," said Lord Ecin looking up from the bench forlornly. He had been fingering a single rose in his blackened hands.

His wise old butler hated to see him like this. "My Lordship if I may be so bold. I have thought this a -" he searched for a less derogatory term than had first come to mind, "foolish endeavour from the start."

"I'm inclined to agree now," said Lord Ecin heavily. He stared straight ahead. His eyes two boiled eggs on a burnt piece of toast. Though his teeth still looked amazing.

"But may I ask if it is important to you my Lordship? Or just a bit of fun to be forgotten about in a few weeks?"

The boiled eggs rolled around on the burnt toast. "I don't think I'll ever live this down!"

"I don't think you should my Lordship," said Resourceful quietly. From behind his back he produced a cloth sack and tipped out five or six cotton sausages with ginger fur on the ends. He gave the sack a further shake and out fell several very long red beards. "I pulled these off the bodies by the lake."

Lord Ecin picked up a cotton sausage turned it over and brought it up about to give it a sniff.

"My Lordship! It's a gentleman's false willy!" cried out his wise old butler.

Lord Ecin threw it away as though it had suddenly bitten him.

"You see what this means?"

"Lord Tig is cheating as usual," said Lord Ecin flatly, "using women when we said we wouldn't."

"My Lordship it allows us some leeway if you'll permit it."

"What are you saying Resourceful? Cheat to win? Be as bad as him? What's the point of that?" exclaimed Lord Ecin.

"My Lordship, I'd prefer to think of it as responding to changing events rather than just giving up. So I respectfully ask you – would you like me to help you win this? Or shall I begin clearing up the mess?" He waited obediently for the answer.

"It's useless with no men," lamented Lord Ecin eventually.

"Your men await you in the courtyard. They have not touched a drop since you left. I've had them eating pork scratchings and most of them are almost sober."

"Really?" said Lord Ecin surprised. "But Lord Dratsab has a wonder weapon called Kaboom! And sherry chocolate biscuits!"

"His lordship ran out of both and has been roundly routed by Lord Tig." His wise old butler thought it prudent to make no mention of Mons Meg at this stage. "Lord Tig believes all he has to do now is wait and your ineffectual leadership will allow him to stroll over unopposed."

"So I'm supposed  to just roll over and take it am I?" asked Lord Ecin angrily.

"From a cheat," said his wise old butler motioning towards the very long red beards and false willies lying at their feet.

"Cheating's intolerable!" spat Lord Ecin. But he still didn't seem ready to rise from his bench.

His wise old butler continued to do his duty. "My Lordship, the blood that built this house, this rose garden, this water feature, placed this bench facing east to watch the rising sun - it flows in your veins too! Your grandfather cut off the hands of a man he caught cheating at cards. What would he have done to a man who dressed women up as men?"

"I dread to think," said Lord Ecin shaking his head. "But it's the principal isn't it? We can't chop anything off nowadays but we can still show cheating doesn't work! Not on this estate!" He jumped to his feet.

"My Lordship we won't be cheating but we will be modifying some of the rules from now on," said his wise old butler patiently.

"Very well. I trust you Resourceful. What do I need to do?"

An hour or so later Lord Tig entered the courtyard with Lord Dratsab's red flag draped over his shoulder. He had with him Mons Meg covered in a huge tartan hood like a falcon and the last of his men. There were about twenty of them altogether swaying slightly and smiling merrily beneath their blue berets. They had been drinking on the way over which they shouldn't have been but this was to all concerned a foregone conclusion. They clumsily spread around Mons Meg like chicks around their mother hen and waited.

Lord Tig surveyed the scene and found it exactly as he had expected. There was no sight or sound of Lord Ecin as he would be by the water feature in the rose garden. The courtyard was littered with loudly snoring servants no good to man nor beast. Most with their pink berets missing. Lord Tig saw why. One of the servants had stacked them all on his head before passing out on a stool. There were so many wine bottles lying around you'd have thought the floor was made of glass and not cobbles. The white flag hung limply from its pole in the corner embarrassed for the losing colour it was.

Though the wall of haybales a little higher than a man behind the flag seemed a bit odd. Also the busty barmaid wasn't unconscious but sitting by her blackboard looking all too pleased with herself.

"Why so happy barmaid?" Lord Tig asked suspiciously.

"Big Beryl's enjoyed herself today your honour!"

"I'm not a judge. You don't have to refer to myself as your honour. I've no doubt in your miserable existence you will be using the term at some point but not today and not now. How many crosses on your board?"

"Nine hundred and ninety nine your honour!" She had wiped the board clean and then added them after Lord Ecin had given her a coin she had heard about but never actually seen before. Then she'd waited dreaming of names for the donkey she knew she could buy with it.

Lord Tig found it very amusing. "Nine hundred and ninety nine? The poor bugger couldn't even manage enough for a charge! Ignored him completely to get stuck into the wine no doubt. And look what it's done to them!"

"Bless 'em!" said Big Beryl slapping the folds of her cotton dress jovially. "Useless they were! Like trying to trap farts in a colander it was!" She was pleased that she'd got that right too. She'd get another coin afterwards now.

"So what are the haybales doing there?" asked Lord Tig.

She didn't know what she was supposed to say now. Lord Ecin hadn't told her. But she liked Lord Ecin. He seemed nice. "I think that's *your* surprise," she said cheerfully.

"Really? What sort of surprise?"

"Don't be silly! It wouldn't be a surprise if I told you!"

Lord Tig pointed to one of his men. "You get the flag!"

His man was just about to take it when Lord Ecin stepped out from behind the haybales. "Piss Off!" he said firmly.

"Ecin it's over. You both lost and I won. Let the man do his job," said Lord Tig hiding his surprise.

"Piss Off!" said Lord Ecin loud enough for it to reverberate around the courtyard.

"Are you going to do it on your own? Is that it? You against all of us?" said Lord Tig most unlike a friend.

"I'm not on my own. You underestimate me again. Men you may awake!" ordered Lord Ecin.

At this the snoring suddenly stopped and all the men in the courtyard miraculously stood up.

"Now I have fifty or so men here just loosened up. You have ten but I'll concede that one of them is Mons Meg so let me help you decide what you should do." Someone from behind the haybales handed him a bottle of scotch which he unscrewed. "Why don't you take off Mons Meg's hood?"

"What's behind the haybales Ecin?" demanded Lord Tig.

"You'll find out if you need to," replied Lord Ecin calmly. "Now take off his hood."

Lord Tig didn't like it one bit. "Has everyone gone mad around here? He'll use you for the toilet brush you look like!"

"That's my look out," said Lord Ecin. "Release Mons Meg!"

"Hey that's my line!" snapped Lord Tig. "Well you asked for it! Release Mons Meg!"

Lord Tig's men hurriedly stumbled away except one who ripped off the tartan hood and jumped out of the way as fast as he could. Mons Meg took a few seconds to look around and then spotted the scotch bottle being held by Lord Ecin. He reached under his kilt to take on another challenger.

But Lord Ecin turned his bottle and poured the golden liquid very slowly out onto the cobbles.

Mons Meg fell to his feet with the sound of clinking bottles. "Wha's the wee gollywog duin? Wha' a waste! Make him stop!" he pleaded to Lord Tig.

"What are you doing Ecin?" asked Lord Tig alarmed.

"Neutralising your main weapon!" said Lord Ecin shaking out the last drops. "Don't like waste do you Mons Meg? I had a Scottish nanny I know."

Mons Meg got to his feet and took a step forward.

"Remember your place!" ordered Lord Tig immediately.

"Make the wee gollywog stop then!" boomed Mons Meg.

"Hood him!" ordered Lord Tig.

One of his men stood in front of Mons Meg and held up a haggis. He seemed immediately besotted with it. The man threw it at Mons Meg and as the two tree trunks that were his arms took it to that great ginger hedgerow two other men quickly hooded him.

"Is this a stalemate Ecin? Shall we call it a draw between you and I?" asked Lord Tig when this was done.

"Let me think about it!" He went behind the haybales to where his wise butler was hidden. Also hidden were three of his female servants naked except for long red beards and a gentleman's sausage each.

"My Lordship it's gone much better than I expected. Everyone has played their part so well but I believe a draw is in fact a victory for common sense. I don't believe your opponent can truly control the loose cannon he has foolishly brought."

"But we can win this!" said Lord Ecin clenching his fists. "And show him for the enormous cheat he is!"

"You could win my Lordship but at what cost? I reiterate your opponent has been very foolish in bringing that big ginger juggernaut. The shipwright can build a whole ship but even he cannot stop its launch once started. Not to mention your friendship with his lordship certainly drowned too? I don't believe he will forgive you for exposing him as a cheat. Is that what you want?"

Lord Ecin shook his head, "No I don't want that. But I would like to beat them both for once."

"You have. You have it in your hand to take victory by declaring for a draw," said his wise old butler remaining patient.

"That doesn't make sense Resourceful!"

His wise old butler tried a different tact. "Please continue with the trust in me you have so graciously shown so far. Would it help if I said I believe your Grandfather would accept the draw to avoid the risk of damage to his house? The risk of damage to the water feature in the rose garden?"

"You think our bench could get broken?" asked Lord Ecin clearly alarmed.

"Very definitely. All that great ginger git would have to do is sit on it."

"Well I'm not having that! But at the same time I feel just like a knight of old! Ready to charge out on my horse, sweep my enemies aside and sweep my lady into my arms!"

"Well I fear throughout history too much blood of the ordinary man has been spilt in the foreplay of the noble."

"Pardon?"

"Nothing my Lordship. Would you like to be a white knight good and kind and strong? Or a black knight evil twisted and weak?" asked his wise old butler still worried his master might make the wrong decision.

"Well a white knight of course!" said Lord Ecin.

"Then be magnanimous! Accept the draw and stop this madness now so everyone wins! You be the one brave enough be like a white knight of old and keep the truth secret for the greater good!"

"Resourceful, who are the best knights *really*?" asked Lord Ecin suddenly.

"The ones that don't play games with other men's lives," suggested his wise old butler.

Not exactly sure why but feeling it was probably the right thing to do Lord Ecin stepped out to accept Lord Tig's offer of a draw.

# CHAPTER 3

## Heaven has no rage like love to hatred turned, Nor hell a fury like a woman scorned

Twenty years or so before Operation Legless took place something tragic happened in Dumfries.

In his mind Ben Burke was one of life's winners. He was young, ambitious, highly intelligent and very deliberately not charging anything like as much as his competitors. The time would come when he could charge what he liked when he had made himself indispensable. On his way to getting the lifestyle he deserved he was taking a small step in the reception area of a farmhouse in Dumfries. It had a reception area because it also let out a few rooms to travellers. He had stayed here only last week but under different circumstances to his visit this morning.

He was about to ring the bell on the small counter to summon the owner when a portrait hanging on the wall behind caught his attention. He was positive it had not been there last week but it looked so right that it would be hard to imagine the wall without it. It was of a woman a little over life-size in the first bloom of womanhood. Simply drawn in charcoal with hardly any frame it was utterly arresting. He stared at the proportions of eyes, mouth and chin trying to figure out why it was so magical. It must of been a stylisation of course because no real woman could be so beautiful. It was so good he looked in the corner for the name of an artist he might recognise. The word "Bonnie" was written in small delicate letters. Bonnie? It's what they called something beautiful up here wasn't it?

The front door swung open and in came the owner carrying a large basket of washing. He was a middle aged man with a friendly face and an instantly apparent pleasant demeanour. "With the wind's help we've beaten the rain today haven't we?" he chuckled to the linen.

He noticed the man at reception and gave a boyish duck of his head. "A little embarrassing being caught talking to your washing!"

He quickly put the basket down and took up position behind the counter. He smiled broadly, "why it's Mr Smith! Back so soon? Though you no longer look like a salesman of saddle brushes but quite the young gentleman! With your shorter hair a different colour, no beard or moustache, and no pipe smoke hiding you like mist on an early morning loch – I would hardly have known it was you!"

"I'm amazed you have. How on earth did you?" asked Ben not sure if he had hidden just how shocked he was.

"So it is you! Welcome back! You can have the room you had before. In fact you can have any room you like! I'm afraid I've more empty rooms than there are grouse on the moor!"

"Mister Henderson," said Ben Burke impatiently holding up a hand for silence, "how did you know it was me?"

"Why your hands sir. You have very distinctive hands," said Mister Henderson still smiling. In fact, he seemed incapable of talking any other way.

"That's very observant of you. The sort of eye for detail I imagine an artist must possess." He looked down at his hand then at the portrait then Mister Henderson's hands spread out on the counter. They were far more elegant than he had been expecting. He squinted at Mister Henderson, "You drew that didn't you?"

"Oh that!" said Mister Henderson dismissively, "I scribbled that out for a promise."

"A promise?" asked Ben Burke intrigued.

"A promise to my daughter." Mister Henderson had stopped smiling. "We can't always keep our promises to our children. That no-one will hurt them. That everything will be alright. But I promised her that I wouldn't miss her when she left home as long as I had her picture."

Ben Burke had no interest in children but he did have a healthy young man's interest in how they were made. "Is that your daughter?"

"Yes. Her name's Catherine -"

"She's stunning – I mean it says Bonnie in the corner though."

"She's always been my Bonnie to me," said Mister Henderson turning to it fondly.

The two men regarded the portrait together with very different thoughts running through their minds.

"But I'm sure it wasn't there last week," said Ben Burke, "I definitely would have noticed it before."

"It wasn't. She thinks I have it up all the time to remind me of her. She lives in London now. Centre of the universe she calls it -"

"I believe she's right," said Ben Burke very definitely.

"Well I can't bear to look at it if I'm honest. It makes me miss her more. So I only put it up when she's at home. So there's another promise I couldn't keep for her," he said quietly.

"You mean she's here now?" asked Ben Burke not interested in any broken promises.

"Why yes. I'll introduce you to her later if you like. Would you like that?" asked Mister Henderson resuming his normal demeanour.

Quite unexpectedly Ben Burke questioned what he had come here to do. He tried to dismiss it like brushing off a bit of fluff from his jacket. "If you can draw like that what are you doing here?"

"Ah, the life of an artist. Even a good one - and I'm not saying I'm any good - is a very precarious affair. One too risky to make sure a daughter has a good education and the security of a roof over her head. It's all a question of a man's priorities in life Mister Smith. Does a man who'd like to be an artist paint on the cupboards or does he put food in them?"

"Let the mother bring up the children and you do what you're good at. You do what you want!" Ben Burke couldn't imagine putting anyone else's needs before his own. It just seemed wrong whichever way you looked at it.

Mister Henderson looked away. "I'm afraid her mother's door closed when Bonnie's door opened."

For a brief moment Ben Burke recognised what empathy might feel like. He still couldn't imagine ever feeling it but he could see how he might.

"Would you like to meet her now?" asked Mr Henderson too brightly for it to be other than a huge effort for him. "She may be able to help you Mister Smith. You've obviously someone important to see today. She's as clever and generous as she is beautiful - but I would say that - I'm her father!"

Ben Burke hesitated. It would be kinder to just do what he had come here to do. Then he stole a glance at the portrait. "Yes, if you're sure she wouldn't mind."

"You stay just there!" said Mister Henderson eagerly coming around the counter and scooping up the washing basket, "we'll be back quicker than a salmon jumps the weir!" He disappeared through the archway that led to the stairs.

Ben Burke resumed his fascination with the portrait but was dogged by the realisation that he must prepare himself for the disappointment that would be coming down the stairs. No woman was going to be that beautiful. Mister Henderson's obvious artistic talents would have provided for his daughter far better than running a small farm with a few letting rooms on Lord Tig's Scottish estate. He felt the writ he carried in his trouser pocket. He shouldn't be wasting his time like this. He could hear footsteps coming down the stairs and took hold of the writ ready to take it out.

Mister Henderson appeared at the bottom of the stairs then stepped aside. "Mister Smith -may I introduce you to my daughter - Catherine de Barnes."

Ben Burke did actually feel something for the first time in his life. Smitten wasn't a strong enough word to describe how he now felt. What word could describe the range of emotions a person felt when they saw someone more beautiful than they could ever have imagined? The portrait didn't actually do her justice. He let go of the filthy horrible thing in his trousers to hold out his hand.

"How do you do Mister Smith?" It was like warm honey being poured down his ear.

"Er, very well thank you," he stammered out.

"I think Mister Smith has some explaining to do - don't you Bonnie?" asked Mister Henderson smiling at him he presumed.

Catherine de Barnes squeezed his hand and fixed him with her beautiful eyes. They reminded him of a big cat. He wondered absently if she played with her food before eating it.

She raised an eyebrow ever so slightly when he didn't answer. He couldn't. He was lost for words.

"Let me help you," said Mister Henderson. "A travelling salesman of saddle brushes spends a few days here as a guest. He talks about business a lot as travelling salesmen do but he also has a lot of questions about my business and the business of the tenants on the estate. Particularly - again and again - the full names and activities of the tenants on the estate. I - being the nice kind of man that I am - tell the travelling salesman what I know. Then a week later the salesman of saddle brushes returns looking like a young lawyer and is most surprised to have been recognised. Why was there a moose trying to slip by as a mouse I wonder? And for what reason Mister Smith? - If that is your real name which I highly doubt."

When her father had finished Catherine de Barnes still holding his hand raised the eyebrow a little more and tilted her head ever so slightly.

He melted before her gaze and couldn't resist what she wanted him to do. Ever so quietly he said, "my name is Ben Burke. I have eviction papers to serve on you. The other tenants will receive theirs too today. The properties were lost in a game of cards. The new owner didn't know what tenants there were but wants you all removed as quickly as possible."

Mister Henderson brought his hand thoughtfully up to his chin before turning away. "Let him go Bonnie."

Ben Burke went to pull down his hand but found it held firmly. He saw a cold fire ignite in her eyes that both enthralled and appalled him.

"Bonnie! I said let him go!" said Mister Henderson turning back to them. Instead, she ran the sharp nail of her thumb across his knuckles digging it in to draw blood. He could pretend it hadn't hurt but he didn't need to. The sense of gratitude was far stronger. To be recognised by her even in that way was so wonderful all he could do was smile. They both knew he would never stand up to her. His hand was discarded as though it were a dirty tissue.

"Of course father."

Mister Henderson looked at his daughter curiously for a second then turned apologetically to his guest. "She's always been high-spirited to say the least! Bonnie, if you promise not to put any poison in this Burke's tea would you make us both one please?"

Ben Burke watched silently knowing no man could control something sent direct from the heavens. Ultimately even its father here on earth would be ignored.

Mister Henderson put an arm around his shoulder, "she wouldn't really poison your tea," and led him into the tiny dining area.

Having waited for him to sit down first Mister Henderson took a seat on the other side of the small table. "May I see the eviction papers?"

He took out the folded paper that he had quite enjoyed handing over many times before but not this time. He watched silently as Mister Henderson unfolded it and read it. There wasn't much to read. There wasn't much a tenant could do other than comply with it. Everyone understood a man's property was his own and anyone given permission to use it did so by his grace and favour. A facility that could be withdrawn at any time. No explanation was needed. It was his property. There were some rules to be followed to make it seem civilised and proper but it wasn't. You were either in or you were out and it was the owner that always decided.

"I see it has been signed by Lord Dratsab," said Mister Henderson handing the wretched thing back.

This was the first work he had done for Lord Dratsab and he knew almost nothing about him.

Mister Henderson regarded him closely. "You don't know about Lord Dratsab do you?"

Ben Burke shook his head to indicate he didn't. Mister Henderson was apparently going to unburden himself of something he knew. To his surprise he felt inclined to listen.

Mister Henderson smiled weakly but knowingly. "I went to his brother's funeral – the nicer of the two as it happens – and if you're wondering why I had been invited – I had done some commissions for him. Horses mostly. Never any of the children. He seemed to like them. My paintings not the children. Never properly paid though! But that's a different story. You know at a man's funeral the vicar will say a few kind words about the deceased?"

"We all know the vicar hardly knew the man," said Ben Burke.

"But it's comforting none the less. Do you know what the vicar did at Lord Dratsab's brother's funeral?"

Ben Burke shook his head politely.

"He climbs into the pulpit and punches the air. Just like that!" Mister Henderson punched the air. "And then he begins his eulogy:

"He's gone! Hallelujah to that! To say that stiff lying in the box before us was a promiscuous plutocrat with a pioneering propensity for all known manly pleasures – is an understatement! He was far worse than that! Ladies and gentlemen the fact he reached his sixties is all the proof you'll ever need that the good die young. We all know that he only smiled at you when he wanted something. All people were stepping stones to the high altar of his own pleasure - and he didn't care to wipe his feet first! He didn't believe in the after-life, he didn't believe in God, all he believed in was "me me me"! Good riddance to bad rubbish! Get him out of my sight!""

"And no-one did anything?" asked Ben Burke.

"We all knew he was right. It's too late for me but you be very careful dealing with Lord Dratsab. Like I say we buried the nicer brother. Though they say you shouldn't speak ill of the dead so I would say his money paid for the deposit on this place. Speaking of which - it doesn't say in here when it will be returned."

Ben Burke suddenly felt quite sick. Mister Henderson noticed, "I'm not getting it back am I?"

Looking down at the table Ben Burke said, "I'm to find fault with a few things. Actually break something if I need to. I'm sorry. All the tenants are to be treated the same -"

There was a sudden almighty crash followed by bits of china and globules of hot tea raining down on him. Tentatively looking up Ben Burke saw a huge wet stain on the wall above him.

Catherine de Barnes calmly walked over. She took the single remaining cup off a tray and placed it on the table, "your tea Father."

"And our guest's tea?" asked Mister Henderson calmly.

"Animals don't drink tea." Without looking at Ben Burke she turned and left.

Mister Henderson pushed his cup across the table, "here have mine."

"That's very decent of you," replied Ben Burke not knowing what else to say or do.

Mister Henderson stared at the empty doorway his daughter had just vacated. "When she was a girl I found her one day with all the buckets she could find lined up on the garden wall. She was standing next to a great big pile of stones. I said, "what are you doing Bonnie?" and she said, "practising!" And I said, "Practising what?" And she said, "Practising throwing stones!" I told her that little girls or little boys for that matter shouldn't be throwing stones - and do you know what she said? She said, "Sticks and stones may break my bones." She'd practise every day and got so good that she could send a bucket flying, put a stone inside it or just gently rattle its handle. And I didn't put two and two together at the time but she never came home crying again about what some of the other children in the village had said about her."

"I think some children know when other children are better than them and they don't like it. Jealousy makes them nasty and horrible," suggested Ben Burke by way of explanation.

"You sound as though you have experience of it?" asked Mister Henderson kindly.

Ben Burke had but he wasn't going to elaborate. "May I ask how her mother died?"

"The cruellest way. The way that makes you doubt there is a God." He breathed out heavily. "Or if there is he doesn't like to make it easy for us."

"You're an artist. You know that every beautiful thing ever created has involved the destruction of something else," said Ben Burke. "And your daughter is truly beautiful."

"I know. I know," said Mister Henderson nodding feebly, "better not to question some things but get on with it the best you can."

"I'm sorry Mister Henderson. Truly I am," said Ben Burke surprised that he actually meant it.

Ben Burke thought seeing a grown man cry was as disgusting as seeing him pick his nose. He didn't think Mister Henderson was going to cry. But if he did he didn't think it would be disgusting - it would be understandable.

"Oh daddy I'm sorry!"

"Bonnie!" said Mister Henderson startled at his daughter's sudden appearance.

She threw her arms around him.

"You're more cat than woman the way you can creep about. And what are you sorry about? We've got plenty of tea cups!" He winked at Ben Burke, the dark cloud leaving his face as he stroked her hair fondly.

"I think I should go sir. I'm sorry for the deceit. I was just doing -"

"Yes, yes," interrupted Mister Henderson pleasantly, "just doing your job. We both know if you didn't do it someone else would. If I were to be angry at anyone it would be Lord Tig for being a lousy card player. I'll show you out." He patted his daughter on the shoulder to be released.

She rose and turned slowly, "I'll show this Burke out father."

"That's a good girl. I've got some letters to write and a lot of packing to do." He stood up holding out his hand. "I'll be honest and say I preferred you as Mister Smith but I wish you well Mister Burke."

They shook hands in a firm friendly manner.

"Most of it is made up as we go along you know. Take care of yourself," he said before leaving the two of them alone.

"I think your father's probably one of the most exceptional men I've ever met," said Ben Burke not daring to look at her.

"Hasn't stopped him being pushed around by the likes of you. But you're not even the musket. You're just a little ball. And I want the man with his finger on the trigger."

"Sorry?"

"So I'm not going to show you out. We're going for a little walk by the loch. And if you don't tell me everything you think I ought to know you'll be going in it and never coming out!" She took his arm.

"Just popping out for a bit dad!" she shouted brightly up the stairs. She dug her nails into his sleeve daring him to say or do anything to stop her.

He didn't and out they went.

They walked down to the loch arm in arm like two young lovers out for a stroll. They didn't say anything to each other but that might be a sign of just how much in love they were to anyone seeing them – which no one did.

When she stopped him he looked around. It was a beautiful spot in the morning sun. The trees had grown noble on the plentiful fresh air and the loch shone with a clarity he didn't realise water could have. Everywhere he looked the majesty of life in the raw was there to see. And then there was her. She was more beautiful than all of it. He didn't know what was going to happen but at that moment it felt like an honour to be there.

She pushed him back towards a large pine tree and tied his hands behind its trunk using a long ribbon from her hair. He was utterly compliant in the act. The way she had shook her hair after taking the ribbon out was probably the most erotic thing he'd ever seen. The calmness he felt at his situation surprised him. Was it something nature had developed to ease the suffering of the captured animal about to be eaten? A calm that kicked in when the chase was over and the game was up? The thought quickly evaporated when Catherine de Barnes looking deep into his eyes started unbuckling the belt that held up his trousers.

Ben Burke had never been so confused in all his life and so had no idea what she would find down there. He inwardly begged his body to get it right because he didn't want to infuriate the beautiful beast that had captured him. He closed his eyes fearing and longing at the same time. He could feel her beautiful fingers brushing the hairs on the front of his thighs. Then his testicles begin to tighten deliciously before she started touching him - there. But it was quickly obvious this was no love act. He opened his eyes to look.

She smiled at him mischievously. "It's quite a nice one actually."

"Er – thank you. It feels a bit different though," said Ben Burke politely.

"That'll be the string of pine cones I've hung from it," she happily informed him.

"Oh. Just so I know."

"Yes we need to do that to play Catherine's Exploding Cones." It was a bit creepy how she made it sound fun for only one of the players.

She walked away and removed a bucket of stones from behind a tree. She took one out and tossed it gently up and down in her hand. "With just the right amount of spin on something like this I've taken the head right off a rabbit. You know little fluffy bunny rabbits that we girlies are supposed to love. Muscle, bone, sinew - clean through the lot of it. Have you ever played Catherine's Exploding Cones Mister Smith?"

"No I can't say that I have." It was remarkable how serene it all seemed to him.

"It's very simple. I have to smash those cones dangling between your legs with these stones." It was clearly a lot of fun to her.

"And what do I have to do?" he asked calmly.

"Hope I don't miss." Her beautiful eyes narrowed dangerously. "Are you ready Mister Smith?"

"My name is Ben Burke. I'm sorry for deceiving your father. You really don't have to do this. I'll help you and your father however I can Bonnie." He wasn't begging. He was still very calm. But it provoked an enormous reaction from her.

Her eyes went the colour of the blackest flint honed to the sharpest edge stabbing him directly in the heart. The stone leaving her hand an instant later making a horrible thud he heard and felt as it hit the tree a short distance above his head. She curled her beautiful mouth cruelly, "Don't ever call me that!"

She bent down to take another stone from the bucket.

"Bonnie!"

She stopped abruptly unable to believe he had disobeyed her. A black wrath malevolence of hair and dress swirling to face him. He felt his balls horribly tighten at the sight of it.

"Bonnie!"

She let go the stone with a speed and fury and accuracy that again seemed heaven sent at the one who had dared call her that when she's said no.

"It wasn't me!" shouted Ben Burke.

It had been too late. There had been a sickening thud like a man's skull being horribly broken open beyond repair.

"Oh you poor girl. What have you done?" gasped Ben Burke. For the first time he struggled to be free from the tree.

Catherine de Barnes watched him confused. How could he struggle?

"It was your father! It was your father! Help him! Untie me! Please!"

Catherine de Barnes slowly turned to see the prone body of her father lying on the ground nearby. She'd killed enough things to know what death laid out looked like.

She fell to the ground covering her face and began to wail. I don't think for the rest of her life she ever truly stopped.

# CHAPTER 4

## You never know what's around the corner

"You can't enter! It's not allowed!"

"Now look here! You step aside or face the consequences!"

"I won't let you in!"

"Step aside you silly girl or get a slap!"

"Slap me all you want! You're not going in!"

"Right! Step aside or I'll throw you down the stairs!"

"You wouldn't dare!"

"Wouldn't I? It'd be your own fault!"

*Oh please Natalie - whoever it is just let him in* thought Sam. The noise of the two of them arguing outside his study door was a filthy end to a filthy slumber. He ever so carefully felt the bump on his head. It was tender to the touch so he wasn't inclined to have too much of a feel. He brought his hand down to have a look at it. There was no fresh blood on his fingers. If the pair of them would just shut up he'd be alright in a few minutes! Then there was the sound of soft skin being slapped by a calloused hand followed by a hurt whimper.

"There's your warning girl! Next thing kissing that pretty face of yours will be the bottom step!"

That was totally unacceptable! Only he was allowed to make such threats to his maid. He slowly rose from his chair to open the door and speak firmly to this intruder in his house.

The door swung open before he got to it revealing a tall coachman dressed in black with Natalie hanging off him. She was squealing, "You nasty man!" and ineffectively beating at his chest.

"Take a look at your master and tell me again I'm nasty!" he ordered.

When she turned her head to look at him her reaction quite frightened Sam. She instantly dropped off the coachman and stood rigid in shock.

"Don't just stand there! Get some hot water and some clean cloth you silly girl!" ordered the coachman. "Beelzebub's Beard! Now!"

"Sir I'm so sorry," began Natalie sounding as though she was about to cry.

The coachman grabbed her by the arm and shoved her through the doorway. "Hot water! Clean cloth! Now!"

He turned to face Sam. "Now sit back down and tell me how many fingers I'm holding up?"

Why the devil ask that? Was he practising his technique in admonishing his fellow road users and valued Sam's opinion on the matter?

"Two," he answered quietly. The coachman was an unknown quantity, quite intimidating, and he had a large whip.

"Excellent! Now can you wiggle your fingers for me?"

"I can - but I'm in no position to play the piano if that's what you're thinking," said Sam doing as he was told.

"A sense of humour? Best medicine there is! Now do you mind if I have a little feel?"

Sam stiffened in his chair. He wasn't sure about that. He wasn't sure a sense of humour or anything else would be much protection against the pain that could be induced by someone poking around the bump on his head.

"Ssshh," calmed the coachman seeing his fear. Sam suspected he would calm one of his horses the same way. "I'll start at the back of your neck and stop the moment it causes any discomfort. So we have a deal?"

It appeared we did as the coachman's hands were already at the base of Sam's neck before he had finished speaking. His hands felt wonderful on him. It was remarkable how they instantly conveyed strength knowledge passion and trust. It must have been something to do with working with animals perhaps. Sam relaxed letting him explore feeling totally reassured. It was strangely disappointing when the coachman stepped back removing his hands.

"Now I think that's all I dare do for now. Until we've cleaned you up a bit. But I think there's no serious wrongdoing done. Can you tell me how it happened?"

"You probably know as much as I do," said Sam feebly raising his arm to point at the window.

The coachman surveyed the scene before bending down to pick up the blood-stained note from the floor. He read it carefully. "I'm not sure Doctor Psycho and his wife Pat are going to be on many of your neighbours' guest lists in the coming months," said the coachman holding the note out to him.

Sam didn't want to touch it. That was his blood on there. "I've never heard of them," said Sam quietly.

Natalie entered the study carrying a small bucket of steaming water in one hand and some clean cotton cloths in the other.

"That was quick!" said the coachman.

She looked rather nervously at him. "I'd just boiled some to do some cleaning." But it wasn't him that frightened her. The look of concern and worry when she glanced at her master was abundantly clear to the coachman.

"Don't worry," he smiled reassuringly, "it looks much worse than it is. A man has a lot of extra blood in his head. It's where he keeps it when it's not needed for special occasions. That's why a man can't think straight when he's got a -"

"Are you being rude?" demanded Natalie. "Because if you are I'll stop talking to you right now!"

The coachman couldn't hide his surprise. Normally maids were always up for a bit of harmless fun with him. "I thought a bit of banter might put you at ease. But there's no point in trying to take a roll in the hay with a hayfever girl."

"You are being rude! I'm not that sort at all! And even if I were do you think I would - thingy - with a man who threatened to throw me down the stairs? Well?"

The coachman gave a little chuckle. "No you're quite right. Being thrown down the stairs probably isn't a good prelude to *thingy*. Perhaps a bit of a spanking - now that's a different matter entirely!"

"That's it!" said Natalie slamming the bucket down but carefully placing the cloths on the rim of it so they wouldn't get dirty on the floor. An attention to detail the coachman admired. "You stop being rude or you leave right now!"

"Yes yes," laughed the coachman holding up his hands in mock surrender. "No more mention of *thingy*." How she described a bit of how's your father held much amusement for him. "My rudeness shall be a thingy - THING! of the past!"

"Good!" said Natalie picking up the cloths and bucket.

"Now you be very gentle," warned the coachman. "We don't want to start that wound bleeding again."

"Of course!" said Natalie beginning. Soon there was no doubt to the gentleness and care in her work. The coachmen had seen butterflies more bombastic.

"Will he be alright?" she asked presently.

"Yes he will. I've seen far worse. Horses are much bigger than us with nothing like as much brains. They don't mean it. I'm sure they don't mean it. Not like bulls. Don't ever go into a pen with a bull without a pitchfork! You think he's not paying you any attention but all the time he's waiting to get you between him and the wall. Then the first you know about it is when he's using his weight and that wall to squeeze the very life out of you. A horse wouldn't do that. But it will kick out for no other reason than you've farted behind it or picked your nose. Then a man's skull - or worse a boy's - isn't much of a helmet against a hoof the size of a spade with a quarter a ton of leg behind it. Then again you'd be amazed at what some people can survive. But I think rest is the key. So that's why I'm unsure as to what to do next."

"Well what are you supposed to do?" asked Natalie finishing.

"First let me have a look at your wonderful handiwork." He went across.

He was very impressed. "You're a natural at this. You've done a wonderful job -" He stopped. Her eyes were a colour he'd never seen before. "I'm sorry I don't know your name."

"It's Natalie," she replied dismissively. "I suppose it's polite to ask yours?"

"Colin. At your service ma'am." He took a small respectful bow. "Though my friends call me Knobby!"

"Why if your name is Colin do your friends call your Knobby?" asked Natalie bemused.

He thought about it. He really did. Any other maid he would have shown. Actions speak louder than words and all that. But not this one. "You really don't know much about how men can behave do you?" he asked pleasantly.

"Why would I? I'm a woman," said Natalie making it clear she thought it an odd thing to ask.

"I'm not a horse but I know what they're like!"

"It's a simple enough question – why if your name is Colin do your friends call you Knobby?" asked Natalie wanting an answer.

Colin was intelligent enough to realise he wasn't being made a fool of. She really did seem to have led a sheltered life. He looked at Sam questioningly. He looked back with a wry smile. Colin deduced he had his approval to educate his maid - within reason.

"Well men are quite good at making something boring more interesting for themselves. And one of those ways is with names. So for instance a chimney sweep might be referred to as Chris the Chimney. Or Chris the Chimney could be a tobacconist. Sam Spade is a man whose main tool of employment is a shovel or someone who talks a load of poo. Carlos Chippie doesn't fry potatoes for a living – he's a carpenter. Or he can be a miserable so and so bitter at life. It gets a bit more obtuse with the more skilled type of tradesman. So for some reason Malcolm is very often an excellent miller or a wearer of bright clothes. And a Ben can be an adequate blacksmith, a very good bricklayer, or a piss-poor grocer."

"It makes absolutely no sense whatsoever," said Natalie shaking her head.

"I know! But it gets better!" said Colin enjoying his subject. "There are some names that cut across all the trades because it's something about the person rather than what he does. Paddy for instance. Paddy doesn't have an important role in the production of mattresses or cushions. Paddy is any drunken prat who likes shouting off stupid questions in an inn and answering them with his fists. Then there's a Knobby like me. Knobby's are quite well en -" he stopped looking at her pretty innocent face - "ENtrusted - with handling horses."

"Well recovered!" said Sam smiling at him knowingly.

Colin accepted the compliment with a slight nod of his head.

"What?" demanded Natalie.

"Nothing," said Sam. "That's enough on the subject now. I want to know what am I to make of a coachman that slaps my maid but sees to my injuries? Well?"

"Natalie?" Colin gave her a very pleasant smile, "do you have any material suitable for bandages about five or six feet long?"

"Do I?" enthused Natalie gleefully clapping her hands. "I've just the thing!"

"Well hurry girl! Let's get your master well as quickly as we can!"

"Yes! Yes of course!" said Natalie fairly bouncing out of the room.

"She's a good girl. Far more important to me than she realises," said Sam fondly looking after her. He turned to face Colin sternly. "But what *is* going on?"

"Do you mind if I sit down?" asked Colin reaching to remove the tray of soup.

"Of course not. If it gets me some answers," said Sam waving his hand for him to carry on.

Colin placed the tray on the floor and sat down on the stool so they were face to face.

"I don't honestly know what's going on. I'm to take you to the man in the tree. Like the others."

"Man in the tree? Like the others?" spluttered Sam. "Who are you?"

The coachman put a friendly hand on Sam's arm.

It was rather familiar behaviour for a coachman to take with a gentleman. Sam eyed the hand suspiciously enough for Colin to gently take it away.

"Sorry. My mother tells me I was always tactile and helpful. Wasn't surprised when I wanted to be a doctor."

"But you're a coachman!" pointed out Sam.

Colin gave a sad nod. "It's a long story."

"Will it help me understand what's going on?" asked Sam abruptly.

"No," answered Colin smiling.

"Then save it for another day! What do you know?" demanded Sam.

Colin took no offence from Sam's manner. "I really don't want to worry you but I've taken three men from various parts of London and brought none of them back. I go to collect them at the correct time only to be told "it's been taken care of" by one of his carpenters."

"What men?" asked Sam not believing his ears.

"Bookkeepers like you -"

They were interrupted by Natalie bounding into the room like an excited puppy.

"Look Colin! An old tablecloth too thin to make into curtains and too thick for hankies! But just perfect for bandages!" She was red faced and happy holding out her bundle.

Although the interruption was an irritation they both smiled at her. One of them excited by her youthful beautiful exuberance and the other because of her adorable thrift.

# CHAPTER 5

## Be careful what you wish for

Lord Ecin pointed at the card. "So that Queen of Spades is worth thirteen points which is added to Tiggy's score. But although he has the most points now - he's just lost the game! That seems very strange."

The three Lords were in another one of the plentiful rooms of Lord Ecin's house. Lord Dratsab had been quite sulky for a few weeks after his defeat and had been making excuses not to join them. Lord Tig liked Lord Ecin but found him much more interesting in Lord Dratsab's company so had suggested a game of cards. Something he knew Lord Dratsab would find hard to resist as he loved recounting how his father had won a Scottish estate from Lord Tig's father in a game of cards every time they played. Lord Tig thought the "ribbing" would be a price worth paying to have Lord Dratsab back in the fold.

After a delightful dinner with some jolly memories of past exploits (with courteously no mention of Lord Dratsab's recent defeat) and some fine port the main event had begun between the two of them. Lord Ecin didn't play cards or like to gamble. He was there as a happy host to fetch another glass of port or another slice of pork pie or to make a flippant remark when he felt the other two might be forgetting it was just a game. And right on cue he just had.

"Yes thank you Newton!" said Lord Tig scooping up his cards and shoving them on the deck. He braced himself for the jibe coming about his family's poor luck at cards.

"Too right Ecin! Strange and boring! And bloody stupid to gamble doing it!"

"Pardon?"

"What?"

"You heard me! Our fathers must have been bloody stupid!" said Lord Dratsab before taking an angry slurp of his port.

Lord Ecin and Lord Tig looked at each other very confused.

"Are you alright?" asked Lord Tig.

"You did just win," pointed out Lord Ecin.

"So?" demanded Lord Dratsab. "Bits of card with pictures and numbers on! For twenty years my family has been enjoying a return on Scottish property because your father happened to turn the wrong piece of coloured card over! Seems ridiculous doesn't it?"

The other two Lords looked at each other. This was serious. Lord Ecin mouthed at Lord Tig, "shall I call the doctor?" Lord Tig shook his head.

"You haven't just been brooding for a couple of weeks have you? You've been up to something?" he asked carefully. He was easily the most perceptive of the three.

"Might have been," replied Lord Dratsab enticingly.

"What then?" asked Lord Tig.

Lord Dratsab leant forward resting his elbows on the rich green baize of the card table. "Gentlemen. What are we actually doing with our lives?"

Lord Ecin and Lord Tig exchanged a bemused look.

"Waiting for a war! And if no war comes and our twenties pass us by what then?" demanded Lord Dratsab.

"I'm not waiting for a war!" said Lord Ecin. "I think war is a horrible thing."

"It doesn't matter what you think. It's what those in charge think," scolded Lord Tig.

"We're Lords!" We're supposed to be in charge aren't we?" demanded Lord Dratsab.

Lord Tig smiled with relief. Lord Dratsab was behaving normally again.

"Who would you like to start a war on?" he asked. "You've only had a few weeks so is it cheesemakers? Or those robbing vintners? Or estate agents? God we all hate estate agents!"

"You can mock Tiggy but I've found an enemy that will always be worth fighting!" said Lord Dratsab puffing up, "Poverty!"

Lord Tig spat out his mouthful of port making Lord Ecin come rushing around to his aid. Lord Tig waved the silly sod away. "What? Have you gone completely mad?" he blurted out.

"Poverty!" repeated Lord Dratsab emphatically, "why should anyone have to be poor?"

Lord Tig threw his hands in the air. The remaining port in his glass spraying out behind him. "We'd have let you win if we knew this would happen!" he said shaking his head in utter disbelief.

"Go on," said Lord Ecin very interested in what Lord Dratsab had to say.

Lord Dratsab turned earnestly to Lord Ecin. "People like us could still be rich. But nobody has to be poor. Look! There will always be differences in wealth but you get rid of anyone being poor!"

"So you want a war on the peasants?" asked Lord Ecin not sure.

"No!" said Lord Dratsab smacking his forehead in frustration. "You get rid of poverty so there are no peasants!"

"And how would you do that? Get rid of poverty?" asked Lord Ecin clearly wanting to know how it could be done.

"Commerce!" lauded Lord Dratsab. "Commerce! A human's ability to take something and make more of it for everyone to share! Commerce!"

Lord Tig rolled his eyes. "You do know most peasants like being peasants? You can't actually polish a turd! You do know that?"

Lord Dratsab ignored him holding Lord Ecin's attention. "Ecin you need to speak to the man I've been speaking to. He'll explain how it can all be done."

"What's his name? Where's he live?" asked Lord Ecin enthusiastically.

Lord Dratsab pulled out an envelope from his jacket pocket. "It's all in here. A letter of introduction and directions to his place. I'm sure you'll like Colonel Peru - he has bears!"

At the mention of the name of Colonel Peru the penny dropped with Lord Tig. He stayed silent. He chose not to warn his friend because they'd called it a draw but he knew Lord Ecin had beaten him too. He also knew Lord Ecin had loved bears ever since childhood.

The number of times he'd bored them about how at the Globe Theatre there would be bear-baiting as well as Shakespeare's plays. How the county symbol of the great man's birthplace was a bear and ragged staff. How jolly exciting it must have been to see a great bear fight off those brave dogs. And what a shame that sort of spectacle can no longer be seen. On and on and on.

It came as no surprise that Lord Ecin said he would leave straightaway. He was so excited to see some real bears. He thanked Lord Dratsab profusely for such a wonderful opportunity and bade them make full use of his house whilst he was gone. He left the room more excited than they'd probably ever seen him.

"You are a complete cad do you know that Dratsab?" said Lord Tig when they were alone.

Lord Dratsab put on his favourite mask, the Machiavellian one, "and you are a complicit git. Now pass the port over."

It was a long ride for the remainder of the night and most of the next day. Lord Ecin was so excited he was unable to sleep in the carriage or take a nap in a chair when they rested the horses at an inn. Eventually though they were travelling up a very long drive to a very secluded house. The trees around it huddled so close it was as though their branches were there to hide it. From his carriage window Lord Ecin glanced nervously at his wise old butler Resourceful.

"Everything correct my Lordship?" asked Resourceful.

Lord Ecin tapped a pocket of his jacket. "Yes I have my letter of introduction written by Lord Dratsab."

"And your betting money my Lordship?"

He tapped another pocket of his jacket containing his purse. "I don't think I'll be betting if I can help it."

"It will be expected my Lordship," suggested Resourceful.

"Well if I have to. Just to be polite."

"Just imagine my Lordship. You're going to see something you thought you would never see. It's almost as if you are a time traveller travelling back in time!"

The carriage stopped with a jolt and they waited for their driver Welly to jump down.

"Thank you Welly," said Lord Ecin taking his hand to help him out.

Resourceful stepped out taking a considered look at the house before turning to Welly. "It looks like you need to go around to the left. If they've any manners they should feed you something hot. But I've a feeling you'll be needing that cold pie from Cook. You made sure to bring it?"

"Yes sir."

"I don't know how long his Lordship will be. It's almost dusk now." Resourceful seemed fascinated by the house taking another long considering look. "Don't untie the horses just yet Welly. Understand?"

"I understand sir. Three calls on you whistle and I'll be there in a flash." He climbed back up and moved the carriage away.

Resourceful joined Lord Ecin at the front door who was looking for the bell-pull.

"Can you see how we ring to get in?" Lord Ecin asked him.

The bell-pull was made of brass about eight inches long and shaped like the talons of an out-stretched eagle claw about to strike.

"I see how my Lordship," he said about to pull on the ghastly thing.

"Wait!" ordered Lord Ecin. "We're to pull it three times wait for thirty seconds then pull on it twice."

"Do you know why my Lordship?" asked Resourceful concerned.

Lord Ecin tapped his pocket. "Lord Dratsab's instructions."

"Do you wish me to proceed my Lordship?" he felt it his duty to ask.

"Why do you ask?" asked Lord Ecin nervously scratching the back of his head. Then throwing his hand down. "But I'd love to see some bears!" Then looking up at the house. "But it seems such a cold unwelcoming house. So much different to ours don't you think?"

"We could be back home before supper tomorrow. It would mean another night ride but Welly has not untied the horses. We could leave right now my Lordship if it pleases you."

Lord Ecin was clearly in a dilemma. "I do have an odd feeling now we're here. But nothing worthwhile is ever easy or straightforward is it? It's always easier to turn back than go on."

"Not always my Lordship," suggested Resourceful. "Sometimes it's far harder to admit you were wrong and turn back."

"Do you think I'm wrong about this?" asked Lord Ecin.

"My Lordship, I think we should all look for answers." Resourceful took another concerned look at the house. "I'm just not sure what we'll actually find here."

Lord Ecin looked at the house too. "No niether am I."

What he would have done was suddenly upended by the front door opening and a servant hoping with anxiety jumping out at them.

"Are you two from the agency?" the servant begged. "Because someone's going to be thrown from the roof if this isn't sorted soon!"

"Resourceful, what's an agency?" asked Lord Ecin hurriedly of his butler.

"A flea that sucks its host dry my Lordship," said Resourceful to his master. He held up his hands for calm, "My good man this is Lord -"

"Sssh! Are you mad? We don't use names here! If you're not from the agency do you have a letter?" It was incredible to see a servant act with no regard for the presence of one of his betters.

Lord Ecin took out the letter from his jacket handing it over.

It was snatched away and inspected so vigorously the servant risked it falling to pieces in his hand.

"Oh dear! This isn't normal either!" He thrust the letter back at Lord Ecin.

Lord Ecin couldn't understand what could alarm a servant to such a degree.

Resourceful took the servant by the arms as firmly as he dared. "Calm down my good fellow. Calm down and tell me what is going on."

"Are you mad? Tell you what is going on? Do you know what he would do to me?" The servant shrugged Resourceful off and snatched the letter back. "I need to show this to the boss. It looks like the scrawl of Pegasus." He slammed the door shut.

"Do you think we should go?" asked Lord Ecin not looking away from the door barely inches from his face. "Do you think he's mad? And who is Pegasus?"

"Which question would you like me to answer first my Lordship?"

Lord Ecin turned to him, "who is Pegasus?"

"I imagine that is how Lord Dratsab is referred to here."

"Why?"

"So when things are whispered about what goes on here real identities are protected."

"Is that servant mad?"

"No he's panicking over something."

"Do you think we should go?"

"Very definitely. But it is not my decision to make my Lordship."

"Oh I hate not knowing what to do for the best."

"It's a lot harder than it looks."

"This hasn't felt right from the moment we got here. I don't know what to do. I really don't know what to do."

"You could toss a coin my Lordship. You have plenty about your person."

"It's an easy way out though. Like asking God."

"Perhaps."

Lord Ecin looked down at the ghastly eagle claw bell-pull. He thought about pulling on it and realised he didn't want to. Then he thought of the bears. Real bears! He didn't necessarily want to see them fight. Just see a real bear in front of him! He would wait to see what happened next and then decide what to do. Resourceful seemed to understand what he had decided and waited patiently too.

They didn't have to wait long. The door flung open engulfing them in the overpowering smell of brandy.

"Well well well. Pegasus flaps his great wings overhead and drops a saddlebag on the front lawn," said a big confident man. "Do you know how many Bob's he's borrowed over the years? I don't suppose you have them with you?"

"I'm sorry. I don't what a Bob is -" began Lord Ecin.

"A Bob! A Bob! What do you call a gardener where you come from? A ponsy Green-Graham I suppose!" The words bellowed out of his great bushy beard.

"If - *Pegasus* - has been borrowing staff and not returning them to you then I'm sorry - but it is not the reason for my master's visit this evening," said Resourceful tilting his head respectfully to indicate no presumption of right or wrong on the matter was intended.

"Hey! When I want the monkey to talk I'll throw it a few nuts," warned the big man firmly.

Resourceful nodded his head respectfully and felt for the whistle in his pocket.

"Now I've cleared that up what am I going to call you?" said the big man looking Lord Ecin up and down. "Athena I think."

"But Athena was a woman wasn't she?" corrected Lord Ecin politely.

"Well you remind me of a woman so what's the problem?" He gave a hearty laugh then fixed Lord Ecin with his black eyes indicating it would be very much a good idea for him to find it funny also.

Lord Ecin smiled broadly as best he could. "And I am to take it you are -"

"Your worst nightmare if you don't follow my rules!" growled Colonel Peru cutting off all pretence of humour. "Now come in!"

Lord Ecin hesitated looking at Resourceful.

"You in charge Athena? Or the monkey?" growled Colonel Peru.

"Well I am of course," spluttered Lord Ecin. He made a snap decision and stepped into Colonel Peru's hall.

"Not the monkey! Round the back with the other monkeys!"

"My Lordship?" asked Resourceful looking at his master unflinchingly.

Lord Ecin nodded for him to do as he was told.

"Very good -" Colonel Peru abruptly slammed the door shut before he could finish.

On the other side of it Colonel Peru put a big arm around Lord Ecin's shoulder. "Do you want to see the bleeders first? Or shall we organise a fight straightaway? Dogs? One on one?" He bent his head down close, "if money is no object I've trained a woman that fights 'em naked."

Lord Ecin gulped clearly intimidated by Colonel Peru. "The woman or the bear?"

"The woman of course!" roared Colonel Peru down his ear. "Whoever heard of a bear wearing clothes?" Then he suddenly straightened rubbing his crotch. "Mind you there might be some mileage in that," he reflected. "Yes I'll have to give that some thought Athena."

Outside Resourceful very deliberately straightened his collar and brushed down the sleeves of his jacket sweeping the recent rudeness off him. Then he began walking with a wry smile "to join the monkeys." He had almost reached the corner of the house when his smile fell away at the sight of an anxious Welly running towards him.

"What is it lad?" he asked.

"Sir! Sir!" Welly hissed, "You need to come with me!"

"Well of course if you think so. Show me the way."

Without warning Welly scooped him up. "Forgive me sir but we need to be quick!" Welly easily ran with him passed the stables across a large courtyard to a small empty piggery. Welly put Resourceful down and anxiously looked back to make sure no-one had followed them. "You need to speak to him sir!"

"Speak to whom Welly?" asked Resourceful kindly.

Welly pointed into a sty. "He's in there!"

Resourceful bent down to peer into the gloom and nearly shit himself at what he saw. He jumped back as fast as he could.

"What are you doing you fool? That thing's a bear!" he exclaimed at Welly. "We need to get out of here!"

"But it can talk!"

"It can talk?"

"It can talk!"

"Listen hear lad. Bears can't talk."

"They can sir! That one keeps saying, "help me" - Listen!"

Resourceful took a deep breath before bravely leaning towards the sty again. Quite remarkably he heard a voice thick with sorrow repeat over and over, "please help me."

Resourceful got up putting an arm around Welly leading him away. "Right lad! What do you know? Tell me exactly what happened."

"I pulled into the courtyard and was just getting down when I felt the coach give a little lurch as though someone had got in. I thought it unlikely so I ignored it. But I could tell the horses weren't happy about something so I opened the door. There he was! Sitting right in his Lordship's chair - a bloody great bear! Before I knew what would happen next my fist decided to punch it! Shouldn't have been in my coach. But instead of jumping at me and ripping my head off it fumbles with the other door handle and jumps out. Then my stupid feet decide to chase it and it ran in there." Welly pointed at the sty behind them. "Then I goes in to make sure he understands that if he wants a ride in my coach he should ask for it rather than just getting in. And I must have hurt him that bad that it's like he's trying to pull his own head off. And he starts begging me for help. Then I felt really bad sir. That I'd done that to him." Welly hung his head. "Don't know me own strength sometimes -"

Resourceful placed a comforting hand on Welly's shoulder. "You're a big kind lad without a bad bone in your body. But punching a bear and living to tell the tale doesn't quite ring true for me. I fear our host might be some kind of pirate."

"A pirate?" breathed in Welly amazed, "how clever to do that this far from the sea!"

Resourceful was more interested in getting to the bottom of this than explaining an analogy to Welly. "You keep watch there's a good lad."

"And you will say I'm sorry!" implored Welly.

"If I'm right about this then we can do more than say sorry - we can make amends." Resourceful turned and entered the sty quite confident he wasn't about to be mauled. A little while later he appeared leading the bear out by its paw. "Welly this is Graham. He graciously accepts your apology."

"Oh that's wonderful! I'm really sorry Graham! Honestly I am!" said Welly relieved. "And I've not seen sight nor sound of anyone sir."

"Excellent - Now you take Graham and put him in the coach exactly as you found him," said Resourceful handing him Graham's paw.

"In his Lordship's seat? Are you sure sir?" asked Welly.

"I guarantee his Lordship won't mind," said Resourceful, "quickly now."

Welly took Graham's paw telling him, "Come on Graham. You heard."

Resourceful sneaked back towards the house most concerned about the dogs. You didn't have bear baiting without dogs. Colonel Peru, unknown number of staff anxious or otherwise, unknown number of dogs and an unknown number of bears. A straight fight would clearly be suicide. To successfully retrieve his Lordship and make their escape he would have to think like a male spider trying to get laid.

Welly led Graham the Bear around the large courtyard by his paw grateful for the dark patches the quickly coming night provided. They moved to one, checked no-one was about then moved silently to another. When they had reached the stables Welly felt much more comfortable in familiar surroundings. His coach was within sight. As they had seen or heard nothing he decided it would be the appropriate moment to apologise to the bear personally. Instead of leading the bear towards the coach he led him into an empty stable block and let go of the bear to sit down on a haybale. The bear plonked itself down on another haybale

"Look Graham I just wanted to say sorry for earlier. I'm not someone who normally sorts things out with his fists."

"Got anything to smoke?" asked the bear.

Welly found it quite funny how the bear spoke without moving its lips. He assumed the lips were moving but he couldn't see properly because of the dim light.

"Yeah of course I'll pipe up." He took out his pipe and his pouch of tobacco and got it ready whilst the bear watched silently on.

"Shouldn't really be smoking in stables of course," he said striking the match before drawing on the pipe to get it well lit. Satisfied it was ready he handed it to the bear who took it rather clumsily in its paw. The whole thing nearly disappearing into the bear's mouth.

"Don't swallow it!" Welly warned.

The bear seemed unperturbed and breathed in deeply. The tobacco glowed so much it lit up all those big yellow teeth in the big mouth.

Welly decided it was probably a good idea to let the bear do more or less what it liked unless Resourceful said otherwise.

"So what's it like being a bear?" he asked.

"Terrible mate," said the bear before taking a long drag and breathing out the smoke slowly. "I used to have proper jobs."

"I didn't know bears had jobs," said Welly.

"You don't know the half of it mate." The bear took another long drag and breathed slowly out. Welly watched as the smoke came out of the bear's mouth at the sides up around his head and seemed to jiggle around his great hairy ears before rising into the air.

"So what do you find the worst part of being a bear?" asked Welly always eager to find out how other jobs compared to his own.

"Not seeing the grankids," lamented the bear.

"Your cub's cubs? Blimey! How old are you then?" asked Welly surprised.

The bear didn't answer straightaway as it took another drag, lighting up those big yellow teeth. "Forty seven."

"And is that good for a bear?"

"A few of the fellas are older but it's mostly a young man's game I have to admit."

Suddenly the bear started coughing and the glowing pipe came shooting out of its mouth. For such a big lad Welly was surprisingly quick. He was able to jump up and retrieve the pipe in mid-air before it could land and be broken or worse cast hot embers everywhere.

"Lucky," he said sitting back down waiting for the bear to stop coughing. "Do you want some more?"

The bear shook its great big head, "I've had enough mate I really have." He let his great big head fall into his great big paws.

"I know - my mum says I smoke too much."

"No mate!" sobbed the bear into his paws, "I mean I've had enough!"

Welly had seen his dad act like this a lot before he'd disappeared off the bridge. Being a dad, being a bear, it was obvious there are a lot of hard jobs out there.

"My mum says you should talk about things that are bothering you. She says it's what my dad should have done. I just think he should have used the ferry – you can't get blown off the ferry."

The bear gave an odd little chuckle not looking up. "Is that what she told you?"

Welly waited in polite silence but when it seemed too long he asked, "Is there something you want to talk about?"

"Don't do it son. No matter how desperate you get - don't give up all hope and do this."

Welly shook his head. "I'm sorry you'll have to explain. I don't know what you mean."

The bear sat up putting its paws on its legs in a very human manner. "Where do you think us bears come from lad?"

Welly thought about it. "Well I know the English bears are all gone. So from abroad somewhere."

"Very expensive to ship bears in from abroad when all that's going to happen to them is being ripped apart by dogs?"

Welly knew he wasn't the brightest person around but he did try so didn't like it when he didn't have the right answer. "Well you tell me. You're the bear. Where are you from?"

"Basingstoke," answered the bear.

Welly tried his best guess, "Is that in Hungary?"

"Well it begins with an "H" - Hampshire."

Welly folded his arms. "I know Hampshire's not abroad."

"Look kid I'm not trying to give you a lesson in geography – though I suppose it is in the ways of the world. Most of us swim along with the current and everything's normal and normal things happen to normal people. But for some people that can't keep up or the current dumps them on a barren shore or for some bizarre reason just pushes them the wrong way - things stop being normal. And then when your wife has left you and your children no longer want anything to do with you taking with them the most precious things in the world then you can find yourself doing what you wouldn't have dreamed yourself doing in your worst nightmares."

Welly had had no idea just how involved a bear's life could be. The bear was unbelievably descriptive with his paws now too – it was almost- well it was almost as though Welly was listening to another person.

"So when you think you've hit rock bottom having sullied yourself on the way down through drink, hurt and begging you're not going to say no to any suggestion – you've done most other things anyway. A man from an agency knows where there's a month's pay for a few hour's work. It might be the start of getting them back even. Yeah count me in! But when you turn up. What's that? I've got to fight off a pack of dogs? That wasn't mentioned at the interview. But you're here now and do you want to tell Colonel Peru no? Rather you than me mate. So you do it. Even though no-one including yourself expects you to survive the experience intact. How desperate is that? But lo – you do survive. And worse you're very good at it. Every crushed little skull and mouth of teeth smacked away, every little whimper as I squeeze the life out of them, is me clawing back at the sides of the filthy tunnel I slid down."

The bear's great head fell again. "Except it's not. All I've done for six months is gouge my way deeper in. And now there's no light left in my tunnel. Any light there was I've snuffed out."

"Burrow," said Welly, "I think a bear probably lives in a burrow rather than a tunnel. I think a tunnel is a man-made thing."

The bear turned to look at him saying nothing for a few seconds.

"Yes burrow's probably right," said the bear quietly.

Then his fist surprised Welly again. It decided it would be a good idea to open out and lead his arm around the bear's shoulders.

"Pitiful isn't it?" sobbed the bear.

"No," said Welly. "It's thinking you're on your own when you're not. Come on Graham. I think you're coming home with us."

# CHAPTER 6

## The goose that lays the golden egg

Natalie had bandaged Sam's head so he now looked like "a Sikh from Bengal" as Colin put it. To which Sam had replied, "That is appropriate for it is knowledge that we seek!" This had made them both laugh but Natalie had looked on bemused. Colin hurriedly finished telling Sam all he knew. Sam asked a few more questions and then asked Natalie to make them a cup of tea. In her absence he asked Colin some more questions. When she returned they had decided to proceed because they didn't know enough not to. Sam wasn't going to flee for his life from a shadow. That would be absurd. He needed to find out what was going on and then decide what to do. However, they had arranged a method for getting Sam out of danger. It was with this in place Sam felt brave enough to proceed.

A little later Sam gave Natalie some instructions for assembling certain items together and how they could be made suitable for quick transport. Then he hurried downstairs to Colin and his waiting coach. He rode up top with Colin rather than inside so they could converse freely some more. Not far from their destination Colin stopped the coach for Sam to climb down and get inside so as not to arouse any suspicion from those waiting for them. Inside the stuffy rocking box Sam's bravery started to run from him like soap suds down a drain. He wasn't sure he wanted to do this after all. If the journey took much longer he was quite sure he would bang on the coach ceiling for it to stop. As it was they lurched to a halt before that feeling got the better of him.

He waited for Colin to open the door. Normally when using a coach he would climb out himself. He knew it was a flimsy attempt to preserve his sense of safety a few seconds longer. Colin opened the door and seemed to sense his trepidation.

"May I help you down sir?" He reached in and quietly whispered in Sam's ear as he helped him down, "remember - you have balls."

"Thank you my good man," said Sam grateful for the friendly reminder and the secret little squeeze Colin gave his forearm.

Colin respectfully saluted someone before climbing up and taking the coach away.

Although he had been primed on what to expect Sam still felt very alone and nervous. He knew he would be dropped at the base of a huge oak tree - there it was. He knew on a big bow in the oak tree would be a medieval depiction of death without the sickle sitting in a chair - there he was. He knew there were two carpenters - he couldn't see them. And finally, he knew that the other bookkeepers Colin had brought here he had not brought back.

The hooded figure addressed him. "There is more blackness within this cloak than in the soul of the blackest pirate on the blackest ocean on the blackest night! What say you to that?"

Sam had never heard a voice so absent in human emotion. It did cross his mind that he was looking at a real demon. The courage it took to remain standing there felt like a drop of rain on a windowpane - it could just suddenly fall away without warning. Then he remembered his balls.

"I fear my demons but I do face them when I must," he said bravely. "I don't profess to know what's in store for me today or for what reason. But I am an Englishman so though I fear what is to come I will not shirk from it!"

"You know God favours the English do you not?" asked the cold emotionless voice.

"I believe we have been blessed with many fine resources and more importantly the necessary qualities of mind and spirit to make use of them. Perhaps he might," suggested Sam.

"It is because you make him laugh."

It was so direct and so cutting Sam felt inclined to take a step back.

"Do you like my shoes?" asked the foul beast.

"I'm afraid I can't see your shoes - though I'm sure they're very nice." It was very disorientating to not be able to see the face of whom you were addressing. He would normally have used a choicer word than "nice".

"Here is a little secret - the first one of the day - the finest shoes deserve the finest polishing on the inner thighs of a Flander's girl. The shoes must be rubbed until the girl's soft skin is broken and the blood mixes with her little tears of pain falling down."

"That's outrageous!" spat Sam taking a step forward.

"Yes but very effective."

"No shoe is worth that you monster!" said Sam taking another step forward raising his fist.

"There is not enough blood and tears in a Flander's girl for riding boots of course. That requires a brace of sisters or ideally twins."

Sam moved forward until he was almost directly below the fiend. "I hope your wretched shoes walk you off a cliff!"

There was a cold stiletto laugh just as a hessian snake jumped from the earth around Sam's feet and flung itself around his ankles. Within a second he was flat on his back wondering what on earth was going on.

"Congratulations. You have proven you have spirit. You have also shown several weaknesses that strengthen me. So in return and to help you learn - at no point did I say that mine were the finest shoes."

Sam felt his cheeks redden with the realisation he had been very easily tricked. He would only look more foolish trying to wriggle and squirm so he didn't.

"Hammer time," summoned the hooded figure on the bow.

The crack of a twig demanded Sam to turn his head to the side. Two burly carpenters looking very elongated appeared from behind the trunk of the tree. Here were the two carpenters he had been told to expect. They were definitely not "bodgers" who worked in the woods turning out simple chair legs. The men's demeanour suggested an absolute confidence in their abilities. Sam prided himself on recognising talent and as they approached he uncomfortably realised they could probably turn their hands to almost anything. The fact they were carrying a chest between them big enough to hold a man and the one on the left held a spade did not seem to bode well. A lesser man might have started wriggling then but Sam had already resolved what to do and would stick to it.

They placed the chest and the spade down and grabbing an arm each lifted Sam to his feet as easily as they might lift a flagon of cider.

"Search him."

Not daring to make any eye contact Sam allowed himself to be searched quite confident they would not find his balls.

"Only a satchel," said one of them holding it up. "Do you wish me to search his bandages?"

Now Sam became acutely aware of his balls.

"No. I can see that they have been done by a woman's hand that no-one here can replicate afterwards. Offer the man apologies for a corner that should not have been cut."

"Sorry for using a lousy messenger," said the carpenter with a sneering smile.

"Hammer - the satchel."

So the one with his satchel was Hammer. Sam watched impressed as he expertly threw his satchel directly into the hooded figure's lap.

The three of them waited in silence below as the contents were examined. Sam watched as intently as he dared at no time seeing a face or any hands. The contents appearing and disappearing in black folds of material as expertly as a barn owl flitting across the night sky. He knew there was a notebook, a few quills, some ink in a pot with a lid to stop it leaking, some plain sheets of paper, and some notes on his fees etc. If that demon was looking for the secret to his recent success he wouldn't find it in his satchel. His secret was still at home getting some things ready for him and then she'd be scrubbing floors and making do.

He had not risked watching all the time and only knew the examination was over when the satchel kicked up some dirt as it landed smartly at his feet. He bent down carefully to pick it up not wanting to topple over with his ankles tied.

"Chisel pluck the cock."

When the other carpenter whom he now knew was called Chisel pulled out from his apron a knife so big it was almost a sword Sam dropped his satchel. Fortunately, Chisel was very quick in making his intention with the knife very clear by expertly cutting through the hessian snake. His satchel was also politely handed back to him.

"Thank you," stammered Sam.

"Don't mention it," said Chisel in a strong Birmingham accent. Then he took all of Sam's clothes off. Taking the satchel back off him as well.

The only slight relief for Sam as this was done being the observation of Hammer at the large coffin chest. He had pulled out a wondrous mechanical object. It appeared to be two metal tubes a foot apart connected by many short metal chains. It looked wondrous and what it might be used for was a welcome distraction for him to think about. But it was soon put away along with his clothes. He stood there as naked as the day he was born. Apart from the bandages covering the top of his head. He hadn't been born with those of course. Though it might be useful if a baby came out too quickly perhaps? What a strange thought he thought.

"Hammer the dressing."

Hammer opened the lid of the chest again. He took out a pair of soft white gloves and carefully put them on. Then he took out a white cotton bag, undid the drawstrings, and carefully removed a long tube of black material.

"Hammer show him the dressing."

Hammer came across to Sam and held out the black material as though it were the shroud of a fallen hero. Sam reached out to touch it.

"Woh! woh-woh-woh – Can't touch this!"

Sam looked up confused at the hooded figure on the bow.

"Do you see how the light is frightened to touch it but it cannot resist?"

Now that he understood what he was not allowed to do Hammer brought it back within Sam's reach. It was indeed a strangely alluring material. The blackest thing he'd ever seen and yet shining as though it were wet to the touch. He'd never seen it before but it seemed so familiar.

"Do you like it?"

"What is it?" asked Sam.

"Hammer hold it up."

With the utmost respect and leaning forward so there was no chance of it catching on the tools sticking out of his apron Hammer held up his arms and let the wondrous thing unfurl.

It was a robe exactly the same as that being worn by the demon above him.

"Do you like it now?"

Sam could not speak. As he gazed in wonder it felt like the night had peeled back for him to gaze upon all the secrets of the universe. He didn't think he was religious but looking at it he thought of Eve and the apple and how he could almost forgive her. He desperately wanted to put it on.

"No-one knows where they are from. No-one knows where they are going. Unless they can wear one of those."

"There are only two in all of England," whispered Hammer from behind it.

"Chisel describe such a robe."

"Millionaire munk!" said Chisel nodding appreciatively.

Again the cold stiletto laugh. "Trust a Warwickshire man to put into two words what a thousand wizards in a thousand years might have taken to create."

"Thank you sir," said Chisel doffing his cap.

"One of those silly sods would not have the ambition to wear it."

"Sorry sir? A wizard or a munk?" asked Chisel looking up.

"Shut up!" hissed Hammer at him.

"They choose simple clothes to help them lead a simple life. The right clothes can make one feel good. The wrong clothes can make one feel bad. Clothes create an impression to others. A piece of coloured cloth can bind men together in battle. It is also that coloured cloth that tears them apart in battle. So in order to truly see the man inside you first have to remove his clothes. Now with that understood – Put the cock in the oven."

Much to Sam's disappointment Hammer respectfully furled away the beguiling robe and put it back in its cotton bag. He joined Chisel at the coffin chest. They took out the wondrous mechanical object at each end and then pulled. It made a regular clicking noise as it grew between them. Chisel let go of his end allowing Hammer to spin it and place his end on the ground beneath the branch. It was a ladder! The chains were rungs! But how could the sides grow like that? The ingenuity of it!

"Is that made by wizards too?" Sam asked.

Chisel turned to give him a knowing look. "Made in England mate!"

Sam's hands had been trying to protect any privacy he had left but at this welcome news he clasped them to his mouth. How he loved his countrymen! When they were at their best they were the best of anyone!

Chisel disappeared behind the tree trunk and reappeared carrying a chair without legs slung over his shoulder. Up the wonderful growing ladder he went and with a little banging attached the chair securely to the branch. Meanwhile Hammer had picked up the shovel and dug up a small chest. He brushed off any lingering soil on the lid with a brush from his apron.

It was an attention to detail Sam noted and admired. "Are those provisions you've kept cool for as long as possible?" he asked.

Hammer looked at him not answering.

"You seem to have thought of everything?" suggested Sam.

"We like to think so," said Chisel coming down the ladder. Hammer handed the chest to him and he took it back up. Very quickly it was attached to the branch as well. He came back down but to Sam's surprise removed the wonderful growing ladder. He and Hammer squeezed it back down and replaced it in the coffin chest. His satchel went in there as well but the cotton bag came out. Then they carried the chest out of sight behind the tree trunk. Then Hammer filled in the small hole and hid the spade in a nearby bush. Then the pair of them stood to attention and waited.

"Let the cock fly."

Hammer and Chisel came across to him taking a wrist each.

"You can't be serious surely?" pleaded Sam.

They bent down taking a firm grip on each ankle.

"You have a magic ladder! It's in the chest for pity's sake! Why?"

Any further protests were tipped out of him with the first swing. Hammer and Chisel began to sing:

"A leg and a wing to see the king!"

Sam shut his eyes tightly.

"A one! ... A two! ... A jolly! ... BIG! ... THREE!!!"

The pressure was released on his wrists and ankles, there was a period that seemed to stand still when he had never been more terrified in his life, and then an abrupt thump in his back that signalled his successful arrival in the chair. Hot molten anger instantly kicked in the door of relief. "What was all that about? I could have been killed!"

"Yes."

"Yes you say? Yes you say?" Sam noticed a familiar bouncing motion in the black material now near him. "Are you laughing? Do you think it's funny?"

"Yes."

It was like bellows on a blacksmith's hearth. "Come here! I'm going to box your ears!" He stupidly lurched oblivious to all danger. But their chairs were too far apart and he couldn't reach. Even in his red mist he noted how the hooded figure had not flinched or recoiled in the slightest from him.

"But this is not funny for you. You should look down."

Sam wasn't hot-tempered by nature. He had been surprised by his reaction and was already ashamed of it so it was easier than it might have been to look down. Chisel or Hammer it could have been either - it didn't matter - was placing an arrow in a bow then drawing it and taking direct aim at him. The reason it didn't matter was because the other one had been pointing an arrow with his name on it already.

"Do you want to behave?"

Never had Sam felt more naked or vulnerable. But that was the idea wasn't it? Being him he tried to analyse how he felt before replying.

"I need to know if you are lucky. One either is or is not. It is an element in even the best of plans. Something I do not underestimate so I have devised a simple test for it. A test I admit I do enjoy. Now you have passed we can continue – Or it ends right now."

No man with a voice like that could have a heart. Sam suspected this man would give treading on an ant more consideration.

"Well?"

"Has anyone ever said no to you?" asked Sam.

"Probably not enough."

It wasn't going to be Sam today. "I am your complete servant Sir," he said.

"Good. Hammer and Chisel. Your loyal promptness is always a delight to behold."

Both bows were lowered and Sam felt his eyes blink. It would appear he had been staring wide-eyed at the bows since he had first seen them.

"There is a belt in your chair. Attach it around your middle. Watch you do not catch anything."

Sam did as he was told.

"Hammer throw my guest the cotton bag."

It landed precisely in Sam's lap.

"Do not put it on. We will see if you earn the right to wear it later. Now enjoy the view whilst I give my men their final instructions."

The hooded figure began to talk in some foreign language Sam didn't recognise. Whatever language it was (for your benefit dear reader I can tell you it was Glaswegian) the man hidden under that black cloak made it sound cold and emotionless and sterile. He looked down at the cotton bag in his lap and felt a tingle up his spine at the thought of what it contained. Curiosity and the prospect of putting the robe on made him inclined to cooperate as much as he could. Was that shameful?

He looked up at the broad canopy of leaves and branches above. They came further down than he had realised from the ground. You would have to be standing right underneath to see them on the branch. Yet he could still see out easily across the huge great field with the trees off in the distance. He twisted in his chair to look behind. It was the same there. They were like two birds hidden in the hedgerow with a clear view of anything approaching. It should have felt snug but Sam was aware he was a long way from any help. Then he remembered his balls. He had confidence in Colin. He hoped he was right about him.

The cold gibberish stopped. Hammer and Chisel tugged at their forelocks then picked up the chest. They disappeared beneath him. He looked down to see where they'd gone.

"They will watch my back from the trees behind us. I will keep an eye on the front. You will do as you are told."

Sam tried but it was impossible to get a glimpse of the man's face beneath the hood or his hands in the folds of the black material. Any clue as to who or what he was.

"You will refer to me as Crow. Name a bird."

"Eagle?" ventured Sam.

"Predictable. Name another."

"Seagull?"

"Too noisy. Name another."

"Magpie?"

"Too clever. Name another."

"Parrot?"

"Pillock. We are in an English Oak tree. I am Crow. You are..."

"Raven?"

"You impertinent chick," warned an icy blast. "Grasp the pecking order."

"Cock!" It was what he had been referred to earlier. Sam was struggling.

"A generic term."

"Blackbird?"

"Are you black?"

Sam looked down at himself. His pale skin dimpled with either the breeze or fear.

"Goose!" he suddenly blurted out.

"Good. I am Crow and you are a Goose. Now Goose, I like to watch the world go by from my mullioned window sitting on a plump cushion of goose feathers. I am experienced of soft furnishings. I know much of the arrangement of cushions for effect. But too many people sit on the cushions others have stuffed. I want to find out if your cushion is your own. If I am satisfied I might make my cushion plumper with some of your feathers. Do I make myself clear Goose?"

"Well yes I think so," said Sam knowing that he was a bookkeeper with balls.

"Good. I do not need your life story but please elaborate on why you think you are a bookkeeper worthy of London."

# CHAPTER 7

## Dark exists when there is no light

Colonel Peru had a manservant up against the kitchen wall by the scruff of his neck. "Whataya mean you can't find him?" he snarled. He tightened his grip on the poor man. "Do you know what the opposite of a secret is?" He leant his face forward to within biting distance. "It's an idea. Now ideas are dangerous. Ideas can change things. People like me don't want any changes so we keep secrets. How do we keep secrets? By silencing anyone who runs away with the idea that they can tell any secrets! Simple isn't it?"

The manservant nodded desperately visibly shaking with fear.

Colonel Peru released his grip. "Now let me tell you something very slowly so there's no misunderstanding – find Graham and bring him to me. You know what will happen if you don't."

"You will throw me from the roof and my miserable carcass will be eaten by the dogs," said the manservant shaking like a puppy in the cold.

"WELL?" roared Colonel Peru.

"My reminder sir," the manservant whimpered. "You haven't given me my reminder."

"Oh yes," said Colonel Peru. He swung his great arm giving the manservant such a blow it sent them both reeling in opposite directions.

The manservant scrabbled to his feet as quickly as he could and fled the kitchen.

Colonel Peru shouted for someone to help him to his feet. The adult servants present all hesitated not wanting to feel his wrath. Two girls of about ten or eleven dressed in rags that had been chopping onions nervously hurried over to him.

Helped back on his feet he turned to address the kitchen staff that had all stopped to watch him go flying. "Now as you can see I don't like bad news. I also don't like work shy gawpers! The last one of you to resume your work will be joining me on the roof!" The effect was instant.

He threw the nearest heavy thing to hand into the middle of them and left the kitchen. He thumped up the stone steps thinking about what to do. The bloody agency had let him down again. It had been a gruesome week and the one bear in a fit state left to fight had gone walkabout. The thing's I'm going to do to that bear when I find him! he thought clenching his fist. He thumped a vase from its stand. The sound of something breaking bringing him to his senses - The thing is I don't think the bleeder actually wants to see one fight. Just see a bear. The wolfhound had just had a litter of puppies. They were pretty big and pretty hairy. Could he pass them off as bear cubs? Not much possibility of emptying Athena's purse that way though. Nor much of a tale to tell Pegasus either.

"How am I going to get my monkey out of this?" he asked aloud. He had reached his hallway and stopped looking at the front door.

I wonder how much Athena values *his* monkey? It's obvious he's one of those "enlightened berks" that actually looks after his staff. Why he was practically consulting with it over there. Kidnap it and demand a ransom? Any petty villain could do that. You're better than that Peru! What then? Pin something on the monkey and demand retribution? Now we're getting somewhere. The monkey does something wrong. I've never been so insulted in my own house. Of course you'll have to pay for it! No you're not seeing my bears. Now piss off before I release the hounds!

He clapped his hands and rubbed them gleefully. "I'll just make sure my guest is comfortable - then I'll decide what his little monkey has been getting up to."

He opened the door to his study. "Everything in order Athena?" he demanded.

"Yes thank you," replied Lord Ecin turning nervously in his chair to face him. He had decided Colonel Peru bore a remarkable resemblance to Mons Meg. A smaller version of course but probably just as dangerous.

"There's wine in the cabinet over there." Lord Ecin opened his mouth to thank him but wasn't given the opportunity – "If there's any missing when I get back I'll break your arm!"

He slammed the door and hurried off towards his gun cupboard.

At the same time Resourceful entered the kitchen. "Good evening everyone. I was wondering if one of you could help me."

He didn't get the response he was expecting. "You shouldn't be in 'ere you twat!" said a round aproned thing he assumed was the cook. She was so ugly it was a wonder she didn't sour the milk.

"I'm sorry for the intrusion I assure you -" he began.

The round aproned thing was reaching for a large broom with clear purpose. "I don't care whose bloody lackey you are. In my kitchen you're a bloody nobody! Now get out you twat before I shove this broom up your arse!"

"Look madam. I only need some information," said Respectful trying to bring his authority to bear.

"Carrot and Swede hold this twat down so I can get this broom in good and proper!"

Two young men stopped whatever they were doing and started moving towards him.

"I assure you that won't be necessary. I'm leaving now," Resourceful said holding up his hands for calm.

Carrot and Swede looked towards the round aproned thing for what to do next. As she was putting the broom back they concluded that the twat could be allowed to leave.

Having quickly negotiated the steps Resourceful stopped at the top shaking his head sadly. "So many people unhappy in their work," he mused, "why does it have to be so?"

It was unfortunate but he would have to find the study himself. What he would find doing so gave him a little shiver. He was about to begin when he turned at the sound of someone running up the steps behind him.

"Quick!" said one of the piles of rags. "If we can we'd like to help you!"

Resourceful looked into two sweet earnest little faces.

"But you'll have to tell us quick before she notices we've gone!"

"Oh that's very kind of you girls. Colonel Peru will be entertaining my master in his study. Can you show me where it is?"

The girls' faces clouded over with such disappointment Resourceful wished he could have retracted his words.

"I'm sorry we're not allowed upstairs yet."

The other pile of rags now looked confused as well as disappointed. "Alice. If we can't help him he is allowed to punish us?"

"I don't know. Will you have to punish us now?"

"Of course not! Why should you be punished for not knowing something?" asked Resourceful smiling kindly.

They both looked confused.

"Alice - tell him to get it over with!" implored the pile of rags that wasn't Alice. She glanced nervously down the steps to the kitchen door.

"Alright! Alright! But we did try to help didn't we?" They began hitching up the miserable collection of rags that passed for dresses.

Resourceful was utterly shocked. He would rather have watched bears and dogs fighting than witness this. "What on earth are you doing?" he gasped.

"Getting ready to be spanked! But can you be quick!"

"Who spanks you like this?" he demanded. Life was hard and tough. Discipline was a good thing. But maltreatment or injustice was something he couldn't abide. Before Colonel Peru was just an unpleasant man. Now he had become an enemy. He kept his master out of his sight. He was obviously cruel. He had called him a monkey. But much worse than all of that - he abused little girls!

He pushed the piles of rags out of the way and flew down the stone steps into the kitchen brandishing his walking cane.

"You Carrot and Swede will remain where you are!" he bellowed. "You - you warty old croan! Make one move towards that broom and I'll break your hand!"

"I'm not having some old twat tell me what to do in my kitchen!" screamed the round aproned thing reaching for the broom.

In an instant Resourceful had spotted a pile of unpeeled potatoes to his side. He picked up the heaviest and let it fly towards the round aproned thing. She took it as he had intended squarely in the left eye.

"Oh you twat!" she said reeling back clutching at her face with both hands. "Carrot! Swede! Shove that bag of sprouts up his arse! Every last one!"

Resourceful swung his walking cane above his head clattering along the pots and pans hanging from a rack. "I warn you you unappetising side dish I am in no mood to be trifled with!"

"Take no notice!" shouted the round aproned thing from behind her hands. "He's an old twat with no farts left in him!"

"Are you still going to take orders from that hideous creature?" said Resourceful looking at Carrot and Swede.

"She is the boss," said one of them, "and we don't know who you are."

Resourceful brought his walking cane down. "Do you know who you are?"

"The sprouts! The carrots! The turnips! The spuds! Shove them all up his arse! Don't listen to him!" squawked the round aproned thing desperately trying to locate her broom with one good eye. "Stuff him like a Christmas -"

She fell down silent. Resourceful hadn't thrown a potato this time. He'd thrown one of the heavy iron saucepans hanging from the rack.

Carrot and Swede couldn't believe what they had just saw and stood rooted to the spot.

"Well, well, well," boomed a familiar voice from the kitchen doorway, "what a very obliging mischievous little monkey you are!"

Resourceful would have been about Colonel Peru in an instant but for one thing – he was holding out the long barrel of a gun.

"I am no monkey you monster!" said Resourceful with contempt.

Colonel Peru was not intimidated. "Making a lot of noise. Throwing things around. No respect for food. You look like a mischievous little monkey to me."

Resourceful was going to ask him about the two young girls at the top of the steps. Then realised it would be unwise for their safety.

"About to have a little chatter monkey? Changed your mind?" ridiculed Colonel Peru. "Now step away from those pots. That's right. Towards that pair of berks."

"Their names are Carrot and Swede," said Resourceful doing as he was told.

"They're a pair of berks who know they'll either be dead or starving if they don't do what I say. Take his stick off him."

"Can we shove it up his arse?" said the round aproned thing trying to get up from the floor.

"Do you know? I'm not sure I want my food being cooked any more by someone whose got such an obsession with arses. You two berks throw her out first."

"Where?" asked one of them.

"I don't bloody care! Where do you put the other rubbish?"

"We feed it to the pigs."

"Well feed it to the pigs then!" roared Colonel Peru.

They weren't sure about that.

Colonel Peru cocked the hammer on the gun.

The round aproned thing was bundled up and taken out. Resourceful hoped they had the sense to take it to a barn or an outbuilding or the shrubbery or the greenhouse or the orchard. She didn't deserve to be eaten by pigs.

"Now monkey. We need to tell your owner what a naughty monkey you've been. And talk compensation for a cook, a dented pan and a wasted potato. But why am I telling you this? You're just a monkey." Colonel Peru motioned with the gun. "In the larder."

Resourceful saw he meant the heavy door to his left. He walked slowly towards it.

"That's right monkey. Open it up and in you go," ordered Colonel Peru.

Resourceful did as he was told and the light of the kitchen was left outside.

"Now how's that crazy old crone lock it?" he heard Colonel Peru say on the other side of the door.

Resourceful had noticed the padlock hanging on the side going in. If Colonel Peru actually took an interest in his staff he might have known this.

"You two girls in here now!" ordered Colonel Peru.

"Yes sir! Coming!"

"Now you tie her hair around that handle," said Colonel Peru.

"But if I do that sir Alice won't be able to move."

"If you don't do it I'll spank you so hard you won't be able to move for a week!"

Resourceful heard them fumbling and scratching on the other side almost immediately.

"Now you come with me girl," said Colonel Peru.

"But I wanted to stay with Alice."

There was the sound of a hard slap and a cry of pain. In that moment in that small cramped larder Resourceful vowed that Colonel Peru would get what he deserved. Not from the Gods. They could be fickle and slow. But from him tonight.

When he was sure Colonel Peru had left he pressed his cheek against the door, "Alice can you hear me?"

"Yes," said a weepy voice.

"Alice if you stop crying we can help each other. Alice believe me I've been in far worse situations. If you just keep trying. If you never give in then you can always find a way."

"I know," said Alice.

"There's a good girl. Now is your friend good at tying knots? Are you actually -"

"She's not my friend she's my sister silly!"

"Sorry I should have known. You look so alike. But can she tie knots? Have you actually tried to move?"

"No."

"Well can you try it now for me?"

There was a few seconds of silence then a bump on the door and then a yelp, "ouch that hurts!"

"Alice! Alice! Stop! I don't want you to hurt yourself."

"Hoi! What's going on?" It was the sound of a young lad not Carrot or Swede. "Alice what are you doing tied to the larder door?"

"The master did it to keep the monkey in!"

"Cool! We've got a monkey now! Can I have a look at it?"

"I don't know. Can he have a look at you monkey?"

Resourceful smiled as it seemed the Gods were prepared to help him. "Uuh Uuh Arrh Arrh!" he said thumping the door.

"Alice stay still!" said the young lad.

"Uuh Uuh Arrh Arrh!" encouraged Resourceful from inside the larder.

"Almost there!"

"Eee! Eee! Eee! Eee!"

"That's it! Alice out the way so I can open it!"

The larder door was flung open by an eager expectant young lad looking in.

"Thank you young man. I am seriously indebted to you," said Resourceful stepping out.

"That's alright but where's the monkey?" said the young lad pushing passed him.

"I'm afraid there is no monkey."

The young lad's shoulders fell at the realisation there was no monkey. "So whydya do that Alice? Say there was a monkey when there wasn't! And why'd you pretend to be a monkey?"

"Alice wasn't lying. Your master referred to me as a monkey so so did she. And I wanted to get out. So thank you once again young man." He patted the young lad fondly on the head which the young lad didn't like.

"Trusting Tim disappointed again! Nothing new there. Abandoned by his mother to work for a mad ginger git! What else was going to happen?"

Resourceful was retrieving his walking stick from where it had been left on the floor. He stopped abruptly because the young lad reminded him suddenly of someone who had been very dear to him.

"If I promise to buy you a monkey will you help me?" he asked.

"A real monkey?" asked Trusting Tim interested.

"Yes a real monkey," replied Resourceful.

"Depends on what you want me to do."

"Now that's a sensible answer young man!" Resourceful reached into his jacket and took out his whistle. "I'd like you to go to the front of the house and find somewhere you can't be seen then blow on this loudly three times. Not a lot to do is it?"

"When do I get my monkey?"

Resourceful handed the young lad the whistle. "You already have it. That whistle and chain are solid silver."

"But I don't know where to buy a monkey?" said Trusting Tim knowing he only had half of what he needed.

"I can see you're a bright young lad. We can use you for better purpose than serving a ginger git! You do as I ask and join us. You have my word I will take you to a shop in London that sells monkeys as soon as I can."

"As soon as I can - I've heard that one before! We'll see! Not far now! This won't hurt! All of them lies!"

Resourceful bent down and placed a gentle hand on the young lad's shoulder looking him directly in the eyes. "I can see clearly that I need to get you and Alice and her sister out of here tonight. You should also know when I make a promise I do my best to keep it. And my best is better than most. But don't tell anyone I said that." Resourceful winked he hoped in a fatherly way and stood up.

"I don't know what to do for the best," said Trusting Tim looking down at the whistle.

"You have my silver whistle my word and the offer of a way out. It is a very generous offer if you could only but see it. Now you must decide what you will do."

Resourceful gently brought the young lad's head up by his chin to look into his eyes trying to determine which way his life force would likely take him. There were no guarantees. He removed his hand gently and beckoned for Alice to follow him.

Outside his study door Colonel Peru reared over the pile of rags, "I cough three times and you do exactly what I told you."

The pile of rags nodded.

Colonel Peru opened the door and shut it behind him.

"Well Athena!" boomed Colonel Peru.

Lord Ecin stiffened at the sight of Colonel Peru addressing him so accusingly and carrying a gun.

"It seems you've got a lot of explaining to do!" Colonel Peru walked over to the drinks cabinet leaning the gun against its side. "What I've got to say is so shocking I need to have a drink first!"

Lord Ecin had spent his time alone in Colonel Peru's study hating it. It was a ghastly study festooned with the male parts of God knows what animals hanging down from all over the walls and the ceiling. The animal heads - the part of the animal normal people put on their walls – were in enormous glass jars on the floor and every other flat surface. All those black lifeless eyes lolling around accusing him of colluding with the monster that had done this to them. He had had enough time to decide enough was enough! He wanted no more of it! The next time he saw Colonel Peru he was going to inform him of his intention to leave. However, that now seemed more difficult than he had imagined.

"Staff problems?" he ventured. It was a feeble attempt to try to establish some common ground.

Colonel Peru turned on him tumbler in hand. "That's very telling indeed you bad apple!"

"Bad apple?" repeated Lord Ecin incredulously.

Colonel Peru gave a hearty laugh making his great ginger beard sound like a beech bush on a windy day in winter.

Lord Ecin thought it would be polite to join in.

Colonel Peru abruptly snatched up the gun pointing it at Lord Ecin. "Who said you could join in?"

Lord Ecin gulped.

"You don't do anything unless I tell you! Do you understand?"

Lord Ecin nodded thinking this was no way to treat a guest.

Colonel Peru rested the gun against the drinks cabinet. "You see Athena. As far as the authorities are concerned I sell fruit. My real interests -" he motioned with his hand around them, "I make sure are of no interest to them. So you have to listen to what I say carefully to understand what I actually mean. Ready Athena?"

Lord Ecin nodded nervously knowing he was about to begin a test that might have dire consequences for failing. In reality Colonel Peru was amusing himself at his expense – at this stage.

"Interesting you mentioned staff problems. Have a lot of staff trouble do you Athena? Being such a soft rotten fruit yourself? Have a lot of flies buzzing around because you've not been throwing out the rotten stuff quick enough?" Colonel Peru didn't move from the drinks cabinet. "Your cheeky monkey of a butler for instance – been watching him go furry with mould for too long and doing nothing about it?"

"There's nothing wrong with Resourceful I can assure you," said Lord Ecin knowing it to be the absolute truth.

"Just what a slovenly fruiterer would say isn't it?" Colonel Peru finished his drink and poured himself another large one.

"Please - if you can just tell me what you think has been going on. I'm sure we can clear the whole matter up amicably," suggested Lord Ecin hopefully.

Colonel Peru slapped down the tumbler on the drinks cabinet in indignation. "Gonna try and shut me up with a free bag of oranges? Is that it? I've found out you're peddling dirty fruit and you think I can be shut up with a few items gratus?"

"I'll think you'll find the word is *gratis*," said Lord Ecin trying to be helpful.

Colonel Peru snatched up the gun again. "I'll think you'll find any more Latin lessons from a Citrus Orchard Shit like you will result in a loss of your senses AD INFINITUM!"

Lord Ecin didn't dare say anything or move anything.

Cradling the gun over his left arm Colonel Peru took up his tumbler in his right hand. "Now I'm a fair man Athena. I'm going tell you what's upset me about you. Then I'm going to give you the chance to correct it. And if you don't -" he bobbed the gun up and down a bit, "that gives me the right to do what I like with you."

Lord Ecin didn't think it did actually but wasn't going to say it just yet.

"So here's the thing. I take the welfare of my staff - unlike some shitty pallet stackers - very seriously. And when I see someone messing with my carefully stacked fruit arranged thus for correct air circulation to aid longevity I don't tolerate it. Unlike some piss poor wobbly stackers that'll do types like you. Wondering why there's a funny smell and not getting the return customers that you should."

Lord Ecin closed his eyes desperately trying to work out what was being said to him as he'd been told to do.

"Well closing your eyes to it ain't going to work this time sloppy! I've got a sweet juicy plum that's one of a pair. And I don't take kindly to any passing punter fingering my sweet juicy plums as and when they feel like it! Now I'm going to show you my plum and you're going to take a good look at it!"

Had something happened to Colonel Peru's testicles? thought Lord Ecin desperately. What on earth was he about to show him?

Colonel Peru coughed loudly three times. When nothing happened he looked angrily towards the study door and coughed loudly three times again.

"Would you like me to get you some water?" suggested Lord Ecin.

"I'd like you to shut up!" snarled Colonel Peru. He tossed the gun over to Lord Ecin. "Here hold this! Thing's not loaded anyway! As if I'd need it loaded dealing with a brown paper bag shuffler like you!"

He angrily strode passed Lord Ecin and flung open the study door. "Are you deaf you...."

It was all he managed before the heavy tip of Resourceful's walking cane made swift contact with his cranium and he fell to the floor like a mattress being thrown out of an upstairs window.

Lord Ecin jumped up out of his chair to greet Resourceful throwing the horrible thing he held away...

"No my Lordship!" shouted Resourceful. But it was too late. True to form Colonel Peru had lied about the gun. It fell through the air. It hit the floor. It exploded with light and noise and smoke. To Lord Ecin it seemed a feather could fall more quickly to the ground than he could. When the light and noise and smoke had stopped he'd got up pulling against the gravity of Jupiter it seemed. Once he'd stood up he was back. "That was lucky," he said. But it wasn't. Resourceful was no longer standing in the doorway.

To Lord Ecin's horror he was lying on his side clutching at his backside. He hurried over to him in some vile dream. He dropped to his knees bereft of the desire to take another breath with the enormity of what he'd done.

"Looks like this is it my Lordship," said Resourceful in a hoarse whisper, "It's been an honour it really has."

"Don't," cried Lord Ecin softly, "Just don't. Don't go. Don't leave me. What will I do?"

"My Lordship You were the perfect hole for my peg. I will always be grateful."

"Don't Resourceful. Fight it! Whatever's wrong I'll get fixed. But just hold on please."

"I do believe I've been shot in the bum. Unless you can stem the flow of blood in some way - which I wouldn't expect you to do  - then my time is short. Get going sir. Welly should be waiting for you outside. Take the whistleblower too. Treated well I believe he could ultimately replace me."

"Whistleblower?" repeated Lord Ecin. "Is this what happens? Do you start saying stupid things before you go?"

With a great effort Resourceful lifted his head a few inches up from the floor. "He has my whistle sir. A young lad with my whistle - oh no what is it she wants?"

Lord Ecin looked behind him to see a round aproned thing striding determinedly towards them. As she got closer Lord Ecin saw she had a nasty bump on her head.

"Out of my way young 'un. I can help him!"

"You can? Oh fantastic!" said Lord Ecin eagerly jumping up out of the way.

"Yes this will do him no end of good!" said the round aproned thing pulling out a broom from behind her back triumphantly.

For the second time Resourceful cried, "No my Lordship!"

"How's it feel throwing a poor old cook out into the cold now you bastard!"

Lord Ecin began wrestling with the round aproned thing to make her stop when it became apparent what she was doing with the broom. But she was a lot stronger than she looked and so intent about her business he was losing the battle. Only when the broom handle snapped with half of it still protruding from Resourceful's rear did she desist.

"He ain't getting off that lightly! I'm gittin' another broom!" she said storming off.

"Oh Resourceful -why am I so pathetic?" lamented Lord Ecin. "You probably had minutes and now you've only got seconds."

"But look -" said a sweet voice, "his bum's not pooing red anymore."

Resourceful opened his eyes. "She's right my Lordship! I can feel it. The broom handle is stemming the flow! Would you help me up both of you? We can all get away from here!"

"It's a miracle," cried Lord Ecin helping Resourceful to his feet.

"I think you'll find it's a deranged cook misusing a broom but I'm not complaining," grimaced Resourceful. He winced with the pain but vowed not to show it again. "Though I am going to have to be careful how I walk. You young 'un. You find your sister Alice and meet us outside. You're both coming home with us."

"But we live here."

"Not anymore. Your master is dead." Resourceful didn't think he'd actually killed Colonel Peru but he looked dead which would do for the moment. "And I have a wonderful master who will look after you both very well." He smiled warmly at Lord Ecin - as much as the pain would allow anyway. "Get your sister and outside as quick as you can girl. Both of you are welcome remember!"

The pile of rags eagerly hurried off towards the kitchen.

"Is he dead?" asked Lord Ecin looking down at Colonel Peru.

"I don't honestly know and I don't honestly care. We need to leave my Lordship. We've been lucky. It could have been a lot worse."

Lord Ecin understood. "He might be out of the picture but that crazy cook is still on the loose. Come on Resourceful hurry up and follow me!"

Resourceful didn't know whether to laugh or cry - that broom handle might be saving his life but by golly it hurt to walk with it sticking out of his rear.

Outside they found the night air cool fresh and welcome. Welly was waiting with the coach. They were quickly joined by Alice and her sister and Carrot and Swede. All four of them had bundled the cook into the larder and locked her in! All four of them would like to work for the really good master if that was alright? Lord Ecin had introduced himself and hugged them all as they got into the coach. Inside waiting already was Graham the bear, Trusting Tim and a manservant close to a nervous breakdown. Resourceful climbed in last not sitting down like the others but on the floor on his front for an obvious reason but very happy in how the night had eventually unfolded. They had saved a few souls that dark night. If the person who kept kicking the tip of the broom handle every now and then would just stop it then his happiness would be complete.

# CHAPTER 8

## Oh, what a tangled web we weave
## When first we practise to deceive

Sam knew exactly why he was a very good bookkeeper. Ever since he was a child figures had sung to him like a melody. Just as a musical person could identify a bum note so it was with him with an incorrect figure. He had been lucky enough to travel on the continent as a young man seeing new bookkeeping techniques. Over time he'd added his own ideas to improve them further. He was also meticulous and scrupulous and industrious. All of these things were true. So it was surprising to him when he opened his mouth the first word that came out was, "Natalie."

Was he really going to give away his secret so easily? Tell this demon here and now that his maid had such an incredible memory that it enabled him to operate in a way he believed no man could do on his own? It looked like he was.

"Natalie came into my employment like many domestic staff enter service through a petition from a parent. I was having my shirts cleaned by a short toad-like woman who quite frankly repulsed me but always did an excellent job. One day collecting my shirts the woman had proudly summoned a round faced child with a bonnet plonked on top and introduced it as her daughter. Not only that but one day she would be London's most beautiful daughter! I looked at the child then the toad-like washerwoman thinking it highly unlikely even if the father was Adonis. The washerwoman had a proposition for me - if I agreed to take her daughter into my service when the time came she would have the girl collect and deliver my shirts in the meantime. It looked like at least six years of added convenience for me. I would need a maid sometime in the future and judging by the quality of the toad's washing she would teach the girl how to do things well. I was also -"
Sam had been looking at the cotton bag in his lap but at this point felt

the need to look away, "I'm ashamed to admit now but I was also quite curious to see if the daughter became as ugly as the mother. Or indeed was able to surpass it."

He looked back down at the cotton bag. "Do you know? In all that time she was never late or ever anything missing. It was quite remarkable. And how gifted was the washerwoman with foresight as well as with brush and soap! I'm not exactly sure when the transition took place in the years of shirt collections and deliveries but only marvel at the wonder of a rich fragrant rose springing from the bog of the earth. She entered my service as agreed. But then quickly began an uncomfortable period of admirers seeking her attention. She graciously rebuked all of them with a maturity above her years. Even some of my neighbours tried it on which isn't right. A gentleman may stroke your cat on the clear understanding he doesn't try to put his finger in it!"

"ENOUGH!" It was spoken with the cold power of the east wind. The iron finger that pushes hands and face against the blacksmith's anvil without pity.

"I'm sorry. I'm really sorry," Sam felt the need to say.

Crow's hood turning to face him was a chilling sight. The way the gentle breeze playfully tugged at the flaps of the material then seemed to runaway frightened making it worse.

"I have never seen a man go off at such at tangent. Unless -" Sam could feel himself being scrutinised, "you work hard to impress a maid you have feelings for?"

"Oh no I assure you. I've watched her grow from a girl! She is a most diligent maid. That's all!" It did sound as though he was protesting too much.

"I wonder if this can be profitable today," mused the cold voice from the black hole. "Your initial bulldog spirit a lie? I do not need brave bookkeepers of course but I do need them utterly truthful."

The hooded figure dark and menacing brooded on the branch next to him. After what seemed like an awfully long time Sam was told, "Put the robe on."

Sam carefully undid the drawstrings. The consequences of dropping the robe or having it blow away were too disastrous to risk any rushing or clumsiness. Taking the robe out he marvelled again at its blackness and lightness. He tucked the cotton bag under his thigh and slipped the robe over his head. It was incredible how detached he now felt from his surroundings. Yet the material seemed as insubstantial as mist in a morning meadow. He squeezed a piece of it between his thumb and forefinger. It bent like cotton but felt as hard as iron. How was that possible? There was something else. He could feel a desire for clarity permeating through him like osmosis. Except the bandages were interfering with that in a way he knew they weren't supposed to. They were acting as some kind of barrier to the power of the robe. Bizarrely it seemed to be the robe that allowed him to know this!

"Do you think a rose appreciates being pruned for it to flower with more vigour?"

Sam knew how to respond. Knew what the expected answer was. But he also knew that he shouldn't know that. It was like he could unpin his shadow to move around as he liked fooling someone looking at his shadow.

"I don't believe it does. You would also have to know if it had a memory. Whether it thought of it as a regular investment or an unprovoked act of mutilation. In either case I don't think it appreciates it at the time," he replied. He'd added a bit but not too much.

"So we are agreed that some bad is allowed in the name of a greater good."

"Within reason of course," replied Sam.

"Within reason," repeated Crow. "Very important to agree on that apparently. I see it as meaningless. All those kings queens bishops and rooks moving predictably around their squares. What do you think about rules Goose? Would you help someone that wants to kick the whole chessboard over?"

"No I would not. Without rules there is chaos. Nothing good can come from chaos. The only ones who would even suggest such a thing are the shadows and dark things afraid of the light," said Sam knowing it was what he believed.

"Decide yourself you want to remove the hood."

Sam knew that he shouldn't be able to have the choice whether he obeyed or not. He could remove the hood but chose not to because that was what was expected.

Crow waited for a short while. "Remove your hood."

Sam did as he was told and removed the hood.

"Good. Replace it."

Sam replaced the hood.

"You are mine Goose whilst you wear that robe. You cannot lie to me and you will do exactly what I command without any ability to resist. I cannot tell you why that is. I do not know how the sun works but I enjoy its light and warmth. Crows cannot sing like other birds but they can talk of plans. The more they talk the better the plans can become. But if they talk at inappropriate times then plans may be lost or stolen. But I am safe here in my tree and you are mine Goose. I will talk of my plans and you will listen until told to speak. When I say "Okay Goose" you may speak. But only then. With that understood we can begin."

Sam hadn't been given an instruction to say or do anything so he didn't.

"Scotland is a beautiful country. She deserves better than she has had. Better weather. Better respect. Better rule. Her people should not have to leave the place to better themselves. Twenty years ago someone was forced to leave her. They ended up in the West Indies where they would watch the fishermen casting their nets. They began to think how wonderful it would be to have a really big net to catch many fish at once. But such a large net would be too big to handle. So many fish would spoil before they could all be sold. But the sun heated their brain pleasantly in a way it could not back in Scotland. The warm surf tickling their toes in a way it could not back in Scotland. The local rum clearing their thoughts in a way it could not back in Scotland. And one day out all those thoughts tumbled onto the white sand laid bare - people could be caught like fishes in a net.

Not with a big clumsy net too big to handle but with a net one square at a time. You could grow it around them. They would not notice they were being netted. And not to sell them. But to milk them. Small regular amounts that they kept on producing and you collected regularly. So how? You tax them. But only kings and government can raise taxes. So you do not call it a tax even though that is what it is. Your own private tax on people. But how? I will tell you.."

So it began. The more Sam listened the more a sense of wonder grew in him at the ambition and vision a single person could contain. It was a cathedral of a plan! When Crow said "Okay Goose" it felt an honour to lay a stone or craft a piece of timber that could reside in such a structure to man's ability! He admired it immensely and desperately wanted to see it built. At times they stopped for him to have something out of the chest. Some cheese, some cold meats, pickles, a bottle of ale. He did notice that Crow didn't eat or drink any of it. For how long Crow and Sam conversed he had no idea or cared. When they had finished Sam felt exhausted but elated too. Then Crow turned to him very deliberately.

"Okay Goose. Do you remember the very first thing I said to you?" he asked.

"Yes I do," said Sam. "A reference to the blackness contained within your cloak."

"I am afraid it is true." It was the east wind again. "It is the English who are going to be caught in my net. Every last one of them. Once you remove your robe you will forget all we have spoken about. It does not matter because shortly Hammer and Chisel will return. When they do you will be taken down and wiped from existence as chalk is wiped from a blackboard."

Sam hurled back the hood. "Never!" he spat.

Crow gave a visible jolt of surprise. It was the first time he had not looked completely in control. "Okay Goose. Remove the robe." It didn't sound like him.

"What's that about the best laid plans of mice and men? You're not going to get away with this! I'm not letting you sell my countrymen down the river!" If only Sam could have reached him and wrung his neck. That's what he felt like doing right now.

Crow had regained his composure after his initial shock. He voice was its usual cold calm calculating tone, "I do not believe in religion. That is an invention of men and like any of his inventions it is not perfect and he changes it and meddles with it to suit his purpose. But I do believe in something much bigger than us. How it works I have no idea but I believe it respects balance. I am a monster. I do monstrous things. Perhaps I am allowed to do such things because of good people like you. There must be a reason the robe did not work on you. It seems you are to be given the chance to escape."

His balls! Sam have forgotten about his balls! Reaching into the turban of bandages he pulled out two brightly coloured balls the size of hen eggs. He brandished them at Crow like the secret weapon they were. Then holding them out as far as he could he let them drop to the ground.

"My consideration for your comfort a mistake on my part," said Crow. "Can I ask what should happen now?"

"I don't honestly know," smiled Sam apologetically. "The coachman told me to do it when I needed help but not what would actually happen."

Crow's hood shook from side to side unhappily. "How many times? Details! Details! Details! - Wait! I think we might have an answer!" From the far off ring of trees in front of them the coach burst out at speed. "To have seen your balls drop he must have been watching us the whole time. Discipline not normally found in a coach driver."

"I think he wanted to be a doctor of medicine," said Sam wondering how long it would be before he got there.

"A noble ambition. I wonder why he failed. I also wonder who will reach us first." Crow turned to look behind him.

Sam did the same and was horrified to see Hammer and Chisel running towards their position too.

"Just because you are to be given the opportunity to escape does not mean I should let it happen. I also signalled for my men in a less clumsy manner than your own. However, if it works it works so who am I to say? The robe you wear. It is extremely valuable -"

"Yes I know!" said Sam snatching his head forwards and backwards trying to see who was going to win, "one of only two in the country!"

Crow's hood gave an uncharacteristic little dip. "Disappointing you should know that. Can you take it off?"

Sam pointed jubilantly at the coach thundering towards them. "You've been feeding your men too many pies! Look how much closer the coach is!"

Crow was unmoved. "Pride very often comes before a fall. You are not out of the woods yet. It is still in the balance. Hammer and Chisel are almost within range of using their bows. I might not be able to stop them until it is too late."

Sam pinched the material of the robe. "I know this is stronger than armour. I'll be alright."

"It is not you they will be aiming for. They will remove the bigger threat first. Do you want the coachman's blood on your hands?"

Sam had been hoping to get away with taking the robe. But he'd never stole anything before in his life. "If I promise will you call them off?"

"Of course."

"But how can I trust the promise of a hooded fiend like you?"

"Because I am not ready to kick over the chessboard just yet so am bound by rules like everyone else."

The coach was almost beneath them. Stealing something was bad enough but risking someone's life doing it was too much. "Very well. I promise to drop it in the field. How's that?"

Crow graciously nodded. "Undo your belt now," he said before standing up and making a great arc with arm.

Sam looked behind to see Hammer and Chisel stop running towards the tree. A few seconds later the coach thundered to a halt beneath them.

"Jump! Jump!" Colin shouted desperately from the top of his coach.

It looked a long way down to Sam. He hesitated.

"Okay Goose – Jump!" ordered Crow. "And good luck!"

Sam looked at him oddly. Was he finding this funny again?

"Jump! Jump!" shouted Colin again.

"Those figures will never look the same again now. Jump!" ordered Crow pointing down at the coach.

Sam shut his eyes and jumped landing with a thud so hard it bounced the loosened bandage from his head.

"Hold on!" shouted Colin as he abruptly turned about the coach and sped off in the same direction he'd come from. On the roof Sam felt as flung around and as unsafe as a cloth doll in a dog's mouth. He looked behind as best as he could to see Hammer and Chisel now at the tree beneath their master.

"Stop! Stop!" Sam shouted at Colin. "You must stop or they will kill us!"

"What are you mad?" Colin shouted not slowing down.

Sam could barely get his breath with all the bumping and thumping. "It's the robe! If we leave the robe they'll leave us alone!"

"Rope? What rope?" shouted Colin.

"Please! Please! Just STOP!"

Sam slid horribly forward as the coach violently came to a halt.

"You'd better be right!" warned Colin looking anxiously back at the tree. If there was one sign of movement from any of them he was giving his girls the beans!

Sam hurriedly removed the robe though he had barely the energy it seemed to remove a hat. He kissed it and threw it over the side of the coach knowing such a wondrous thing didn't deserve to be treated like that.

"Go! Go!" he shouted at Colin. "Before he changes his mind!"

Colin slapped his girls into action.


Back at the tree Hammer quickly readied his bow. "He's dropped the robe! Take them out now sir?"

"No let them go," ordered Crow above him in the tree.

"Sir?" asked Hammer surprised.

"Yeah what for sir?" asked Chisel reluctantly lowering his bow.

"To keep order for a little bit longer gentlemen. Now get me down."

# CHAPTER 9

## Look after the pennies and the pounds will look after themselves

Lord Dratsab made himself comfortable in the chair in a very satisfied manner. "That's a fine port. Ecin does know how to keep a good cellar."

"Yes. I wonder if we'll ever see him again," replied Lord Tig reaching for his glass languidly.

"Of course we will! Pruvey will just rough him up a bit. Have a bit of sport with the fellow. I don't really wish him any harm. He's a friend!"

Lord Tig regarded him oddly. "I'm not sure you actually have any friends Dratty."

"Well what are you then? Scotch mist?" asked Lord Dratsab smiling.

"At this moment in time I'm more of an accomplish. I allowed you to send our gracious host on a wild goose chase to a known madman." His face buckled. "And on the pretence of the greater good for humanity!" He burst out laughing with Lord Dratsab eagerly joining in. He wiped away a tear from his eye. "All that poppycock about commerce!"

Lord Dratsab suddenly stopped laughing. "I've got something to show you." He reached into his pocket and held out a small clear bottle with an orange label on it.

"What's this?" asked Lord Tig taking it from him.

"Read the label."

Williams Amorphous Nordic Kip (WANK) is a rare and precious fluid to help relieve the strains of modern day living. When you want the fluid of a Scandinavian Beauty in your hand reach for WANK. Collected from only the finest natural buxom blonde women be assured of the quality of WANK. 9 out of 10 bishops swear by WANK! Go for it! Go for WANK!

Lord Tig turned the bottle over to read what was on the back

WARNING: WANK is definitely harmless. Evidence is inconclusive whether repetition of the act it supports can lead to blindness and/or hairy palms. If you are finding it easier to grip things but more difficult to find them. If you are struggling to read this after repeated WANK usage then the makers accept NO RESPONSIBILITY whatsoever. That's life.

"I'm still none the wiser. Though I am reminded of a governess who every night would warn my brother and I that the balls would fall out of an over-polished musket!"

"She was obviously being cryptic!" chuckled Lord Dratsab.

"No I think she was Scottish," said Lord Tig grinning.

"Well whether WANK is harmless or harmful is not important. It's only someone's opinion. The most intelligent man walking the face of the earth can still be wrong. And it will always be the case. But in the meantime – do you know how much people are paying for a bottle of that?"

Lord Tig held it up to the light. "There's not much there. Three pennies?"

"Two schillings! Two bloody schillings!" said Lord Dratsab knowing it must be hard to believe.

"I don't believe it!" exclaimed Lord Tig.

"It could make me richer than all my mines put together!"

"You've invested in this? What sort of profit are you making?" asked Lord Tig handing him back the bottle of WANK.

Lord Dratsab placed the bottle on the table between them in full view. "Nothing at the moment. I'm reinvesting all the profits back in. I have a contact that got me involved and sorts it all out for me. I don't want to be messing about in the day to day business of it. Why would I?"

Lord Tig nodded. "Well I understand that. But how much is this fellow charging you?"

"Nothing! His costs come out of the business."

"Well how much are you in for?" asked Lord Tig hiding his scepticism.

"Price of a good racehorse. That's what I invested initially. I'm told it's already worth three times that! In less than a year!" Lord Dratsab sat back to drink his port.

"So why are you telling me?" asked Lord Tig putting his glass down.

"The inventor of WANK is a French Doctor apparently -"

Lord Tig interrupted him, "But that stuff's Scandinavian!" He pointed at the bottle of WANK on the table.

"He did that in case it didn't work. So it wouldn't be a French product that failed."

"Seriously? Isn't that just typical of the pompous pride of a Frenchman?" Lord Tig shook his head. "I'm not sure I want to hear any more."

Lord Dratsab was eager to continue, "Listen! It's not important. He has now developed something he calls "After Shave"!"

Lord Tig pulled an unimpressed face.

"Come on Tiggy!" implored Lord Dratsab. "What's the difference between rich people and poor people?"

Lord Tig threw up his hands. "Where do we begin?"

"They smell don't they? Poor people smell! Imagine they could buy something that stopped them being so smelly? Something they splashed on after having a shave to make them smell nice. They'd buy a bottle of it every week!"

Lord Tig shook his head in disagreement. "It's been done for centuries – covering up bad smells with something that smells nice. But it's a luxury purchase poor people can't afford. It won't make you the money you think. And do you know why? Because most poor people have got beards! Men and women!"

Lord Dratsab smiled knowingly. "That's the flaw I saw in his suggestion. But I realised something else. It's not just about them smelling nice after a shave – it's about them smelling the same as you!"

"What?" asked Lord Tig sharply.

"It's making them believe they don't just smell nice - It's making them believe they smell like a gentleman or even a Lord!"

"I don't want my gardener or groom or labourer to smell like me thank you!" spat Lord Tig.

"We only need to persuade a few Lords and gentlemen to say they use it. Just enough to make people believe all gentlemen use it."

Suddenly Lord Tig looked very interested. "You mean lie to the buggers?"

Lord Dratsab was grinning in a very satisfied way. "This doctor pretends he wants to do it for equality and fraternity and all that. But he knows about the money. There's money here Tiggy. Lots of it! This is aspiration. This is hope . This is selling a dream. If people are willing to spend two schillings for WANK how much are they going to spend to smell like a gentleman? To splash it on and pretend they're as good as us?"

Lord Tig didn't like that. "Why should we even begin to let them think they're as good as us?"

"We both know there's much more to being a gentleman than smelling nice! That's not the point. The point is we let them believe it to make lots of money!" Lord Dratsab leant forward. "We're only pretending," he whispered.

Lord Tig looked interested again. "Do you think your contact could make this work?"

"No not with Team Wank," admitted Lord Dratsab.

Lord Tig looked visibly surprised with his honesty.

"This is much more ambitious. That's why I've got Crow involved. He'll bring in the expertise they're lacking."

Lord Tig rubbed his chin. "I imagine the only reason you've brought this matter to my attention is because you're looking for someone else with a spare racehorse to put in?"

Lord Dratsab nodded, "and be willing to join me in extolling the virtues of After Shave when the time came."

"And you say you have Crow?" asked Lord Tig picking up the bottle of WANK.

"Someone who always gets things done without any failure. I get him involved pay him his fee and whatever I need to happen then happens without any further involvement from me. I admit this is the biggest thing I have asked him to do so far." Lord Dratsab picked up his port looking at Lord Tig intently, "So?"

"Have you ever met him?" asked Lord Tig rolling the bottle of WANK around in his hand.

Lord Dratsab shook his head.

"No niether did I," said Lord Tig glancing down. "Secretive chap. But I can't argue with what he gets done."

"So now you know whose on board - are you in?" asked Lord Dratsab. "That little beauty you're holding proves it will work. That little beauty is just the start!"

Lord Tig put the bottle of WANK down on the table. "I'm in!" he said smiling. "And our host?"

Lord Dratsab shook his head. "I daresay Crow might have to break a few eggs. He won't be up for that."

Lord Tig nodded in understood agreement.

"Besides his grandfather left him more money than he knows what to do with. Any more would just be a further burden to him," said Lord Dratsab putting down the port to pick up his bottle of WANK.

Lord Tig smiled, "It'll be our little secret then."

# CHAPTER 10

## Red sky at night shepherd's delight
## Red sky in morning the barn's on fire

The tavern was dark but he could see that it was empty. A stale tobacco fog hung in the air too lazy to find a way out from last night. The floor was a patchwork quilt of the debris and filth strangers leave behind for someone else to clean up though *someone else* rarely did. The lithe man dressed mostly in black with a sword hanging down at his side hesitated. They were expensive boots he was wearing.

Proficient at applying his weight gradually he opened the door further and silently stepped in. Next was to consider whether to leave the door open or to close it? In an enforced escape every second could be vital. To have to open a door, or worse, find yourself fiddling with an unfamiliar latch could give failure a chance to come knocking on that door. However, he never underestimated people's ability to be very sensitive to anything out of place like an open door that was normally shut. So, cupping the edge of the door with his hand, he gently pushed with the heel of his thumb until he felt the doorframe on his fingers. Then with his acute attention to detail, he pulled it back slightly to allow a margin for his hand being in a great hurry. He turned and placed his hand across his midriff so his fingers lay poised over the handle of his sword. The door to the living quarters had been obvious from the beginning. He silently began to make his way towards it.

Suddenly the lazy tobacco fog was shoved out of the way by the shape of a woman hurrying through the front door.

"Lucky for me I've got a cock I can rely on in the morning!" said the woman aloud. "I'd have been late otherwise! And the boss would have loved that!"

The lithe man knew otherwise. The silly woman was in fact early. If it were his cockerel he'd ring its neck for giving him bad information!

He would have quickly moved on to deciding to what extent she needed removing from the situation were it not for the truce the filthy windows seemed to have agreed with the light outside in order for them all to get a proper look at her. She had not noticed the lithe man and had immediately began placing beer mugs from the bar top onto a shelf above. The stretching motion pulling the cotton material of her simple dress tight under her breasts. In such a place it was like finding two shiny pennies sticking out of a pile of dog poo.

"Do you always talk to yourself?" he said letting his presence known.

She stopped holding a beer mug in mid-air. "Ooh you made me jump!" A rope of her thick yellow hair fell caressing her cleavage on the way down before coming to rest under her right breast framing it beautifully. She peered into the gloom quizzing him with such big sweet innocent ready to please brown eyes.

If the lithe man had a weakness, if there was a chink in his meticulous armour, if there was a fly buzzing around his ointment - then that fly wore a dress. He loved attractive women. They could delight his every sense. They were no longer pennies he was looking at - they were half-crowns.

"How old are you?" he asked.

She looked coyly at the beer mug. "I'm sixteen."

"No you're not," he said in a way that indicated it was never a good idea to lie to him.

"Do you promise not to tell anyone if I tell you?" she asked meekly after a few seconds. The stern look on his face indicated it was also a good idea not to try and bargain with him. "When I say anyone I really mean him upstairs - the boss." Her big brown eyes were like a doe's.

He nodded so slightly it meant nothing but it was all she required.

She leant over the bar towards him and whispered her big secret, "I'm fourteen."

The lithe man smiled and when he wanted he had a charming cheeky smile. "You're very well formed for fourteen."

She seemed pleased to have told someone. "That's what my mum says. She says I've always been forward with walkin' and talkin' and growin'. And these -" she straightened thrusting out her breasts, "started poppin' out when I was ten!"

"Tell me about him upstairs," said the lithe man looking at them appreciatively.

She was eager to tell. "His name's Trevor and he was really nice when I started. He said being a barmaid wasn't just pullin' pints and letting the punters pinch your bum and giving you a cuddle – sometimes it was like being an angel in times of a lonely man's need. But would you try and put your hand up an angel's skirt? It's pointless anyway. I don't keep anything valuable there - I put the money straight behind the bar. When I asked Trevor about it he did say the tossers were going too far and to tell them – They can go to town to pay for a girl to let them do that sort of thing. So I do."

"Excuse me – a tosser? Could you tell me what a tosser is?"

She lowered her voice, "Trevor says they're all tossers. But it's behind bar talk and we don't let them know that."

She was a stunningly attractive young thing just on the cusp of blooming but quite clearly he was in the presence of a child. It wouldn't be right. "Is there anything else Trevor keeps secret?" he asked regretting being too early.

She quizzed him again with those big sweet innocent ready to please brown eyes. "I like you. You seem nice."

He smiled pleasantly, "I wouldn't go that far."

She leant forward ready to tell him the most shocking thing he was ever likely to hear. "He puts his boggies in the nuts!" She let the enormity of that sink in. "He thinks it's funny but I think it's a horrible thing to do! But when I said something he said – "There's the door!" He says it all the time whenever anyone complains about something or says anything he doesn't like. And he has a pitchfork out the back if they don't go straightaway!"

"Anything else?"

She seemed surprised that that wasn't enough but appeared not to want to disappoint him. "The chicken pies aren't chicken -" she glanced over her beautiful shoulder before earnestly looking back at him, "he collects frogs and toads in the middle of the night and puts them in the pies!"

The lithe man pondered on this incredible revelation. "What would you do if you were released from this cage little bird?"

She shrugged. "Come right back the next day I suppose. There's not much else in Little Piddle."

"That's a shame. What if you couldn't come back? Because the man upstairs was gone?"

"He'll never leave! He's got too many fingers in too many pies around 'ere. I've learnt that much. My mum's told me to say nothing to anyone about what goes on in the snug!"

"Well it would appear he has been messing with venison pie this time," said the lithe man also sharing a secret.

"Venison? What's that?" she asked picking up on the wrong detail.

"Deer meat," replied the lithe man patiently.

"Well if it's dear meat that's why I've never heard of it! We can barely afford rabbit in our house!" She giggled youthful and infectious.

He slipped out his sword holding it aloft in front of her. "Do you know what this is?"

She stopped giggling. "It's a sword of course!"

The lithe man shook his head gravely. "It's an instrument. I use it to push the life out of people. Quickly – if I feel they deserve it. Or slowly - if I think the time spent passing from this world to the next should be more reflective for them."

She laughed not understanding so nervously.

He had no doubt a diver could spend years trawling the tropics and still not find a pearl as beautiful as this one he had found in a dirty ditch in the English countryside. But she was still a girl. And not a very bright one at that. Still, she deserved better than what her life would be living it out here.

"You're a barmaid are you not? May I give you an order?" he said sheathing his sword.

She smiled happily knowing the answer to that. "What would you like?"

"I would like you to walk out that front door and don't look back until you reach London. Find honest work until you're old enough to understand how to make the best use of what you've been given. Don't waste away your life in Little Piddle. Don't spend sovereigns as though they were pennies. And most importantly forget all about the man who gave you this good advice." It was spoken slowly and gently like a well-meaning uncle.

He was disappointed to see her mouth fall dumbly open.

"Shut your mouth. Take the good advice and your chance. If you are still here when I come down then I will have to kill you. I leave no witnesses." Still he spoke like a well-meaning uncle.

"Witnesses?" she repeated it in the same way she had said "venison".

"I like the way I live. I don't risk it by not tying up loose ends. I'm here to push the life out of Trevor and anyone who sees me doing it. Do you understand little girl?"

She had grasped something. She was frightened now, "because he's been putting boggies in venison pies?"

His impatient hand reached down for his sword to remove such stupidity from existence but his greedy eyes knew it would be a crime to cut down such a flower and stopped it.

"Wake up little girl! Use what you have been given properly!" His face looked more dangerous than his sword. "Run little girl! Run and spend your worth wisely!"

She gazed at him paralysed with fear.

"Run little girl! No-one else can do it for you! Now through that door!"

She didn't move. Not a muscle. She stared at him incredulously as though he was the adored family dog that snarling and slobbering had cornered her for no reason.

Suddenly there was the sound of horses arriving outside. The lithe man's head jerked towards the front door listening. Two horses so two men. He looked back at the barmaid putting his index finger on his lips. He brought his finger down pointing at her. "Don't move!"

She jumped up and ran towards his carefully prepared back door flinging it open and disappearing. He could have stopped her. He looked down to see he had his throwing knife in his hand. He hadn't thought about taking it out. He knew her startling beauty had saved her from him. He hoped what he had not taken away she did indeed spend wisely. He eased his throwing knife back into place grateful his ugly nature didn't always win.

"Women! What are they bloody like?" he asked aloud. Then quickly hid in the darkest corner curious to see if these unexpected visitors were interested in him.

The front door began to open very slowly. Someone began whispering through the gap, "Nightnurse – Nightnurse – Don't kill us - We have new instructions for you - Nightnurse – Nightnurse - Are you there?"

Just because someone was using his name didn't mean he wasn't preparing to kill them the moment he could. Something they seemed to understand judging by how carefully they were opening the door.

"Come on - hurry up!" said someone in a Brummie accent.

The door suddenly stopped opening.

Through the gap Nightnurse could hear what was being said. "Are you mad? I'd rather be hunting a lion with nothing more than a 3/8 chisel than what could be waiting the other side of this door. We're good - but this man is a killing machine. That's all he does. Well that and his reputation with the ladies of course."

"Well what reputation is that then?" asked the Brummie accent.

"Don't you know? He's not just called Nightnurse because he prefers to kill his victims in their beds. He takes care of a lot of other things at night too."

The door resumed its slow opening but Nightnurse now knew who they were and relaxed.

The door finally finished opening. Hammer stiffly stood in the doorway. Little flecks of light glistening off some of the hand tools sticking out of his apron.

"Nightnurse? Are you in there?" he said trying to get his voice to carry but being as quiet as possible. "Nightnurse this goose no longer needs cooking. Nightnurse – this goose no longer needs cooking."

Suddenly he was pushed to one side by Chisel. "We'll be here all bloody day at this rate!" he chided as he stepped in.

"Don't take another step!" said Nightnurse's cold voice from the dark.

Chisel stopped but immediately asked, "Why? Have they got them horrible pork scratchin's the yam-yams like so much?"

Nightnurse stood up into view. He found Chisel's bluntness quite comical.

"See Hammer? Not only are us Brummies brilliant at makin' things but we can charm even the most dangerous beasts with our sparklin' wit." He didn't take his eyes off Nightnurse.

Nightnurse put his finger to his lips then brought it away to point at the ceiling. He pointed at the front door to indicate he would follow them out. Chisel did so walking backwards.

"So – what is important enough for you to interrupt my work. Well?" asked Nightnurse when they were all outside.

"Basically Crow's lost a couple of feathers and he wants you to find them," said Hammer.

"Lost 'em? Let 'em bugga off on the top of a coach you mean!" snorted Chisel. "Bin out in the sun too much if you ask me!"

"Look Chisel not here not now," said Hammer as though he had been worn out by Chisel's thoughts on the matter. "We haven't got time!"

Hammer reached into his apron pulling out a purse. He held it out to Nightnurse. "Payment for finding them and something extra for walking away from this one - which we know you don't like."

Nightnurse took the purse respectfully. His manners were quite the opposite of thuggish. He opened it to look inside. He raised his eyebrows at the contents. "Pretty big feathers? Why me? Why not Horace the Hatchet?"

Hammer and Chisel exchanged slightly embarrassed glances.

"You tell him Chisel," said Hammer.

"No you tell me Hammer. I want to be able to understand it," ordered Nightnurse.

Hammer was grateful Chisel had the sense to not rise to the insult in any way. "Well you know Horace always prided himself on being a master of disguise. Well it appears this time his disguise might have been a bit too good. You see he was disguised as a stag and he got shot on a hunt!"

"Wouldn't you have loved to have bin there when they tried to put his head on the wall?" laughed Chisel. "I mean what a berk!"

Nightnurse regarded Chisel coldly so he soon stopped laughing. "Are you sure he doesn't want this one doing? I can still do it and be ready to leave within a few minutes."

"No - This must be a little fish in the scheme of things. No disrespect to you intended of course!" Hammer was suddenly worried.

"Not taken," replied Nightnurse smiling his nice cheeky smile, "a job's a job."

"Well anyway we're to get you back as quickly as possible," said Hammer grateful for Nightnurse's good manners compared to his clumsiness.

"I'm to actually see Crow? That's a first," said Nightnurse putting the purse safely away.

"Well you won't actually see him of course. None of us have," said Hammer.

"I wonder if he still knows who he is under that cloak the way he's bin behaving recently. We could have just popped 'em with a few arrows there and then," said Mr Chisel turning up his palms at the stupidity of not doing that.

"How many times? I've told you - this is a big deal he's working on. Don't know what. But that puts us all under more pressure," said Mr Hammer.

"I don't mind the extra pressure!" retorted Chisel, "it's making stupid mistakes I disagree with!"

"We don't know if it's a stupid mistake! We don't know the bigger picture do we? Perhaps this bookkeeper had to get away for some reason!" said Hammer in Chisel's face.

"Then why are we the next day employing the services of one of the finest killing machines in all of England to find them? Answer me that then clever clogs!" demanded Chisel.

Hammer stepped back not liking to lose his self-control "Look Chisel," he said quietly. "We can pontificate all day long and still not have a bloody clue about what's actually going on. Yes? So we just do what we're told and we do it properly. Which for now means getting Nightnurse back to Crow as quickly as we can. Unless you'd like to look for another employer of course."

Chisel went to reply but was stopped by the creaking of a window opening above them. The head of an odious looking man popping out of it. Nightnurse was angrily reminded of chicken pies and nuts.

"Look fellas. You're more than welcome to come in for a drink. Touch-up the barmaid if you put a bit in the tip jar. Help yourself to the free nuts too. But if not - would you bugger off somewhere else to have your mother's meeting at this time of the morning? If it's all the same - you clowns!" He slammed the window shut.

Mr Hammer caught the look in Nightnurse's eyes and wished he hadn't. "You don't need to," he whispered.

"Oh yes I do. This one's on the house," said Nightnurse. They watched as he glided into the tavern like a snake.

Chisel laughed. "Very good! Did you see that Hammer? It's a tavern. "On the house". Very clever. I like him."

"He frightens you to death you mean," said Hammer giving him a sideways glance.

The window above them flew open. The odious man's panicked face was there. "Help! Help! This man's going to kill me just because I put boggies in the nuts!"

Something dragged him away from the window. Then there was a scream that lasted so long and was so terrible Hammer wished a man could close his ears like he could close his eyes. When it had finally finished Hammer turned to see Chisel looking at him.

"That's why I don't touch anything free on a bar!" said Chisel. "He deserved that."

Nightnurse soon reappeared whistling for his horse.

Hammer and Chisel mounted their horses and waited. Nightnurse's beautiful black beast hitherto hidden came thundering up to his master.

"Oh I admire you for being able to do that. I gave up a long time ago trying to get my horse to do that. How do you do it?" pestered Chisel as Nightnurse mounted.

"The old way," said Nightnurse patiently.

"The old way?" asked Chisel.

"A mixture of fear and respect," replied Nightnurse smiling, "the old way."

"Come on Nightnurse. Crow wants you in his nest for dinnertime. We'll show you the way," said Hammer.

The three of them left the tavern at Little Piddle watched by someone who'd been unexpectedly woken up that morning.

# CHAPTER 11

There are some people to whom a good time
means a drink a meal and a fight The order
doesn't matter nor who they end up fighting

Colin took another frantic look behind him. Sam hung on for dear
life wondering where he was getting his strength from. He felt like an
omelette in a frying pan that someone was trying to flip over. When
the coach started stopping he felt like he was going to slide off and go
splat on the floor!

Colin jumped down from his seat. Sam risked loosening his grip on
the knob, bolt, rail, whatever it was that had become his whole
purpose in life for the last few minutes. Only to grab at it again with
sudden sickening panic as the coach suddenly lurched to one side.

"Here use this!" Colin threw a blanket over him. He was standing in
the open doorway of the coach. "Do you think you can climb into my
seat from there?"

Sam wrapped the blanket around himself on his knees. "Do you
promise to keep the coach still?"

"I'll stay right here and steady it."

Sam under Colin's watchful eye clambered over the backrest of the
driver's seat.

"Well done Sam!" said Colin jumping down.

He quickly joined Sam on the seat. "Budge up," he said taking up
the reins.

Sam shuffled along a bit. "It moves about quite a bit up here doesn't
it?" he said looking uncomfortably over the side.

"You get used to it," said Colin reassuringly. He gave a slap on the
reins and off they moved. Not frantic and violent as it had been before
but not dawdling either.

"I don't think it's safe for you to go back to your house," said Colin looking straight ahead at the road.

"I know it's not safe," said Sam looking at Colin. He hadn't noticed before but he had a very noble profile like one of those Greek or Roman statues. "All my life I've been precise in my efforts trying to corner perfection. Then BANG! one day you get punished for working so hard and everything changes. Just like that." Sam snapped his fingers.

"Do you want to tell me what went on?" asked Colin quickly glancing at him.

"I don't know where to begin. Most of it I shouldn't have understood. And it certainly wasn't his intention for me to walk away with what I knew! Chalk from a blackboard. Bloody scary!" He gave a shudder under the blanket. "Do you believe in magic Colin?"

He glanced at Sam thinking it an odd question to ask. "I believe there are many things we can't explain. But just because we can't explain it doesn't make it any less real. If you want to call that magic then yes I do."

"I didn't. Not until today and I saw that robe. Then when I put it on and I understood so many things. It was like I could fly above the earth looking down on everything," said Sam gazing up at the sky.

"With the shock you've had I don't expect you're thinking straight right now," said Colin glancing uneasily at him.

"Far from it!" said Sam snapping his gaze back to Colin. "I'm more lucid on this subject than I've been on any subject in my life! I'm a dead man! You're a dead man! My God! If they find out about Natalie – she's a dead woman!"

Colin pulled on the reins to halt the coach.

"Don't stop!" implored Sam putting a hand on Colin's arm. "But not that way. That way is London and almost certain death for you and me if we're stupid enough to return."

Colin kept the coach moving. "Where then? Where do we go?" he asked.

"At least to a good hiding place off the road," said Sam sensibly.

"Come on girls – find us a good hiding place," said Colin putting down the reins on a little bar running along in front of him. He turned in his seat to face Sam as best he could.

"Will they do that?" asked Sam looking worryingly from Colin to the horses.

"Don't worry about them. You tell me what you know."

So Sam did. It appeared that a "doer" called Crow had been tasked with a new project funded by some big money. But Crow wanted a new way of "cooking the books" to suck in even more of their money to finance his own devious scheme that he was "piggy backing" on their project. Ultimately he was going to double-cross them and not just take their money but probably become the richest man in England. There was so much money and power at stake that the lives of a few penpushers or any other plebeian for that matter was of no consequence whatsoever.

When he had finished Colin was shaking his head. "It doesn't make sense."

"Oh it does. It's quite wonderful. The death of a thousand years way of life very probably. But quite magnificent," said Sam looking to the horizon again.

"No! Why did he let us go? Knowing that you know all this? Why?"

"I'd made a deal for him to get his robe back," said Sam. "He stuck to it?"

"No. They could have taken the robe and anything else they wanted from our corpses! And this man's clearly a megalomaniac – they don't take rules and deals seriously. No there's something else. Something else that's missing here!" Colin was shaking his head in frustration as though it were the puzzle of a child that should have a simple answer.

"Well I'm sorry I got you involved with this. It's proven to be a very expensive fare for you," said Sam humbly.

Colin stopped shaking his head to look at him earnestly. "No they did. It was them that hired me not you. And we're not going to let them do it!"

"How can the likes of us stop them?" asked Sam more hopelessly that he had intended.

"By surviving for a start! All three of us!" There was strength in Colin's voice.

"Yes of course! Natalie! She is completely innocent in all of this!"

Colin looked at him. "Not completely innocent? She does help you run your business? She will have the sense to flee when you don't return today?"

Sam felt himself go quite pale at his own guilt. Facing something yourself was one thing but knowing another must face danger because of you was something else. "She's more than a maid. She's the reason for my recent success. She remembers everything. And I mean everything! She's the most valuable thing I have. And she doesn't have a bloody clue -" he laughed pathetically, "she doesn't have a clue how valuable she really is."

"Oh dear," said Colin heavily, "she really will be waiting for them like a plump bird ready cooked in the oven?"

"I'm afraid so. I've got to go back. I don't expect you to. Drop me off at the nearest coaching inn."

"And what will you do there Sam? Sell that incredibly valuable blanket to buy some clothes and a horse? It's not even your blanket!" asked Colin wide-eyed.

"My maid does appear to be stuffed," said Sam looking down into his lap.

"No," said Colin defiantly, "nobody's stuffing your maid except me! It's you they'll be looking for tonight. Coachman and coaches are more common in London than bird droppings. I'll go!"

"You would?" said Sam clapping his hands. "She will have got my things ready. I did have the sense to do that this morning. And you will be careful?" Something suddenly occurred to Sam, "Wait! Where will I be?"

"Don't worry! My clever girls have seen to it. This is the road to my sister's house!" He took up the reins to hurry the horses along.

"I don't know your sister," said Sam concerned.

"My sister doesn't know you. But you need somewhere safe to stay. Food, drink, a warm bed whilst I risk life and limb saving your maid." He was only half-joking.

"If you put it like that I've easily got the better half of the deal. I'm sorry for being so thoughtless."

"Think nothing of it Sam. You've had quite a day. You'll like Clare," said Colin looking at the road, "she's quietened down a lot."

Sam wondered what he meant by that but didn't ask. Feeling quite tired he shut his eyes to doze. As much as he dared perched up there like a canary on a swing.

Eventually Colin halted the coach outside a cottage so small they were almost able to look over it. The front door hadn't had a lick of paint in years and the doorframe had been half chewed away. But the smell of bacon from an open window more than made up for that. Colin jumped down. "Wait here. I'll see who she's with."

Sam watched as Colin opened the small picket gate taking only a few strides to reach the front door. He knocked twice.

"Coming!" said a woman's voice from inside. It was quite a shock when what appeared to be a big man wearing an apron opened the door!

"Oh Colin! This is an unexpected surprise!" She gave him a big hug. "I'm doing a bacon sandwich. Do you want one?" She turned to go back in.

"Clare wait! Are you with any one?"

"No we're meeting up later. Why what's wrong?"

"Clare I need to ask you a really big favour," said Colin.

"Anything. You know that. But if it's money I'm a bit short myself this week," said Clare glancing at Sam.

"I've got someone with me who needs our help. His maid's life is in danger - through no fault of his! - and if we both go then there could be three people feeding fishes in the Thames tonight!"

"Really? That serious?" asked Clare putting a hand to her mouth.

Colin nodded. "I'm afraid so. I have to go alone and he needs somewhere safe to stay."

"But I'm going out tonight!" tutted Clare.

"Take him with you!"

"Colin - he's a man!"

"Clare I've seen your friends. Put a bonnet on him and he'll be one of the best looking ones there!"

"Colin - have you fallen off your coach today and had a knock to the head?" asked Clare folding her great big arms over her apron.

"Excuse me?" said Sam politely, "could I not just stay at your house whilst you go out?"

Clare stared at Sam. "You seem very polite so I'll tell you straight - the dog would have one of your legs for dinner and the other one for a midnight snack!"

"Could you not put the dog out for the night?" suggested Sam.

Clare's great mouth fell open.

Colin waved at him with his hand. "Sam sshh please just sshh - Clare can we go inside?"

"I mean whose bloody house is it? His or my dog's?"

"Clare please," said Colin shooing her in, "your bacon will be burning!"

"Oh blimey yes!"

The front door shut. Sam looked out across the open fields and hedgerows clinging on to the last of the day's light. The thought of spending a long night out here in the countryside filled him with dread. He knew he couldn't do it. His imagination would run wild. Things with hooves and horns walked the countryside at night. That's why front door bolts had originally been invented. He knew would agree to almost anything to avoid it.

As he waited he watched the dark stalking him down the lane. When it reached the horses he knew he would have to get down and knock on the door. So it was with a little joyous jump of his heart that he saw the door open and Colin appear carrying a plate in one hand and a bundle in the other.

"Sam," said Colin passing up the plate, "I've got some good news and I've got some bad news."

"Well what's the bad news?" asked Sam in trepidation.

Colin stepped back and held up the bundle letting it unfurl. It was a dress and a bonnet and a shawl. "You're going out with my sister and her friends tonight."

Sam gulped. "And the good news?"

"The dog hasn't slobbered on your bacon sandwich."

Sam looked down at the plate not hungry in the slightest. He was about to say he wouldn't do it when looking up he noticed the dark was so close it had removed the horses' ears and the colour of the dress was indiscernible to him.

"Is there no other way?" he asked putting the plate slowly down on the seat.

"She won't put the dog out. The dog will eat you if you're in the house without her. There are no out-buildings. I need the coach. It is either the hedgerow or my sister's friend's hen party."

"Hen party?" asked Sam trying to latch onto something positive, "will there be chicken to eat?"

"There'll be food and drink and warm company! And your maid safely returned by sunrise!" said Colin trying to help him see the best of it.

"Yes Natalie. I must do it for Natalie. But – we don't tell Natalie. Or anyone else for that matter! That's a promise between us! Yes?"

"Don't worry Sam! Most of the lads round 'ere have dressed up as a woman at one point or other to join in the fun of a hen party! You enjoy yourself! But! – The women don't know that! Whatever you do – don't let them find out you're a man!"

Sam climbed down removing his blanket. With a little help from Colin he got into the women's things.

"You knock three times and my sister will be right out. Don't go in or the dog will have ya! From now until my sister says otherwise you're her cousin Charlotte from Dorset," said Colin climbing up. He held up the bacon sandwich. "Sure you don't want this?"

Sam shook his head noticing the odd feeling of the bonnet's strap under his chin. "Where about in Dorset?"

Colin admired Sam's attention to detail. There was a good chance the three of them would get through this. "I'll let my sister answer that for you. And one more thing – if you pretend you like dogs you're more than halfway to having my sister as a friend. And believe me

Sam - you'd rather have my sister as a friend than an enemy! If we ever get the chance I'll show you the scars."

Sam believed the scars were real even though Colin had been smiling. He could just about see his teeth in the dark.

"Come on girls. I know it's been a long day but we've important work to do." Colin slapped the reins. The coach disappearing so quickly up the dark lane it was like it was made of black smoke.

Sam reluctantly opened the picket gate. At the door he raised his hand about to knock but stopped. He had cold feet. He felt the bonnet on his head, the shawl around his shoulders he could pull up tight to cover his face, the dress that was so baggy he could have been a pit pony and get away with being a woman. But still there was something wrong. He hitched up the hem of the dress. He had no shoes!

"Well hello Charlotte! Glad you could make it!" said Clare throwing open the door.

"Hello Clare! I wouldn't miss it for the world!"

Clare leant her great bulk forward. She wasn't wearing a bonnet and Sam noticed the back of her neck seemed to have a lot more skin than it needed. "Just speak normally. Not all high-pitched. You're going to a hen party not Lady Faversham's bridge evening."

Whilst they were being honest before the true deception began Sam thought it wise to point out he had no shoes.

Clare nodded. Sam couldn't be sure in the dark but she might have had a clump of hairs growing on her forehead like he'd seen on a picture of a bull hanging on the wall of his butchers. "I've only got the pair I'm standing in but I've thought about it and I do have these!"

Sam looked at what she was holding up. "But they're gloves aren't they?" he asked bemused. Gloves the size of his feet it had to be said but gloves nonetheless.

"Moleskin these are. They were my nan's intruder gloves. You need something with good grip that ain't going tear or let you feel any desperate teeth as you squeeze the life out the little bugger."

Sam swallowed hard at how they dealt with intruders around here.

"My nan didn't believe in ignoring intruders like some folk or keeping a clean house so they were less likely to come in in the first place. My nan always said the only good rat was a dead rat and over the years these gloves have done for a few I can tell you." Clare put them down on the floor in front of him.

"Oh I see," said Sam relieved, "but isn't it easier to keep a cat for such things?" he asked. The moleskin gloves fitting his feet much better than he expected.

"Ain't a cat big enough for the rats we used to get around here. Besides they're snooty horrible things." She narrowed her eyes. "You're not a cat lover are you?"

"Oh no. I'm a dog man through and through. Man's best friend. A friend for life always there."

"So what type of dog do you have?" asked Clare very interested to know.

"Oh if only. I live in the centre of London with nowhere for such a fine animal to run around and play. It wouldn't be fair on the little fella. It saddens me greatly that I can't."

Clare put one of her big strong arms around him with surprising softness. "What a truly responsible attitude to take. I like that. We've got time. Come in – you must meet Beelzebub."

"Beelzebub," stammered Sam, "isn't that some kind of demon?"

Clare stopped. "Yes you're right. If he gets a whiff of the blood on your shoes -" She turned him about and closed the front door. "So if you could have any breed of dog what would it be and why?" she asked him.

Sam began stretching out what little he knew of dogs to please her as she led him to the location of the hen party. He proved to be better than he thought he would be and was still going when they arrived. "Now a Beagle always seems very kind to me. A Beagle wouldn't bite you unless you really deserved it. Labradors very good with children- aren't they? - Bloody Hell!"

He'd been cut off by Clare opening a gate and it going off like a gun. "I've never known a gate make such a noise before!" he said ducking.

"It wasn't the gate," said Clare matter-of-factly, "it'll be Sharon taking her turn on the roof with the musket. Bloody stupid if you ask me."

"I'm inclined to agree," said Sam keeping his head down as they walked up the front path.

"One of these days we won't have had much rain and that thatch will go up like a tinderbox. But some of the young lads get curious about what we're up to and knowing one of us is up there with a musket tends to see to that."

"Do you think she suspects about me?" asked Sam worried.

"God no. You'd be dead if she did. She's just showing off." Clare stopped him and guided his hand to the bonnet he was wearing. "Have a feel. You'll find a hole in there that wasn't there when we left."

Sam found it almost straightaway. "She's quite a shot!" he said breathlessly.

"Only when she's had a few. When she's sober she can't hit a barn door. Now remember you're my cousin Charlotte from Weymouth Dorset. None of these girls have even been to Dorset let alone Weymouth. But I'll warn you again - speak nothing to anyone of what you see tonight. And if any of them find anything dangly in your crotch they will hang you up by it! Do you understand? Other than that – enjoy yourself!"

"Clare before we go in can I ask you something?"

She straightened having no idea it seemed of what he wanted to ask.

"Why are you doing this?"

She considered the question thoughtfully then replied so quietly he only just heard, "I don't honestly know - perhaps to properly say sorry to my brother -"

The front door opened without warning stopping Clare elaborate.

"Claremeister!" boomed a woman wearing men's breeches with something big dangling between her legs. There was no time to see exactly what it was, as with great strength the woman pulled the two of them inside as though her life depended on them not being seen on the doorstep a second longer. She was enthusiastic for them to follow her down the hall. There was a powerful smell assaulting Sam's nose: a mixture of hoof and hair. He suddenly longed for the safety of a black hedgerow but knew it was too late now.

At the end of the hall the woman stopped before a big oak door. "So Claremeister! Whose your friend?"

"This is my cousin Charlotte from Weymouth. Bad business with an unwelcome admirer so she's staying with me for a few days. Thought it might do her good to let her hair down with the girls," said Clare putting an affectionate arm around her.

"Yes of course! The more the merrier! And men hey? Can't live with him and can't live without 'em! Welcome Charlotte! I'm Marian and welcome to my daughter's hen party!" The woman flung open the oak door as though it were made of paper to reveal twenty or so milkmaids in the room behind. Each one of them holding or gulping from a large flagon of cider. Each one of them with something big and dangly hanging between their legs.

Sam had never seen steak with the hooves still on. He didn't believe it was possible for the human female form to attain such proportions. All of the milkmaids were huge, with enormous thick necks and shoulders. Big hands too. Really big hands. What could big hands like that do to a man? What would upset them? A man amongst them pretending to be a woman for instance? All he wanted to do now was run out of there! Marian shouted for quiet and all those bovine eyes were slowly moving in his direction.

"You all know the Claremeister!"

They all whooped. The whole house not just the room seemed to shake as they stamped their feet.

"Whoa! Whoa girls! We don't want to shake anyone off the roof again!" shouted Marian.

"Yes we do!" shouted one of them. The stamping increased.

"Whoa! Whoa! Manners girls!" The stamping subsided.

"Thank you. This is Clare's cousin Charlotte from Dorset. Now you all let her find her feet but if she needs anything then we help her out." She turned to Charlotte and whispered, "you'll be alright chick these are good girls." Marion spread out her arms wide to the crowd, "Now raise your flagons while we stiff them!"

"Look! Charlotte be shaking! Can't wait to get her hands on a stiffie!" roared someone stepping forward with a huge imitation leather willy.

Sam shut his eyes, but to his untold relief it was strapped around his waist like everyone else's. He wasn't going to get any different treatment because he was new. A great deafening cheer went up. Then another cheer when the Claremeister was *stiffed*.

When the attention was no longer upon them Clare led Charlotte to a chair in a quiet corner returning a few seconds later with a flagon of cider. "Hide behind this for a bit," she said.

Sam started to pull down the shawl he'd tied around the bottom half of his face. Clare stopped him, "through the shawl's perfectly normal. Ain't pretty what a beast's hoof can do to a mouth."

"I had no idea looking after farm animals was so dangerous." Clare hadn't heard him. A great cheer had gone up and the Claremeister was swallowed up into the throng.

Sam wasn't a regular drinker. He liked it but it affected his work and his work came first so he didn't partake very often. But sipping the cider through his shawl he could feel himself start to unwrap. The heavy coat of a tiring day being lifted from his shoulders. He knew he had to be careful of course. But the more cider he sipped the more he felt everything would be alright. When the flagon was much lighter than when it had been given to him he felt like a sail being smoothed out by a warm wind. So when a great hand fell on his shoulder he didn't give a horrible start but turned smiling to see who it was.

One of the milkmaids had pulled up a chair. She had made her hair into two girlie pony tails but it just made her look like a bull. But she was very friendly holding out a hand introducing herself as Janet. She began telling Sam over the din who was who (they used nicknames mostly) and what was going on. The bride-to-be was Northwind because she couldn't half blow – but don't tell her mum that - and she was over there talking to Gripper. It did seem to Sam that out of all of them Northwind did look like the one with the best chance of finding a husband. But why was the other one called Gripper? Janet told him the reason cows' eyes were on the side of their heads was because Gripper squeezed their udders so hard at milking! None of the lads could beat her at arm wrestling. Looking at Gripper's particularly large arms and hands he could well believe it!

Unfortunately it was also true that marriage didn't happen very often for them. So when it did they really liked to make the most of it with a good hen party. Without being prompted Janet explained the tradition of the hen party, which had evolved over many generations. The willy Northwind wore was in fact a real one. It had been removed from the bullock provided for the wedding feast and was referred to as The Todger. All the others were imitation willys made from leather stuffed with straw. Janet playfully flapped hers about a bit so Sam did the same with his. They were called Stiffies. A very old Stiffy that had passed through the hands of many mothers and daughters was called The Old Man -

"Who be hungry?" Marian roared out stopping Janet explain any more.

The room shook as they all stamped their feet and chanted, "Welshie-Be! Welshie-Be! Welshie-Be!"

"Come on then girls! Let's Welshie-Be!" roared Marion.

They all piled out into the night air with some of them taking flaming torches as Marion had done. Sam followed at the back of the pack. As they rumbled through the night, the boisterous band waved their stiffies in the air or playfully hit each other with them. Amongst this rowdy group Sam felt invincible. A hoofed demon that took this lot on would be sent right back to hell in pieces!

They soon reached a set of crossroads. Marion held up her flaming torch for quiet. She was so big it looked like a tree had caught fire.

"Red Dragon or Welsh Rabbit?"

The group all boomed and roared at once. From a distance, it must have sounded like an approaching thunderstorm.

"Red Dragon it is then!"

The whole group wheeled to the left to follow her. Further along the road, now more of a bridle-path, Sam could see a red light glowing in the distance. As they drew closer, he could see it was a fiery dragon in mid-air! Drawing closer he could eventually see it was a dragon sign on the wall of a brick building. It was very clever how they'd done it.

Through the building's windows he could see people eating at tables with little candles lighting up the underside of their faces.

They arrived at the entrance.

A huge man, only a little shorter than Marion, with a great hairy beard down to his belly button barred the door. "Hen-Party is it girls?" His voice was thick and phlegmatic.

"That's right - BOYO!" said Marion. Her use of the word "Boyo" making everyone fall about laughing.

"How many is it then?" he asked having seen and heard it all before.

"Be counting sheep all day but can't be counting people - BOYO!" shouted Marion sticking two fingers up.

"Fact is see, sheep's easier than people in lots of ways. Less rude for a start," he said eyeing the two offending fingers with disdain.

"Twenty - BOYO! A table for twenty should suffice," said Marion taking the two offending fingers down but sticking one of them up her nose as far as she could get it.

"There's lovely I'm sure," said the bearded phlegmatic man before disappearing into the building.

Marion was so engrossed in picking her nose she hadn't seen Cowpat Chucker and Udder Nose begin a fight near the bins. Very soon they were using their Stiffies quite ruthlessly on each other. Sam expected someone to step in and put a stop to it but the group turned to idly watch whilst they waited. If he had to guess Sam would say Cowpat Chucker was the more relieved when the bearded phlegmatic man reappeared.

"None o' that now girls. See! You won't come in. See!" he shouted towards the bins.

"We'll be good," said Marion finally taking her finger out of her nose.

"You promise? See! Money up front too! See?"

"None of my girls be causing any real trouble," said Marion passing the bearded phlegmatic man some money.

"Let's be havin' you then!" he said stepping aside.

Inside, tables had been pushed together big enough to sit the whole group. Sam's immediate concern was obtaining a quiet seat out of the way. There was one being ignored near the door to the kitchens. He was able to sit there. Marion ordered twenty flagons of cider as everyone fell into loud conversation. Sam was hungry but how would he eat through the shawl? Soup was probably the best bet. Looking at his copy of the menu it didn't look good. Lamb was available for starter, main-course and dessert! But there was no mention of lamb soup.

"You know why the meat is so moist and tender here?" shouted Bigmouth across the table.

Those who heard shook their huge heads in knowing anticipation.

Bigmouth pointed at one of the bearded waiters. 'It's the extra SAUCE they put into it while it's alive!"

Most of the milkmaids fell about laughing. The waiters did not look very happy at all. When the drinks arrived, they seemed to be dropped rather than placed. Also, whilst they decided what to order the milkmaids were not getting plates of toast with melted cheese on as the other diners had done.

"Hey - BOYO! Another twenty flagons of cider!" shouted Marion unbelievably quickly.

When they arrived everyone roared, "THERE'S LOVELY ISN'T IT!"

However, the mood at the other end of the table was turning downright ugly. Tits-Out had made it perfectly plain why she was called that. Two men on an adjacent table, far from being pleased at the sight of what was on show, pushed their plates away in disgust. Sam also heard a couple celebrating their wedding anniversary ask for their coats when something Nose-Picker had produced had been flicked at them. Then Arse-Scratcher started standing up rather than remaining seated when she got the urge. It wasn't nice. Fortunately, the food started to arrive and everyone seemed to settle down.

Suddenly Fussy shouted, "There's an eye still in this!"

She held it up for all to see.

"What be the bloody idea BOYO?" roared Bigmouth.

"Now girls," warned Marion half-heartedly.

It was too late. A flagon of cider spinning about its own axis made an arc above the table. There was a horrible dull thud as it made contact with the skull of the waiter pleading with the anniversary couple to stay. Retracing its path led Charlotte's gaze to the only person now without two flagons in front of them – Janet!

It was the spark that ignited the whole powder keg. Sam stumbled back as the table lifted in front of him. The kitchen door flew open. He was pinned behind it as bearded waiters and bearded kitchen staff came hurtling out. It was like being on a beach watching the waves of a mighty storm crash in. Chairs were being broken over backs. Bodies being hurled onto tables. Beard hair filling the room like feathers from a split pillow. Sam squealed like a girl as a chair came hurtling his way. Gripper grabbed it in mid-air and crushed it in her hands like matchwood then pointed for Sam to stay where he was before grabbing a waiter by his beard and swinging him out of a window. Filthy Temper jumping through it after him shouting really horrible things about her stiffy and the waiter's anatomy.

Just as suddenly as the storm had arrived so just as suddenly it passed. Sam ventured to step out from behind the door. No one with a beard was left standing. Those still left inside were all groaning around on the floor. The other diners were cowering in a corner but mostly unharmed. Marion led the girls out laughing.

Sam followed out last. The other diners not daring to say anything to him.

The mood of the group heading back to Marion's was joyful. The gain of a good fight had easily outweighed the loss of a bad meal. Very soon, secret whispers abounded of what they had in store for the bride. Open talk of their exploits on previous hen nights. Some of the best dirty jokes Sam had ever heard. There was nothing that could jump out of the dark that could harm him and that felt very nice thank you. Then at Marion's command they sprung their surprise on Northwind stripping her naked and tying her to a tree. Then they all had a go at kicking the Todger back to Marion's house.

When the group reached Marion's house Sam was all ready to go in to carry on but Clare discretely held him back. "Come on you. You can help me go back for Northwind."

"Ah come on Claremeister just one more!" pleaded Sam.

"No. That's my friend back there and we should quit while we're ahead. Come on."

Reluctantly Sam did as he was told joining Clare going back the way they had just come.

# CHAPTER 12

## Rings on her fingers and bell on her toes
## She shall have music wherever she goes

Nightnurse dismounted pulling his black cloak about himself. The way he did so you would think it must have been a cold barren place but it was not. It was an English country garden in full bloom at the end of a summer's day. In all the world is there ever a nicer time or place to be? The herbaceous borders to his left and right were a cacophony of flowers shouting at the bees to come visit me first in a profusion of every colour. But it wasn't random. Someone had been methodical and very precise in making this garden look so natural. And if he put that much effort into his garden how much more effort did he put into the more important things? That's why Nightnurse pulled his cloak about himself like he did – he needed to be on his guard.

Hammer and Chisel dismounted then joined Nightnurse walking up the garden path.

"He's like a spider at the centre of his web here. His eight legs resting on strands that eminate out in all directions listening and disseminating and deciding whose gonna get eatin' next." Chisel hadn't specified to whom he was talking. "It's a beautiful garden isn't it? But I'll tell you something - you won't find any other spiders in this gardin'. He doesn't allow it."

They went around to the back door which had a little wooden arch protruding out with climbing roses lounging over it. The day had been warm enough for a jasmine nearby to let it be known that when all the noise had died down something sweet would be available in the dark.

Hammer opened the back door. "It's the door on the left. If it's open you can go straight in. If it's shut then you knock and wait. We'll wait here."

Nightnurse nodded. At the end of the short hall the door was open so he went straight in. It wasn't what he was expecting. It looked like the room of a pleasant old lady. Crow sitting behind a small desk in his black robe looked very incongruous in such a place. It was like a young man had known his granny was away and had sneaked in to do something he wouldn't dare dabble with at his own house. There was an empty dining chair in front of the desk.

Nightnurse felt himself being very closely observed where he stood. It was very odd. He almost felt it was in *that* way. Eventually, a great black sleeve indicated he could sit on the chair.

"There is more blackness within this cloak than in the soul of the blackest pirate on the blackest ocean on the blackest night! What say you to that?"

"I think that once you get to a certain shade of black it doesn't matter any longer," said Nightnurse coolly. "All of it is black on black."

The black hood nodded reflectively, "I think that is the best response I have had."

"Thank you," said Nightnurse smiling charmingly.

"You have a very endearing smile."

Nightnurse was less sure how to respond to that.

"Attractive legs, clear upper body elegance, thick black hair. Why you are almost a panther in human form. Tell me - that bulge in your crutch. Is it where you have tucked your tail or something else I should be interested in?"

Nightnurse had not come here to be toyed with! But he was sensible enough to not let his confused annoyance show. "I'm not a panther," he said still smiling.

"Pity. I like cats very much. And to stroke a cat as big as you."

"Well if I were a cat I'm a Tom and not a Tiddles," he said calmly and pleasantly.

There was a cold stiletto laugh that aroused Nightnurse's curiosity. But what occurred to him was so fantastic it couldn't be asked.

"Would you like me to say sorry for playing with you?"

Nightnurse knew that voice had never been sorry in its life even as a child.

"You wouldn't mean it if you said it so why ask me?" He wondered if he'd been wrong about Crow. Was his reputation undeserved?

Crow thumped the table. "I never say sorry! I have nothing to be sorry for. All of them! All of them will be sorry when I have finished with them!"

Nightnurse nodded prudently.

"Do not nod at me like that! Get up! Take a look at your chair. You are so clever why sit in a chair like that?" Crow demanded.

Nightnurse jumped out of the chair sensing danger. There was nothing obvious to see. He ran the palm of his hand very carefully over the cushion noting nothing untoward other than the terrible flower pattern. Then he inspected the legs and here was something strange: the back two were clearly hinged at the base by discrete metal hinges so it would appear the chair was designed to pivot. There was a thin metal wire running from the top of the chair down its back and disappearing through a tiny hole in the floor. He gave the back of the chair a hard shove but it was quite firm. Looking at the base of the two front legs he noticed metal hooks digging into the wood. He spun round behind the chair to take a look at the rug lying directly behind it.

"You are getting warmer," he was told.

Reaching down he tried pulling back on the rug but it was firmly attached to the wooden floor. For a second he was thrown but then he understood. He walked around the rug. He knew on this side he would be able to throw it back. A trap door big enough to swallow a flailing man was revealed.

"Try jumping on it. It will not open. I promise you."

It was some sort of test between them. If Nightnurse jumped on the trapdoor and it opened would that be confirmation he was too stupid to be of much use? Or if he didn't jump on it would that indicate he wasn't one to follow orders? What would be the correct thing to do? And he had no doubt how long he took to decide would be duly noted. He bent his knees readying his pounce. He bent them a little further and then pounced but not upon the trapdoor but twisting in mid-air to land directly in front of the desk reaching out for the only object upon it: a small silver candelabra. He yanked it hard expecting it to swing in his hand but it did not move.

"So very close," said Crow even more coldly than normal. "Keep your hand where it is but do not move it."

Crow rose out of the chair gliding over to the trapdoor. Then to Nightnurse's amazement began to dance upon it. Gentle little taps at first but then quickly rising to great stomps giving the trapdoor an awful bashing. He was making so much noise that Hammer and Chisel came hurrying along the hall.

"Sir! Sir! Is everything all right?" they shouted above the din.

Crow stopped dancing. "Yes my concerned little chicks go back to eating your corn."

Hammer and Chisel quickly surveyed the room from the doorway then went away as they had been told.

Crow glided off the trapdoor. "Why the candelabra?"

"The mechanism needs a trigger within reach. It is the only object on the desk but I admit I was mistaken." Nightnurse went to remove his hand from it.

He was told, "Leave it be." He watched Crow glide behind the desk to stand right next to him. "A weaker thing might score some petty victory at this point but your intuition should be rewarded. My openness with you now should make you more inclined to be open with me in the future. And it was quite a sight to see you pounce like you did."

Crow was now close enough to have the hood ripped from his head. Nightnurse was very curious to see what was underneath it.

"Move you hand a little further up. That is correct. Now gently twist to the right."

Nightnurse did as he was told surprised and shocked at the smallness of the twist required. The trapdoor not just falling open but disappearing as though it had been blown open by a tempest. The chair eagerly retching backwards to disgorge the occupier into the black hole afterwards.

"Very impressive," said Nightnurse liking the feel of the shaft in his hand uninclined to let go of it.

"The rug is a very good rug. One of my favourites hence the need to make sure it does not disappear too."

"A strange consideration if I may say so," replied Nightnurse. "Does it ever snag on the -" he wanted a choice word, "user?"

Crow sat down in his chair. "Again I could attempt to impress or frighten you but in all honesty I have never used it. Hammer and Chisel - whose wonderful creation it is - assure me it would work well with pigs in the pit. There is enough of a fall to facilitate broken bones. Deep enough to make attempts to climb out futile for those lucky enough to not break any bones."

"So why the need for pigs?" asked Nightnurse.

"I can see you are not used to cleaning up a mess. They will eat everything apparently. But I do not have the need to make it fully operational – *yet.*"

"How does it reset?" asked Nightnurse.

"Hammer and Chisel will sort that out afterwards."

Nightnurse sat on the edge of the desk. He felt he could. "You know it's only a very little turn. If I had been a bit clumsy whilst you were doing your little jig?"

"Did you like the way I moved?" asked Crow. The cold thawing out of his voice.

"I thought it had energy," replied Nightnurse. He knew he was right about something. As fantastic as it seemed he knew he was right. He wanted to find out. He slowly reached out for the robe Crow was wearing.

The hood jerked urgently towards the doorway, "Lock the door!"

Nightnurse jumped off the desk shutting the door and locking it with a bolt at the top.

"The one at the bottom too. They are big fellows."

Nightnurse bolted the one at the bottom. As he stood up he turned to see Crow seductively peeling back the hood of the robe.

"I knew it," he whispered. "I just knew it. The second I walked in."

He was looking at perhaps the most beautiful woman's face he had ever seen.

"What are you?" he asked irresistibly drawn over.

"Anything you want me to be," she purred.


Out in the garden Hammer and Chisel were sitting on a bench by the back door.

"I'm telling you it's not feasible to have pigs in it. It would stink!" said Hammer.

"What if we had a small tunnel so they could go in when they needed to and then leave when they'd finished?"

"That would compromise the whole building. If it's big enough for a pig it's big enough for a man. Imagine what they could hear under that room!"

"Why don't we forget pigs entirely and use rats instead? All we'd need is a pipe in and out! A man can't squeeze through a pipe!" said Chisel eagerly.

"Would you really want rats running around the place with a taste for human flesh?" asked Hammer shaking his head at so stupid a suggestion.

"Well at the moment Hammer it's half a job if we're honest and that rankles."

Hammer leant back and shut his eyes to enjoy where they were for a bit. He hoped Chisel would hurry up and do the same. He didn't.

"This bookkeeper's cleverer than we gave him credit for. I thought it'ud be a cert for him to show up at his house. So must the boss for him to send Sneaky Simon to keep an eye on the place."

"We should of used Sneaky Simon and not Handfisted Harry to make the initial contact," said Hammer not bothering to open his eyes. "Then he wouldn't have had a bandage on his head and the robe would have worked properly."

"You think that's what it was then?"

"What else could it be? The robe's always worked before. Those robes are special mate. They're the nearest we'll ever get to heaven."

"I wonder where he got them." Chisel glanced at the back door. "Do you ever wonder where he's from?"

"No," said Hammer flatly with his eyes still closed. "And if you know what's good for you you won't try to find out."

"Hold on! Can you hear that?" asked Chisel looking at the back door.

Hammer opened his eyes. "There was something but it's gone. No there it is!" He looked at Chisel with a disappointed expression, "It almost sounds like a woman being pleasured."

Chisel laughed into his lap. "Do you think Crow has sneaked a present in for Nightnurse?" He looked up with a better idea. "Or do you think both of them are giving the wench a spit roast right now!"

"Sssshh!" ordered Hammer.

"Whatever's going on she's enjoying it! Shall we take a look?" asked Chisel starting to get up.

"Sit down!" ordered Hammer, "you know "eat your corn" is the code for under no circumstances disturb him. What are you going to do? Knock the door and say, "Excuse me. I'm a bit of a pervert do you mind if I watch?""

"Alright keep your hair on!" said Chisel. "Just thought it would be a bit of fun that's all!"

Hammer was no longer trying to relax. "I must admit I don't understand how some men have to complicate business with a bit of how's your father. Business before pleasure! Just stick to that simple rule! Women that's the problem. They're a bloody distraction. Most men would like to get the shed built, get the horses shoed, fix whatever needs fixing. Then say "okay that's a job well done – a pint and a poke would be nice!" But women! If that fire starts a crackling down below then that floor ain't gonna be swept! That cheese ain't gonna be made! That girl's flying out of that buttery hell bent on getting her own butter churned! And no mistake! And you've got your hammer in your hand and she's standing there offering out hot buttered buns. Well there aren't many men that can resist having a nibble and getting their own tool out. And where's that leave the job? Hey Chisel? Where's that leave the job?"

"I bet Nightnurse knows all about bun distraction," said Chisel.

"What?" said Hammer really saying: "haven't you listened to anything I've just said?"

"He must think he's a piss-poor baker he gets that many buttered buns thrown at him."

Hammer abruptly got up to shut the back door. He sat back down irritably.

"And they can see he's dangerous. I bet that helps too."

"Shut up Chisel!"

# CHAPTER 13

## It's something to do

Colin had collected Natalie with the things Sam had instructed her to assemble in a sack. There had been a short conversation with Cook about her options. She had said she was old enough to retire and would go to live with her sister in Margate. She wished them both luck and to tell the master not to worry about the wages she was owed – she would take as many of his possessions he was leaving behind as she could carry on her sister's husband's cart. They had left not seeing Sneaky Simon skulking in the shadows watching them and ridden through the rest of the night. Finally stopping after dawn at a small coaching inn.

"So it's not much further to your sisters now?" asked Natalie wringing her lovely hands delicately.

Colin was slumped in a chair opposite her, barely able to keep his eyes open. He'd drunk half of the tankard of ale on the table and that had been it. Little tiny sailors had attached ropes to his eyelids hauling down those mainsheets for all they were worth.

"Not far. The horses needed to rest. I needed to rest," he replied with a lot of effort.

"I don't know how you can just sit there as though you've just had Sunday lunch when my master is in peril." The thought upset Natalie and she rubbed her pretty nose giving a little sniffle.

"He's perfectly safe with my sister." That took a lot of effort to say so he brought his hand up to rest his chin in the palm of his hand and his elbow on the arm of the chair.

"Well how much longer will we be?" asked Natalie pushing his arm so his head fell out of his hand.

"Hey! That's not nice," mumbled Colin putting it back.

"How much longer will we be?" demanded Natalie.

"As long as the lads take to feed and water the horses. Do you want them dropping down dead in front of us?"

"Could that really happen?" asked Natalie obviously concerned for their welfare.

"Or I could drop off and break my neck." He opened one of his eyes fully. To his disappointment that appeared to be of no concern to her.

"Oh what a mess," she lamented leaning back in her chair. "My master attacked in his own study! Then having to flee for his life! He doesn't deserve it. He really doesn't deserve it!"

"Things happen to people they don't deserve all the time unfortu - unfortu - " he really didn't want to make the effort to say such a long word, "It's hard cheese!"

"Open your eyes! It's rude to talk to someone with them shut!"

Colin wondered how she could be so alert? She had ridden up top with him so he knew she hadn't slept. All she'd done was go on and on about getting back to her master. He'd never seen such devotion in a domestic. She'd only shut up when the clouds had cleared to reveal all the stars. Then she'd been quiet. The fact he couldn't open his eyes proved to him just how tired he must be. Under normal circumstances he would have quite happily looked at Natalie all day.

A dishevelled man appeared at the table.

"Don't waste your time with him gorgeous. Look at the state of him. He'll be no good to you in the sack. Me on the other hand," he gave a thrust of his dirty baggy trousers, "I've been getting my candle ready ever since you walked in. How would you like to light my wick with that pretty little mouth of yours?"

"OUT! OUT!" shouted the barman suddenly appearing from behind the bar. He had a round jovial face that seemed pained to be dealing with such things. "Honestly - You don't learn do you Lecherous Len?"

"Aw come on! It's such a bloody waste someone as good as her with someone like him!"

"That's not for you to decide. Now OUT!"

"But I haven't finished my pint!"

"You should have thought about that before bothering one of the customers. Don't make me come round there Len!" He was wiping a tankard. He put the cloth down to show that he meant it.

Lecherous Len took a long dirty look at Natalie before reluctantly leaving.

"Sorry about that folks!" shouted across the barman taking up his cloth and waving it in a friendly way.

Colin held up his free hand lazily to indicate everything was alright.

"I don't believe that! You just sat there as though nothing was happening!" said Natalie folding her arms.

"Nothing was happening was it?" murmured Colin.

"You pig! You absolute pig!" said Natalie abruptly turning her head away from him.

The barman saw the way her beautiful hair flounced as she did. Such pretty features that drew an alluring profile. A wild spirit that needed taming. He decided rules or no rules he was going to have a go himself.

"Hey - can you do this with your tongue?"

"Sorry?" asked Natalie turning to face the barman. She liked his very clean white apron.

"Can you do this with your tongue? It proves if you're a royalist or not!" He stuck out his tongue and rolled up the sides to form a little tube.

"How on earth could that prove if you were a royalist or not?" asked Natalie bemused.

"Ah, I see the suspicious denials of a potential roundhead!" laughed the barman.

Natalie noticed that his teeth were almost as white as his apron. His mouth had a nice shape that arranged them very well when he smiled. "I don't know. I've never tried."

Colin didn't move but was alerted by mild curiosity to open his eyes.

The barman was handsomely rewarded as Natalie stuck out her tongue trying to roll it up at the sides.

"Not quite! I'm still not sure I could trust you with any royalist secrets!" laughed the barman.

"Show me again how you did it!" enthused Natalie.

Colin glanced up at the barman. The way he stuck out his tongue and rolled it up he could see that this was no child's game. Did that make him jealous? He wasn't sure. In the short time he'd known her she did seem totally oblivious to her stunning beauty. Almost like a horse wearing blinkers. Although he had no doubt the poor sod had no chance of getting her out of the paddock let alone over a few jumps. He shut his eyes once more.

"That's better!" he heard the barman say. "Now imagine you're rolling it around something."

*Yeah right* thought Colin.

"What do you mean?" he heard Natalie ask sharply.

*She ain't stupid mate* Colin inwardly chuckled.

"Well you know like a tube or something round like an egg?" suggested the barman.

*Or something that looks like a walnut with hairs on it?*

"Are you being rude?" demanded Natalie.

"No of course not! Just trying to make you do it better!" said the barman. The confusion at how it had gone so quickly sour all too apparent in his voice.

Colin heard Natalie stand up. "I don't tolerate any rudeness. I know that bees buzz around flowers and birds fumble in their nests but I don't! That's for the animals and people who want to behave like animals! I find beauty in the exploration of our minds not our bodies! So good day to you sir and please be about your business!"

*Well that sounds about right Bloody Unusual! But I think it explains a lot.*

"But they are one. How can you possibly separate them out?" asked the barman.

*Fair point!*

"I said be about your business sir!" repeated Natalie.

"No seriously lady! I'd like to know how you can even begin to think like that? Is that how you've managed to deal with being so beautiful by denying its existence?" asked the barman. There wasn't any anger or judgement just a desire to know.

Colin heard Natalie drop down into her seat as though she had been slapped. He opened an eye to make sure she hadn't. The poor barman had such a kind earnest face. He couldn't blame him for trying his luck. Although it took a bloody unwelcome effort he decided to intercede. He straightened up in his chair.

"Young man! I have only known this lady a day or so myself. And I can honestly say I've never seen such beauty before. Not in any sunset or in any flower. But I think such rare beauty operates on a different level to the rest of us. Whether God puts truly beautiful people amongst us to punish them or reward them or punish us or reward us I don't know. But they're different in ways that us ordinary people will never understand. What we may see as a wonderful gift might be to them a terrible curse. So it would be wise of you to look upon Natalie here as probably the most beautiful woman you will ever see. But bizarrely it seems the likelihood of you or anyone else taking her out for a canter and over a few jumps are unlikely. Now that seems a waste, that might seem unfair, or even plain ludicrous, but that's the way it is. Like a beautiful sunset enjoy what you can see but don't expect to understand it or to hold it."

He was tired. It had been an effort to say. He didn't really know if any of it made sense. But there it was he had said it.

The barman who had been nodding attentively whilst Colin spoke gave an appreciative final nod, "very wise words sir."

Colin gave a gracious tilt of his head.

"And as you say," suggested the barman, "I can think of her next time I'm boning my girlfriend."

Colin smiled. That's not what he thought he'd said but an awkward situation has been avoided it seemed.

"Would you like a refill sir?" asked the barman.

"Why not? Natalie?"

She folded her arms looking away.

"Just one for me then," said Colin smiling.

"Coming right up!" The barman took up his tankard, "And for giving such good advice this one's on the house!"

"What a splendid fellow you are!" said Colin getting ready to snuggle back into his chair.

"What do you mean by that?" At the barman's departure Natalie had turned to face him.

"Can't I just have a few moments to rest?" he pleaded with grizzled eyes. "I've just helped you out haven't I?"

"Helped me out? Because of you he'll be thinking of me when he's boning his girlfriend. Whatever that means."

"It's when you two people get meat ready for the pot. Perhaps he thinks you'd be good at it."

Natalie looked at Colin suspiciously. He could feel her eyes burrowing into him unpleasantly. It was obvious he would get no peace.

"Here we go sir your drink on the house!" said the barman arriving.

"So what do you get up to in an area like this? You're a long way from the smoke." It wasn't a conversation he wanted but it was preferable to an interrogation.

"I know what you might think. It's not like living in Swansea.." began the barman jovially.

Colin interrupted him. "Swansea? What's Swansea got to do with anything? It's bloody miles away in Wales isn't it?"

"But surely," said the barman bending closer quite unnecessarily as there was only the three of them in the bar, "you know it's got the largest red light district in the whole country! Swansea does it all. It is said that when a man is tired of Swansea he is in fact shagged out!"

This made Colin laugh.

"I don't like the way you're laughing! More rudeness I expect!" said Natalie getting up, "I'm going outside!"

The barman leant closer to whisper in Colin's ear. "Lecherous Len will be skulking outside. I don't think that would be a good idea."

"Sit down!" ordered Colin.

"You can't tell me what to do!" Natalie was defiant. Her eyes sparkling deliciously. He was tempted to tell her again.

"No I can't. But your master's safety depends on us working together for him. Every second is precious. If I have to waste my time looking for you outside that could be the time that puts your master in danger." He was relieved to see that although she wasn't happy she did sit back down.

He turned to the barman. "So forgetting about Swansea - what is it the young men get up to around here?"

The barman straightened very enthusiastically.

"There's all sorts of things we get up to! All the local inns get involved. And we organise ourselves properly into leagues with rules on classes and sizes and distances and all that sort of thing."

"Ah," nodded Colin, "something the English are very good at – finding something to do and organising ourselves properly to do it. Can you give me an example?"

"Well at the moment we're been playing shadow noses. That's where you have to turn really quick to see your nose's shadow on the wall. But I think it's boring. My favourite is "Acorn Squirrels." That season starts in the Autumn. It's a man's sport but the girls love to watch! You have to see how many acorns you can get your squirrel to swallow!"

"Sounds a bit cruel?" suggested Colin half-heartedly, really only for Natalie's benefit.

"Oh no not real squirrels! Bastards are too bloody quick. No the squirrel in your crotch. Better than waffling on I'll show you! I like it so much I practice all year round!" The barman eagerly left them to fetch something.

Colin took the opportunity to close his eyes not understanding what had just been said to him. He began to get a horrible sinking feeling that an interrogation from Natalie would have been preferable after all. He didn't know whether to warn her or not of what they were about to witness because he wasn't sure himself. Instead he held onto the comforting thought that he had in fact fallen asleep and was dreaming.

The barman returned placing a large bowl of acorns on the edge of their table. He removed his very white apron with a flourish undoing the strings holding up his trousers to let them fall. "I'll just get my squirrel ready." He gripped the tip of his penis with his thumb and forefinger stretching it out as far as he could.

*Yep. I'm definitely dreaming* thought Colin.

"You get points for how many acorns your squirrel can swallow and then bonus points for how long before he's sick. I normally compete in Class Eight so obviously I've got to get my squirrel to swallow nine acorns."

Colin had no intention of asking the barman to explain why nine acorns in class eight? But he did watch as the barman squeezed nine acorns into his foreskin and pinched it shut.

"Now you start counting. It won't be the same with just two – normally it's a whole inn full."

As he was clearly dreaming Colin decided to join in, "One! Two! Three!" At fifteen the barman shut his eyes with the effort he was making. At twenty-two there was a red bloom to his neck under his ears that at thirty-seven had quickly spread to the whole of his face. And wasn't he now shaking? Surely it wasn't that hard? At forty-two Colin had a real sense the barman was struggling uncontrollably. Sure enough at forty-five the barman let go gratefully shaking out the acorns like lice from a blanket.

"Damn!" he gasped, "I'll never beat Big Bill until I can get into the fifties!"

Colin looked at Natalie curious to see her reaction at such a sight. It surprised him. She rose out of her chair to begin picking up the acorns from the floor.

"You don't need to do that miss," said the barman.

"Yes I do. You've made a mess," replied Natalie. But it wasn't a problem. She'd soon have it cleared up.

Colin took it as another sign he was dreaming. Nothing as beautiful as Natalie could behave in so servile a way ignoring what she had just seen surely?

"I could do a minute," he said.

The barman was pulling up his trousers. "I'd like to see you try stranger. It's a lot harder than it looks."

Colin stood up pushing away his chair behind him for more space. He undid his belt pushing his stout leather trousers down over his riding boots. "Is there a time limit for feeding your squirrel?"

The barman shook his head. "It's just assumed you'd want to be as quick as you can."

"That's where you country bumpkin amateurs are going wrong then!" said Colin confidently. "And what about the acorns? Can you pick any you want?"

"Of course. An acorn is an acorn isn't it?" replied the barman surprised.

"Really?" Colin tipped out the bowl of acorns onto the table. "I wouldn't do this in competition. Too obvious. I'd constantly practice picking the smallest acorns out from a bowl so in competition it just looked like I'd taken them at random. But these nine little beauties would have been shouting at me to be picked. See? See how they are noticeably smaller than the rest?"

The barman looked at the neat line of nine acorns Colin had lined up on the table. "Yes! Yes! I see it! It seems so obvious now!"

"Now let's see what my squirrel is made of shall we?" said Colin rubbing his hands together briskly, "don't want the little fella clamming up with a cold touch do we?"

The barman watched intently as Colin picked up the first acorn carefully scrutinising it. Then he poked it down taking the time to seat it exactly where he wanted it. Then the second, then the third and so on. He had been like a bull at a gate in comparison. He doubted a real squirrel could be more precise with the placement of his nuts. It was a revelation to watch. But how well would it work?

"Now my good man," said Colin calmly pinching his foreskin shut after the last acorn had gone in, "begin counting."

"One!" shouted out the barman.

"No. No. Save the showmanship for competition. This is where we learn to win. Gently."

"Sorry! Do you want me to start again?"

"Seven!" said Colin.

"Hey that's..." then realising what Colin had done, "eight - nine."

At twenty seconds Colin was still supremely confident that this would be easy. He'd thought it through, spotted the competitive advantages, taken them, and now it was just a question of showing this amateur how a professional did it. There really should have been some money involved. So when the barman had counted to thirty it was quite a surprise to suddenly get the sensation that a shirehorse had sat on his testicles. It made no sense whatsoever but it was something he couldn't resist. It was all over and he was shaking out those acorns as though they were made of jagged glass!

The barman gave him a hearty pat on the back. "That was so impressive for a first attempt! I really drop my trousers to you sir!"

Colin keeled over not knowing what was worse - losing when he expected to win or the small Shetland pony standing on his gonads. At least it was no longer a shirehorse. He was vaguely aware of Natalie busying herself picking up his spent acorns. Then vaguely aware of the inn door opening.

"Master!" screamed Natalie suddenly, "You're safe! But what have they done?"

"Just in the nick of time too! What's going on?" asked an unhappy looking Sam in his dress and bonnet.

Colin made the hard effort to straighten. "Don't worry. It's not what it looks like. I was playing Squirrel Acorns."

"Acorn Squirrels," corrected Natalie, "making a right mess they were."

"Would you like a drink sir?" asked the barman hurriedly picking up the bowl of acorns.

"No! He had quite enough last night," said Clare stooping to get through the door. "I thought I might find you here. And I thought this one could walk off his hangover."

"Oh my God," breathed out the barman.

"Nice to meet you too," said Clare used to such a response but still not liking it.

"Thank you Clare. Thank you so much for looking after him. I'll take you back now," said Colin pulling up his trousers.

"No you won't. You look dead on your feet. Get in your coach and get some sleep. I'll look after this pair." Clare turned to Natalie. "Did you bring some clothes for him? If he stays any longer in that dress he might start to turn."

Natalie laughed unsure of how to behave. "They're in the coach with his other things."

"And some money?" asked Clare.

"Oh yes plenty of money," said Natalie wanting to please.

"Good! Because I'm famished and I'm sure we could all do with a good breakfast. Colin you'll have to wait and look forward to a good lunch. Now away to your coach with this pretty little thing." After Colin and Natalie had left she put a great big arm around Sam. "This might prove to be a little bit dear for you. I do like a big breakfast."

Sam didn't mind at all. "After what you've done for me it will be my pleasure. And we'll see if they've got some big bones or sausages for your dog. What about that?"

"What a sweet man you are," she said almost squeezing the life out of him.

The barman apologetically stood in front of them. "Could I just squeeze through? I need to fetch the chef."

They stood aside so he could pass. He opened the front door shouting out, "Len! Len! Inside now! We need breakfasts doing! Hurry Up!"

# CHAPTER 14

## You think you've had hard time

Hammer and Chisel had been sitting in silence on the bench long enough for Chisel to begin taking out tools from his apron to give them a wipe with an oily cloth. Hammer looked deep in thought. Normally it would be Chisel who would bore first but suddenly Hammer leant forward resting his arms on his legs.

"Do you think if you were made in happy circumstances that's what makes you a happy person?" he asked solemnly.

Chisel stopped rubbing the blade of a 3/8 chisel with the oily cloth. "And if your mother had been raped you'll always be a miserable sod?"

"Something like that," nodded Hammer.

"I've never given it much thought." He nodded towards the back door. "If you're right and that wench gets pregnant - the babby will be as happy as a lark!"

Hammer didn't find it amusing. He abruptly stood up. "There's an hour or so of light. I'm going to the workshop."

At the bottom of the garden was a large shed where Hammer and Chisel made things for Crow.

"What if he calls us?" asked Chisel.

"Well you don't have to come. Stay here."

Chisel put the chisel and cloth back in his apron. "I'll come as well. That seal's getting on me nerves. If he wants us he'll know where we are."

He followed Hammer down the garden path to the shed watching him open the doors realising what was probably bothering him. "You missing your dad again?"

"No of course not! What's the point?" said Hammer defensively not making eye contact.

"No good comes of wallowing in the past!"

"Rubbish!" spat Hammer. "It's what's brought you to where you are!"

Chisel took his hands off his hips and went in. "Come on then. It's obviously time again."

"Time for what?" asked Hammer picking up a plane unnecessarily.

"Time for you to tell me your dad's life story again! How hard it was and how unfair. That time! About every six months it seems. But I'm not just listening to it. We'll keep ourselves busy. Come on - we'll finish off "Project Stretch."" Chisel chivvied at Hammer to make room for him. "You normally start with the terrible night of his birth. Your grandma an ironing maid in the service of some terrible Colonel. Some git that loved his animals more than his staff. That's right ennit?"

Hammer put down the plane picking up something more useful for Project Stretch. "He was a git an' all! The imminent arrival of a baby was no excuse for not having a selection of ironed shirts in the morning. All the other women servants unable to help. The stablelad presumed to be the father scarpering at the first signs of a growing bump. My poor grandma left all alone to give birth and finish the ironing! A contraction and a cuff all through the night. Can you imagine it?" Hammer stopped what he was doing to shake his head. "The merciless hunger of the ironing board not caring an inch for her labour pains."

"Come on! We're better than that mate! We work to a sixteenth of an inch!" said Chisel trying to cheer his mood. He gave a hard blow to remove some wood shavings from the frame of Project Stretch.

"Do you do it on purpose?" asked Hammer looking at him threateningly.

Chisel's cheeks were still puffed up from blowing. He looked to the side as though there might be someone else there who could have upset Hammer, "what?"

Hammer couldn't blame him for being a Brummie git. It hadn't been his choice after all. He softened putting his head down to pencil in an area of wood he was going to remove. "Finally just before dawn the basket of ironing was empty and the baby was out. But at some point in the night she had left the hot iron on one of the shirts. It was ruined beyond repair!"

"This is when he kicked her out? But keeping the baby as compensation for the shirt?" Chisel shook his head, "chores put before children. When will it end?"

"She was never seen again. And had nothing to do with her son because she'd burnt some toff's shirt! You can't credit it can you?"

"Time's moved on. I don't think it would happen today," suggested Chisel. "Now they'd soak the shirt in brine and flog her with it – that's all."

Hammer picked up a small saw. "Perhaps. Well my dad's first job was cleaning dishes in the scullery. As soon as he could make hand movements in a bowl of water. When he began toddling he was given a romper suit of goose feathers and boarded into chimneys to clear them of soot. Getting down from the roof by the use of a precarious drainpipe apparently. As a small boy he progressed to cleaning the downstairs windows with his tongue. He could get right into the corners to get rid of all the little annoying bits. He was so good at it they attached two wooden stilts to his legs so he could do the upstairs windows as well. He learned how to repair guttering, replace roof tiles, prune trees, pick blossom to decorate the hall, or even smack birds for singing too loudly outside that git's bedroom window. In fact there were so many jobs that the stilts were never taken off my dad."

"I meant to ask you this before - how would he get into bed wearing stilts?" Chisel stepped back to see if he was happy with what he'd just done.

"Bed!" spat Hammer. "Bed! Do you think he had a bed to sleep in? When he finished his sixteen hour day my dad was placed along the bottom of the barn door as a draught excluder!"

"No wonder you don't feel the cold," suggested Chisel.

"I think I get that from my mum but that's not the point! Then one fateful day something went wrong picking blossom. Not yanking a guttering back into place or stamping on rats in the yard. But picking blossom!"

"Is this where one of his stilts got stuck in a rabbit burrow? And there was a magpie that come chattering out of the branches at him like a stagecoach? Throwing up his arms and losing his balance he hit the ground with a sickening merciless crack? The wrenched petals of blossom falling around your dad like little pink tears." Chisel did find this bit bad luck.

Hammer nodded heavily. "His right leg had been torn apart as easily as cooked chicken. He was too far from the house for his screams to be heard. He was found later with barely a breath left in him. They'd only looked for him because of a particularly rebellious robin that had been asking for a good slap all day. Do you know they were happier to find a falcon's egg wedged in the wound than my dad alive?"

"Because of the git's love of falconry!" knew Chisel.

"Any man who could help the git pursue it was treated sparingly. The egg was left where it was to incubate and two weeks later it hatched. Imagine - your leg has been torn to pieces and you can't move for two weeks in case you break a bloody egg left in it!"

"That's where you get your determination from," suggested Chisel.

"Now the egg had hatched my dad could be left to die. He was only spared because the git saw the chick liked the taste of him. My dad said that chick saved his life twice. It ate all the rotten stuff in his leg and the maggots. The stilts were removed and my dad joined the falconry staff. They were the lucky ones. They were almost fed regularly and had a bed to share in the bottom of the aviary. My dad said he would get shat on through the night but there was still a lot of protein left in it. On his diet of mutes my dad grew into the best falconer that git had."

"The git died though didn't he?" said Chisel more interested in examining a length of dowel.

"I'd like to think he was murdered but we'll never know. Hand me that sandpaper would you?"

Chisel put down the length of dowel to hand Hammer the sandpaper. "So how did he end up in Bristol?"

"The git's son never liked my dad. Ever since my dad had seem him through an upstairs window polishing his musket. He was more or less given away. Like a wonky chair. Or a broken mangle. Or a threadbare rug from the hall."

"Working for the dodgy dressmaker in Bristol." Chisel grinned and began singing, "Gordy Georgie pudding and pie kissed the girls and made them cry. But when the boys came out to play he kissed them as well he was funny that way!"

Hammer put down the sandpaper and rubbed his forehead exasperated. "Subtlety's a bit lost on you Brummies isn't it?"

It was a frequent jibe between them and Chisel responded as he always did, "Hey you don't make the best stuff in the world by chance! It's facts, figures and focus which I wouldn't expect some Cambridgeshire carrot cruncher to understand!"

Hammer wouldn't mind but he wasn't even from Cambridgeshire. He picked up the sandpaper resisting the urge to use it as a flannel on Chisel's face.

"Well go on. How's a falconer with a gammy leg gonna get on at a dodgy dressmakers?" asked Chisel brandishing the length of dowel.

"Are you actually going to do anything with that?" asked Hammer.

"I suppose I could find somewhere nice and tight to stick it! Do you want to bend over and see if anywhere occurs to me?" asked Chisel widening his eyes.

Not for the first time Hammer did wonder why he'd not set himself up as a sole trader rather than enter into a partnership. But he'd give it some thought later rather than now.

"As you know the dressmaker wanted to try something new with my dad." Hammer looked up daring Chisel to say or do something. Chisel put on an exaggerated prim face saying nothing. "He put a black velvet sack over my dad's head." Again Hammer looked at him. It was much more of an effort this time but Chisel didn't crack. "And made him put on a dress."

"To stand in the shop window," Chisel said calmly. He'd done ever so well not to laugh at this point like he normally did.

"That's right," nodded Hammer pleased. "Immediately two women passing the shop stopped to look at the dress my dad was wearing – the other dresses draped on the shop window floor being completely ignored. The dressmaker knew everyone would soon copy his idea – which they do. But my dad was the first."

"And I found out why when I knocked one over once it groaned when I picked it up," said Chisel pointing thankfully at him.

"You must have been in a cheaper ladies clothes shop. The expensive ones charge enough to use wooden dummies. Everywhere else it's real women. They're far cheaper than wooden ones. But my dad's talent was not limited to standing very still in a hot shop window for hours on end with a black velvet sack over his head. It had started one night at closing with a whispered suggestion to the dressmaker. Such impertinence rewarded with a cotton reel shoved up his nostril! Unperturbed my dad made the suggestion again the next night. This time receiving a cotton reel up his other nostril. The next night a thimble rammed in his ear. The fourth night the dressmaker finally giving in to what my dad was suggesting."

"Lucky for your dad's orifices," suggested Chisel under his breath.

"Soon Bristol's most fashionable women were beating a path to the dressmaker's door because of my dad's suggestions. Though never, not once did the dressmaker ever let on where the true inspiration lay. Soon the dressmaker's ability had spread much further than he could ever have imagined. One evening just before closing a sweet smelling man with a thin moustache twirling a small cane entered the shop. He glided around liking more and more of what he saw. – Pass me that hammer would you?"

"One Brummie scalpel -" said Chisel handing it across.

"Well this man was from Rome. My dad standing in the window heard the whole conversation." Hammer gave one precise hit with the hammer and placed it down on the bench. "He represented someone who was bored with the mediocrity of Milan. The pretentious of Parisians. The downright falseness of Frankfurters! He wanted to shake up the old order with the bonfire blazing in Bristol. This would be the dressmaker's chance to set the whole of Europe alight!"

"This is where he goes on about all that fashion twaddle isn't it?"

Hammer nodded agreeing completely with Chisel's derogatory tone. "I'll condense it for you. They wanted flowing lines but not too much movement, lots of gold but not ostentatious, height but not over-bearing, traditional but brought bang up to date, civilised but with a deference to ethnic influences - " Hammer had to stop. "Can you imagine what it would be like if that lot had to make something important like a bridge or a ship?"

"Well it would look nice," suggested Chisel.

"Yeah but would you want to go over it or go to sea in it?"

"Probably not. Not if I didn't want to get wet."

"Well unbeknown to the Roman the man who needed to know all this wasn't the one he was talking to but the velvet hooded figure in the window. When the dressmaker heard what the Roman's boss would be willing to pay if he was pleased with the results he nearly fell over. It was a stupendous figure but to my dad about as relevant as being told there was salt on Saturn."

"If your dad wasn't going to be paid anyway what did it matter how much it was?"

"Just because you don't understand something when you first hear it doesn't mean it won't become relevant later on. You for instance. At some point you heard that you came from Birmingham. Only later realising it explains your unnatural appetite for pork scratchings."

"I think you'll find that's someone from the black country. If you're looking for a culinary eccentricity about Brummies then we don't put butter on our sausage sandwiches!"

"Well that's as maybe," said Hammer waving a hand not interested.

"Oh - and I've never seen stera milk anywhere else either," added Chisel helpfully.

Hammer was curious to know what "stera milk" was but wasn't going to ask because he didn't want a lecture on the fact that obviously God wasn't a Brummie but everything he used was probably made in Birmingham if God had any sense.

"Well my dad's efforts were about to make a man wealthy. It's just a shame it wasn't him. The dressmaker could either do everything he could to make sure it took place or make plans to spend it."

Chisel nodded knowingly. "We're talking about a dressmaker here not an engineer. He was in every jewellers in Bristol!"

"Jewellers! Haberdashers! Coach Dealers! If it had a large pound sign in the window the dressmaker strolled right in! But back in his own shop my dad was working his nuts off day and night! The dressmaker getting so lazy he couldn't even make sure my dad had all the materials he needed. Desperate my dad went out to find them himself. How eager everyone had been to supply what he needed in return for a chat about who he worked for and what he wanted them for and *how much?* It wasn't his fault. He had no comprehension of money or the funny words tradespeople used. Free sample? Set up an account? Pay me now or pay me double at the end of the month? Didn't mean a thing to him. He had been surprised at how easy it was to get the things. How many people had known the dressmaker. But other than that, all he cared about was finishing the garments he was working on. He wasn't to know he had stumbled upon the dressmaker's biggest creditor in the process."

"Always dangerous not knowing who you're talking to," said Chisel holding up a piece of wood to see if he'd taken enough off.

Hammer wasn't going to acknowledge such obvious advice. The fool might as well of said – don't clean your teeth with a saw or don't use a chisel to get the wax out of your ear. "That night the dressmaker burst into the workroom at the back of the shop all red-faced, "You stupid cretin! Why you been blabbing your mouth off all over Bristol? Do you know what you are? You're fired! Get out you bitch!""

"I wish I'd of bin there Hammer. I really do," said Chisel with a thick set jaw.

""But where will I go? I don't even have my own clothes," pleaded my dad.

"I don't care! Get out now!" My dad had tried one of the Roman robes on to see if it moved in the way he was looking for. He was that good.

"And this!" said the dressmaker hurling a crook from the Autumn shepherd collection at him. "And you'll need something to shit in of course!" A beautiful white and gold mitre commissioned by the local bishop was tossed at him like a plain ball of wool. "I don't ever want to see this again!" said the dressmaker blowing his nose on the black velvet sack and throwing it at him. Then he was hurled into the street like an empty box."

"Each time this bit makes my blood boil!" said Chisel menacingly.

"I do believe even the greatest of men must allow themselves a few tears in such a situation. As long as it's in secret. Whether he did or not my dad never said. But I wouldn't blame him."

Chisel decided to take over as Hammer did have a tendency to fill up at this point.

"He went to see the friendliest person he'd ever met – not knowing it was the dressmaker's biggest creditor. When he got there he knocked several times but there was no answer at the back door to the shop. But it was unlocked so he went in. At first he wondered how the friendly man could possibly find anything. It was such a mess. It looked like two donkeys had been arguing over a carrot in there. Then as his eyes became accustomed to the gloom he could see the friendly man slumped over the sewing table with many buttons all spilled about him. He went over to speak to him but there was something sticking out of his ear – a number eight knitting needle! But before dying the friendly man had managed to spell something out in buttons on the sewing table: THAT LYING CHEATING BASTARD FROM DOWN THE ROAD DID THIS BECAUSE HE WON'T PAY UP DON'T LET MY DEATH GO UNPUNISHED SIGNED ARTHUR PRICE."

Chisel took a sneaky look at Hammer then stopped to rub the back of his head. "I've never understood. He did all that in buttons. It must have taken him ages. Why not just go and get help?"

"Who knows what goes through the mind of a dying man?" asked Hammer.

Chisel smiled deliciously. Hammer had fallen right into his trap. "In this case - a number eight knitting needle!"

Hammer looked at Chisel. "You know what happened in a haberdashers in Bristol could happen in a workshop in Buckinghamshire too. And I'd go back to mess up any message the dying man left behind."

"I know you would – though I did get you!"

Hammer graciously nodded admitting he'd fallen for it. But moving quickly on with the story to not allow Chisel to gloat.

"My dad wandered aimlessly down the high street in his gold robe and mitre carrying his crook. It was mostly deserted at that time of night except for the drunks being thrown out of the taverns. One of them blundered into my dad giving him a right earful. Couldn't a man get pissed and stumble home unmolested? What is it with you bloody religious types? Why couldn't you just stay in the pulpit? Creeping around catching sinners doing it wasn't fair!

"Sounds like a right mouthy git, not a happy drunk at all," chided Chisel.

"My dad didn't know what he was wearing made him look like an important religious type," said Hammer in his dad's defence.

"I don't know what's worse – religious types – drunks that want to take on the world – or sloppy drunks that want to kiss ye to death. They're all a pox!" remarked Chisel unfavourably.

"All the noise he was making brought the landlady out to see what was going on. Taking one look at my dad she knew something special had just landed on her doorstep. She told the drunk to beat it sharpish and took my dad around the back for a little chat by the bins. She'd been toying with an idea for some months now and knew my dad was the missing piece. In his situation he was putty in her hands."

"I know she was a conniving unpleasant woman but I do think a lot of her ideas could catch on." Chisel looked up because Hammer was staring at him not wanting an interruption. "Sorry!"

"Oh she knew what she was doing alright even if my dad was too trusting to see. She told him to see a local farmer who was looking for a shepherd. But he wasn't a shepherd! my dad told her. It was easy! she said. He'd got a big robe a big hat and a crook. That was all he needed! She told him where to go again but on no account was he to tell the farmer she'd sent him. Just pop back and see her after his first payday. My dad said he went thinking his luck had finally changed. He didn't think he was going to be abused again."

"We know we'd definitely pop a lot of the people in this story if we ever met 'em. Do you think we'd pop the farmer?" asked Chisel holding up a chisel that happened to be in his hand.

"He just sounds like a berk to me. I mean I know come my dad's first payday he'd made so many deductions my dad now owed him money. But most employers do that in the first year. But to see what was going on and believe what my dad was telling him. He must have been a berk. If we did pop him it would be to put him out of his misery."

Chisel liked the part of the story coming up next the best. It contained the ideas he could see catching on. "So remind me again of the landlady's scheme," he said putting down his chisel.

Hammer liked this bit too. "She was going to attract a better clientele by introducing something she called a "theme" to her pub. She was going to put wool mats on the floor of the lounge and the heads of collie dogs on the walls of the snug. Whole stuffed sheep instead of stools to sit on in the dining area. Only lamb on the menu every day. And complimentary pots of mint sauce everywhere. But her biggest innovation was going to be proper indoor toilets! Separate ones for men and women! And so everyone would know which was which. There would be a ram's head on the gent's toilet door! And a ewe's head on the ladies!"

Chisel joined in with Hammer's growing incredulous laughter. "Sheep to sit on yes! Complimentary pots of mint sauce yes! But indoor toilets?!"

"I know!" said Hammer wiping away a tear.

When they have both calmed down Hammer continued with a smile on his face. "Well of course all this was going to take a lot of sheep. But to make it a surprise for the farmer they wouldn't tell him until it was all finished. They'd keep it a secret by taking a few sheep at a time and pay him for what they'd taken on the opening night! She reckoned a whole sheep could be hidden under my dad's great gold robe, maybe even two."

Chisel let out a guffaw. "I know he's your dad and that – but do you think he might have been a bit thick at this point?"

Hammer held up the saw he was holding like a sword.

"That one's too short. You could do a lot  more damage with the one behind you," suggested Chisel smiling.

Jokingly Hammer went to reach for it.

"I mean binding a frightened sheep to your leg under a great flowing robe. It's no wonder it's going to start biting down on whatever's nearby," laughed Chisel.

Hammer wanted to laugh too but this was his dad not some stranger. "It was over a week before he was in a fit state to try again."

"Just think – if sheep had really sharp teeth you wouldn't be here!"

"Alright. Alright. Don't you want me to get to the rustlers?"

"Oh yes the magpie gang!" said Chisel eagerly.

"Each night my dad would tie a sheep to his leg under his great flowing robe and take a casual stroll into the village. If he saw a villager out late walking their dog he would give them a friendly nod with his mitre. What a polite young shepherd they all thought. So much nicer than the other ones the miserable bastard normally tricked into working for him. Then when all was clear a quick slip for a landlady exchange by the bins. But although the farmer was a berk he had noticed his flock was getting smaller. My dad had to tell him something."

Chisel began chuckling in anticipation.

"A gang of sheep rustling magpies had moved into the area. They were led by an old crow. One of the gang a jackdaw was always finding clever ways to distract him before the whole magpie gang swarmed into view to carry off another sheep!"

"Just how many magpies would it take to carry off a sheep?" laughed Chisel.

Hammer shrugged his shoulders. "Like I say I think the farmer must have been a berk. Unlike the pigs."

"Oh yes the pigs," nodded Chisel seriously, "they soon put a stop to it all. But they are wonderful though. Bacon, ham, sausages, black pudding, pork pies and crackling off a Sunday joint." He licked his lips lovingly.

Hammer nodded in full agreement. "Not only ridiculously tasty but a lot more intelligent than any sheep or goat. Spurred on by the success of The Leg of Lamb the landlady wanted to open another pub called The Trough. This time my dad's skills were required to procure pigs. She invented some plausible reason for him to be doing it and off he went to the local pig farm. But on his very first raid he didn't notice one of the clever old sows slip out from her pen making straight for the pig farmer's back door. Her trotters – making an excellent supper when delicately boiled by the way – banging out the alarm. The pig farmer on the other side of the door waiting for her message to stop before waking two of his burly sons to join him at the scene of the crime."

"Are pigs really that clever?" asked Chisel.

"I may have exaggerated that bit a little," suggested Hammer.

"I do like pigs."

"They are quite delicious," Hammer admitted freely.

"We need to stop. It will make me hungry."

"The pig farmers found my dad playing with the little darling piglets like puppies. He was enthralled by them and they obviously adored him. They didn't give him a good kicking but took him to the piggery's owner."

"That's where your dad was able to impress him so much he took your dad on as a pig farmer. Your dad met your mum who was a maid in the big house. She was from Swansea originally where she'd worked in the entertainment industry. And they had you. Then when you were eight your dad got swine fever and told you his life story on his deathbed. He told you it don't pay to do the right thing. It's a mug's game."

Hammer nodded. "Very succinctly put if I may say so."

"Well it's almost dark. I don't want to light the lanterns and attract the moths." Chisel gave a shudder. "Bloody creepy things."

"I do believe we're done," said Hammer stepping back. He pretended to look at Project Stretch but he was somewhere else.

"You know the best way to put right your dad's life is to remember what he told you on his deathbed – doing the right thing is a mug's game. He's right!" said Chisel sincerely.

Hammer said nothing still apparently admiring what they had finished in the fading light.

"That's exactly how he wanted it!" said Chisel quickly moving on. "It'ull break down into three pieces so it's easy to move from place to place. And it'ull work on anyone from four foot to six foot two. Tension easily adjusts. And nowhere is there any chance of being pricked by a splinter."

"It's a bloody rack!" exclaimed Hammer suddenly back to normal. "Do you think the poor bastard strapped to it will be worried about splinters?"

"No but I do! I wouldn't want him thinking it was poor quality workmanship he was on."

Hammer put a caring hand on Chisel's shoulder looking at him admiringly. "Do you want me to strap you in and see how much this baby can take?" he asked smiling.

Chisel pushed him away calling him something nasty.

# CHAPTER 15

## All work and no play makes Jack a dull boy

Colin stepped out of the tavern knowing he could finally give in to those sailors. Sam would be safe with his sister. Natalie would get Sam's things from the coach and then he could climb in and sleep. It would be wonderful!

"Hey mister!" It was a stablelad. "Do you know one of your horses has cast a shoe?"

Colin's heart sank. "I don't believe it," he muttered under his breath. It was something he couldn't ignore. It also explained why the poor girl had been struggling. He handed Natalie the key to the coach door. "Get what you need and lock it back up would you?"

"What are you doing?" she asked taking the key.

"Trying to beat the county record for how long a man can go without sleep it seems," said Colin rolling his blood-shot eyes.

She grabbed his arm. "I'll do it. You need to rest."

"You'd do that for me?" asked Colin surprised.

"Of course! What do I have to do?" She started leading him to the coach.

"Go with the stablelad. He'll take you to the blacksmith. If he's a good lad give him a tip -"

"How much should I tip him?" interrupted Natalie.

Colin remembered who he was talking to. "Two pennies. Nothing if he's a cheeky so and so. Then watch the blacksmith to make sure he does a good job."

"And how much should it cost?" she asked unlocking the coach door.

"Well we're not in London so no more than half a schilling."

Natalie reached in taking out the sack of Sam's things. "You get in and rest. I'll make sure the blacksmith does a good job."

"Thank you Natalie. I'm sure you will," he said thinking *the poor bastard.* But he didn't care. Those sailors were piping him aboard that dark vessel ready to sail him off to warm waters.

"Wait a bit please!" she shouted at the stablelad. She went inside to give Sam his sack and ask for the money she'd need. He told her to be careful and asked her what she wanted for breakfast. She asked for a full English but could they make sure to keep the tomatoes separate from the eggs using a dam made with the sausages? Clare asked her why? Wasn't it obvious? No! So the eggs didn't get all soggy. Oh! Clare asked for the same on her breakfasts.

Natalie joined the stablelad outside. "You take me and the horse that needs a shoe to the blacksmith. If you do it politely you'll have two pennies. If you're a cheeky so and so you won't get anything. Is that clear enough for you?"

"Crystal clear!" said the stablelad tugging on a forelock of his hair. "I shall not speak unless spoken to. Your horse is this way Miss."

He led her to the entrance to the small stable block. "Wait there Miss and I'll bring her out."

"Ooh she's lovely! What kind brown eyes," said Natalie seeing her. "May I lead her?"

"Of course Miss. She is a nice one this one. She won't give you any trouble." He handed her the short rope.

"How far do we have to go?" asked Natalie wondering how long the anticipated pleasure might last.

"Only down the lane," replied the stablelad.

"Come on girl. That's what you say isn't it?" said Natalie excited.

The stablelad nodded. "This way Miss."

As they walked gently down the lane Natalie kept looking up at the horse thinking what truly noble creatures they were. Wasn't it wonderful to be so close to one? How wonderful must it be to work with them like this young lad did every day?

"So how long have you worked with horses?" she asked leaning underneath the horse's chin to see him on the other side.

"Since I was five Miss," he answered politely.

"And how old are you now?"

"Twelve Miss."

"Seven years. Lucky you! You must love it!"

"Not as much as I love fingering girls!" he said enthusiastically.

She abruptly brought her head from underneath the horse's chin. His head immediately replacing the space. "Do you like being fingered Miss?" he asked pleasantly.

"No I'm afraid I don't." Natalie thought it might be something rude. But he was such a polite young lad.

"Shame. I mean horses are great. But fingering somebody up in the hayloft. That's better!"

"I'll give you three pennies if you don't say another word until we get there," suggested Natalie.

"Very well Miss," nodded the stablelad surprised but agreeably. He tucked back out of sight.

They walked the remainder of the way in silence.

"Here we are Miss. The Blacksmiths. That'll be three pennies please," he said politely. He held the rope whilst she took out the money from a little pocket in her apron. With the coins in his palm he clasped his fist firmly shut and began laughing.

"What are you laughing for?" asked Natalie sharply.

"You'll see!" he said handing her the rope and running off. He stopped well out of reach. "You'll see!" Then ran off again.

She thought about chasing after him but what would happen to the horse? And why? He hadn't actually been a cheeky so and so. He'd done as he'd been told. Instead she led the horse into the cobbled yard of the blacksmiths. In the centre was a hearty hearth with a little roof above it. There was a horse tied to a post to the side and a big blackened blacksmith in a huge apron with his back to her. Being a blacksmith must be really hot work because he wasn't wearing any trousers. The knot - the size of a child's fist - holding on the apron resting above the blacksmith's naked buttocks! She coughed hoping to attract his attention.

The blacksmith turned rearing up like a great sail filling with wind. She was relieved to see his apron was big enough to cover the things that shouldn't be on show. His hair had slid down the sweaty sides of his huge head to be stopped in two great clumps above his ears. His face was blackened around the edge and red in the centre. He looked like a dartboard with a bigger bull's eye than normal.

"What is it girl? You've stopped me graftin'." His voice was so big and powerful Natalie felt she was feeling it rather than hearing it.

"I was just hoping for a few moments of your attention," she said nervously.

"Attention? No attention in my life! Grafted to find a nipple! Grafted ever since!" The cobbles seemed to rattle against one another with the power of his voice.

"Oh," said Natalie regretting her good deed.

"Oh? Oh you say? Eight in a litter and you say – OH?"

"Nice to have a big family around you?" she suggested.

"Big family around you you say?"

With one giant step he was right in front of her. Though she didn't want to be accused of staring she couldn't help notice the man's face had a strange concave look about it.

"Big families need big feeding!" he boomed in her face. His breath smelt rusty. "All dead before earning their keep! Me left to graft from dawn 'till dusk so Ma could make some more with the milkman."

"Must have been hard for you," said Natalie resisting the urge to throw down the rope and run for her life!

"Do you want to learn something girl?"

"Yes," replied Natalie. She clung on to the rope hoping the horse wouldn't allow anything bad to happen to her.

The blacksmith took the rope from her. He tied her horse to another post. Back at the hearth he arched his back to take in an enormous barrel of air. "Bellows!" he boomed. He leant forward expelling hard over the coals with all his might saving a final bit of precious air, "are not grafting!"

The black coals sprang eagerly to a red life. He arched his back taking in another great barrel of air. This time after blowing with all his might informing Natalie that bellows were "the thin end of the wedge." Again and again he released a hurricane over the coals saving a precious tailwind to enlighten her. By the time the coals seemed to glow almost blue she had been informed that bellows via hammers and other soft tools might tempt you into thinking you deserve a day off now and again and imagine the madness of that!

"That fire is so hot!" said Natalie barely able to stand the heat form where she stood.

"It'ull have to do," said the blacksmith standing right next to it. How could he do that?

He reached into his giant apron to pull out a horseshoe.

"Leaving these on the bench 'till they're needed," he said sneeringly. "Howzat gonna break your back?"

He tossed the little iron vessel onto the fiery sea. In spite of the heat Natalie was enthralled to watch as the waves hungrily licked it to a lovely cherry glowing red.

"Metal Tongs!" boomed the blacksmith, "aren't graftin'! Wooden ones are graftin! Got to be quick before they burn - see?"

Natalie couldn't see any tongs anywhere in the yard.

The blacksmith bent forward reaching a great blackened hand behind him. Natalie turned away desperate not to see where he kept his tongs.

"ARRRGGGGHHHHH!" screamed the blacksmith.

She looked up at the sound of the hot cherry shoe clanging on the anvil.

"A hammer? I think not!" shouted the blacksmith.

She saw him thump his great head down hard on the shoe. The thud of hard bone against hard iron sickening her to the very pit of her stomach. She turned away unable to watch.

"Frightened of seeing...

THUD

a man graft..."

THUD

"are you girl?"

THUD

"What's this...

THUD

country coming to?"

She found the courage to look again. The blacksmith was tossing the hot shoe from one hand to another over to the horse.

"Back with me girl?" sneered the blacksmith. "Nails in a pouch? Like a woman's purse? Makes me sick! I swallow these while they're still hot!" He belched loudly and something shot out of his mouth into his great blackened palm. He then seemed able to *push* the nail - for that's what it was - into the horse's hoof! Seven or eight times he straightened to belch out a nail then bend over to push it through the shoe into the horse's hoof. A few times using his teeth to bend the shoe into the shape he wanted. Natalie had never seen such a demonstration of strength.

"All done girl," said the blacksmith straightening to his full impressive height.

"That's incredible," said Natalie. "You didn't use a hammer to push those nails in!"

"A HAMMER?" boomed the blacksmith so loudly several tiles from the roof clattered onto the cobbles. Her horse gave a start which he easily checked with a great arm around its neck. "DO YOU SEE THE TOOL OF THE IDLE SOFT GOBLIN?"

"No sir! Not at all sir!" spluttered Natalie. Her horse was going nowhere. The blacksmith could clearly move it around as easily as she could a washing basket. "I can only thank you for such a wonderful demonstration of grafting. It shall remain with me forever. Thank you very much sir!"

The blacksmith released the horse. His face erupting into a grotesque pumpkin smile. This is it thought Natalie - I've either said the right thing or he's going to eat me!

"Very kind of you Miss. Appreciate it."

"Thank you again for letting me watch," said Natalie. There was just one more fence to jump. "Is half a schilling fair payment?"

The blacksmith nodded his big blackened head. "Exactly fair Miss. That covers the shoeing and the cost of bum ointment."

Very greatly relieved Natalie dropped the money into his great hand.

"Good day to you Miss," he said handing her the horse's rope.

"Good day to you sir," said Natalie eagerly taking it. She led the horse out of the yard as quickly as she could but being English not so quick that it would appear to be rude.

As she led the horse up the lane the simple enjoyment of doing so returned to her. By the time she reached the stables she felt much wiser for the whole experience. The stablelad was waiting for her eating an iced bun.

"How did you get on?" he asked with a cheeky knowing grin.

Natalie smiled very pleasantly handing him the rope. "Creep!"

It wiped the smile of his face. "Ooh you learn quick don't you?"

"Yes it appears I do," she said thoughtfully. "Enjoy your bun."

As she stepped inside the tavern she found the barman making a mess with acorns again. This time with her master. Clare found it highly amusing. Natalie had no doubt she would have loved to have joined in if she only had the equipment. She decided she wasn't going to pick the acorns up again even if they were her master's and sat down at a table a little way off.

"Oh Natalie," said Sam pulling up his trousers (he had changed into some of his own clothes from the sack), "we were just trying one of the local sports whilst we waited for breakfast. Did you sort out the horse satisfactorily?"

"Yes sir. All done," she said in an unusual perfunctory tone for her.

Sam was visibly surprised but didn't have the chance to respond as the barman had suddenly disappeared and reappeared carrying four large plates, two in each arm. "Lady your timing is almost as beautiful as you are! My guests your breakfasts are ready!" He put the four plates down on the table. "One for you sir. One for you lady. And two of your three -" he glanced at Clare and she looked at him very interested in what he would say next, "madam!"

The barman had no idea where it came from but she liked it so that was all that mattered.

"I'll just get some knives and forks," he said hurrying behind the bar.

"Come on Natalie! Tuck in!" said Clare beckoning her over.

"Come on Natalie. You don't want it going cold," said Sam pulling up a chair. He sensed a change in her but couldn't begin to guess what might have happened just getting a horse shod so would speak to her later about it.

She sat down with them rather pleased at what she saw. It was a wonderful looking breakfast just as she'd asked with a sausage dam. The barman handed her a knife and fork. "Try that brown stuff there." He pointed to a patch on her plate. "Taste's lovely!"

"What is it?" asked Natalie.

"Len calls it his "brown sauce" but I think he's going to have to come up with a better name if he wants it to catch on. But it does taste lovely with a fry-up. And egg and chips." The barman scrunched up his face, "but not apple pie!"

"Do you have any tea?" asked Sam interrupting him.

"Yes of course sir."

"And a pint of cider for me," said Clare. It was quite incredible but half of her plate was already empty. She didn't seem to eat but to tip it in.

Lecherous Len appeared carrying Clare's third plate of breakfast.

"Just put it on the bar. I'll grab it when I've finished this one," said Clare with a mouthful of food.

He put it down not taking his eyes off Natalie. "Is everyone enjoying their breakfasts?" he asked smiling. Natalie wished he would just leave staring at her like that.

"Very nice. I like your "brown sauce" very much," said Sam giving him a quick glance, "very tangy!"

Lecherous Len nodded gratifyingly still staring at Natalie. "Not too salty?"

The barman who was halfway through pouring Clare's cider abruptly stopped looking horrified at Lecherous Len. After a few seconds he looked to see if anyone had noticed. Fortunately they hadn't. "Right Len! Cup of tea please! Now!"

"But I wanted to see that gorgeous thing eat my sauce!" protested Lecherous Len still not averting his gaze.

The barman hurried across to him. "Now! I need to show you where I keep the tea!"

"But I know where we keep the tea!" said Lecherous Len trying to look around the barman at Natalie.

"I've moved it!" said the barman grabbing hold of him. He bundled him through the door to the kitchen.

"You always know where everything is Natalie. Never have that problem with you," said Sam popping in a bit of sausage he'd dipped in brown sauce.

"No sir." It was nothing specific or clear but something told her it would be a good idea to leave the dollop of brown sauce on her plate exactly as she'd found it.

The barman presently returned with a pot of tea and cup on a tray and Clare's cider.

"Everyone happy?" he asked pleasantly.

Sam and Clare nodded. Natalie noticed him taking a keen interest in her plate seeming visibly relieved to see her untouched brown sauce. She'd eaten enough anyway and pushed away her plate. The barman stiffened as though expecting some accusation. Clare picked up her plate. "Don't want that love?" When Natalie shook her head Clare tipped what was left onto her plate. "Waste not want not!"

"Sir – do you mind if I have a little doze on the bench outside? The sun's up now and I imagine it would be quite pleasant."

"Of course. Of course. It's been a very trying day and night. You go and rest girl," said Sam looking at her fondly.

She left to sit on the bench which was already warm with the summer morning sun. She sat down looking at the coach a little way off. Then further out to the fields and the hedgerows and the space of it all. All so different to the density of London. The smell of the stables tickled her nose gently – a mixture of hay and sweet urine. She closed her eyes enjoying how the strong sun made her see red not soot. She brought her feet up to tuck them underneath her dress. She gave a little shiver as though she had feathers and then fell fast asleep.

She was awoken by Colin standing over her.

"Sorry," he said, "I didn't mean to wake you. I brought you out a cup of tea but didn't want to wake you. But I didn't want to leave you either."

"That's alright. We're quite safe here aren't we?" she said sitting up. She couldn't see Colin's face properly as the sun was behind him. "You sound better."

"Amazing what a few hours' sleep can do. May I?"

"Of course." She moved to make room for him on the bench. "So where's my tea?"

"Oh that went cold a long time ago," said Colin tipping upside down an empty cup.

"Well how long have you been there for?" asked Natalie covering her eyes with a hand so she could look at him more clearly.

"Dunno."

"Well didn't you get bored just standing there?"

"No. I think it's a beautiful spot." She watched him as he looked to admire the view. "And you're the most beautiful thing in it." He was still admiring the view when he said it.

She pretended she hadn't heard. He seemed to know she would. "But we'll have to leave tonight as beautiful as it is."

"Will my master ever be safe?"

Colin still seemed captivated by the view. "It boils down to something very simple when you're on the run - you either evade capture for as long as you can or you destroy the thing that's chasing you. Does that make sense?" He turned to look at her.

"If you accept it doesn't make sense for being chased in the first place then yes."

"You can only destroy something if you first know what it is and second have something to destroy it with. I think the three of us fail on both counts. Ergo our only choice is to evade capture as long as we can."

"That seems so unfair! My master is a bookkeeper not a master criminal. He's never murdered anyone or taken anything he shouldn't have done. Why not talk to these people and sort it out sensibly?"

"Because the world doesn't work like that. I think some people are born bad and get worse as they get older. They like to mess it up for the rest of us. You'll never explain it because they don't understand it themselves. Don't even try. Best avoid them in the first place. Unless you get unlucky like we have."

"Then you run like frightened mice from a broom!" said Natalie folding her arms.

"Or live to enjoy another day!" said Colin smiling. "Even the people chasing us have something they can't outrun. It'll surely get them in the end. And they won't know how much nicer their own lives could have been just enjoying each day as it comes rather than tearing through each one. But I do. And that makes me better than any of them silly sods." He stood up. "I'll get you a fresh cup of tea." He jiggled the empty cup.

Natalie reached out to stop him leaving. "What are we going to do?"

Colin sat back down. "Your master and I and my sister have talked. She talks a lot of sense my sister. It's just a shame for most of her life people have been inclined to flee from her rather than listen to her. But that's by the by. We're going to head for Wales. Not Swansea either like the barman kept suggesting."

"You spoke in front of the barman. Was that wise?"

"Don't worry. My sister will have a word with him before we leave. He won't dare tell anyone what he knows after that. She doesn't live very far from here remember."

"But will she be alright when we're gone?"

"She won't come with us if that's what you mean. She won't leave her dog. Besides there's nothing to tie her to us. Only this place. And as I've already explained they won't be saying anything to anyone."

Natalie nodded reassured. "So how do we get to Wales?"

"Not by my coach unfortunately. They'll be looking for that. A London coach out in the sticks heading west will stick out like a sore thumb. Clare knows someone who'll buy it off me. That's where we're going tonight. I'll be sorry to see my girls go but your master's lost a lot more. Then we'll buy a couple of dobbins to get us to Wales. We'll take it from there."

"I'll try my best but I don't think I'll be able to keep up with you two on horses," said Natalie resolved to it.

Colin shook his head. "Why has such a beautiful thing been taught to think like that?"

Natalie went to say something but he held up his hand firmly. "After I've taught your master how to ride you can pick which one you want to ride pillion with. Stop being so servile! You're much more than that!"

He got up to indicate that was all he was willing to say or have said. "I'll get you another cup of tea."

# CHAPTER 16

## One man's meat is another man's poison

Hammer and Chisel strolled up the garden path to the back door.

"I love that smell of the earth when it's just gone dark," said Chisel breathing in deeply to enjoy it more.

"Hello," said Hammer sounding agreeably intrigued. "We have a message."

A magpie was pacing back and forth outside the back door. It fluttered its wings impatiently at the sight of them.

"Someone's not in a good mood," said Chisel not really caring.

"I'll take it. I'm quicker than you anyway," said Hammer reaching into his apron to pull out a small notepad and pencil. He clicked his fingers three times.

The magpie regarded him with a beady black eye doing nothing else.

"Why haven't you started?" asked Hammer staring back at the bloody thing.

"Because three clicks was last month. This is a four click month," said Chisel.

"No it isn't. July is a three click month."

"Well why hasn't it started then?" asked Chisel folding his arms.

"It didn't hear that's all."

"Didn't hear! That thing can hear better than you. See better than you. I bet it could even dance better than you!" Chisel was impatient. He clicked his fingers four times.

The magpie hopped across to him pecking at his shoe. It appeared to be random but presently Chisel began whispering. "It's from Sneaky Simon. Sighting made. Target followed. He has a location. A small cottage near -" Chisel had to wait for the magpie to tap out a long word, "Twickenham! The address is -" Hammer wrote the address down. "He'll wait for further instructions there."

The magpie stopped pecking at his shoe to flutter up to his shoulder. It began tapping at his neck.

"He wants paying," said Hammer.

Chisel reached into his apron taking out a shiny sixpence holding it out in his palm in front of the magpie. The bird swallowed it before flying off into the night. "What do they do with real money?" he asked watching it go.

"Birds that clever probably have it invested on the stock market," replied Hammer looking down at his notebook. "He'll want to know about this. They must have had enough nookie by now surely?"

"Only one way to find out," said Chisel opening the back door. "Cor! Can you smell that? Sex sweat or what!"

"Alright. Alright. Let's just see what he wants doing," said Hammer following him in.


The next morning Nightnurse, Hammer and Chisel left to spend most of the day riding to Twickenham.

"We'll tie the horses here and creep the last bit on foot," said Nightnurse when they were almost there.

They had entered the far end of the lane that had frightened Sam with its creeping darkness.

Chisel noticed even in the dim light of the high-banked lane that Nightnurse didn't dismount a horse like most men but kind of oozed off. He would have said like butter running down a thick crumpet but this was more. Something smooth attractive to watch but also threatening. A whisky cream with nutmeg drizzling down the side of a large chocolate cake? That was closer. What about a big spoon of sherry trifle dribbling down a woman's thigh...

"What are you doing you gormless Brummie git?" hissed Hammer in his ear.

Chisel's eyes widened. "Shit! I didn't even know I was doing it!"

"Well stop staring at him before he sees you!" warned Hammer.

Chisel dismounted his horse thinking in comparison he probably resembled a sack of coal falling off the back of a wagon.

Hammer and Chisel tied their horses to an old stump giving them a long rein so they would be able to nibble on anything tasty in the hedgerow. Nightnurse tied up his horse with no such consideration but it didn't seem to mind as it stood there motionless and aloof.

Nightnurse crouched over silently creeping up the lane. Hammer and Chisel copying his posture followed him. They had barely gone twenty feet when there was a loud crack. They all instantly stopped. Hammer and Chisel had cowered down but Nightnurse had done the opposite. He stood up turning to face them.

"That fallen branch now lying in two pieces under your right foot – you didn't see it?"

Chisel felt a cold chill enter the lane. If it had been almost anyone else he would have replied, "I did but I thought I'd step on it anyway." But this was Nightnurse. He could lower the ambient  temperature around him it seemed. "Would you prefer it if we stayed here?"

Nightnurse nodded grandly.

They watched as the silent shadows welcomed him in as one of their own.

"I never thought I was one to scare easily," said Chisel when he thought Nightnurse must be out of earshot.

"Lucky he finds you amusing," said Hammer taking out a sandwich wrapped in a little bit of white cloth from one of the pockets in his apron.

"Bostin' idea! I think that's what's wrong with me. I'm hungry," said Chisel taking out a sandwich from his apron. "What have you got?"

"Cheese and onion," replied Hamer before taking a big bite.

"Swap you a black pudding and carrot for one of your cheese and onion."

Hammer hurried up his chewing so he could reply, "piss off!"

"Good for you! Alright - except the carrot - but I like the taste."

Hammer swallowed hard eager to say something. "Let me get this straight. You're telling me the good bit on your sandwich is the black pudding and the questionable bit is the carrot? Is that right?"

Chisel nodded as he wasn't going to hurry his chewing for anyone. Well anyone apart from Nightnurse maybe.

"Only a particularly thick Brummie git could come to that conclusion!"

Chisel was having known of that. He swallowed hard. "How many carrot crunchers do you know can make a gun? Or a cannon? Or a length of chain long enough and strong enough to hold a ship with each link exactly the same as the one next to it?"

Hammer proffered his sandwich out. Chisel went to take it. "I'm not swapping it you berk! I'm making a point! What about windmills? Or carts? Or big barns? Carrot crunchers seem to make them alright!"

"Pah! That's wood! It takes a lot less skill to fashion wood than metal."

"You're joking! Some of them beams must weigh over five tons. You don't move them around like a little bit of tubing on your workbench!"

Chisel was about to take another bite of his sandwich but stopped himself. "You're right. I've never really considered the weight before. I've always laughed when some chippie says sixteenth of an inch is precision engineering. But you've done that on a couple of beams each weighing five tons that's some going!"

"And at height remember. Out in the elements," added Hammer pleased he'd made Chisel see his point of view for once.

"Yes there's somehat very special about the people of these islands. Carrot crunchers, yams-yams, geordies, jocks, sheep-shaggers and the rest. I think it's our climate you know..."

"What was that?" interjected Hammer suddenly. He hadn't heard anything but he didn't want to hear another rendition of Chisel's theory on a variable climate breeding an adaptable people. Each time it seemed to get longer as Chisel added to it like an old codger collecting worthless coins.

Chisel quickly pushed in the last of his sandwich. Even with the potential for danger it seemed the most important thing to do.

Hammer made out as though he was intently listening. When he thought he'd done it for long enough he said, "Nothing. Just the wind."

Chisel turned his head from side to side to satisfy himself that Hammer was right then took out another sandwich.

"What does it actually taste like - black pudding?" asked Hammer watching him. If he didn't point him in another direction there was a risk he would remember where they'd been.

"You mean you've never tried it?" exclaimed Chisel.

It had worked.

"Well there are lots of things you don't have to try to know they're probably not good for you," said Hammer. He was wondering if he fancied another sandwich.

"Yeah but that's throwing yourself off the church roof to see if you like flying. Or seeing if you can save time by shaving with a sword. But food's different. You've got to try different foods. When I was a kid and saw an animal for the first time I didn't think - ooh what lovely feathers or I wonder how fast that can run or is it dangerous? I used to wonder what it tasted like." He grimaced, "not always a good idea when you lived near a duck pond."

"Nothing wrong with duck. Tastes lovely!" said Hammer surprised.

"Not duck. I couldn't catch them bleeders! Frogs, toads and newts. I could catch them. But some of 'um could have you shitting for weeks!"

Hammer laughed.

"It's not funny," said Chisel. "But you live and learn! I tell you what. You try one of my black pudding and carrot sandwiches and I'll wash your apron next time I wash mine!"

Hammer made a face as though it was an offer he couldn't refuse but then went, "nah!"

"Very funny!" chided Chisel. "Do you know who you looked like then?"

Hammer shook his head.

"Bad Ben!"

"Bad Ben? Who the bloody hell's Bad Ben?" Hammer decided he would like another sandwich.

"You know Bad Ben! The twat from Dorridge."

"Oh him?"

"Yes," said Chisel nodding his head as though it was the most obvious thing in the world.

"I don't look anything like that twat," said Hammer. "Little short git for a start."

"You did when you pulled that face!"

Hammer stopped unfolding his sandwich. "How can I look like someone who has an upside down nose?"

Chisel spluttered on his mouthful.

"Steady tiger – mind your fingers," said Hammer not in the least concerned.

Chisel recovered. "How can anyone have an upside down nose?"

Hammer looked at him oddly. "Are you telling me that when you used to watch him taking snuff and when he sneezed it went straight up making his hair move – you didn't think something was amiss?"

"No," said Chisel, "you meet all sorts on a job."

Hammer was visibly irritated. "When it was dusty he could wipe his eyes and blow his nose at the same time? You never noticed that?"

Chisel pondered for a few seconds, "no."

"You never heard how he fell through a shopfront window and sliced his nose clean off?"

"I thought that was Flat Face Fred," said Chisel.

"No it was Bad Ben!" exclaimed Hammer.

"But it doesn't make sense," said Chisel calmly.

" *What* doesn't make sense?" asked Hammer.

"How could he have an upside down nose if it'ud bin cut off?"

"Because my little toad chewing font..."

Chisel immediately interrupted. "Did you say funt?" Hammer nodded. "That's alright then. Carry on."

"...of facts! He found it in the dirt and got one of the shop assistants to sew it back on for him. But they all hated him so they sewed it back on upside down!"

"So that's why his sneezes went up!" enthused Chisel.

"By jove the thick Brummie git's got it!"

Chisel tucked into his sandwich very happy to have something cleared up. A hard working bumble bee landed for a rest on a leaf near him. "Hello little lady. You're out late this evening," he mumbled at it.

"Are you going to eat that?" asked Hammer.

"Yeah very funny! But even a committed carnivore like me can see it's better to eat the honey and leave the bee." Something suddenly occurred to Chisel. Rather excitedly he asked, "do you think that's why they're called bees? In the old days when they were finding things out someone would go to eat one of these and someone else would say, "It's them that make that sticky stuff that tastes bostin' so let it BEE!""

"Possibly," said Hammer flatly. "Though I do struggle with the concept that the word "bostin'" has been involved in any tiny let alone great advances in our understanding of the human condition."

"Hey?" asked Chisel looking up from the bee.

"Nothing," said Hammer looking up the dark lane. "Do you think he's been gone a long time?"

"Dunno'. How long does it take to dispatch a coachman and apprehend a bookkeeper? It's hardly knee trembling stuff is it?"

"Put it like that then no. But so far they have proved to be no ordinary coachman or bookkeeper."

There was an unexpected noise in the lane that was close enough to make both of them jump up immediately drawing out their swords.

"It's a badger!" exclaimed Chisel.

"What do they taste like?" asked Hammer replacing his sword.

Chisel was more wary holding out his sword in the badger's direction.

"What are you doing Chisel? It's a badger!"

"Know much about badgers do you? Well do you?"

"I know they come out at night and their favourite food is hedgehog. And being near a boring Brummie git makes them stand perfectly still like that." said Hammer pointing at it.

"So you don't know their front paws can crush a man's chest like an acorn? That they can bite off a man's hand even if he's wearing armour? And their skull? Their skull is so thick that wagon's have been upended riding over one and the badger's just trotted off as if nothing happened?"

Hammer now found their unexpected visitor a lot more alarming than he had done. "So just tell me - would you recommend a 3/8 or a 5/8 chisel or not mess about at all and stick an arrow in the stripey git?"

"You stick an arrow in its middle and I'll clear up the mess with this." Chisel brandished his sword.

The badger which had been standing motionless watching them appeared to understand English. It abruptly disappeared into the night once more.

"Just hope he hasn't gone to get his mates," joked Chisel.

"What's taking him?" chided Hammer irritably after replacing his sword. "Shall we take a look?"

"And risk upsetting him? No fear! We stay here just like he wants."

"Unlike you to do as you're told?" suggested Hammer.

"I'm a very good team player actually. It's just I'm a team player that think for himself as well."

"Sounds ideal," said Hammer. "But like every superhero you do have one weakness."

"No I don't!" said Chisel.

"Yes you do," replied Hammer. "Black pudding! All an enemy would have to do is cut off your supply of black pudding and within hours you'd be powerless."

"It's not the only thing I eat stupid!"

"That's true - you'll always eat it with something else! Bacon, eggs, sausage, carrot or swede..."

Hammer stopped at another unexpected noise. Something much bigger than a badger was barging towards them down the dark lane. Nightnurse's horse which was normally so still and aloof turned to face the direction of the noise snorting nervously. Hammer nodded for Chisel to move to the other side of the lane into the bushes before he slipped away to his side. After a few seconds they both jumped out as the perpetrator of the noise arrived within striking distance.

"Will you pair of amateurs stop pratting about!" snapped Nightnurse.

Hammer feeling a little foolish replaced his sword. Chisel replaced his two biggest chisels in his apron (he'd expected it to get animal and nasty) and resented being called an "amateur".

Nightnurse was clutching at his midriff with his left arm as though he had been injured there.

"Are you alright?" asked Hammer.

"Is that your blood?" asked Chisel. Even in the dark lane they could now see he was covered in a dark matte film as though he'd fell in a river of it. And the smell! A sickly heavy iron smell of suffering and death.

"Really?" spat Nightnurse contemptuously. "There's been enough blood spilt tonight to last me the month. But if you really think any of it was mine then you're even dumber than you look!"

Chisel didn't like that. Without thinking he reached inside his apron for the first thing he could lay his hands on. Fortunately for him he pulled out a wooden mallet.

"Couldn't even get that right could you?" said Nightnurse. "If that had been anything dangerous you'd be dead now."

Hammer had been amazed to see Chisel do something so stupid. Then amazed even further to see an apparently injured man act so quickly. Nightnurse straightened unsheathing his sword swinging it perfectly to within an inch of Chisel's Adam's apple waiting to see what he did next.

"You've obviously never banged your thumb with one!" said Chisel carefully.

The sword remained perfectly still poised in front of Chisel's throat. Then it was gone.

"You do make me laugh," said Nightnurse.

He moved towards his horse which obviously imbued discomfort because he reluctantly clutched at his midriff again.

Hammer silently indicated for Chisel to put away his stupid mallet to help Nightnurse onto his horse.

Fortunately this wasn't one of the occasions when Chisel could be slow on the uptake.

"Do you want a hand?" he said going over.

Nightnurse said nothing but put a hand on his shoulder to indicate he would accept that. Chisel's strength allowing him to practically throw Nightnurse into his saddle which was unorthodox but effective.

"So what went wrong?" asked Chisel.

Nightnurse pulled something he had kept hidden under his coat. He handed it to Chisel who held it up for Hammer to see.

"What is it?" asked Hammer.

"Almost certainly one of Sneaky Simon's thighbones," said Nightnurse.

Chisel threw it away with a disgusted groan.

Hammer noticed that an uncharacteristic weariness seemed to suddenly weigh heavy on Nightnurse. The air in the lane suddenly heavy and oppressive irritated with the petty tribulations of men. He just wanted to leave.

"Sorry. What -" began Chisel.

"Chisel!" snapped Hammer "Just get on your bloody horse!"

# CHAPTER 17

## Snips and snails, and puppy dog tails

Natalie didn't like the jostle and bumpiness inside the coach. To her it seemed preferable to be up top with Colin where you could see what was going on. She'd been told to enjoy it. It would be her last chance to ride inside the coach because they were on their way to sell it. But being told to enjoy something just because you should didn't seem sensible at all. Just like something else didn't seem sensible now troubling her more than the coach ride.

Natalie liked remembering things and placing them precisely so she could find them again whenever she needed. It pleased her and she was very grateful for it because it helped her master. She was happy to help him because he had kept his word to her mother and given her a home and an occupation. She respected him. He was precise and methodical and wanted to do things properly. He seemed wise and understood how things worked in a way she did not. He looked after her so she tried to look after him as well as she could. An order to everything and everything in its place.

The only thing that sometimes concerned her were what she called her "womanly feelings." These were things that jarred out of place. Something like seeing a stray cat and wanting to take it in. But it would make a mess bringing dead things into the kitchen and annoy the neighbours pooing in their gardens. The only reason it could have occurred to her to want to look after it was because of her "womanly feelings." Then there were her more worrying "womanly feelings" about what men and women could do with each other. She didn't know much about it but it sounded messy. She knew that's where babies came from and if she wanted a baby that's what she'd have to do. But she didn't want a baby. On the rare occasion that she thought about men in "womanly feelings" ways she could instantly dismiss it knowing she didn't want a baby so had no need to think about it further. To the best of her knowledge, which was so accurate in its recording it must be so, she didn't think she had ever seen a man's "baby thingy" until today.

Until today....

Today she'd seen three of them in quick succession! She looked at her master asleep on the seat beside her. He didn't look as much in control or precise as he had done now she'd seen his "baby thingy". And she'd seen the barman's "baby thingy" and Colin's "baby thingy"! Every time she closed her eyes she saw Colin's "baby thingy" in all its wonderful detail. In desperation she began reciting her times tables under her breath. It was her ultimate defence. All her previous unwanted "womanly feelings" had been beaten in the same way.

Up top Colin resisted the tiredness that gnawed at him like blown sand. Knowing this would be the last journey he'd make with his girls almost making him give in to it to get it over with. But they didn't know the way. He wondered if they'd still pull if they knew it was to their parting? He wasn't arrogant enough to believe they wouldn't. His sister had told him this "Thomas" would pay a fair price and was a fellow animal lover. He'd been quite lucky to get it sorted so quickly. They could soon be on their way to Wales not attracting any attention. He took out the map his sister had drawn him. Her broad brutal strokes amusing him fondly. Not much further now.

They arrived at a modest but prosperous house about an hour later.

Thomas's wife was a lovely woman. She was so excited to see them. Her husband had been after such a coach and horses for a long time! She was sure the price Colin wanted was no problem. After seeing to his horses – soon the be ours! – she said the two of them should join her for dinner to await her husband's return from work. Their maid could join her servants in the kitchen for something to eat. She only had a few nothing grand but they would look after her. Even if they had an alternative it was a very agreeable proposition so they both accepted her kind offer.

Sam and Colin were sat at the dining table with Thomas's wife just finishing their first course when all of a sudden the dining room door burst open. In lunged a big shouldered man with a quick face half covered in brick dust.

"What the bloody hell's going on here woman? Where's me dinner? Are these bastards eating it?" He sat down at the head of the table.

Far from being shocked or appalled his wife laughed, "Oh Tommy what are you like? These gentlemen are here to sell their coach and horses. The Capital type you've always wanted."

"You're kidding! The one on the drive! It's a beauty isn't it? I was just looking at it!" said Thomas very excited.

"At a good price Tommy for a quick sale!"

Thomas clapped his hands making a little cloud of brick dust. "Wonderful! It's a deal! Well tuck in! Then we can all get shit-faced later to celebrate!"

Thomas got up.

"Tommy where are you going?" asked his wife.

"I'm going to wash my hands and get a bigger bowl for my soup! This is a celebration night!"

His wife clapped her hands with joy looking at Sam and Colin. "Oh you've made him so happy!"

Sam coughed nervously. "I don't mean to be rude madam but we'd prefer to settle our transaction and be on our way. Your hospitality does you proud but we are pressed for time."

Thomas's wife looked at him sharply. "It's not stolen is it?"

"Of course not! It took me three years of hard saving to buy it!" said Colin clearly telling the truth.

"Yes I'm sorry gentlemen for even suggesting such a thing." She looked distressed her recent joy evaporating.

It wasn't something Sam and Colin wanted to see but didn't really know how to end.

"I've not seen him so happy in months! I'll give you another two guineas if you celebrate with him. It would mean such a lot to him."

"When would we get the money?" asked Colin more callously than he intended, "sorry. I didn't mean to be so rude."

"I can see you're tired. Think nothing of it. Surely a good meal and a few drinks doesn't seem so bad?"

"How can we refuse such a charming lady? Of course we'll stay," said Sam.

"Excellent! As soon as Tommy tells me he's had a good night you shall have your money and be on your way. Another bread roll?"

Thomas reappeared carrying a big bowl of soup with clean hands. "Is that your maid in the kitchen? She's a bit of alright ain't she?"

"Oh Tommy! What are you like?" laughed his wife.

Thomas sat down with his soup. "I'll tell you something for nothing – if either have you have got lads tell them to be plasterers! Three bloody jobs going begging for the sake of a bloody plasterer! Jobs that could have helped pay for my new coach and horses!"

It was the theme for the rest of dinner.

When a maid had finished collecting their empty pudding dishes Thomas turned to his wife. "Right woman. Get THE KEY."

Colin stole a glance at Sam. He assumed he was thinking the same: that it was the key to the safe and their money.

"I will Tommy but remember to go easy. It's a week day and can I speak to you about Mrs Penderel first. She really is insistent about you finishing her extension before next week!"

"Oh! So I'm really going to listen to you babble on when I can have a celebratory drink am I? I don't think so. So remove yourself poste-haste and fetch me THE KEY now!"

"Look Tommy I'm glad you're having a drink to celebrate your new coach and horses but we do need to sort out what I'm going to tell Mrs Penderel first."

"You heard him woman!" said Sam from the other end of the table.

"I like you already! But I'll tell my wife what to do in my own house if you don't mind." He turned back to his wife cupping her hands in his. "Tell Mrs Penderel that me and the lads will be there on Saturday and will stay until the job is done. How's that my dove?"

"But I wanted to go shopping for bed linen on Saturday."

"For Pete's sake! I can do more than one thing at once! Will you get THE KEY woman?"

Appearing to think it rude of her to impede any further on the entertainment of guests she decided to leave it at that and fetch THE KEY. Returning a minute or so later kissing her husband on the cheek before leaving them.

"Finally!" exclaimed Thomas rising out of his chair.

"What we got?" asked Sam.

"What haven't we got? replied Thomas going over to a huge cabinet and unlocking it.

Much to Colin's surprise Sam was very enthusiastic in joining in with Thomas's drinking. He himself was reluctant at first but as Thomas regaled them with stories of "all the punters he'd screwed" Colin found himself being drawn in. The more they drank the funnier the stories seemed.

Later on when Colin had had so much to drink he was having trouble focussing properly Thomas climbed onto the table. "Right! I'm going to show you my impressions!"

He dropped his trousers. "Right! The rules are simple. I'm going to do some impressions and you soft puddings have to guess what it is. Right?"

Thomas reached down contorting his genitals into a shape Colin could not make out.

"I know!" said Colin, "It's like a cock only smaller!"

"Wrong! And that's three points deducted for offensive behaviour."

"Offensive behaviour?" asked Sam drunkenly. "How much more offensive behaviour can it be than getting your tackle out standing on a dining table?"

"That's two points deducted for you for having no imagination."

"Hold on hold on – How come he gets two points deducted and I got three?" asked Colin pointing his finger a lot.

"Look are either of you going to tell me what it is or is there going to be a time penalty coming as well?"

Sam and Colin shook their heads. "You'll have to tell us."

"That is Sam the Snail!" Thomas informed them. "That's ten points to me."

"This sounds rigged," said Colin unhappily taking a large swig of whatever it was he was drinking.

Thomas pulled his large scrotum completely over his penis. "Come on gentlemen this is an easy one."

Colin tried very hard to focus to see something he might recognise.

"I've got it!" exclaimed Sam. "It's a handbag!"

"Ooh so close," said Thomas letting his scrotum go. "But it's another ten points for me for not correctly guessing it was a toolsack."

Colin turned to Sam across the table. "Ask him if he's had a good night so we can go."

"Now gentlemen the bonus round worth twenty points.."

"I will after this. Come on it's worth twenty points," replied Sam putting down his drink.

Thomas stuck his tongue out concentrating very hard to get his impression right. "Right gentlemen what is that?"

"A smoking pipe?" suggested Sam.

"Ooh so close again gentlemen," said Thomas bringing his hands away. "It was in fact a heavy field gun! That makes the twenty bonus points mine to give a total of forty! You losers!"

"Have you had a good night?" asked Colin.

Thomas was climbing off the table. "Been brilliant! Got a new set of wheels and forty points in the bank."

"Good! Would you tell your wife?"

"I will if you tell your maid to stop spying on us through the window."

"What?" said Sam looking around to the window. Natalie was clearly standing outside looking in. "Oh that's nothing. She often goes for a walk in the evening."

"Should have drawn the curtains if you were going to do that," said Colin not happy.

"In my own bloody house!" said Thomas incredulous at such a suggestion.

"Colin – where is bed tonight?" asked Sam.

"A local tavern with rooms," replied Colin.

Thomas came down to their end of the table. "You'd best get a move on. Your best bet's the Chestnuts but they'll be closing soon. Come on I'll get the wife to pay you and have one of the maids show you the way."

"If it's no bother," said Sam getting up groggily.

Colin got up clumsily too. "Thank you. It's been an unforgettable evening. You will look after my coach and girls?"

"Of course. Come back in a few months when I've put some new wheels on it!" Thomas walked his way along the table using it for support. Opening the dining room door he shouted into the rest of the house. "Wife! Wife! I've had a really good night! Let's pay these gentlemen and let them be on their way! Quicker that creepy maid of theirs is off the property the better! Come on woman!"

Two hours later the three of them were ensconced in the Chestnuts. Two of them snoring in two beds in one room. The third in another room lying awake on a bed desperately repeating her times tables.

# CHAPTER 18

## Good manners cost nothing

Lord Ecin was looking out of his study window very happy to see a bear wandering across his lawn. His wonderful butler Resourceful knocked on the open door and entered.

"What's my bear doing now?" asked Lord Ecin still looking out of the window.

"He's looking for nuts and berries. Says he's got to fatten up for the winter!" Resourceful gave a little chuckle. "He does play his part very well but he won't find any yet. The dogs are a little wary of him still but they'll come round."

"My own bear! I always wanted my own bear. And there he is!" Lord Ecin reluctantly dragged himself away from the window. "How are the others getting on?"

"Very good my Lordship. It's only been a week or so so it's early days. According to Cook Alice and her sister are a joy to have in the kitchen both not afraid of hard work. The two lads Carrot and Swede likewise."

"And the lad with your whistle?" asked Lord Ecin.

Resourceful frowned a little. "I'll have to work a bit harder with him but I'm sure he will come good. I think there's a great talent there for something my Lordship. It'll begin when I get a monkey on his shoulder."

Lord Ecin looked at him earnestly. "And you Resourceful. How are you?"

"Oh I'm alright my Lordship. Cook is very good with the goose fat which helps a lot. But I think it's safe to say my riding days are well and truly over."

Lord Ecin put a friendly hand on Resourceful's shoulder.

"There's really no need to be so familiar my Lordship," said Resourceful taken aback.

"Yes there is," said Lord Ecin not moving his hand. "I don't think I will ever be able to repay you for what you did. I do believe you saved my life."

"Oh no my Lordship. I don't believe things were that bad," said Resourceful very touched. "You've paid for my operation. I don't see what more you could do for me."

Lord Ecin took his hand away not wanting to make Resourceful feel uncomfortable. "Make a few more changes that's what I can do for you!"

"My Lordship?" asked Resourceful bending forward.

"Sit down Resourceful," said Lord Ecin pointing at one of the chairs.

"But your Lordship I'm a servant it would be inappropriate," said Resourceful not moving.

"Sit down in that one Resourceful. It has the softest cushions. It's one of the changes I'm going to make. From now on I'm going to recognise you as my counsel as well as my butler. I need you comfortable so you can think clearly."

Resourceful didn't want to disobey but didn't want to rip through years' of correct behaviour either. "My Lordship a servant will serve you best remaining standing ready for action."

"Not with what you've been through. Not with what I'm going to ask you to do. Now sit. Don't make me order you." It was the most authoritative manner Lord Ecin could muster.

"Very good my Lordship," said Resourceful sitting down in the chair like it was a throne that wasn't his.

"Good," said Lord Ecin showing he was pleased and there was nothing to be afraid of. "I'm right in thinking we've heard nothing from Colonel Peru or his household since our visit?"

"Nothing at all. May I suggest it would be Lord Dratsab who could tell you more on that score my Lordship."

Lord Ecin gave an uncharacteristic snort. "Don't talk to me about Lord Dratsab! He's another change I'm going to make. I don't ever want to see the bounder again! He's not actually a friend but a louse! A louse I'm going to keep off my rug!"

Resourceful's surprise grew even more to hear Lord Ecin refer to Lord Dratsab in such a way. Lord Dratsab had been a terrible influence on Lord Ecin ever since the day they had met. The money went one way and the favours went one way. The only thing that ever came back the other way was trouble.

"Resourceful I want you to tell me what you know about Lord Dratsab. All the things I'm going to remember when that louse tries to crawl back onto my rug!"

"Would that really be wise my Lordship? It's not like mopping up a spilt drink – it's more like burning down a house."

"Precisely!" said Lord Ecin eagerly sitting down in the chair opposite. "There must be loads of stories. I want them all as nails in his coffin!"

Resourceful felt in a quandary. He was programmed to obey. He would do anything for Lord Ecin. He thought Lord Ecin was right. But he was a young man who'd been humiliated. He was sore at the moment. That would pass. What if he then regretted the dirt under his fingernails he couldn't wash out? As ever Resourceful knew what to do – he would give Lord Ecin a few tacks. But no nails that would permanently keep a coffin lid down.

"Resourceful I can see you're unsure what to do. But I want to know. There's not a malicious bone in your body. You've always had my best interest at heart. I'm giving you permission to proceed." Lord Ecin raised a finger. "But no innuendo or rumours. Only what you know to be the truth."

Resourceful admired that immensely. Most people in the circumstances would have not cared if the stories were true or not. How could he now refuse?

"You are the very best of employers my Lordship. But there are many who believe that because you employ a person that it gives you ownership of their mind and tongue too – which of course it does not. Such arrogance undoes an employer from within."

"Sorry Resourceful. I'm a bit confused. Is this part of a story about Lord Dratsab?"

Resourceful smiled patiently. "I'm trying to explain where most of them come from."

Lord Ecin leant forward in his chair paying attention.

Resourceful continued, "You look after your servants well so they would not think or talk of anything that might be inappropriate – should it even occur in the first place. But there are lots of employers who deserve no such loyalty and have servants who talk freely to anyone who will listen."

"That's very decent of you to say. That means a lot to me," said Lord Ecin smiling.

"So it should my Lordship it's the truth."

Resourceful had found something appropriate to begin with. "When Lord Dratsab arrives for an evening engagement some of his servants will have worked very hard in the previous few hours to make him presentable from the last one. He doesn't make it easy for them."

"How could one make it hard?" asked Lord Ecin frowning.

"In the afternoon a servant will be dispatched to his study to rouse him. Knocking the door several times but receiving no answer he will push the door open to be greeted with a smell so dire he will have to immediately cover his nose and mouth to stop himself gagging. Lord Dratsab will invariably be in his favourite wing-backed chair with his legs spread-eagle dangling over the arms. Too close to the fire that he has made far too big he will be red-faced and sweaty. The servant will politely make his presence known. If Lord Dratsab didn't have too much to drink he'll get the response, "What do you want? Can't you see I'm roasting my chestnuts!" Something he finds highly amusing. But most of the time he is unconscious. The servant will approach with extreme caution. Lord Dratsab is so close to the fire and can fart so strongly that several servants have lost eyebrows and hair at this stage."

Lord Ecin held up his hand. "How can servants be losing eyebrows and hair?"

"Apparently Lord Dratsab's legs will suddenly stiffen into the shape of a V - sometimes with such force his shoes fly off, then there will be a fart so strong the flames will momentarily blow back into the hearth.

Then his fart will catch light as it must to come shooting back out like a great dragon tongue lashing out at everything within range. The servant is then expected to throw himself in front of it to protect Lord Dratsab."

Lord Ecin shook his head in astonishment. "Why would any man get so drunk he wants to be a crumpet?"

"He's actually drying his trousers my Lordship. He can't be bothered to relieve himself in the appropriate place so does so in his trousers. He further can't be bothered to change them so dries them off in front of the fire."

"Whilst still wearing them?" Lord Ecin clearly found it disgusting.

"It can be worse. If he has let loose a fart of shoe flying proportions even he can't sleep through he will demand, "Who did that?" If the servant tells him the truth then the servant is beaten on the spot with the toasting fork and bawled out. If the servant suggests, "A sudden downdraught sir," then he is not beaten but has the horrible job of removing Lord Dratsab's trousers and cleaning him up. It's not much of a choice. Most prefer a beating with the toasting fork rather than cleaning him up so will resort to calling him a "windbag," if they have to. But I don't believe that part. I think they are trying to make out they are braver than they are."

Lord Ecin thought for a bit leaning back in his chair. "It's pretty disgusting. Definitely unfair on the servants. But not enough for someone to fall out with him over."

"I have another that may be of interest to you," suggested Resourceful.

Lord Ecin leant forward, "Well go on Resourceful. I'm listening."

"Do you know of a cousin of Lord Dratsab's known as Typhoon Tim?"

Lord Ecin grew excited. "I do I do! They were in the army together. A real fighting man apparently. Once he was cornered unharmed surrounded by four men. He tore the arm off the first man and beat them all to death with it! Imagine that? Being beaten to death with your own arm?"

"That's the version Lord Dratsab regales. What he omits to mention is that they were his own men coming out of the mess tent," said Resourceful sadly.

Lord Ecin swallowed hard. "That puts a different light on things - but that's hardly Lord Dratsab's fault?"

"No not directly. But it points to a lack of discipline which is ultimately the commanding officer's responsibility. Anyway it's an aside. I wanted to tell you this. One day Lord Dratsab and Typhoon Tim were hiding in a tree trying to evade capture."

"So he has seen some real action then?" asked Lord Ecin not believing it before.

"Of course not! They were hiding from Colonel Beetroot and his men."

"That's the one they call Colonel Beetroot because he's always angry. The one with a very attractive wife."

"The very same," replied Resourceful. "Lord Dratsab and Typhoon Tim had gone to Colonel Beetroot's Hall in his absence for a "spit roast" with his wife. Colonel Beetroot had unexpectedly come home early. Though why he should be so cross forcing them to flee for their lives over a "spit roast" alludes me. It is only good manners to feed your guests surely?"

Lord Ecin looked at Resourceful curiously. Clearly his butler had never been to Amsterdam. Did he divulge what he knew? Did Resourceful need to know that two men and a woman having a spit roast wasn't the three of them tucking into a nice bit of beef?

"Is something wrong my Lordship?" asked Resourceful presently.

"No carry on," said Lord Ecin realising he'd had to concentrate to say it properly.

"Hiding in the tree Typhoon Tim had fallen asleep instantly. Lord Dratsab was worried that he might start to snore and give their location away. He wasn't snoring but it was a constant worry for him. When it became clear they would have to wait until nightfall to climb down and escape a pressing need overtook Lord Dratsab. The same pressing need that can overtake any man in a pressing situation."

Lord Ecin nodded knowingly. "Something too big to look like a bird had done it."

"Exactly my Lordship. He knew he couldn't let it fall out of the tree but he didn't want it next to him either. He looked over at Typhoon Tim's large gaping mouth. A mouth still not snoring but for how long? Looking down at the thing he had produced he was struck at how much it resembled a cigar. He had an idea. He was lucky it was such a warm day. Gently blowing on it as well it was soon firm enough to handle. Picking it up he sidled along the branch towards Typhoon Tim."

"The bastard," remarked Lord Ecin, "he put it in one of his pockets didn't he? A joke cigar you can't light!"

"My Lordship?" asked Resourceful a little bemused. "He wanted to be rid of it and stop the possibility of Typhoon Tim snoring. He put it in his mouth!"

Lord Ecin convulsed forward retching.

Resourceful jumped up as quickly as his recent injury would allow. "I'll get you a glass of water as quickly as I can."

Lord Ecin clutching at his midriff with one arm beckoned for him to sit down with the other. Although his mouth was wide open he couldn't speak.

Resourceful sat back down when he could see Lord Ecin was no longer in danger. "I'm sorry to have produced such an effect in you. I heard that straight from one of Colonel Beetroot's men. He had found them and saw it all."

Lord Ecin found his voice, it was quiet but he had found it. "Why didn't he raise the alarm?"

"It goes back to what we were talking about earlier. He'd seen what happened when people informed the Colonel what his wife got up to when he was away. Talk about shooting the messenger. It was safer for him to not find them. That was best done knowing right where they were and not letting on."

"But surely Typhoon Tim noticed? Surely it woke him up having that – thing! put in his mouth?" asked Lord Ecin.

"You would think so. But the man had seen Lord Dratsab precariously perching himself above an open a pocket on Typhoon Tim's coat trying to make a deposit several times. Each time not able to get it right. It was only failing to do that he had resorted to doing it on the branch. None of this had woken Typhoon Tim. He must have been out cold. Although the man wasn't there to see it he believes Lord Dratsab must have bashed Typhoon Tim on the head when he wasn't looking. Or -"

"Or what Resourceful?" asked Lord Ecin jumping on his reluctance.

"As well as being his cousin Lord Dratsab was his commanding officer. He might have known what was expected of him and feigned his unconsciousness. Of course we'll never know for sure."

Lord Ecin stood up. "Well thank you Resourceful. It's been most useful. How could any man be trusted who would put his bum cigar in his cousin's sleeping mouth? That will be all."

"Very good my Lordship," said Resourceful slowly but gratefully getting out of the chair.

Lord Ecin went to the window to remind himself of what was good in the world. Within a few minutes of watching a man in a bearskin search in vain for nuts and berries on his lawn he felt at peace again.

# CHAPTER 19

## Tails you win heads you lose

Nightnurse would let Hammer and Chisel report to Crow. He headed home hating the smell of dried blood upon him every inch of the way. What a beast it had been! All the more dangerous for being disturbed eating. How it had come at him! Nature's fang against man's wit and steel. That first lunge sending him flying to the ground like he'd been hit by a cannonball. It would have had a chunk of him in its mouth if not for his leather waistcoat. Then the pounce up close snarling gnawing for his throat. Then he'd got his blade in for the first time. Felt the thing shudder but not give in. That's when he knew he was in for a proper fight. At an elemental level it was just a question of who was the bigger beast and wanted it more. And what was more? To live of course! To not die there. To not die losing a fight.

But he hated the mess. The blood the gore. It was clumsy and vulgar. It lacked finesse and precision. The revulsion at letting the beast do his work for him was far greater than any regret he felt for the life he'd taken. He had thought in the past of wearing a mask or a specific hat when he was working. Something he could take off so he wasn't the person who did those things the rest of the time. But he knew that would be a lie. It was him and he did what he did. He wondered if he would sleep when the time came. Or would he wriggle and writhe as unbecoming sleep mixed with evil memories and cold dark currents dragged him away from civilisation to play with him on a far flung desolate beach? That happened sometimes. It was an occupational hazard.

It was the next day.

"It is not often I find myself in this position but with you I thought I would probably never..."

Crow was sitting at his desk fully robbed and hooded. It was the pretence that he was a man when they both knew different. It needed to be because Hammer and Chisel were still in the room. Nightnurse was sitting in the chair that tipped into the pit. He sat motionless and mute.

"...so what do you to say for yourself?"

Nightnurse remained mute staring at him.

"Now we have to decide whether you are being professional in the circumstances or a little bit foolish do we not?" asked Crow.

Still Nightnurse sat motionless and mute in his chair.

"I understand that even in a machine of lies there are some rattles of truth that cannot be ignored. I do not punish people for bringing them to my attention. Just tell me what happened," said Crow very precisely.

Nightnurse broke his silence, "To me it makes no difference. But there are lots of people who won't take orders from a woman. It doesn't make any sense to me but there you go. What can you do about it?"

"What's that got to do with the price of fish?" asked Chisel.

"You two can go!" ordered Crow.

"Are you sure?" asked Hammer looking warily at Nightnurse's back.

"I said go!" There was no question it was an instruction that must be obeyed.

Hammer and Chisel turned to leave the room.

"Shut the door on your way out!"

They left shutting the door.

Crow took down the hood. "Bolt it! Bolt it now!"

Her features were so finely chiselled she was like a porcelain doll but she had the presence of a panther. Nightnurse jumped up to bolt the door. Then they made love again. Not like the first time when they were almost trying to outdo each other as two apex predators. A trial of stamina and depravity. This was more like a union of like-minded souls that had finally found one another in the dark. They hardly made a sound.

When they had finished they shared a clay pipe passing it back and forth as they spoke. He had replaced his trousers but Crow was completely naked totally uninhibited in front of him.

"You are so dangerous. Would you have told them?" she asked. It was like a low feline growl purring around his ankles.

"Why do you do it?" asked Nightnurse taking the pipe from her lips.

"What is a woman with ambition to do? Wait for the world to change or change her world?" She took back the pipe playing with the tip briefly before inhaling. Her voice was up from his ankles caressing his inner thighs.

"Why not do what every woman of ambition has done for centuries – marry a powerful man and tell him what to do?"

She laughed. A cold hunter's laugh with pure intent. "Because I am better than that!" She looked at him with her big feline eyes. She was in the best part of his trousers. He could feel her in there.

"So what happens now?" asked Nightnurse surprised at how outwardly calm he seemed. But then why? He had spent a lifetime hiding his emotions and true feelings.

"I pounce upon you and play with your sorry corpse from one side of this room to the other!" She smacked away the pipe from his mouth.

When she had finished with him he found the pipe relit it and they began talking again.

"Is this bookkeeper really that important? What can he actually do?" asked Nightnurse taking a drag then passing her the pipe.

"I did not get to where I am without tying up loose ends," she said exhaling the smoke in his eyes.

"And where are you exactly?" asked Nightnurse waving the smoke away.

"By this time next year I shall be the richest woman in the country. And I will have done it my way! Knocking every empty bucket off the wall!"

"That's a strange way to put it," said Nightnurse taking the pipe.

She jumped up. The exact right amount of fat on her hips needed to make them almost perfect quivering deliciously. "Fancy a competition? If you win we leave the bookkeeper alone. If I win we chop off his head next time he pokes it above the wall?"

"I have no affection for the man but I'm not going to back down from a competition with a girl!" he said playfully. But he saw how she really didn't like that. Living with her would be like living with one of those big cats from Bengal. Exciting but your life would always be in danger. She would never be anyone's pet.

She had lined up four of the pretty china ornaments on a shelf at the opposite end of the room. Then out of the desk she took a bowl of small rounded pebbles. She sat down on the floor with them next to him.

"She how many it takes you to smash the two on the left. I will take the two on the right." She knew she would win because she'd been throwing stones since she was a little girl in Dumfries.

# CHAPTER 20

## There is no shame in falleth but in lieth long

Sam and Colin were walking across a field two abreast in the late afternoon sun. They were on their way to the local millers because they'd been told at the tavern that he had two horses to sell. They were ambling along still under the influence of the night before.

"I must tell you this," said Colin. "I once heard of a woman in Newbury who each Sabbath would urinate the Lord's Prayer in Latin in the dust of her pew!"

"And they kept letting her do it?" asked Sam wondering what his feet might be treading in.

"Would draw quite a crowd apparently. Of course that soon led to competition from the other churches in the area. For a time a man who could shit animal shapes around the edge of the font gave her quite a run for her money. Birds, dogs, cats and the like. But more often than not it was just "the python" yet again. His attraction soon paled."

"I imagine they would pale as they dried out," said Sam mischievously.

Colin laughed, "I walked right into that!"

"Yes, it's what I might walk into that concerns me."

"Oh, I don't think this is a livestock field. It looks more like oats."

"I don't know how you can tell," said Sam brushing at the things coming up to his waist.

"Good for your horse. Gees them up a bit. But not too much or you can't stop them."

"I'm sorry you had to let them go. You were obviously very fond of them."

Colin tutted. "Well it's done now. Shall we have a look at the map?" He stopped walking.

"Oh yes," began Sam knowingly, "the map drawn by a cartographer quite clearly suited to being a publican."

Colin knew what he meant. "It does have quite a rustic charm that's for sure." He imitated the voice of the landlord mockingly, "Just follow the instructions on that map and you'll be there in no time!"

"What a bloody joke!" said Sam staring down at the map he had taken out from his pocket. "How do they cope without street names?"

"They use landmarks. You know that's why a horse race is called a steeplechase? Originally it was a race between church steeples."

"I don't know much about horse racing. In fact over the last few days I've realised there's an awful lot I don't know about anything – Do you think those trees could be those trees over there?"

Colin took the map from him laughing. "He's drawn the tavern – I know it's the tavern because he's drawn a man vomiting outside it. Then some trees. A squiggly line past the trees. Then the windmill. We know it's the windmill not because it has sails on it but because he's drawn the miller standing outside looking like a clown." He handed the map back.

"I was going to ask you about that. Why has he drawn the miller like that?" asked Sam looking at the map sideways.

Colin began walking again so Sam quickly put the map away.

"This is just conjecture you understand. This will be the first miller I've actually met. But apparently there's a lot of whirring cogs and wheels in a mill that wear away the miller's hair in the middle. Then there's all the flour dust that gives him a white face. Then all the wind from the sails gives them big red lips and noses. And they need big shoes to rest the sacks of flour on."

"It makes you wonder what job there is that doesn't have some detrimental effect on the human body. My chair cost a fortune but I was getting such a bad back in the old one." He suddenly stopped walking.

Colin hadn't noticed straightaway. But when he did he stopped and turned around. "What is it Sam?"

He wasn't quite sure why he had to stop. He didn't feel thirsty. He couldn't feel anything actually hurting. But he had to stop. They were under the arms of a large oak in full leaf. He looked up at it. He'd been in one of those a few days ago. Right up in its branches with a strange figure in a cloak who wanted to take over the world. And ever then since his whole world had been turned upside down.

"Are you alright Sam?" asked Colin walking back to him.

Sam was a precise man. A man who believed in the power of figures over the subterfuge of conjecture. Absolutely everything could ultimately be understood if we worked hard enough and applied ourselves properly. There was really no room for things that made no sense at all. So when it began with a slight itchiness in his eyes he thought it dust blown up by the warm wind. But when it continued until his vision became blurred Sam could not understand. Why on earth was he crying? He felt his shoulders slump knowing that his knees were ready to buckle. He decided he wasn't going to let them but it was such an effort.

He was vaguely aware of Colin's arm around his shoulder then him whispering in his ear. "I know we're not supposed to – but I'm amazed it's taken this long. Let it out. It's better than drowning in it."

Above the caring oak seemed to murmur for everyone to be quiet whilst this little fella tried to sort himself out. Sam felt very grateful to them both.

"Sorry," he said eventually.

"There's nothing to apologise for. It's just the drink," said Colin gently.

Sam took out a handkerchief to dry his eyes. "A man shouldn't cry. It's a sign of weakness."

"At the wrong time very definitely," said Colin.

Sam put his handkerchief away. "I haven't thanked you for saving my life."

Colin put a firm hand on his shoulder. "Sam I haven't yet. Come on!"

Sam for something to do in an awkward situation took out the map. He noticed a small pair of lips underneath the clown's feet. They were quite high up and at the bottom of the sloping field he thought he saw a kissing gate! Perhaps this might be their little break for him not giving up!

"Come on Colin I think it's this way!" He strode out through the crop of the field unconcerned as to whether it was barley, wheat or oats. It didn't matter! Vaguely he had a notion that tears must be very heavy because he now felt so much lighter. He didn't understand why. But do you know what? It didn't matter! So he'd lost his expensive chair? It didn't matter! So he'd lost most of his possessions. It didn't matter! He might not see his next birthday. It didn't matter!

What mattered was he was still here today doing what he could! He would do what he could until someone else stopped him. He wouldn't be the one responsible for stopping.

He shouted out as he strode happily through the whatever. "Thank you Sky! Thank you Sun! Thank you Birds! Thank you Wind! Thank you Trees! Thank you - little buzzy flying things! Thank you all! Thank you all for just being there! I love you!"

A startled Colin followed him smiling.

# CHAPTER 21

## Nice to get away for a bit

Lord Dratsab and Lord Tig were in Lord Dratsab's study. It wasn't as salubrious as Lord Ecin's or if you looked closely anything like as clean. They were sat in large wing-backed chairs by the fireplace. The fire wasn't lit as it had been another gloriously warm summer's day.

Lord Tig was looking at his glass of port disdainfully. "Where did you get this Dratty?"

"It's Moroccan. What do you think?" replied Lord Dratsab holding up his glass of Moroccan port to the light.

Lord Tig put his glass down on the small table by his chair. "I think I prefer their dates."

Lord Dratsab put his glass down too. "I'll get some decent stuff out in a bit."

"So what have you been doing with yourself? We've not seen you for a few weeks," said Lord Tig pleasantly.

"Well as a persona non grata is that any surprise?" Lord Dratsab's eyes had a devilish twinkle in them.

"He'll come round. He always does."

"Do you think the Colonel went too far?"

"A gentlemen can't be blamed for the actions of his staff. The crazy cook hardly stuck that broom into someone important. I could understand Ecin's annoyance if he'd been lanced with it!"

"You know he loves that butler of his almost like his own father. Perhaps it was stupid of me sending them there. We all know the Colonel isn't a full tray of eggs."

"Nonsense!" said Lord Tig. "You were doing a friend a favour and one servant misbehaved with another servant. That's the end of it as far as I'm concerned. And so it will be with Ecin when he comes to his senses. Now forget about it and tell me where you've been."

Lord Dratsab clearly not wanting to be bothered with the matter any longer clasped his hands together sitting forward eagerly. "I've been in France!"

"What did you want to go there for?" asked Lord Tig clearly hoping for somewhere more exciting. "Not Tahiti or The Bahamas?"

"How could I go to Tahiti and back in a few weeks? Do I look like I have wings?"

Lord Tig wriggled in his chair. "Are you going to get out some decent port or not?"

Lord Dratsab stood up. "You will find it interesting when I tell you what I found out."

"The better the port you bring out for me the better your chances of keeping me interested!"

Lord Dratsab went over to the drink's cabinet. Lord Tig knew what he was doing. He was resisting the urge to break out anything too expensive. Ecin didn't give it a second thought. There was a simple reason they mostly met at Lord Ecin's house. "Come on Dratty! I want some fine Portuguese port. Not Icelandic. Not Egyptian. Not Chinese. Not Japanese. Not..."

"Alright alright it's coming!" said Lord Dratsab flapping his arm.

"And a cigar! A Cuban one!" shouted Lord Tig. "Not one from Nepal. Not one from Zanzibar. Not one from Timbuktu."

"That's enough!" shouted Lord Dratsab very irritated. "You'll get a cigar served in the manner of the Colonel's cook if you don't shut it!"

Lord Tig knew it was time to ease up on the reins.

"Here!" said Lord Dratsab thrusting a glass of port at him. "If you want a cigar they're over there!"

Lord Tig inwardly laughed at how easily Lord Dratsab could be riled. "Do you want one?" he said getting up.

"No!" Then abruptly changed his mind. "Yes! The better ones are in the box on the right."

"Thank you for letting me know," said Lord Tig smoothly.

He presently sat down handing Lord Dratsab a cigar. They lit them with their own matches.

"You just spoil it sometimes," began Lord Dratsab irritably, "I've got something interesting to tell you and you faff about first!"

Lord Tig held the cigar in his first two fingers picking off a piece of leaf with his thumb and little finger from the tip of his tongue. "Sorry old chap. But with a proper glass of port and a proper cigar I'm all ears."

Lord Dratsab exhaled his cigar smoke in Lord Tig's direction. When you were smoking one of his cigars he was allowed to do that. Or you could leave.

Lord Tig smiled through it taking a drag of his own.

Lord Dratsab seemed satisfied. "You know I showed you that bottle of WANK. Told you about the French Doctor and his "after shave" which is the real money maker."

Lord Tig nodded pleasantly. "You're already in for one racehorse and are thinking of putting in another. Want help with a few whispers when the time comes. I remember. It's only been a few weeks since you told me."

"Well I thought I'm at a bit of a loose end. A few day's break would do me good. Why not use it as an excuse to meet him?"

"Sounds reasonable enough. What did you think when you met him?" asked Lord Tig.

Lord Dratsab sat back in his chair with an odd look on his face.

"Well?" asked Lord Tig.

"I thought it would be more productive if I didn't meet him as myself. You know – make sure I wasn't being *done*."

Lord Tig was intrigued. "So you had some form of disguise?"

Lord Dratsab nodded as though it was something he couldn't wait to tell.

"You speak fluent French. Did you go as a French Count? What? What disguise?"

"I went as an English salesman of glass bottles! How clever was that!"

Lord Tig was surprised at his friend's gall. "I wouldn't have thought you had it in you!"

"I did!" enthused Lord Dratsab. "But I must tell you how I got to meet him! Talk about over-estimating your own importance."

"Well we all know they're good at that. Come on then let's hear it. But none of the boring bits of paper bits. Just get to the pertinent points."

"Don't worry. I don't like the paper bits either." Lord Dratsab put his cigar in the ashtray. "The doctor's place of operations is a secret. To get there I had to escorted by some of his men through the night. As I may be someone potentially important the "Dijon brothers" had laid on a horse for me instead of walking. They told me in broken English - I didn't let on I could speak French to anyone -"

"Sneaky," interrupted Lord Tig nodding, "beat them at their own game."

" - that it was the local miller's horse used to pull the mill cart. I'm waiting in trepidation for the thing to be brought round expecting it to be the size of a haystack."

"You make it sound as though he had a leg missing?" suggested Lord Tig.

"Just after dusk I'm with the Dijon brothers around me all "armed to the teeth". I'd been told I would have nothing to fear. These were the doctor's best men. I expected them to be bristling with pistols and muskets and silver bullets for werewolves! In reality the weapons they had that relied on gunpowder to function amounted to none! My batman was the only one with a loaded weapon."

"Wait! You took your batman?"

"Of course!" nodded Lord Dratsab. "I wasn't going to fly solo out there! I didn't tell anyone he was a batman. I told them he was the works foreman."

"And you did all this yourself?" asked Lord Tig leaning forward wanting to see Lord Dratsab's eyes more clearly through the cigar smoke.

"With some help from my batman," admitted Lord Dratsab.

Lord Tig knew there were some excellent batman in the army. Lord Dratsab always did have remarkable luck finding them. "So no guns but surely knives, daggers, a sword tucked into every available belt?" he asked.

"Not quite. Two of the Dijons had a pitchfork each – a bit too large to tuck into a belt. The short Dijon brother had a stiff bristled broom in each hand – again a bit too large to tuck into a belt. And the last brother had a large blanket – that was definitely too big for any belt. He had that thrown over his shoulder. But crucially the servant acting as guide did have a candle."

"Not even a lantern?" asked Lord Tig.

"No not on his pay. He grumbled about his pay a lot all through the journey."

Lord Tig shook his head. "Never satisfied are they?"

Lord Dratsab let out a raucous laugh. "They were there to protect me against all comers - and they looked like they were going to tidy the barn!"

Lord Tig laughed too then gathered his thoughts. "So what was wrong with the horse again?"

"It was no bigger than a child's pony with a dry rasping cough!"

"The flour getting on its lungs I imagine!" laughed Lord Tig.

"The flour would also explain why it was BRILLIANT WHITE!"

Lord Tig slapped his thigh so hard in glee the ash fell from his cigar.

"I was being taken to a secret location in the night away from prying eyes and the horse they were using was BRILLIANT WHITE! It also had a cough that could wake somebody in Paris - and we were in Normandy!" Lord Dratsab excitedly crossed and uncrossed his legs. "The miller confessed to the brothers he had been trying to clean it off all day but it was just too ingrained! They're all jabbering away in French with lots of hand waving and pouted tutting. "What about the blanket?" asks one of them. "No," says the miller, "trying to cover Wind with a blanket will just frighten him." I almost give myself away at this point. I nearly ask them - "Wind?" At least he's fast then?" But it turns out he's called that because he's full of it!"

"Come on Dratty! You're making this up!" laughed Lord Tig.

Lord Dratsab placed his hand on his chest. "Hand on heart it's all true. I was able to mount this fantastic beast by simply stepping over it!

Gently lowering my weight the damn thing produced a cough and a fart at the same time! This amused my batman so much that he asked me to get off and do it again!"

"Did you?"

"Of course not! I was trying to find a position where I could cover as much of its white as I could. Those garlic berks shouting out suggestions in broken English didn't help. Each time I adjusted my position the damned thing farted or coughed or both! I could see my batman losing it big time! Eventually I think I ended up on my back with my legs hooked around its neck. My arms dangling underneath holding onto something firm."

"You know what that was don't you?" asked Lord Tig clearly enjoying the story.

"Honestly I was past caring I really was."

"So how long did you have to put up with that?" asked Lord Tig.

"Until the smell got too much to bear!" laughed Lord Dratsab.

"You couldn't stand the coughs and the farts any longer?"

"It was Wind who couldn't stand them any longer."

Lord Tig scratched his nose holding the dangerous end of the cigar expertly away from his face. "I'm confused. The horse is the one producing all the smells but he's the one who couldn't stand it any longer?"

Lord Dratsab smiled getting ready for Lord Tig to enjoy this even more. "Imagine the scene. I'm draped over Wind his rein held by the miller. Around us in a tight circle are the Dijon brothers. Up ahead is my batman with the servant with his candle. We've all just emerged from the dark trees onto a large moonlit field when suddenly - the night air is broken by a large crack!"

Instant alarm spread through Lord Tig. "Musket fire? You'd been spotted?"

"I've no doubt something got spotted," laughed Lord Dratsab. "One of the Dijon brothers had just let off an enormous fart! Then the smell that wafted across. It seemed to break down a great dam of desire in all of them. The silent night air shredded by a great cacophony of botty burps, breech belches and crack gas! But what was worse was the giggling. I don't know who cracked first but very quickly we were all giggling uncontrollably at each and every fart. The worse the sea shanty got the more we were laughing. My batman backtracked to see what was going on. Then starts shouting for the guide to bring his candle."

"Were you mad?" asked Lord Tig bemused. "To toss away a sneaky passage for a group lighting botty burps session? Talk about playing with fire!"

Lord Dratsab picked up his cigar from the ashtray. "We didn't get that far. I felt Wind stiffen beneath me and we collapsed to the ground."

"Musket fire! Wind had been shot!" said Lord Tig with his overriding interest in guns ignited.

Lord Dratsab eyed him through the cigar smoke. "Have you bought a new gun you want to tell me about?"

"Not recently no. To stop spending so much at the gunsmiths I've even stopped going into London," said Lord Tig looking wistfully out of the window.

"I think the poor thing was already shot a long time before I was on its back. The miller had its head cradled in his arms. His nostrils were grossly enlarged with a liquid oozing out. In the moonlight we couldn't tell if it was blood or what it was. It was such a shame. The laughter had stopped but none of them seemed able to stop their inconsiderate arses."

"Shame," said Lord Tig distracted thinking about guns. "What do you think had happened?"

"Oh I think that Wind liked his own gentle lullaby. When the Dijon brothers struck up their French horns in such close proximity it was deafening for him."

"Such noble creatures are horses," said Lord Tig thinking of the engraving on the stock of his current favourite gun.

"I can see now the miller rubbing his chest and blowing into its mouth. He must have loved it because its teeth were horrible. Then one of the Dijon brothers puts a hand on the miller's shoulder. "That's an ill wind. That blow's no good." It sounded quite beautiful in French. It would have been quite poignant if he hadn't farted so loudly afterwards."

"So what did they do?" asked Lord Tig thinking stuff it! I'm going to London soon.

"Well rather cleverly the four of them got their Wind up each tucking a leg into a boot. The two at the front holding up his head. It was all very compact and I did wonder how I was supposed to get back on. When I tried they all got a bit miffed."

"You didn't try to get back on?" admonished Lord Tig.

"The damn thing was only there to carry me!" said Lord Dratsab in all seriousness. "Anyway they got their revenge on me!"

Lord Tig stopped thinking about London and guns. "How?" Looking at Lord Dratsab he was pleased to sense this was something he was less keen to relay. There wasn't the previous mirth when Lord Dratsab spoke.

"We hadn't gone far when the miller suddenly says my disguise is not good enough. It needs to be improved as we draw close to our secret destination. I now need to look like a man who has toiled in the woods all day. But regard! The solution is at our feet. He points to the pebbles and grit in the bed of a millpond. We must put some of those in my crutch so I will walk like a woodsman! They all insist it has to be so. I'm in their hands so I agree. I let the miller pull open my trousers to scoop some of it in. He's there quite a while getting it the way he wants. It was only when he'd finished when I try to walk that I understand what he's done. God how things pinched and rubbed down there! I had to take each step very carefully I can tell you!"

"You think they were toying with you? Blamed you for what had happened to the horse? Punishing your rudeness for trying to get back on?" asked Lord Tig who was always very perceptive.

"At the time I thought it necessary. Now? Yes I think they were being petty." Lord Dratsab took a considered drag in his cigar. "What's your knowledge of French millers?" he asked.

"The same as English millers – nothing," replied Lord Tig. Then he had a thought. "They always add a lot more to the price when they find out you're English!"

Lord Dratsab waved such an obvious truth away. "Let me give you a few facts about your typical French miller. When he mills his flour it makes a lot of white dust which covers him from head to toe. There's nothing unusual about seeing a French miller out and about with a very white face. Those big sails on a windmill make a hell of a draught. Working in that draught gives your French miller very ruddy cheeks and lips. Then there's a part in milling that involves being so close to a big revolving wheel that it rubs at his hair so he has to wear a beret to keep his head warm. So to sum up - the bread a French miller bakes he likes to butter on the other side to most people."

Lord Tig nodded in complete understanding. He was pretty sure his father probably preferred buttering his bread on the French side. He saw such behaviour as just another type of thread that it took to weave the rich tapestry of life. Though it was good manners to never be seen picking at it!

"This was a steep learning curve for me. I'd hobbled on as best I could with the help of my batman. We got to the mill first with the Dijon brothers carrying the horse understandably slower. The mill gate barring the path just wouldn't budge for us. I get behind my batman trying to give him a hand. Both of us pushing and humping at this gate but still the bloody thing wouldn't budge! Then there's a loud bang of a door being thrown open and we're engulfed in the light of a flaming torch. We both jump back like boys caught scrumping!

"Ooh la la darlin'. Look at you naughty boys up my gate!"

It's the miller. Beret, white face, big red cheeks and lips. But he's a mountain. He'd have no trouble opening the gate we'd been struggling with.

"You've got the wrong idea mate," says my batman.

"So you're naughty English boys! You all need a good spankin'!" says the miller in broken English.

In broken French because I'm not sure how close the Dijon brothers are I tell him we'd just like to be on our way.

"Oh I don't think so my young English fox. You see me and my special friends have been watching you," he says in broken English. "You see tonight Duckie I have two special friends over! And there we were idly looking at the stars when what do we see? A group of men come out of the woods with a horse they like to kiss! And two of them have to stop at the water to give into their lust in full view of everyone! And you weren't coming to see us? I don't believe you!"

"Honestly mate!" says my batman. "You'd be the last people we'd be coming to see!"

"Poppycock! I've seen what one of you did with just one handjob! Now you two are both at it again up my gate! You're insatiable you naughty boys. And I want a piece of English muffin!"

"English muffin? Look mate I've got a gun!" my batman warns him.

"I know and I bet it's a big one!" replies the miller. His horrible white face all lit up excitedly under his beret. "Enough of these silly games! If you want to use my bridge then there's a toll to pay! I've never seen men with such wheat in their sacks! Stop playing games! Come in to have it properly milled!"

The Dijon brothers arrived with the horse and the miller. At the same time a man shouted from inside, "Are they coming in or not Pierre?"

"I don't know Henri. I think they like playing games."

There was a shriek of hellish laughter. "I know Nicholas! Fox and hounds! How exciting!"

"With real English foxes this time boys!" said the miller.

"You know the rules," said one of the Dijon brothers in French. "You give us two hours. You can do anything you like to us if you find us. But only if you give us two hours to hide!"

"I know! I know!" said the miller clapping his hands gleefully. "I'll get the key to the gate."

The Dijon brothers turned on each other jabbering away in the French they didn't know I understood. "What were the English fools doing coming this close to the mill? I mean the silly sods would stick to the two hours. But they had Wind to carry. They'd have to drop these tools. And tomorrow one of them would have to run the risk of sneaking back to get them. They were still arguing when Pierre and the two other millers appeared. They were massive, wearing berets, had ghostly white faces and hands, and shrieking and giggling like excited schoolgirls.

"Remember two hours. Then it's fair and not a sin." said a Dijon brother.

"Wouldn't dream of it darling. Cat wants to earn her cream!" Pierre unlocked the gate and swung it open.

"What's going on?" asks my batman. I whisper to him to follow the others through the gate. The guide with his candle, then the Dijon brothers full with Wind, then the miller, then my batman and me last. As I pass Pierre he gently pinches my bottom telling me, "You saucy young fox!"

"You naughty old hound!" I said pausing to face him. I could be brave knowing about the two hours' start. His head was massive. His white face like a loaf with two red apples for cheeks. His lips like a big squashed tomato. But in the moonlight I could see such an innocent young joy in that grotesque face. He was going to say something else. I thought it might be something like good luck or may the best man win. Something like that. But he opened that big squashed tomato of his and said in perfect English, "Now run me beauty!"

It was though he'd slapped me! My legs shot off and the rest of my body bits followed because we were attached to them! But oh the pain as the gravel and pebbles ground in my crutch. Desperately I reached in trying to get the damned stuff out trying to keep up with them. Do you know in a desperate situation things become very clear and simple of purpose. It doesn't matter you are an excellent horseman - you have no horse. Doesn't matter an excellent shot - you have no gun. Doesn't matter you are rich - your money's not with you."

Lord Dratsab looked unusually wise. "In that moonlit country lane I realised something about life."

"And what is that?" asked Lord Tig thinking about guns again.

"It's not about coming first all the time. You can't do it. No-one can. It's about not coming last. Don't ever come last!" said Lord Dratsab solemnly.

"Well for someone who normally leaves the room when the truth walks in I find that very refreshing." said Lord Tig. He held up his glass of port. "A toast to your new found enlightenment!" He emptied his glass. "A whole glass of port and we're not even at the doctor's yet!" He held out the empty glass. "Come on. Put a shift in!"

# CHAPTER 22

## Sorting it out over a pint

Chisel put down his pint on the table top. They were both sat outside in the beer garden of a nice country tavern just after breakfast. "What do you reckon's going on then?"

Hammer rubbed his earlobe with his thumb and forefinger. He only did it when something was troubling him. Chisel didn't like watching him do it. "I don't honestly know."

A farmhand entered the beer garden and caught Chisel's eye. "Morning Chief," he said.

"Morning mate," replied Chisel.

The farmhand walked towards the farthest bench and sat down. He looked around as though he'd forgotten something. A small dog came scuttling in, decided it needed a poo, did one right in the middle of the path, did that stupid kicking of its back legs thing then jumped into the farmhand's lap. He gave the dog a friendly rub on its head. Picking up his pint he offered it to the dog first. His big tongue flicking in and out spilling most of the beer from the glass which only made the farmhand smile.

"Disgusting," said Hammer to Chisel.

"I know. My missus went on for ages about getting a puppy and I kept saying no. Then one day she just brought one home and seeing how happy it made her and how cute it were I said alright then. You can keep it. Trouble is puppies grow don't they? When his shits were bigger than mine I told her he'll have to go. She told me if the dog went she went. So that's why I'm single now." He took a satisfied sip of his beer.

"No. It's disgusting we're not being kept in the loop! All this dangling in mid-air, not knowing what's going on. Doesn't sit right with me. It goes right against the grain." Hammer picked up his pint taking a gulp as though it were medicine and not something to be enjoyed.

"You know what they say. Give one man two sixteenths of your trouble, a second four thirty twos, a third eight sixty fourths and a fourth sixteen one twenty eighths and you'll feel better by half," said Chisel nodding to encourage Hammer to take another sip of his pint.

Hammer brought his glass down examining Chisel with exasperation. "Wouldn't it have been easier to say a trouble shared is a trouble halved?"

"Hey! We're master craftsman! We're much more precise!" Chisel looked at him taking a gulp of his ale absolutely confident there was no answer to that.

"Have you heard of a chap called Isaac Newton Mr Chisel?"

Chisel lowered his glass a little wary of where this might be going.

"He's a chap from Lincolnshire who is so clever he can explain why when you drop a hammer it bashes you on your big toe rather than floats back onto the bench. Why when you throw it against the wall it doesn't just slide down but bounces right back at you. Why when you bend over and fart - you immediately straighten up. Apparently it's all to do with forces. And he knows how all these forces work."

"Really? That's incredible," said Chisel genuinely enthralled. "How clever must a man be to know all that? Wonderful really."

"Well here's the thing – do you think he loses any sleep worrying about what you might be working on? You know – the competition you might provide him?" Hammer took a satisfactory sip of his pint.

"You can be a right sarky sod when you want to be can't ya? I was only trying to help. And I had heard of him."

Hammer brought down his pint. "You hadn't heard of him."

Chisel took another sip of his drink wondering what was troubling Hammer so much.

After a few more sips of his pint Hammer began talking again. "Did you know the Elizabethans believed in a wheel of fortune with good luck at the top and bad luck at the bottom? The wheel never stopping so a person could expect both but neither would last for long. But do you know what? It only partly explains it for me."

"How'd ya mean?"

Hammer wasn't looking at him but off into the distance. "Perhaps luck is more like a clock with lots of different wheels inside. I don't understand how a clock works but I can tell the time with it when I've been shown. I don't have to understand how all those complicated wheels do it. But of course -" He turned to face Chisel. "You can lose or drop a clock and watch it smash into pieces right in front of you."

Chisel confused rubbed his chin. "What's ya point?"

"A pint of brown please!" quipped Hammer because it was too good an opportunity to miss even though he was being serious.

"Ha Ha very funny," said Chisel. "But what *is* your point?"

Hammer rubbed his ear in the way Chisel didn't like. "I thought I knew what the time was. But taking the back off this clock and seeing all those whirring around cogs and gears and wheels I've realised - I don't know which one we are."

"So what's ya point?"

Hammer rubbed his brow struggling to understand something himself let alone explain it to someone else. "I don't know how a clock works but I can use it to tell the time..."

"Yeah you've said that," interrupted Chisel impatiently.

"I don't know how luck works but I use it or deal with it however it comes. But there are people called watchmakers who do understand how clocks work. Just like there are people who decide how much happiness or grief we get in our lives."

"Yes!" said Chisel emphatically. "They're called women!"

"No!" said Hammer banging the table. "Our watchmakers! The people who put us in their creation. I can't put my finger on it. I can't explain it. But I'm telling you – something has changed!" He turned to Chisel with a worried expression. "I don't think our clock is the same anymore."

Chisel shook his head. "Why bring luck and clocks into it? Why not just spit it out?"

"I'm trying to you thick Brummie Git!"

Chisel looked away noticing the farmhand looking over at them at Hammer's raised voice.

"Hoi! Your dog took a shit there mate! Carry on looking over and I'll rub your nose in it!"

The farmhand who was young and in a vest had arms on show that looked as thick as tree trunks. Though he did find it odd that the man had pointed out his dog had taken a shit as that's what dogs do, he looked away as it had been a bit rude of him to have been staring.

"I've got a complete set of chisels in this apron you know!"

"Chisel. The guy's looked away. Leave it!" admonished Hammer.

"Well you shouldn't call me a thick Brummie git in public!" said Chisel bobbing his head in that curious way men can do in such a situation.

"But at this moment you are a thick Brummie Git in public!" said Hammer firmly.

Chisel decided to hide behind his pint.

"Did you order the lamb?"

Hammer turned around to see who it was. He'd thought it was a woman but now he wasn't so sure.

"Did you order the lamb?" it repeated.

It appeared to be a talking apron. There were two clogs poking out of the bottom of it and a mass of bushy hair poking out of the top.

"Not us I'm afraid," said Hammer.

"Try Mister Nosey over there!" suggested Chisel.

The apron went over to the farmhand. "Did you order the lamb?"

"Yes I did," said the farmhand.

"Well the poor thing had been raped. The cook's refused to cook an animal that suffered like that and given it a proper burial in the herb garden," the apron informed him.

"Well how would the old bat have known?" asked the farmhand.

"I don't know. But she's forever going on about the cruelty of man to animals. Do you want a fry-up?"

"Will I get it if I order it?"

"Oh yeah! She hates pigs!"

"I'll have a fry-up then."

The apron disappeared back into the tavern.

"Do you fancy a fry-up Chisel?" asked Hammer.

"What? Cooked by a woman off her trolley and served by a hairy apron? Not likely!"

"You're probably right."

"More often than you give me credit for!"

"Very well. You're Isaac Newton and you have to explain what's going on. How would you do it?" asked Hammer giving his pint a little tilt towards Chisel.

"Well I wouldn't do it here for a start. Don't know who's listening."

"Oh come on. You can't get out of it that easy. There's a beefy young lad waiting for his fry-up and us two. Don't use any names and keep your voice down and explain away Newton."

Chisel put down his pint. "Alright then. As I see it it's like this. Our boss is working for unknown others who want to introduce a new concept of taking money from people through the sale of a certain item. They need a new way of managing it all using figures and books in a way that hasn't been done before. But the people who understand these things best want to stay on the right side of the law so they're not interested in getting involved. So some of the best of them have effectively been kidnapped, had their brains picked in a tree and then been thrown away to keep them permanently quiet."

Chisel lowered his voice even further. "But one of these clever chappies was allowed to escape because something went wrong with the cloak. As you know – why he was allowed to escape is beyond me. But they can't have someone who knows the plan running around. Now what should have been a simple collect and dispatch has got complicated because a coachman of all people seems to be as clever as the boss. So they got a professional involved. But lo and behold he's proved no better at finding them than the two handsome workmen. So what do they do now? Press ahead with the plan and hope this guy just stays quiet? Or put the plan on hold - if indeed they can – until he's found and silenced?"

Hammer stopped nodding digesting what Chisel had said. "Do you want another pint yet?" he asked.

"I hadn't finished," said Chisel indicating for Hammer to lean closer which he did. "What have they been doing with everyone involved after they've finished with them? Hey? Do you think eventually it will include the two handsome workmen? A year that's all! That's how long we've worked for him. And what do we really know about him? Nightnurse -"

"Shush shush shush!" said Hammer flapping his hands down.

"Sorry!" cursed Chisel. "I should have said *the professional* is a bigger fish than the two handsome workmen. Big fish eat little fish."

Hammer pulled away deep in thought.

Chisel followed him leaning across. "I've got a lot of respect for your instincts. I think you explain them like a frog trying to get out of a bucket mind - but they've saved us more than once. If you think something's changed then it probably has." He sat upright. "Pint of mild please."

Hammer suddenly turned to Chisel very excited. "How many times has Crow laid on a bit of crumpet for his guest's entertainment like he did for - you know?"

"I don't know. I've lost count," replied Chisel.

"And have you ever seen any of this crumpet?"

"He's got a secret passage he gets them in and out with."

"Pah!" said Hammer. "It's us that's half rebuilt that cottage! It would have been us who built a secret passage! And have we?"

"But what are you saying?" asked Chisel frowning.

"Do you want me to call you a thick Brummie Git again in public?"

"I think you're going to have to. I really don't know what you're getting at."

"What if it ain't a bit of crumpet making all that noise? What if it's Crow!"

Chisel scoffed turning away. "Sounding like that? Sounding like a -" He stopped turning back to Hammer with his mouth hanging open.

Hammer raised his eyebrows. "When have we ever seen him uncovered? How many times has he just done something that seems odd? What about the cushions? And the curtains? And the ornaments? He always smells nice. How friendly he can be one minute and an absolute bastard the next?" Hammer put his hand under Chisel's chin closing his mouth. "Stop gawping and tell me what you think."

"We could have just popped the bookkeeper there and then. I even said it," whispered Chisel so shocked when the farmhand glanced over at them he gave him a friendly wave.

"What's it Mick the Misogynist says - The best man is better than any woman -"

Chisel finished it for him, "But the worst woman is worse than any man."

"Exactly! Why do the bookkeepers have to die?"

"Er - I've got to stop you there," said Chisel holding out his hand. "It's us been doing that."

"But on whose orders?" demanded Hammer in a tone indicating where the real responsibility lay. He picked up their empty glasses going inside.

Chisel looked to the far end of the beer garden seeing something that gave him a horrible cold shiver because he saw it just then. Right after what they'd been talking about. It was a magpie surveying the beer garden from a small tree. Seeming satisfied it flew right at Chisel landing with a chatter on his table.

"One for sorrow hey boy?" said Chisel gulping. Rather reluctantly he clicked his fingers four times.

The magpie began tapping out a message on the table top. Chisel glanced across to see if Mister Nosey was taking any interest. He wasn't. The bird had finished and was gone when Hammer came out carrying the two pints.

"We've just had a message," said Chisel letting Hammer sit down first.

"Oh yes?" said Hammer picking up his pint. "Will I have time to finish this?"

"Yes. We're to meet someone this afternoon."

"Oh yes? Who?"

"Our professional friend." Chisel picked up his pint raising it at Hammer to thank him for it. He took a big mouthful and put it down. "What are we going to do?"

"For the moment what we're told. After that we'll have to see." Hammer raised his glass. "To your continued good health sir."

Chisel picked up his glass frowning. "Up Yours Sir!"

# CHAPTER 23

## You should never judge a book by its cover

Lord Dratsab sat down after topping up their glasses. "So where were we?" he asked puffing on his cigar.

"You've just had your bottom pinched by that naughty French hound on your road to Damascus," suggested Lord Tig.

Lord Dratsab smiled. "How very clever of you."

"Thank you," replied Lord Tig graciously tilting his head.

Lord Dratsab wasn't going to let him bask too long. "Up ahead I see Wind's white body disappearing into the night. But I can't run that fast. Of course I'm cursing millers - I haven't touched a bread roll since - but it hurts too much to run! Fortunately my batman sees my predicament and hurries back to scoop me up. I imagine we must have ran for half a mile or a mile. It was hard to tell in the dark."

"You're waffling," said Lord Tig curtly. "And you promised you wouldn't. And you're starting to look like Winston." Winston had been one of the dogs they had known as children. A bulldog with a sad face they had spoilt immensely because they were always trying different ways to cheer him up.

Lord Dratsab stood up walking behind the wing-backed chair puffing on his cigar. He put both hands on the back of the chair peering over it. Finally, he sat back down. He took the cigar out of his mouth.

"They're a funny lot over there you know. They won't let their little princes climb trees but whenever they paint one of the little buggers it's always with a sword. Now you tell me - what's the more dangerous thing for a boy to be learning? Hey?"

"I've hardly been. You're always there. I'll have to take your word for it that's what they're like."

Lord Dratsab got up again walking towards the fireplace putting his hands above his head on the stout chimney breast. He puffed on his cigar so enthusiastically it jiggled up and down.

"What happened at the doctors?" asked Lord Tig thinking it must be serious. "You have a pocket full of rabbit feet you're that lucky. It wasn't that bad surely?"

"Luck's not a rabbit foot! Luck's found in a mine! And it takes a lot of hard work and brains to dig her out! Any luck I've had I've earned!"

"I didn't mean to offend you," said Lord Tig sipping his port carefully.

"Well you haven't! Why would you even think that?" snapped Lord Dratsab taking his hands off the chimney breast.

"Because look at you. You seem so – animated all of a sudden."

Lord Dratsab took the cigar out of his mouth looking at it. He went over to the study door. Opening it he took a long look at the hallway outside. Then he shut it bolting the two bolts top and bottom. He sat back down.

"How do you think your port came over from the Iberian Peninsula?"

"You know I don't like riddles," said Lord Tig unhappily.

"Humour me," ordered Lord Dratsab.

"Oh, in a ship I suppose."

"But within the ship the port would have been stored in..."

"The hold?"

"Within the hold the port would be in...."

"Barrels?"

"Yes barrels – thank you! People are like barrels. Some made by good coopers with good wood which never leak. Some made with driftwood by bad coopers which will always leak. Then they get filled. Some with good stuff right to the brim. Others destined to roll around empty all their lives."

"It was France you went to and not Mount Olympus?" asked Lord Tig. "I had no idea being chased up a muddy lane in the middle of the night by a French miller could have so profound an effect on a man."

Lord Dratsab ignored the comment. "Of course what you want is a good barrel made by a good cooper full to the brim of good stuff."

"Now I don't need to be Plato to know that that is a rare thing! Ecin's the only one I know who comes close."

Lord Dratsab didn't ignore that comment. "Yes the fool! But what do you do with a bad barrel?"

"Are you going to lecture me on how to manage my staff?" asked Lord Tig wearily. "Because if I want to hear that rubbish Ecin can do it much better than you."

"Of course not! Wouldn't dream of it. All I'm saying is a good barrel can have bad stuff inside it and no-one would know!"

Lord Tig now understood. "You thought you had a barrel made out of strong shiny wood well banded but you've opened it to find something dark and sticky?"

Lord Dratsab looked like Winston again. "You won't believe it when I tell you."

"You've been trying to put it off for long enough now – tip it out man!"

"I don't trust doctors. You know cutting up cadavers in the middle of the night? It's not normal behaviour is it? Leeches? When a wretch already feels poxy how is covering the poor sod in leeches supposed to help? Surely that's when you need your blood the most! All I'm saying is a doctor is no more correct than the rest of us. They're made of wood just the same." It appeared Lord Dratsab was still struggling to get to the point.

"You should know by now you're speaking to the wrong person. I admire those brave enough to be reaching out into the dark on our behalf," said Lord Tig unusually honest.

"I know! I know! It just seems to me that when you put a doctor and a sick man together in a room all you're going to get a few hours later are some lucky leeches, a richer doctor, and a biscuit!"

"You really don't want to tell me do you?" asked Lord Tig looking very hard at him.

Lord Dratsab shook his head despondently. "No but I have to."

"Because you want my advice afterwards I imagine?"

Lord Dratsab nodded unwillingly.

"Then I need to know all the pertinent facts. You understand? Only what's relevant but all that's relevant."

Lord Dratsab gave a final sorry nod and began. "When I get to the doctors I pretend to be feint and listless brought on by my trouser injuries. The Dijon brothers deposit me on a bunk in the washroom. I'd almost fell asleep when suddenly there was an overpowering smell of garlic."

"Is this relevant?" demanded Lord Tig.

"Of course I've got to tell you where we met! It will become very relevant!"

"Very well," said Lord Tig, "proceed."

"My plan had been to pretend to be ill, come round, engage him in conversation and get him to tell me a lot more than he realised. As far as he was concerned I wouldn't remember half of what had been said. But it didn't quite work out like that."

"He saw you weren't ill?" asked Lord Tig.

"That was easy. He asked me in English, "Under the feint young man?" I just groaned a bit. Then he came round the bunk to open my eyelid. He thumb was really soft and smelt of butter. Then he said, "There's a free fry-up with as much free beer as you can drink in the scullery today!" Then he leant closer, "with lashings of gravy!""

"Was there?" asked Lord Tig thinking it did sound splendid.

"I don't know."

"So why did he say it?"

"I can only presume it was something he considered a normally functioning Englishman would find irresistible. When I didn't respond he seemed quite satisfied I must be unconscious. I was just ready to start coming round when he let go of my eyelid saying in French, "Good you stupid Roast Beef. I have more important things to do in this room than look after you!"

"He didn't!" exclaimed Lord Tig.

"He did! Then he just goes off in French, "You stupid Roast Beefs of the lower classes never learn the French. That is good. This means we nod and we smile and all the time we taking the piss out of you!

Regard that suit. Grey? Grey? It is russet this year! Grey was over five years ago you dummy! And the buckles on those shoes. PAH! But I digress and waste my time with you. You're just a Roast Beef after all! I have work for France in this room. Important work that will change the world. You see the people are divided by the class. And you tasteless sprouts are worse than anyone! Well apart from us maybe. But this must end! And it can if we all smell the same!""

Lord Tig held up his hand covering his mouth with the back of his other hand.

"Is something wrong?" asked Lord Dratsab peering at him.

Lord Tig brought his hands down. "Oh no. I'm getting quite a picture. But I need to ask – this French doctor doesn't know you can speak French and is sure you're unconscious because you refused a free fry-up and free beer?"

"I think he felt the refusal of lashings of gravy was the absolute proof," pointed out Lord Dratsab seriously.

"You've got to go on."

Lord Dratsab cleared his throat. "In this room the washing is done once a week. The basket over there for the men, a basket for the women. And over there a basket for the lady of the house. A lady of noble birth from England. That is good news. A good doctor can make a thorough examination. Not of you! You pork scratching! Why would you put such things in your mouth? Put simply so even a Yorkshire pudding – which is not even sweet!  - can understand. In France we have the finest food. We have the finest wines. We certainly have the better weather. The very best of everything the French deserve. Or so we thought. For there is something in that basket that is better than we have in France. And we shall take it! For we deserve it more than you. You sickly treacle tarts and custard. And what it is this spotted dick for Christ's sake? Why have you named a pudding after a disease? I am now bored with trying to educate a weak brown stew. It is time for my diagnosis.""

"How could a diagnosis be performed on the washing basket of a lady?" asked Lord Tig enjoyably bemused.

"He lifted the lid with such reverence it was as though he was expecting a genie to rise out of it. Then he solemnly bent over it breathing in deeply. "Magnificent!" he moaned out. "You see my little island of clumsy chefs," he said as he began rummaging through the contents. "It is my job to take what I find in here for France. I the great Doctor Eau de Toilette! You see you pork pie there is nothing finer. Truly nothing in the world that can compare." He found something pink placing it over his head. "To the special scent of an English lady's GUSSET!""

"No!" exclaimed Lord Tig. As perceptive as he normally was he had not seen that coming.

Lord Dratsab nodded his head regrettably. "The doctor had placed a pair of her knickers over his head adjusting them so the thin centre ran down the middle of his face. He was breathing in so hard the material was going up his nostrils. Through the leg holes I could see his eyes going all fluttery! It was like a drug to him. But it's gets worse! After a while it's not enough. He viciously rummages in the basket pulling out a red basque. "This one is not for France. This alone is for me!" He lovingly puts it on and starts rubbing the breast cups so vigorously he keeps on having to adjust the knickers. Then that's not enough! He rummages in the basket again. "I caught a glimpse of your wicked rouge. I must have you! English Lady," he pulled out something red. "I just love your red camisole knickers!"

"I didn't realise there are so many different types of lady's undergarments." said Lord Tig still reeling.

"When the doctor started thrusting his hips back and forth I just wanted to get out. But how could I? Then suddenly the door knob rattled with someone trying to get in! He shouts, "I am a doctor with my patient. On no account must we be disturbed! Go away! Then a woman's voice says, "It is the Lady of the House! Open this door immediately!" "Lady Martineau?" he gagged. "Yes. I want to come in! I wish to see how my countryman is doing. Now open the door!"

"Er no my lady. I am at the crucial stage of investigation!" In a panic he yanks off the knickers pushing them deep into the basket.

"He's going to be alright isn't he? There have been too many deaths recently. In fact they've got worse since we've had you as a doctor. Open this door immediately. I want to see what you're doing!"

"Of course my lady! If I may just concentrate just now!"

Watching him I knew what he was really concentrating on - removing all her underwear without ripping it or breaking his neck!

"Open the bloody door!" she shouts rattling the door knob frantically.

"Indeed my lady." Taking a last furtive look at the basket he unlocks the door. "Ah my Lady. May I say how radiant you look today!" he says in English.

"You're so sweet. Is the little terrier alright?"

"As right as your English rain. May I escort you back to the drawing room?"

"Thank you doctor but that won't be necessary. I've brought some biscuits for when he wakes up. I'm going to leave them on the table. You continue without me."

"You English. You treat your animals and servants so well. Adieu my lady."

As soon as he was gone she shook me really hard. "Is that pervert going through my washing basket? Come on! I've got three boys. I know when someone's pretending to be asleep!"

So I "woke-up" and as we ate the biscuits I told her what I'd seen. In return she told me what she knew about her strange in-house doctor."

The last thing on Lord Tig's mind now was a trip to a London gunsmith. Looking at him you wouldn't know the difference but he was very interested to know a few things. "So this doctor has no laboratory of his own?" he asked.

"No," said Lord Dratsab clearly needing his stiff drink.

"His after shave is based on the smell of an English lady's gusset?"

"It appears so," replied Lord Dratsab after a large mouthful of port.

"His men arm themselves with pitchforks and brooms like a mob?"

"And a blanket. Don't forget they had a blanket!"

"He is an amateur!" Lord Tig got up abruptly.

"Where are you going? You haven't told me what to do!" said Lord Dratsab hurriedly putting down his drink.

"Do I really need to?" asked Lord Tig staring at him. He walked towards the bolted study door then stopped. "Your contact? You mentioned a contact who got you involved with all this. Who is he?"

"You know that's crossing a line Tig. You know I can't tell you."

Lord Tig wondered how well he actually knew his friend. Would he find out when he said the name on the tip of his tongue? Would he be able to read Lord Dratsab's reaction to it?

"Colonel Peru," he said clearly.

Lord Dratsab said nothing trying to remain unreadable. There were after all certain rules that everyone was expected to follow.

Lord Tig unbolted the door.

"The important bit of rope is the bit that's around your neck. That's the bit you need to worry about. You don't need to see where it's hanging from."

He left.

Lord Dratsab flopped down in his chair wondering how much money he was now going to lose by pulling out. He had no inkling that someone else would take the news so badly they would want him to pay with his life.

# CHAPTER 24

## Dangerous Appetites

Colin and Sam were still on their way to the miller. The kissing gate had proved to be a bit of a red herring. Sam had expected to pass through it to have the mill magically appear before them. It hadn't so they had trudged on a little deflated. Climbing a small hill which was no small effort in the warm sun they had reached the top to see it open out like a great green blanket.

"This looks like Maureen's Moor to me. On a smaller scale of course," said Colin.

Beside him Sam looked around catching his breath. It looked quite pleasant. It was a bit blowy but it was a warm wind. It was lovely to see so much blue sky without any chimney pots or rooftops.

"You say it with a sense of foreboding," said Sam. "Is that deliberate?"

"There's a story they tell around those parts about what happened there," said Colin looking up at the clear sky.

"Is it a long story? Something to pass the time. Because I can't see a mill around here."

"I imagine if they put a mill up here it would get blown off!"

Sam chuckled. "Yes I do imagine it can blow a bit up here in the winter. Nice on a day like today though. I can feel it sucking the soot out of my lungs. Shall we continue?"

Colin nodded and they began walking abreast. After a few steps he said, "I'm not even sure I'd call it a story. It's just something they say happened there."

Suddenly Sam stopped grabbing his arm. "It's not a ghost story is it?"

The thought this intelligent specific man might be scared of ghost stories amused Colin. "You don't believe all that rubbish do you?"

"Let's just say I have an open mind on such things." Sam began walking again.

So did Colin. "It's more a story about a witch. Long ago the moor had been a forest. There was only one man who lived in it called Frank."

"Did he wear any clothes?" asked Sam.

"Pardon?"

"Did he wear any clothes? Was he naked?"

"I don't honestly know. It seems a bit of an odd question to ask though," said Colin thinking about it.

"Really? Doesn't it annoy you that artists and storytellers always cover people up when there's no need? This Frank - with only the animals of the forest to see him he could stroll around naked as the day he was born. But I bet you if the story became well known and we needed a picture of Frank - he'd be wearing a loincloth! Stop everything jiggling around as he ran through the forest. But I bet you that feels great. That's how you'd want to do it if you could."

"I'd never really thought about it. But what about when it's cold? You'd want to be wearing something then?" suggested Colin.

"Wear a fur when it's cold of course. But still be naked underneath. If I was going to be free in the forest I'd want everything free. Not feel the need to have anything about me covered up!" Sam sniffed the clean air. "Never happen of course but that's what I'd like – to jiggle and bounce around naked without a care in the world. I imagine that's what any man given his freedom would like to do - be completely naked!" He smiled apologetically. "Sorry - has that shocked you?"

Colin shook his head amicably. "I found it very interesting. All of us seem to have this yearning deep inside to live simply in a forest. In reality I think it could be a nightmare. But there must be something in an attraction so powerfully deep-rooted."

"Sorry I've made us digress. Carry on with the story," said Sam.

Colin thought Sam was full of surprises today. But where the conversation might go was for another time in front of a roaring fire with a few beers. The story would be better for now. "One dark night people arrived with axes and shovels. They started to cut down the trees to make huts and furniture and burn. All the time never enough wood for them to burn. At night they would huddle around a great fire. The women singing gently to their children. The men telling stories and roasting their chestnuts. But Frank wasn't happy. They were destroying his forest. At first he tried to persuade them not to harm the trees and live like him. But they looked at his blue body and dribbling nose and decided they preferred being warm. It made Frank very sad. But then it got worse. The men got bored roasting their chestnuts by the fire. They started hunting the forest animals! Frank tried to stop them. He tried to show them how vegetables could be fashioned to look like squirrels and hedgehogs and rabbits. But they wanted the real thing!"

"A stew without meat is a soup. Mind you I like my soup. But I think Frank's the odd one out here. Did he know what the animals tasted like?" asked Sam.

"He was set in his ways. In desperation he went to see his best friend. A badger who was so close to Frank he called him Brian. Many moonlit evenings they had wondered the forest together looking for grubs and hedgehogs – Brian's favourite food."

"Hold on!" interrupted Sam. "You see this is another thing that annoys me. It's alright for the animals to eat each other. That's only natural isn't it? But if a man decides he like the taste of hedgehog too he's the monster that's going to ruin everything!"

Colin nodded. "The berks telling you with a mouthful of chicken sandwich!"

"Why is it some animals like chickens get eaten and some animals like hedgehogs get sainted? It doesn't make sense."

Colin shook his head. "Another debate for another time I suppose."

"Yes sorry," said Sam. "I've made you digress again."

Colin continued the story. "Their walks together through the forest were full of doom and gloom now. Brian didn't even have the heart to tear apart a hedgehog that Frank had found for him. It made Frank very sad to see Brian so off his food. It wasn't right! Those people were ruining the forest where he had lived all his life! Taking a walk on the wild side he went to see Maureen."

"*Maureen*?" asked Sam.

"Yes. Maureen Jenkins lived in a hut on the edge of the forest. She had ragged black hair and beady black eyes. She smelt things by licking them with her tongue. She drank tea made from the eyes of frogs. Frank didn't like her at all."

"I'm not surprised," said Sam.

"Frank didn't mind any of that. Frank didn't like her because her favourite food was badger. Over the years Brian had lost two sisters and a brother to her. Brian's only consolation was his brother had managed to take two of the bitch's fingers before she killed him."

"Badgers aren't fearsome animals are they?" asked Sam. "How would she have lost two fingers?"

"You need to understand. Their front paws can crush a man's chest as if it were an acorn. You can't catch them in the open. They have to be dug out of their set inch by inch. That's the easy bit! After that comes the fight to the death. It has to be a fight to the death because badgers take it very personal when you try to eat them. They're not going to leap away like a relieved deer or bound off like a grateful rabbit. He's going to take you to task for trying to do that to him. But to kill him you've got to break that thick skull. Again and again beating down on it. All the time he's trying to rip your throat out with his claws and his teeth. Just when you think after the fiftieth or the eightieth or the hundredth blow you've done it - he can jump back up from the dead and surprise you! That's how Maureen lost her fingers. Swore she'd never touch badger again. Just use the Chippy from now on. Except on Fridays when it got busy and wasn't worth the stares she got."

"The "Chippy"?" asked Sam.

"Yes the Chippy. Haven't you got one? A bit of battered fish and some chips. Nice hot cheap meal."

"No I can't say I've heard of such an establishment."

Colin licked his lips. "I'd love some fish and chips right now. I think it's my favourite meal. Tell you what! When this is all over and we can I'll buy you a bag of fish and chips from our Chippy. You won't find any better."

Sam smiled quite touched. "I look forward to it."

"That's a deal then," said Colin happily. He continued with the story. "But deep down she missed her badger meat. When Frank went to see her she agreed to help him on a terrible condition."

"That he'd hand over Brian?" suggested Sam.

"Yes," replied Colin. "In return for killing every last one of the interlopers she wanted Brian served up on a platter – with a full accompaniment of root vegetables."

"Did Frank do it?"

"For two days and nights he didn't sleep struggling with the choice he had. Should he save his beloved forest or should he spare Brian - even though he only had a few years left anyway? But it was Brian? But those bastards! Every day another tree. How many rabbits, hares, pheasants and squirrels? What about the deer? What if they discovered venison? He would have to agree to her demand. It was Brian on one side and everything else on the other. On a dark moonless night the deal was struck. She would sort the people out the next night and have Brian delivered the night after that."

"How did she do it? Kill all those people?" asked Sam.

"In a way I don't think she intended," said Colin luring him in by stopping.

Sam stopped walking turning to face him.

"She flew into their camp on her broom brandishing a bit of stick she called a wand. She landed muttering something under her breath when one of the men grabbed her knocking the wand out of her hand. "Hold on!" he says. "You're the cow that keeps pushing in at the Chippy? You are aren't ya?" She's more interested in trying to retrieve her wand. Before she knows it she's surrounded by all of them. Then you have to see it from their point of view. Beady black eyes? Smelling with her tongue? Drinking tea made from frog's eyes? Owning a broom but her place was a tip? The evidence was overwhelming. They tied her to a stake gathering all the wood they had around her. Then they lit it! But they were in for a shock! She didn't just burn she exploded! It was like she was made of gunpowder! Everything in a mile radius was flattened. All the people! All the trees! Even Frank's home with him in it! Everything! The only thing that survived was Brian in his underground set. After that they always called it Maureen's Moor."

"You'd have thought they would have named it after Brian because he was the one that survived," said Sam.

"Brian only survived for another night," said Colin grimly. "On the night he was due to be delivered he was found dead outside his set surrounded by an accompaniment of root vegetables -" he paused for effect, "with two of his claws missing!"

"Oh yes?" asked Sam sneering. "Who found Brian? I thought everyone had been blown up? It sounds like a made up story. But that isn't!" He pointed excitedly. "If I'm not mistaken I do believe that is a mill!"

Colin smacked him on the back. "I do believe you're right!"

They both began hurrying towards it.

# CHAPTER 25

# Damn!

Crow was meeting Raven in a secluded scab of woodland that was their emergency contact point. She wore her hooded robe and Raven wore his. Sam had been told incorrectly there were only two of them in the country. In fact there were twelve with Raven's possessing more power than Crow's.

"I want rid of it without getting any shit on my hands. What do you propose?" Raven said angrily.

Crow was grateful to have her face covered so Raven could not see the angry resentment she felt.

"Well?" asked Raven.

This project was the big one for her. The one that would allow her to join "them". "Them" - the few that actually ran things. Now one of "them" was telling her to end it all? Just because a lousy bookkeeper was taking a little bit longer to apprehend than they'd expected? It was pathetic. If he was typical of "them" then they didn't deserve to be running things. Perhaps the force that had put them there was spent. They'd grown lazy on their fathers' backs whilst she'd been on her back having to earn what they'd inherited. She wanted to kill him. She wanted to tie him to a tree and stone him to death.

"You want to put a stop to the whole thing?" she asked calmly.

"You were told to find a clever way of hiding the money I was planning to make. At no point did I mention topping off every bookkeeper you sort help from to do it! What on earth made you think that was a good idea?" demanded Raven.

"Tying up loose ends properly. I was being thorough."

"Thorough?" shouted Raven. "I like making money! I like keeping my money! I don't like ghosts haunting me! I like a good night's sleep!"

Crow was really tempted to tear off his hood to tell him what a cock he was!

"It's still something you can make a lot of money from. I have put too much into this to just let it go." She was inwardly struggling to remain calm but she would do whatever it took to get through their meeting with him believing he was still in charge.

"You should of thought of that before pretending you were Boudica running your chariot through my plans!"

This was unwelcome startling news to Crow. "But Boudica was a woman!" she said.

"Don't try and be clever! It obviously doesn't suit you. I know you're a woman. I don't know how you do the voice. Under that hood you could be talking through a duck's arse for all I care." Exasperated he walked away. His black robe billowing out like an angry thundercloud. He turned shouting louder. "I picked a woman because she wouldn't leave a trail of dead bodies! I thought she'd be clever. I thought she'd be sly. This was something that would suit the gentle touch of a woman. Why did you do it? Why did you go against nature?"

"So how would you have done it? Who do you think you are?" she asked needing to know who he was to begin her revenge.

"Don't take me for some clumsy fool who'll let things slip when he's angry! You don't know who I am and that's how it will remain! You got carried away with your own importance. You got careless." He stopped to whistle loudly for his horse. It came over to him instantly. He began to mount. "Did you see that? She's a mare. She does what she's told."

He got himself comfortable in his saddle making Crow wait almost daring her to say something. "You won't see me again. This is put to bed. I'm finished with you. You will leave the two robes where I told you to find them by sunset tomorrow." He leant down towards her looking like the grim reaper. "Make any further trouble or attempt to steal my robes then I'll have you sorted out in the way you seem to like so much."

He snapped the reins and left her. She watched him go letting her body begin to tremble with rage. She knew how the trembling would stop when he was gone – with an almighty scream to the heavens. When it was out of her she flopped down on a grass hummock to think. She reached down picking up a stone pulling up the sleeve to examine it in her hand. Her practised eye told her exactly how it would behave in the air. She turned it over. Then dropped it. Just like that. It landed without a sound. It was only a small stone after all. Quite useless unless she decided to pick it up again. Looking down at it she knew without question that she no longer had a boss.

Then her thoughts turned to Nightnurse. Something unexpected had happened there. She'd taken him as a lover because he was useful but unlike any previous lover she had fallen for him. Hadn't it been delicious to have the hands of death and the tool of life exploring her in ways she had never been explored? Hadn't it made her feel a woman and a monster at the same time? Hadn't it been wonderful to look into those dark malevolent eyes at the point of letting go and recognise herself in those glorious fireworks? And then do it again. And again until they had nothing hidden from each other about their true nature. She didn't need "them" she had "him".

She looked around making sure no-one was about. It was very unlikely that's why they met there. Satisfied she slowly removed the hood exposing the bandages she had wrapped over the top of her head. There was nothing wrong with her but she had had an idea. She didn't understand how the robe allowed you to "know things" but did understand that Raven's robe was superior. She had hoped by wearing the bandages she could keep things "hidden" from him. What she hadn't expected was when she'd asked, "Who do you think you are?" her robe had let her know. She now knew that Raven was Lord Tig. She was also sure he didn't know she knew.


Raven's black robe billowed out behind him as he rode. He abruptly pulled up his horse just before he hit the turnpike dismounting snatching at the robe irritably. He obviously wasn't going to ride all the way back wearing it. It wouldn't be clever wearing a disguise that shouted disguise. Lord Tig was too clever for that. There was no doubt in his mind about how clever he was. But he had been bloody stupid this time!

He roughly folded the robe shoving it into a small satchel hanging from his saddle. He was about to remount when he stopped hitching his horse instead to a nearby tree. He pulled out a pipe from his jacket preparing it for a smoke. He sat down on a conveniently fallen branch puffing on his pipe like a little thinking engine. There was no-one watching but if there had been they would instinctively know here was a troubled man.

His thoughts turned to the previous evening and the private business dinner he had attended. It had begun badly. The cat of the host's mistress had jumped up on the table proceeding to wash itself thoroughly in full view.

"Excuse me gentlemen whilst I remove this muff from our midst," said the host picking it up by the scruff of its neck.

"Not where one's trying to eat," said Henry looking disdainfully at the bag of hanging fur. Henry! What a waste of space he is! thought Lord Tig puffing on his pipe.

"Useful on board ship though or on a farmyard – keep the rats down," suggested William in the general defence of felines. William! Wouldn't trust him to warm the bed without setting fire to it! thought Lord Tig regarding the glowing tobacco in his pipe when he breathed in.

The host opened the dining room door throwing out the cat into the hallway. "I hate the way he always lands on his feet. One day I might try bouncing it off the ceiling to see if he still lands on his feet then! Danielle wouldn't be very pleased. But then again Danielle doesn't need to know!" He shut the door.

"So we're here to discuss our strange French doctor?" said Henry carefully cutting off some fat from his piece of lamb.

"In what way is he strange?" asked William.

"He means," said the host answering for Henry, "he's not a reliable lantern to use in a dark alley."

"Sorry?" asked William.

The host picked up his knife and fork. "Henry you tell him what he did at Hyde's."

"Hyde? Whose Hyde?" asked William.

"It doesn't matter. Just listen!" snapped the host.

Reluctantly Henry put down his knife and fork. "Hyde is someone I know who could produce the stuff here. For various reasons it makes sense to have a production capacity here in England. I took the doctor to meet Hyde over dinner. Except Hyde's very attractive wife joined us unexpectedly. The doctor was all over her like a rash. Then she excuses herself feeling ill. The doctor quickly follows her out to see if he can help. Hyde and I carry on talking for the rest of dinner when a servant arrives to whisper something in his ear. He jumps up all excited flying out. I'm left alone so get up to enjoy a view of the grounds from the window where a minute later I see the doctor's naked buttocks glistening in the moonlight as he flees across the lawn!"

"What had he done?" asked William. "Had he been in the wine cellar?"

The host gave a hearty contemptuous laugh. "William you're priceless!"

Lord Tig reluctantly stepped in. "For a husband there is a worse room to find an uninvited guest than the cellar."

"Not just their bedroom! All over the house! In the space of a few hours!" The host found it highly amusing.

"Well Hyde has obviously pulled out. Says he can't work with someone like that. So there it is." Henry picked up his knife and fork.

"Shame that – you know – it – pops up to complicates things," said William.

The host shook his head. "I really don't know William if you're a saint or a fool."

Henry put down his knife and fork. "I like Hyde. It's a shame his wife has more masts take refuge in her harbour than Portsmouth. But that's not really for us to make fun of is it?"

Lord Tig wanted to get on with business. "So it will always be whilst there are dogs who can't ignore a well chewed bone. The loss of our own production capacity is what is of relevance here gentlemen."

"I'm afraid there's something else you should all know," said Henry. "Hyde did find out how the doctor produces Wank. It's not what we expected."

"It's bosom sweat from Scandinavian girls! I mean that's what he's been charging a fortune for!" said the host slamming down a glass of red wine.

Henry looked down at his plate. "Not quite."

"What's he been doing then? Because there's something in those bottles!" demanded the host.

Henry took a deep breath well aware they were all watching him intently. "They put a female moose in a sauna and scrape the sweat off her teats."

The host writhed in his chair as though some annoying insect had suddenly crawled under his clothes pulling out a bottle of Wank. He looked at it disgustingly in his hand before throwing it into the fireplace.

"What's a sauna?" asked William.

"A very hot room," explained Henry.

Lord Tig shook his head. "He's not been telling the truth but he's not been lying either."

The others looked at him.

"It is the fluid from a Scandinavian female," Lord Tig pointed out.

They nodded in tacit agreement. Henry continued. "The problem is the moose doesn't survive the sauna."

"What's important about that? He can sell the meat can't he?" asked the host.

Lord Tig enlightened them. "Because it's unsustainable. Daddy moose need mommy moose to make baby moose. You only need one male to make lots of babies. It doesn't work the other way round. I would rather they were sticking a male in there and scraping it off his testicles. What a stupidly short-sighted thing to do!"

"But they've got more moose up there than a cat's got fleas!" said the host.

Henry shook his head. "For now. But unless you bred them specifically - which would take a lot of time and money - then this isn't a viable long-term business."

Lord Tig let them sit in silence letting the disappointing news sink in.

Presently he spoke. "Which begs the question - how was the crazy bastard going to make the after shave?" He hadn't expected an answer but William surprised him.

"Oh I know!" said William.

"You? How do you know? You don't know anything about production," said Henry.

"But I can put on a good spread. When the doctor came to my house he was eating and chatting away like a good 'un. I couldn't grasp all of it with his funny accent. Then I showed him my wine cellar and he loved it! Joked that for ten of the best bottles in there he would give up his biggest secret. I told him to take his pick and he told me how he was going to make the after shave. I was a bit disappointed actually. I wanted to know how to make a good baguette."

"So why haven't you told us this before?" asked Henry.

"It's never come up before!"

"Didn't you think it might be important?" asked Henry.

"Well I can tell you now."

"I can't believe you haven't brought this up before," said Henry.

"Fool," said the host. "I've decided you're a fool."

William looked confused.

"Gentlemen. Are you going to let this man tell you or not? Or would you prefer to harangue him unnecessarily for a bit longer?" asked Lord Tig.

Gratefully relieved William told them. "He used some words I didn't understand. He was quite excited as he was pulling out the bottles - but I think he said he was going to open a chain of - launderettes? where ladies could get their underwear cleaned. But he was going to keep the water they used and - distil it?"

The host looked at Henry solemnly. "How much were you in for again?"

"Too much. You?" replied Henry unhappily covering his head with his hands.

"The same."

"Well that's taught us a lesson then," said Henry not gloating, not pleased, not anything.

"Does that mean I've lost my money then?" asked William innocently.

"Yes it does," said the host. He turned to Lord Tig. "Sorry old chap. You win some you lose some. Would you let your friend know for us?"

Lord Tig shook his head. "Not this time. He doesn't know I'm involved."

The host nodded. "Well he's a good chap. He'll understand when I tell him. Of course you can disassemble the administration you were constructing now Adolf*. And you Henry. No need to investigate production capacity any longer."

Lord Tig sat there surprised at the thought running through his head. There was a bookkeeper right now on the run whose life had been turned upside down for something they weren't going to progress any further. Could he make amends? Could he atone himself in some small way with the man?" He reached for his glass. Nah! Stuff him! They were out of pocket for thousands of guineas believing a crazy French doctor! How did that compare to an inkpot scratcher? What really began gnawing at him then was the decision he'd made. Why the bloody hell had he chosen a woman? How bloody stupid had that been? Not only that! A woman pretending to be a man? Was there anything more likely to let you down?

"It's not just the money of course," said Henry. "There is the matter of the elephant in the room."

"Oh my God yes," said the host. "He doesn't take bad news well does he?"

"Colonel Peru?" asked William.

"So he is involved?" asked Lord Tig.

"I'm afraid so," replied the host.

"And whose bright idea was that?" asked Lord Tig.

"Mine," replied the host not looking at him.

"Well it was nice knowing you. You like daffodils don't you? I'll plant some on your grave next time I visit you. Thank you for dinner. Good evening gentlemen."

The host stood up holding up his glass to propose a toast. "Gentlemen! We lost this one. But here's to the next adventure!"

That was the spirit! That's what made them special. They wouldn't give in! Lord Tig stayed to join in the toast then left. They would commiserate by getting pissed but he wanted the matter closed. He had a meeting to quickly arrange and get over with.

Lord Tig was back to the present tapping out the last of the tobacco on the heel of his boot having had his meeting. He was no longer troubled. She'd been told what to do. As far as he was concerned  that was the end of the matter.

* Lord Tig's first name

# CHAPTER 26

## Hit and Run

Catherine de Barnes hitherto known as Crow was surprised to see Nightnurse sitting in the chair waiting for her. "I didn't request your presence. What are you doing here?" she asked him coldly.

Nightnurse languidly turned to face her. "I was wondering how you got on so I decided to pop over and see."

"No-one comes here without my invitation. Do you understand?" Her eyes glowed like polished ebony the way he liked so much.

"Arrhh," he mocked. "Are you still annoyed at being beaten at your throwing game?"

She glanced at the china figures still there remembering what had happened. He'd picked out four stones bouncing them in his left hand. I don't like that one's hat. Bam! His arm flicked like a scorpion's tail and the hat was gone. When the figure had stopped rocking he asked if that one of hers was pointing at him? Bam! The figure no longer had a hand. That's an ugly face. Bam! That figure no longer had a head. That basket looks a bit heavy. Let's help her with it. Bam! The figure's basket was gone. Then he'd turned to her smiling. "I imagine you've been throwing stones since you were a girl? Let me tell you – when I was born I made a slingshot out of my umbilical cord!" She'd hated being beaten but she loved to see such ability in a man.

"There's no way I'm doing what the pig wants," she confided in him. "This is too good to let go!"

"You've been building a machine. But how will you run it with no levers?" asked Nightnurse taking out his pipe.

She snarled at him like a cat cornered. "What I've constructed is good enough to do anything! I'll use it for something else! You just watch me!"

He watched her pace up and down like a cat itching to get her claws into something. Her long raven hair shimmering in anger. Her body a beautiful bow bent on action.

"Why do you want to rule the world? Why not be less ambitious but much happier? Why not buy a bit of sun rather than try to make a sun?"

She stopped pacing looking at him. "What do you mean?"

Nightnurse lit his pipe first before replying. "Rob them. They're all very rich. Kill them if you want whilst you rob them if it makes you happier. But rob them. Then with the money buy yourself an island in the sun. When everyone you hate are all shivering in November you'll be swimming in a turquoise sea." He proffered out his pipe for her to smoke.

She padded over warily reaching for it. He grabbed her scooping her into his lap. "This is no climate to grow old in. Why should you if you don't have to?" he asked squeezing her.

"Would you help me?" she purred.

"Of course that's my job." He took a drag on the pipe.

"How much does an island cost?" she asked clearly liking the idea.

"Depends on how big an island you want," said Nightnurse handing her the pipe.

She took a long slow thoughtful drag breathing it out slowly. "We'll rob them all to be on the safe side. I think there are five of them. I've got one name. Give me a few days and I'll get the others. And what they've got worth stealing!"

"Pick up the scent and track it back to where its hiding. Hunting is simple in essence."

She briefly examined his face with her large feline eyes before suddenly throwing away his pipe. He heard it snap as it hit the wall but he didn't care. She was a ball of desire and fury so hot he needed oven gloves to handle her!

Afterwards she produced a rug and a new pipe from somewhere. They talked and smoked lying naked on the rug. Them doing what they wanted to do was all that mattered. They could do it too. Between them they had everything they needed. No-one could stop them! "Hit and run" she called it. They made love again to celebrate their partnership. A far stronger way to seal their bond than any document signed and witnessed. Then they began in earnest. She gave him the name. He would leave immediately. She would send a magpie for Hammer and Chisel to meet him there also deciding Nightnurse would have to "fire" Hammer and Chisel at some point. She would do what she needed to joining him on the road as soon as she could. He warned her about packing any "stupid ornaments" when she packed her things and left.

# CHAPTER 27

## Honey is sweeter than beef dripping

"Well that was a ride and half," said Chisel to Hammer. They were hidden lying prone at the base of a hedge near an impressive house. They had left their horses in a small copse creeping the last hundred yards or so on foot. "Do you think this is it?"

"We can hardly ask them can we? Er excuse me is this Lord Adolph Tig's residence? We're a couple of handymen come heavies that have been instructed to meet a very effective assassin here. What do you think? Shall I ring the bell?"

Chisel looked at Hammer disdainfully. "I shall forgive you that bout of sarcasm because like I say it's bin a long ride."

"Don't you talk to me like a wife telling off her husband!" hissed Hammer.

"Cor blimey! You are touchy! Have you ran out of goose fat for your piles?" said Chisel a bit taken aback.

"I haven't got piles!" said Hammer looking away.

Chisel looked away too wondering what to do. After a few seconds he said quietly, "well I've got some goose fat with me if you need it for anything."

Hammer didn't say or do anything at first but then whispered, "thank you."

"Do you want it now? I can go back to the horses and get it?"

Hammer held up his hand indicating that he was grateful for the offer but didn't want to linger any more on the subject.

Chisel felt a bit clumsy. To avoid an uncomfortable silence he wracked his brains for something to say. "I bet that house has an inside bath."

"What?" asked Hammer reaching underneath him to adjust a tool in his apron digging in.

"That house looks big enough to have an inside bath. I put one in myself once. A Lady Marmaduke. By all accounts she used it as a honey tub for officers."

Hammer stopped observing the house through the hedge resting his head on his hand to face Chisel. "How on earth could a bath be used as a honey tub?"

"Well she was a good looking woman was Lady Marmaduke. And if you were lucky she'd run you a bath showing you herself how all the plumbing worked. Her husband the silly sod thought that's all she was doing."

"How do you know all this?" asked Hammer.

"I was having to fix it all the time! It was obvious pipework were taking an hammering in there!"

Hammer looked a little sad. "Shame isn't it? How far do you have to go to find a faithful wife?"

"I think mine was faithful," said Chisel.

"That's because she smelt of swarf," said Hammer.

"Nothing wrong will the smell of swarf. Show's she knows a thing or two about metal."

Hammer unhappily rolled onto his front. "In my experience the more you do for them the less happy they get. Until you find out the gardener she wanted is not only ruining your herbaceous border but pottering about in your bedroom as well!"

Chisel had been digging in the flowerbeds of other men's gardens for years. Poor creatures left at home feeling lonely and neglected whilst their husbands were away. What purpose did it serve to let any flower wilt in such a way? Anyway men and women were often dishonest with each other planting gardens neither had any intention of staying in.

"Marriage is a complicated game. Some follow the rules to the letter and others like to break them when they play."

"Cheat you mean!" said Hammer taking out his eyeglass.

"Following rules can get a bit boring can't it? When I was young I was told if you play a game you should play it properly or not bother. But then you find out that the winners are always bending rules. And there's a bigger game of not being found out. That makes any game more exciting. We all have to find the games we're happy to play in the way we wish. When there's work to be done work we must. But when there's not we can play! What is work and what is play is the hard bit we must work out for ourselves."

Hammer rolled on his side to face him. "Well if you forgive me – that sounds like a recipe for chaos."

Chisel pushed himself up onto his knees spreading out his arms. "And all this is organised I suppose?"

"Get down you thick Brummie Git!" snapped Hammer. "Remember what we're doing!"

Chisel lay back down. He felt he needed to say something. "I'm sorry your wife did that to you. But you know I was never green fingered with her."

Hammer snatched the eyeglass away from his face. "Good God Chisel! Of course I know that! – She was a cow not a lunatic!"

"What's that supposed to mean?" asked Chisel pulling on his arm stopping him replace the eyeglass.

"She couldn't understand a word you said and hated the sight of you! Now let go," said Hammer tugging his arm away.

If he'd turned to look at Chisel's face he would have enjoyed it. His brow furrowed trying to retrieve something with a hook when what he really needed was a net.

"I never liked her either," he said.

"Well that makes two of us at the end then doesn't it?" said Hammer surveying the house with his eyeglass.

There was something else Chisel decided he needed to say. "You might have shagged like a lion but afterwards you could feel lower than a kitchen cat," he said quietly.

"Can you hear that?" asked Hammer.

There was a noise coming from the other side of the hedge down to their right. It was where the long drive of the house joined the main road.

"Does that sound like.." began Hammer.

"A mob! It can't be? What on earth..."

Hammer irritably waved his hand for Chisel to shut up and listen. It was. There was the sound of footsteps, raised voices, metal implements clanging and the very specific whoosh sound of burning torches.

"It's a bright sunny afternoon! What is it with the torches?" asked Chisel. "I really don't get it!"

"Come on Chisel! It's not a proper mob without torches! But what's a mob doing here now?"

"Do you think we should go?" asked Chisel trying to work out how many they sounded.

"No we're well hidden. Let's see what's going on."

The mob came into view marching up the drive. There were about twenty of them all carrying either a pitchfork, shovel or torch. What looked to be the ringleader was carrying something else though. It looked to be a large jar of honey. Chisel silently pointed this out to Hammer who nodded to indicate he'd seen it.

The mob reached the front door. The ringleader stepped forward shouting out. "May the master of the house show himself so justice may be done upon him!" The mob cheered clattering their metal things aloft.

The front door remained firmly shut.

"May the master of the house show himself and justice be done upon him!" shouted the ringleader again.

Still the door remained firmly shut.

The ringleader turned to the mob. "Right. Whoever's got an axe come forward!"

There was a lot of murmuring and head turning but no axe apparently.

"Nobody's brought an axe!" cried the ringleader.

"Thought it was a bit unnecessary!" one of the mob shouted.

"Didn't want things getting out of hand!" said someone else.

"What sort of mob is this?" whispered Chisel to Hammer.

"Fair enough!" said the ringleader. "Well has anyone got a horn or a drum or something loud like that?"

There was a lot of murmuring and head turning but nothing noisy came forward.

"Ring the doorbell!" someone shouted in a Brummie accent.

"Chisel what are you bleeding doing? Stay out of it!" hissed Hammer giving him a clout. Chisel covered his mouth stifling his laughter.

"Yes ring the doorbell! Ring the doorbell!" chanted the mob.

The ringleader strode up to the front door giving the doorbell a hefty pull.

The ringleader turned to the mob. "Not long now. We'll soon have justice. Just as soon as someone answers the door."

The door remained firmly shut.

"Ring it again!" one of the mob shouted.

"Hold on! Give 'em a chance. It's a big house!" said someone else.

"Come on! It's been long enough now. Ring it again!"

"My torch is going out. Anybody else's torch going out?"

"How much fat did you put on it?"

"It's not the fat! It's how he's holding it. Look at how he's holding it!"

"Come on ! Ring it again!"

The ringleader held up his tub of honey. "Wait! I hear footsteps!"

The mob fell quiet.

"I can't hear anything!"

"Of course you won't under that hood! What did you wear a hood for? That could be seen as very provocative. You do know you're the only one wearing a hood!"

"No I'm not. Jack's got a hood on!"

There was a loud "Sssshhhh you berk!" from Jack presumably.

"Silence!" shouted the ringleader. "The door is being opened!"

It was. The sound of bolts being undone was followed by the door slowly opening. The mob waited patiently.

"Good morning gentleman. Can I help you?" said a very well dressed servant.

"And ladies! There are ladies present too you pompous pig!"

The ringleader turned to someone in the mob. "Come on June there's no need for that."

"Justice!" shrieked June. "We want justice! We want justice! We want justice!"

The ringleader held up his hands for the chanting to stop which it did very quickly allowing him to say, "Call forth your master so that justice may be done upon him."

"I'm afraid that is not possible sir. He is away looking at guns in London."

A worried murmur passed through the mob.

"He's lying!" someone shouted.

"I beg to differ! Lying is not in my make-up. The master is indeed away in London. As if we didn't already have enough guns to clean."

"Do you promise me you're telling the truth? You're not just trying to frighten us?" asked the ringleader.

"I'm insulted sir that you needed to ask that."

"Nibbard's a good egg! He wouldn't lie to us!" one of the mob shouted.

"So your name's Nibbard is it?" asked the ringleader.

"Indeed it is sir."

"Can you give your master a message from us on his return from London?"

"Indeed I can sir."

"Can you tell him that the tenants aren't happy with the rent increases this year? It's got to stop. It's the sixth year in a row. Would you tell him in the strongest terms you can Nibbard please?"

"I will of course. But I will need every one of your names. He will demand to know who was it formed a mob on his drive."

"I told you! You all thought me and Jack were being stupid but now who's sorry?"

"You'll be sorry if you don't stop pointing me out you blitherin' idiot!" shouted an unhappy Jack.

"This is rubbish!" shrieked June. "We knew this would happen! Nibbard here is not going to deliver a message. He's going to be the message! Come on girls!"

The mob spat out June and four female accomplishes from its centre. They were carrying ropes, stakes and a hammer.

Nibbard tried to shut the door but the ringleader quickly put his foot in the doorway to stop him. "Sorry old bean. I'm quite curious to see what they're going to do."

"Give me that!" said June snatching the tub of honey from the ringleader. "A token of friendship my arse! Do you know what we're going to do with this? We'll bloody show you what we're going to do with this! Get him on the lawn girls!"

"Ladies. Ladies. I really must protest. This is most unbecoming," wailed Nibbard uselessly.

The accomplishes carried Nibbard to the nearest bit of grass. The mob watched curious and apprehensive.

They were now closer to Hammer and Chisel who were watching open-mouthed.

"Now stake him down!" ordered June.

The accomplishes soon had Nibbard staked to the ground with his arms and legs spread out. Though he wriggled and pulled he was utterly at their mercy.

"Now cut his clothes off!" ordered June.

"What are you going to do?" implored the ringleader.

"Shut it softie! You had your chance!" said June leaving no-one in doubt who was in charge now.

The accomplishes produced small pocket knives proceeding to cut poor Nibbard bare.

"How does that feel Nibbard?" taunted June standing over him.

"You wait. You wait you ruffians. You wait until the master hears of this!"

"Oh that sounds a bit sour. You need something to sweeten you up a bit. Something to make you less tart." She was unscrewing the tub of honey as she spoke. She turned to the mob. "Shall I?"

"No! Set fire to him!" someone shouted in a Brummie accent.

There was a gasp of horror from everyone present including June. "I don't know who said that but you need to look inside yourself!" She turned to reassure Nibbard. "Don't worry. Your life's not in danger. Your willy's out for all to see but we wouldn't set fire to you."

"Do your worst!" said Nibbard defiantly.

"Do it June! Do it June! Do it June!" chanted the mob.

"Treacle that bastard!"

"Let the master find a message on his lawn he'll never forget!"

"Suck on his sausage roll! He'll hate that!" someone shouted in a Brummie accent.

June paused clearly wondering whether it was worth going through the mob to find whoever it was saying such horrible things.

"I'm telling you Chisel. You're pretty good at throwing your voice but a couple of them have started looking over here." warned Hammer.

June poured out the honey over Nibbard. "Tell your master from us his golden days are over."

"Never! He's right! You can suck on my sausage roll!"

"Oh Nibbard. I didn't know you had it in you! You feisty fool. But my work here is done." She bent down giving him a kiss on his forehead. "Oh that tastes much better! Good luck you lap dog!" She stood up. "It's only a suggestion. But I think it would be a good idea if we all got out of here right now!"

The mob followed her lead down the path and out of sight.

"Now there's a sweet lady." It was Nightnurse standing right over them.

"Good afternoon Nightnurse." Hammer hoped he had masked his surprise seeing him.

"Mister Hammer. Mister Chisel. Good afternoon to both of you. Who said the only worthwhile entertainment was in the West End? But are we to gather that the master is not at home?"

"He's in London getting another gun. Should have gone to Birmingham," said Chisel getting up slowly.

"You think our sweet naked friend over there is telling the truth then?" asked Hammer getting up.

"Nibbard wasn't it? - I wonder," said Nightnurse rubbing his chin. "You two stay here."

Nightnurse expertly slunk around the hedge.

"Do you think he'll kill him?" whispered Chisel.

"I'm not sure I want to watch this," said Hammer. "To see him do what he does in broad daylight."

Peering through the hedge they both watched as Nightnurse kneeled down talking to Nibbard expecting at any second some fatal blow to befall the poor fellow that had done nothing more than answer his front door.

They seemed to be talking an awful lot. Hammer and Chisel began to get bored watching. Finally, Nightnurse stood up taking out his dagger.

"This is it," whispered Chisel. "He's gonna do it now."

Nightnurse leant down cutting through the ropes releasing Nibbard from his bondage. Nibbard got up shaking Nightnurse's hand profusely in thanks. Then remarkably they embraced like long lost friends.

"Well I've seen everything now," said Chisel looking at Hammer. "What do you make of that?"

Nibbard ran back towards the house whilst Nightnurse slinked back to them behind the hedge.

"It's only Naughty Nibbard!" said Nightnurse happily. "We were best friends as kids! What are the chances of that?" It was the most human rather than resembling a machine they had ever seen him. "That felt so good. Come on gentlemen. It's obvious I'm meant to do this!"

Hammer and Chisel let him walk off a little way.

"I think he's more frightening when he seems nice," whispered Chisel.

Hammer looked concerned. "I feel another ride coming on. When you get an opportunity will you let me have a bit of your goose fat?"

"What are friends for?" asked Chisel smiling warmly. Then the smile abruptly left him, "But I'm not rubbing it in!"

# CHAPTER 28

## Plenty more fish in the sea

Natalie was sitting in the saloon area of the Chestnuts. She'd eaten breakfast gone for a short stroll returned because it was very warm eaten lunch had a nap and now sat waiting for the return of Sam and Colin. There had been no-one else other than the landlord coming and going until a handsome man about her age had strolled in. He ordered a drink then came across asking if she minded if he sat down?

"It's a free country," said Natalie.

"I sometimes wonder," he said giving her a lovely smile.

A woman would have to be made of stone to not feel a ball of energy arrive from somewhere at such a smile. "My name is Natalie. What's yours?"

He held out his hand clearly comfortable in his own skin. "Phillip. Pleased to meet you Natalie."

"Do you like horses?" she asked him. "That's what your name means – lover of horses."

"Now I didn't know that," he said smiling. It was clearly very easy for him to smile.

"I do! I think I've found out today just walking one up the lane."

"You didn't go to the mad blacksmith did you?" asked Phillip in mock horror.

"I did!" she replied very pleased.

"Well you're a lucky girl. He usually eats his customers!"

Natalie looked shocked.

"I'm joking I'm joking!" laughed Phillip. He suddenly stopped laughing with something important to tell her. "It's the miller you've got to watch out for!"

Natalie sprang to her feet. "I've got to warn them!"

Phillip laughed pleasantly. "I'm joking I'm joking! The landlord told me your master has gone to see him."

His smile was like a lighthouse light - something safe but it did mean danger was nearby.

She sat back down. "They've gone to see him about buying some horses."

"Oh I see," said Phillip. "See a man about a dog."

"No dog. Just two horses."

Phillip was about to explain it was just an expression then realised he'd be wasting his time. "He's an unusual man is Burt." He took a leisurely sip of his pint.

"What's unusual about him?"

Phillip beamed. "You want to know unusual? Let me tell you about Trevor. Now he *is* unusual!"

He didn't wait for Natalie to agree.

"I think there are several ways you can judge a man - what he does for a living - how he treats his wife if he has one - his children if he has any - But perhaps a really good way is to study what he chooses to do in his spare time."

"Spare time?" asked Natalie as though the concept was foreign to her. "What does Trevor like to do in his spare time?"

"Ah well it's what he used to do. He was stopped eventually. The locals thought it inappropriate for the church."

"What exactly was he doing at church?"

Phillip suddenly felt he might be attending a job interview rather than trying to chat up an attractive lady in a bar but he persevered. "He was sneaking in just before they shut the doors."

"That doesn't sound inappropriate," said Natalie.

"He'd be wearing a bonnet."

"So? I wear men's boots to mop out the backyard."

"And a shawl."

"Perhaps it was cold in there and he couldn't afford a proper coat."

"And tights."

"Builders will wear women's tights under their trousers to keep themselves warm in winter."

"And a dress! How many builders do you know wear a dress?" asked Phillip annoyed at her quick sensible responses. She was supposed to find the story amusing not be dissecting it!

But Natalie had heard enough for her conclusions. "I think it's strange behaviour but not inappropriate. He might have lots of sisters for instance. He might be the only man in the house. They might be too poor to buy man clothes so he has to share theirs."

Phillip decided she was attractive enough to try one more time. "I couldn't agree more. You should wear whatever you feel comfortable in." He sipped his pint thinking quickly. "It's what he used to do on the back row I think they found inappropriate."

"Singing too loudly?" suggested Natalie.

"It involved the singing yes."

"Getting the words wrong and putting everybody off?" suggested Natalie.

Phillip regarded her. "You're never stuck for something to say are you?"

She looked at him suspiciously. "You make it sound like a bad thing."

He shook his head. "No! Far from it! That wasn't my intention at all. I think a beautiful woman with a wonderful mind is probably the finest thing there is in nature." He gave her a lovely smile to indicate he meant it. "It's a very rare thing of course!" he added cheekily.

Far from rebuking him in some way as he expected she nodded.

"You don't think that's an odd thing for me to say?" he asked at a loss.

"No," she replied. "Beauty is a rare thing in nature. Most of it is savage and cruel. We're the only ones with a chance to make sense of it all."

Phillip picked up his pint drawing the conclusion he was wasting his time with this one. It was a shame because she was lovely. But he had no interest when there were plenty of others far less complicated.

"So what was he doing?" asked Natalie when he wasn't forthcoming with any more.

"It's not important." He'd finish his pint then try his luck at the Three Horseshoes.

"So what was Trevor doing on the back row in a dress and bonnet the locals found inappropriate?" asked Natalie.

"Can't you guess?" he asked amazed.

"Guess?" she repeated as another foreign concept to her.

He abruptly got up. He hated leaving an unfinished pint but he had to. "See you Frank!" he shouted towards the landlord. He left as quickly as he could feeling very confused.

Natalie suddenly felt quite alone not understanding how the man had wanted to leave when they appeared to be getting on so well.

# CHAPTER 29

## Snakes and Ladders

The three of them were riding abreast which was unusual as normally Nightnurse rode out in front deep in his own thoughts. They hadn't seen much traffic on the road and even when they did it seemed to get out of their way well in advance of their approach. Nightnurse's horse seemed to have this sort of projection that beamed out keep away there's more bull in me than horse. He was a big black intimidating hulk of a beast. Chisel could sense his own horse wary of him being so close. But Nightnurse had been the most convivial they had ever known him. From the beginning of the journey he had placed Velmax (his horse's name short for Velocity Maximum) between the two of them talking about his childhood! Chisel had liked this new Nightnurse almost warming to him but Hammer had been more reticent. He was naturally more wary than Chisel anyway but more pressing was the absence of goose fat that was so agonisingly close in Chisel's saddlebag. His contributions to the conversation had mostly been pressed one syllables.

Nightnurse was talking. "When I was a boy I thought girls were a nuisance. Only there to get in the way and have their hair pulled when they stamped their feet. As I got older I began to realise their hair was for stroking not pulling. There was treasure to be found in their chests! But a man cannot spend all of his time in their company so when I miss them I play a little game I invented."

"Does this game have a name?" asked Chisel.

"You're a mouthy Brummie Git! Why not suggest one now? That would be fun!" said Nightnurse turning in his saddle to face him.

Chisel was a little taken aback. Firstly, only Hammer was allowed to call him a Brummie Git! Secondly, Nightnurse had just used the word fun. He was quite sure Nightnurse was incapable of having fun. Cold ruthless satisfaction definitely but fun? And thirdly, Nightnurse was asking his advice? Nightnurse never asked for anything. "Er yes. But I need to know how you play this game?"

Nightnurse sat a little more upright in that cool assured manner of his.

"I am the only man trapped in room with all the attractive ladies I can think of. We discover we only have a few hours left to live. Everyone agrees we should spend our last precious hours making love. As the only man present it is up to me to do what I can."

Chisel took the risk of sneaking a worried look at Hammer who gave a little grimace back.

"I can't sleep with all of them of course so I've got to put them in some sort of order. So I ask them all to strip. Very often I can spend so long watching them do that that the game ends there. But if it doesn't then I have to arrange them with the most pleasing ones at the front and the unlucky ones at the back."

"What criteria do you use? Do you have a points system? Perhaps borrowing from a recognised methodology for accurately assessing conflicting factors to perform such an exercise?" asked Chisel.

Nightnurse turned to look at Hammer. "Did the thick Brummie Git just say that?"

"Yes."

"Are you alright?"

"Yes."

Nightnurse turned back to Chisel.

"I don't know why you're so surprised," said Chisel before he said anything, "there's a lot of other stuff needed in making things. It ain't just thumping things together."

Nightnurse nodded appreciatively. "So it seems."

"So what criteria do you use?"

"When I first started playing it was easy. The thing between my legs always thrust his opinion strongly into the debate and the bigger her buns the nearer the front of the queue she'd be. Now I'm older I find I consider other less obvious attributes. Can she be discrete for instance?"

"You mean you've matured. You need laughter - intelligent conversation - a breast to lay your head on - a gentle woman's touch to fill in the cracks of your wall?" suggested Chisel.

"Shut up you berk!" said Hammer in an unusually long sentence for him that afternoon.

"He's right Chisel," said Nightnurse almost regrettably. "After all these years it's still **BIG BUNS** that make this baker want to get out his rolling pin. Give me a couple of big baps and I've got the meat to make a lovely sandwich!"

Chisel found himself quite unpleasantly surprised at such a blunt remark.

"So what about a name then Chisel?" asked Nightnurse.

"Bap Bakery?" he suggested half-heartedly.

"Too boring! I've got an hour to kill I think I'll play "Bap Bakery". No that won't do. Think of another," ordered Nightnurse.

Chisel suggested another half-heartedly, "Loveline?"

Nightnurse looked coldly at him. "I don't love these women! I'm putting them in the right order to screw!"

Chisel didn't like glimpsing those dark eyes. This didn't feel like fun. This felt like come up with a good name or get stabbed. Desperately he rummaged in his toolbox to come up with something good. "Screwdriver!"

"Screwdriver?" repeated Nightnurse interested.

"Very useful tool is a screwdriver. Puts a man in control when he's got a good screwdriver in his hand," said Chisel trying to sell it.

"A screwdriver is a real thing? Have you got one? Can you show me a screwdriver?"

Chisel reached into his apron pulling out his best screwdriver. Nightnurse snatched it from him as though it were the key to a treasure chest. Chisel and Hammer secretly exchanged a baffled glance.

"You've never sin one before?" asked Chisel carefully.

"So how do you use it?" asked Nightnurse regarding it intently.

"May I?" asked Chisel holding out his hand.

Nightnurse handed it back to him watching as Chisel held it by the handle making a twisting motion with it.

"You do that to somebody's eyes? Their teeth? Or is it their arse? How do you get them to talk with it?" asked Nightnurse eagerly looking with those dark eyes from the screwdriver to him.

Chisel gulped. "No it's not like that. You screw things with it."

"You do that to a woman with it?" asked Nightnurse looking back at the screwdriver.

"No bits of wood and stuff. It's a hand tool not a weapon or a pleasure stick," said Chisel worried that Nightnurse might think he was toying with him.

"A pleasure stick?" repeated Nightnurse interested. "Are you saying you can get people to talk by doing something nice to them?"

Hammer closed his eyes wishing he could close his ears as well. Talk about unintended consequences. It should have been obvious to Chisel that Nightnurse was a killing machine that never switched off. Chisel had somehow spilt blood in the water and Nightnurse was homing in on it. Although his arse felt like it was in a toaster he had to intervene on behalf of his partner.

"Nightnurse if I may explain? I think there's been a misunderstanding. It always happens when dealing with thick Brummie gits. You screw screws with a screwdriver. Little bits of metal like nails. That's all that is. And nothing more."

"But he said it puts a man in control when he's got a good screwdriver in his hand," said Nightnurse not pleased.

"He meant you'll put things together well. - Not get what you want."

Nightnurse looked grim. "People! Each time I try to engage they let me down!"

He gave Velmax a dig with his heels. A couple of hours of bonding blowing away on the breeze.

When he was safely out in front on his own where he belonged Chisel put the wretched screwdriver away. "Thanks Hammer I owe you one," he said gratefully.

"You can pay me back now. Get that goose fat out. I could toast muffins with my arse!"

"Funny how it flares up. You're alright for months on end and then out the blue a grumpy sod that don't say much," said Chisel rummaging in his saddlebag.

"There's gratitude for you."

"Sorry. Didn't mean it like that. There you go." Chisel handed him a little round tin of goose fat.

"Do you mind riding ahead for a bit?" asked Hammer snatching it greedily.

"I ain't catching him up if that's what you mean!"

"Oh no don't! You leave him well alone for a bit! Just enough to give a man a little privacy."

Chisel obliged carrying on when Hammer brought his horse to a stop. He made sure there was no danger of catching up with Nightnurse who looked even more angular and pointy sat on Velmax than normal.

"Thanks mate!" said Hammer catching him up proffering the tin.

"Urrghh! You keep it. I know what you've bin doing with that!" Chisel nodded towards Nightnurse. "He just turns dun he?"

"I thought you'd been making remarkable progress until then. He's said more to you this morning than every other day put together. There's something changed though. You mark my words there's something changed."

It was the last they said to each other for some time. They rode in contemplative silence like two drops on a windowpane awaiting more drops from above.

"Do you get fed up with pulling socks out of the drawer with holes in them?" It was Hammer sounding most unlike him.

"How else you going to put your feet in 'em?" asked Chisel pleased with his quick wit.

"You know what I mean," said Hammer not smiling. "We're good at making things. How did we end up helping someone like him do his dirty work?" He gave a disapproving jerk of his head towards Nightnurse riding in front of them.

"The money of course! We make ten times as much doing this as we would doing honest work." Chisel gave Hammer an encouraging look.

"You look even more of a gormless git when you do that than normal." said Hammer unmoved.

"You always get like this when your arse is playing up. You've got your throbbing orifice and I've got this Brummie accent. We've all got our cross to bear."

"I know which I'd rather have at the moment!" said Hammer standing in his stirrups for some relief.

"Yours is temporary. This is permanent! I could be the cleverest surgeon in the land. But can you imagine it? - Alright Mister Smith. I've done this procedure many times before. You're in safe hands. It's going to be bostin!" Chisel had exaggerated his Brummie accent for effect. "They wouldn't want me anywhere near them! It's a home counties accent or nothing!"

"It works in reverse you know. Some smooth Surrey plumber will never fix your tap properly. Sell you an insurance policy. But not fix your tap so it won't leak. There's a reason we make the judgements we do." Hammer sat back in the saddle as it wasn't fair on his horse to keep riding in the stirrups. "And you could have elocution lessons."

Chisel was aware that some men had a very narrow set of steps from their mind to their mouth. Some men had the added protection of a rope handrail curling down the steps. He'd never been like that. The steps from his mind to his mouth could easily become so wide and steep they became a slide. When that happened many thoughts could be swiftly sliding out of his mouth with no chance of stopping them. Aware of this he firmly pictured a stone stairwell with a rope handrail deciding he wouldn't go down it until he knew what he wanted to say. They rarely talked openly about why they did what they did and he wouldn't mind trying to understand why. To do that he would have to let Hammer take the lead.

"Are you alright?" asked Hammer presently.

"You're a man of reason Hammer. Give a man of reason the cushion he desires and he will willingly sit on it!"

"What?" spluttered Hammer.

"But a true man of reason is not interested in cushions. A true man of reason is only interested in the hard bench of truth! And how can the truth be anything but the truth?"

"You're not a surgeon because of your accent! You're not a surgeon because you're a berk!" said Hammer not meaning it as a joke. "The truth is everyone would rather sit on softly upholstered cushions than hard benches all the time!" He rose in the stirrups again. "How I would love a softly upholstered cushion right now."

Chisel had done it again. He had just been trying to prepare the ground for an honest conversation. Perhaps he was a thick Brummie git after all!

Up ahead Nightnurse suddenly stopped indicating they should get off the track. Fortuitously the trees were thick and plenty with bushes at their bases so they were quickly hidden.

"What do you reckon it is?" whispered Chisel to Hammer.

"Not a normal road traveller. It'll be something that's alerted his predator instinct. Keep your horse still!" They were both peering through the branches and leaves trying to watch Nightnurse and the track.

"Look Hammer. There's a ladder resting up against that tree over there. So someone's about."

"Oh yes so there is. Can't see anyone though. Hold on! What's that?"

There was the unmistakeable sound of something charging through the undergrowth on the opposite side of the track.

"A big boar do you think?" asked Chisel.

"Yes you are. But I'm not going to break up our partnership over it," said Hammer looking intently at where he expected the thing to appear.

Chisel was about to rebuke him when a lad red-faced and clearly in a panic flung himself onto the track. Urgently picking himself up he seemed in some dilemma as what to do next. Take the track left or right or into the trees opposite?

"A schilling says he doesn't see the ladder," said Hammer.

"A schilling says he does," replied Chisel instantly.

"You're on," said Hammer reaching across for them to shake hands but not taking his eyes off the lad.

With the bet agreed Chisel shouted out, "Hoi mate! There's a ladder there! Use that!"

Hammer slowly turned to look at him. "That's not very sporting is it?"

Chisel was beaming with his audaciousness but Hammer knew how to fix that. "I've just lost a schilling but it's not me you're going to have to explain yourself to is it?"

Chisel's face was like a boys that had climbed a massive tree to retrieve an egg then placing it gently on the floor had stepped back to admire how high he'd climbed only to tread on it. "I forgot about Nightnurse."

"That's right you impetuous Brummie git. You forgot about Nightnurse. What's the first rule?"

"Not to get involved," said Chisel sheepishly.

"Not to get involved," repeated Hammer enjoying his partner's concern. "And what have you just done? Again?"

"I just got involved," said Chisel now looking worried.

Hammer turned away because if he looked at Chisel any longer he would start laughing at him. "Well the lad is in the tree and had the good sense to kick away the ladder. But we still don't know what he's running from. No wait! What's this?"

Across the track a big bulk burst out from the undergrowth.

"What on earth is that?" asked Chisel.

"I don't honestly know," gasped Hammer. "Could it be a gorilla?"

"It's more like a bear but it's like its body is too small for its skin." said Chisel incredulously.

"Do not under any circumstances shout out! Do you understand?" There was real concern in Hammer's voice.

"Are you joking? Look at it! I'll be having nightmares for weeks over that!" hissed Chisel.

"It hasn't seen the lad or the ladder," said Hammer watching intently.

"I can't see either of them either," said Chisel bobbing his head from side to side for a better look.

"Stop doing that!" ordered Hammer. "Just stay quiet. I think it's going."

The bear looked up the track both ways strangely lifting its head with a paw to do so. Clearly not able to see the lad it slunk back into the trees from whence it came.

"Might be worth rubbing that lad for luck?" suggested Chisel. "Because he's bin very lucky to get away from that!"

"I wonder what Nightnurse will do. Come on let's see," said Hammer slapping his horse forward.

"I hope his mood's improved," said Chisel worried.

Nightnurse was waiting for them on the track. He eyed Chisel with his dark eyes. "Hoi mate! There's a ladder there use that!" he said with contempt.

"We had a bet.." began Chisel.

Nightnurse held up his hand not wanting to hear it. "There's something about this that's making my palms itch. You saved the little bird. See how it sings," he ordered.

"What do you want to know?" asked Chisel relieved he was going to escape punishment.

Nightnurse glowered at him. "If I go in there I will surely wring its little neck for slowing us down. Now get off your horse and find out why my palms are itching!"

Chisel hurriedly dismounted entering the trees not knowing how he would satisfy Nightnurse.

"Alright there! It was me who shouted about the ladder. Are you alright?" he called out.

Soon his foot stubbed the ladder lying in the carpet of leaves. He looked up at the nearest tree at a youth still visibly frightened. "Now I'm gonna put this ladder on the branch so you can get back down. Sound like a good idea?"

"Has it gone? Are you sure it's gone? I don't want to come down. It's too dangerous!"

"How old are you son?" asked Chisel picking up the ladder.

"Fourteen. I'm fourteen."

"Ever run for your life before?"

"Not like that. I really thought that was it."

Chisel expertly placed the top of the ladder against the branch beckoning for the lad to use it. The lad didn't want to. If it wasn't for the fear of Nightnurse's reaction he would have left him there. But he knew that wasn't good enough.

"Look son. Me and my mates are tooled up enough to cope with a small army. You come down and tell me what's going on."

"I'll tell you but I'll stay here," stammered the lad.

"That's fair enough. So what's happened? And be quick about it! We ain't got all day."

Chisel needn't have worried. The boy's anxiety was so great that it flowed out of him very quickly. He had started his new job that morning at the big house. The place seemed in a state of disarray and confusion. He'd spent most of the day hanging around. He'd needed to go to the toilet and had pushed on a likely door in the yard. But when it opened there was a bear on the other side taking a pee! He'd screamed in horror and ran out. The damned thing had followed him chasing him all the way to here!

All this of course wouldn't explain Nightnurse's itchy palms. So Chisel had asked why he thought the place was in a state of disarray? The lad told him everyone was saying a magpie had arrived that morning with news someone was coming to kill the owner! Chisel had heard enough.

"Right son. This is a fifty-fifty moment for you. I'm going to leave now to be told what to do. I don't honestly know what that might be. But it could be curtains for you. You decide if you want to wait to find out."

"Sorry! You talk funny! Could you say that again? asked the lad.

"You cheeky bastard! Look! The ladder's there. Use it if you want to see your mum again. But lay it back on the ground when you've finished with it!"

Chisel turned his back walking away. He'd already broken one rule and now he'd broken another.

Nightnurse listened to what Chisel had to say suspecting he was being told more slowly than he needed to be. Although it was very interesting how these petty people had petty things happen in their petty lives it wasn't explaining his itchy palms until Chisel had nearly finished.

"Do you know of anyone else who uses magpies?" he asked Hammer.

"No. I believe we're the only ones," replied Hammer.

"You believe?" demanded Nightnurse.

"Well of course I can't be one hundred per cent sure. You would have to ask Crow," replied Hammer surprised at the worry Nightnurse showed. It was obvious he thought he'd been betrayed.

"Where exactly is this lad?" demanded Nightnurse getting down from Velmax.

"I'll show you," said Chisel.

"No you two will stay here."

Chisel pointed at a large bush. "Go in there for about twenty feet then he's on the right."

Nightnurse walked across to the bush then disappeared.

"I hope that lad's luck holds out," said Hammer solemnly.

"If the lad has any sense I'm hoping it won't need to," replied Chisel with a grave look on his face. "I'm just worried where he's going to find that ladder."

"What did you do Chisel?" asked Hammer alarmed.

Chisel didn't answer but quickly mounted his horse. "If he comes out all angry because he found a ladder up a tree get ready to run!"

"Why?" asked Hammer taking up the slack in his reins in preparation.

"Because I ain't in the business of killing boys!" hissed Chisel.

"We wouldn't get away. There's a better way of doing this," said Hammer suddenly dismounting.

"What are you doing you fool?" asked Chisel.

Hammer didn't reply but went across to the large bush. Inside the copse he found Nightnurse pacing around looking up at different trees. The ladder lying on the ground soon became obvious to Hammer perhaps as a vein would have been obvious to Nightnurse.

"The ladder's there!" Hammer shouted so there was no danger of Nightnurse reacting badly to being sneaked upon. "The lad must have been in that tree. He must have jumped!"

They both stood by the ladder.

"That's over ten feet! Why would he risk it?" asked Nightnurse.

"He wanted to get away. Chisel has that effect on most people who meet him," said Hammer.

"You don't think Chisel helped him?" asked Nightnurse giving the ladder a little kick.

Hammer shook his head. "Chisel's thick but he's not stupid. Besides I doubt it would have occurred to the lad to lay the ladder back down afterwards. Why would he think to do that?"

Nightnurse nodded.

"Do you want us to try and find him? He can't have got far." It was a question Hammer didn't want to ask but knew it would be suspicious if he didn't.

Nightnurse said nothing clearly distracted.

"I'll go back to Chisel," said Hammer.

Nightnurse said nothing so Hammer assumed it was alright.

Hammer joined Chisel on the track. "Telling that lad to lay the ladder down afterwards has probably saved both your lives." He mounted his horse. "You did didn't you?"

"Does he suspect? Do we need to get out of here?" asked Chisel not releasing the tension in his reins.

No sooner had Hammer sat in his saddle than he dismounted. "I'm just going to," he was feeling in his apron with a pained expression, "take a pee first."

Chisel knew what Hammer really wanted to do reluctantly letting him disappear into the bushes.

Nightnurse appeared.

"Hammer says the lad's gone?" asked Chisel as casually as he could.

"Where is Hammer?" asked Nightnurse.

"Taking a pee," replied Chisel holding his reins very carefully.

"You two carry on. Don't do anything until I get there," said Nightnurse mounting Velmax.

"How long will that be?" asked Chisel.

"As long as it takes. You do nothing until I arrive!" Nightnurse kicked his heels into Velmax. In a cloud of dust and black they sped off down the track.

"What sort of instruction is that?" asked Chisel under his breath waving away the dust assaulting his face. "Can't do anything properly with vague instructions."

# CHAPTER 30

## Is it a draught or fresh air?

Resourceful was in the room where the staff could find him during the day. He didn't call it his office as he felt that was unnecessary. He was sitting at his small desk looking out through the small window towards the lake. It was his favourite view from anywhere in the house. But not today. Sat on a thick cushion that had been a necessity since Colonel Peru's house he had just finished reading a letter. It was news that an old friend (and he had had precious few over the years) had died. His poor wife would be beside herself with grief as they had been inseparable since the day they'd met. In the letter one of the sons had let him know the name of the churchyard and the amount Resourceful now owed towards the flowers. Looking at the amount he was reminded of a line from Shakespeare: "Good wombs have borne bad sons." The figure would probably pay for the whole funeral. Resourceful wasn't a "soft touch" but he would send the amount asked for because he had admired his friend and felt for his widow. He let the letter fall heavily onto the desk then got up to reassure himself with the view from the window.

Almost immediately as though it had been waiting for him a magpie appeared on the windowsill outside. Resourceful had had one piece of bad news was he going to get the other two as quickly as today? As he struggled to pull up the stiff sash window he repeated aloud, "one for sorrow, two for joy, three for a girl, four for a boy, five for silver, six for gold, seven for a secret never to be told." Outside the magpie was clearly impatient to get in tapping on the glass and squawking loudly.

Resourceful stopped pulling on the window listening for how many times the magpie tapped. It stopped at seven and tapped no more. With a reluctant final heave the window opened letting the magpie hop inside. It flew onto his desk as though it were his own.

"Good morning Aristotle. You have a secret to tell me?" said Resourceful still standing at the open window.

Incredibly the magpie nodded seeming to understand what he'd said.

"Just give me a moment to shut this bloody window," said Resourceful taking hold of the brass handles.

The magpie stamped its right foot three times. It wasn't a loud sound but it was very clear to Resourceful what it meant. As it should – he'd trained him to do it! Resourceful always had an affinity with birds beginning with falcons. He soon understood that while man had realised long ago that chickens were tasty he hadn't realised birds could be used to send messages quickly. Resourceful had tried at first with falcons but they were easily distracted by hunting on the way. Then he'd tried to train some pigeons because they were clearly very fast. But they had proved to be such gormless gits only interested in three things. None of which involved learning new skills. Then he had found a young family of magpies. What a revelation it had been! They weren't as quick to fly as falcons or pigeons but they were far quicker to learn! They proved to be so intelligent he named the five of them Aristotle, Plato, Socrates, Pythagoras and Archimedes. With his hard work and their receptiveness they became very effective messengers for him. Then his employer found out about them and they were confiscated. Lord Ecin wouldn't have behaved in such a way. Used for nefarious messages for a time then lost in a card game.

The two females had quickly taken the hump with him using the excuse he'd given them male names. They knew as well as he did there hadn't been any female Greek philosophers. Why hadn't they just admitted they wanted to start families? It was perfectly normal. The three males however, no matter how many employers they passed through had all kept in touch. Looking at Aristotle on his desk Resourceful was pleased to realise they had known each other for over ten years even if he was probably the bearer of bad news today.

"So it can't wait," he said coming over to sit down.

The magpie tapped with its beak three times on his desk then bowed.

"I'm so glad you agreed that was a good idea. It looks so polite," said Resourceful smiling. He caught sight of the letter still lying on the desk. He picked it up putting it out of sight in a drawer reminding himself there will always be bad things and less often good things but you should let the good things shine bright. Whilst he was in there he pulled out a small black notebook from the very back.

"I have our secret codebook as requested," he said holding it up.

The magpie fluttered its wings impatiently.

"Alright. Alright. You take it steady and we'll get there in one go," Resourceful said gently.

The magpie tapped its right foot three times. Resourceful opened page three of the codebook. Then the magpie did a little dance hopping a number of times on its left leg then its right leg then its left leg again. Resourceful watched carefully. You had to go down with the right up with the left and then down with the right again.

Resourceful looked up with a young cheeky expression in his old face. "London bridge has fallen down? That can't be right!"

The magpie tilted its head observing him with a beady black eye.

"No time for even one little joke?" asked Resourceful cheerily.

The magpie gravely shook its head. His black beak looking like the shiny handle of a small saucepan.

Resourceful looked at the codebook properly this time. He looked up startled. "Can this be right? Three men coming here causing mischief?"

The magpie nodded.

"But it's not the secret is it?" asked Resourceful rubbing his chin.

The magpie shook its head before beginning another little dance.

Resourceful watched closely then consulted the codebook. He flicked through the pages several times struggling to make sense of the message. The magpie waited leaning up a small vase that held his pencils and pen. When it crossed one leg over the other Resourceful noticed and had to stop. Such almost human behaviour delighted him. He broke off a bit of cheese form his half eaten breakfast offering it to the bird. "It's your own fault. You have improvised here."

The magpie straightened taking the cheese swallowing it whole. Then it gently plucked the codebook from his grasp. Laying it out it stamped on a very specific point on the page. Resourceful craned his neck to see. "I see loose cannon on deck," he said.

The magpie carefully turned a few pages over with its beak then stamped on a part of that page. Resourceful looked and repeated aloud, "pirates coming to steal treasure." He looked at Aristotle. "I understood that part too."

The magpie turned back a page. Resourceful didn't need to look. "Yes I understand that too – danger very soon." Resourceful leant forward gently turning a few pages. "But - "watch out the lady's on her period"? What do you mean by that?"

The magpie nodded at the cheese with its beak.

Resourceful broke off another piece handing it to him.

"Aristotle you were always the cleverest one. There's obviously something you need to tell me that we didn't expect. But I'm sorry I can't see what it is."

The magpie began tapping with his beak as he would if it were Hammer or Chisel. After thirty seconds or so Resourceful stopped him by gently stroking his back. "That's something very clever you've learned but I don't understand it. If only I was as quick as you on the uptake." He stamped a fist on the desk. Not hard that wasn't his way but hard enough for a pencil to jump out of the vase. It caught the magpie's eye. Resourceful knew that look in Aristotle. Not believing it would work he looked down taking out a plain piece of paper from a drawer. When he looked up Aristotle already had the pencil in his beak his head on one side in the way that comes very easily to birds. Resourceful placed the piece of paper in front of the magpie. Incredibly it began drawing.

When it had finished Resourceful pushed his plate of breakfast over to Aristotle whilst he looked at the picture. Of course it was crude but he'd seen three year olds do worse. It appeared to be a girl wearing a cape pushing eggs out of a nest. There were three birds in the picture all flying away from the tree.

Resourceful looked over the picture at Aristotle who was rolling a tomato around the plate. He wasn't trying to eat it he could have picked it up easily enough. Resourceful knew he was keeping himself busy rather than worry about what Resourceful thought of his picture.

"You are such a bright thing. It has been such an honour to know you," said Resourceful heavily. "But I understand now. There's a woman in charge who's ruining everything and you guys are off." He brought the picture to his lips his eyes watering. "Two goodbyes in one day. It's too many."

Aristotle tapped his beak three times then bowed. Resourceful understood there wasn't the attachment to goodbyes in the animal world that we have. They were much more likely not to see each other ever again from one day to the next so refrained from making a fuss about it.

"You're right," said Resourceful smiling as best he could, "it's time to go." He slowly stood up then bowed respectfully to the magpie.

To most people magpies were black and white. But Resourceful saw all the colours of oil on water as Aristotle flew out. He hurried after it as quickly as he could watching him disappear across the lake and over the trees. "Fare thee well clever Aristotle! And your brave messenger brothers," he whispered staring from the window.

He starting shutting it feeling so sad that he would never see him again.

"I'm not going to ask why do we bother? It's what we do. But closure never gets easier does it?" He pushed down harder. "Especially with this bloody thing!"

It snapped into place. After only a few seconds contemplation so did he. There were lots of things that now needed doing. He would mourn when he could.

# CHAPTER 31

## Live and let live

Chisel was waiting for Hammer to come out of the bushes wondering about it all. The summer evening sun yellow and friendly on his face he felt they'd earned a pint or two. Hammer appeared looking a lot happier.

"Has he gone?" he asked getting ready to mount his horse.

"We're to carry on and do nothing until he gets there," replied Chisel helpfully holding the reins of his horse whilst he mounted.

"What sort of instruction is that?" asked Hammer lowering himself gently onto his saddle.

"Useless! That's what!" said Chisel contemptuously. "Fancy a pint?"

"We'll have the time. He's got to go all the way back. Find out what's going on. And then come back. In fact - there's a very small possibility we might not ever see him again."

"Do you really think so?" asked Chisel quite enamoured with the idea.

"If he finds out Crow has double-crossed him in some way do you think he'll leave it at that?"

"Do you think he she it whatever it is has done that?" asked Chisel letting go of Hammer's reins.

Hammer threw up his hands. "I don't know. But we've got all night to discuss it. If he is coming back it won't be until tomorrow morning." A strange naughty expression fleetingly passed over his face too quick for Chisel to notice. "You say you fancy a pint? I know just the place nearby."

"Bostin!" said Chisel eagerly. "A few pints sat outside watching the sun go down. We'll soon have it all sorted!"

"We're here," said Hammer.

"This is it?" asked Chisel not impressed. "I can't imagine he gets much passing trade. You'd hardly know it was here."

Hammer gave him a knowing look. "I think you'll find that's the idea."

"Will we be able to get something to eat?" asked Chisel seeming unwilling to get off his horse until it had been confirmed.

"Trevor always puts on a very good spread," said Hammer dismounting.

"So you know him then? Are you a regular here?" said Chisel getting down.

"I'm not a regular here but I've done a fair bit of work for him over the years. You'll like him. He's quite a character."

Right on cue the tavern door opened.

"Is that you Hammer? It's been ages! Come on! Let me have a good look at you!"

Trevor was about thirty with a ballet dancer's physique and a kind open cheeky face. His eyes seemed to sparkle and caught by the gentle evening sun they shone out warm green light. He was dressed as a traditional innkeeper in breeches and an apron. Some days he liked to wear a bonnet and a dress but not today. He might tomorrow it depended on how he felt when he woke up. Or not wait until then and slip on a dress later. Who knew?

"Come on! Whose your friend?" he asked bouncing with vigour.

Hammer obliged. "This is Chisel. He's my partner now."

"Partner?" asked Trevor cocking his head like a bird. "Don't tell me you've seen the light!"

"Business partner," said Hammer looking at Chisel who was eyeing Trevor warily.

Just then their attention was drawn to a small pony and trap approaching the tavern.

"This is my new barmaid," explained Trevor. "I've not seen her yet but I've been assured she's very good!" He fizzed like the wine he liked to serve.

A farmer's daughter type of about sixteen but very attractive got down from the trap when it stopped. "Thank you dad I'll see you later," she said.

Chisel watched the trap leave noticing the left wheel was wobbling. The bearing clearly needed sorting out.

"My God you're gorgeous! I'm so jealous!" said Trevor to the girl who smiled awkwardly. He walked slowly around her. "What a lovely pearl for a pirate's chest! You're going to have to show me how you do your hair! Your nails!" He slapped her on the bum. "Just as I thought. Tight as a drum! Come in! Come in my beautiful Lucinda! Let's see how many of them we can confuse in there!" He offered up his arm the girl taking it with a little giggle. "Come on! Let's show you off!" He nodded at Hammer and Chisel to follow them. "And you guys fed and watered!"

Before Hammer could move Chisel held him back. "Is this a *funny* pub?" he asked.

"Yes," replied Hammer freely. "And I guarantee you'll love it! Come on."

Chisel cautiously followed them in never having felt such a wave of warmth wash over him stepping into a building. The tavern was much bigger than it looked from the outside with people sat at the bar on stools and some at tables and an eating area it seemed towards the back. He guessed there were about twenty or so people in there altogether.

"Everyone! Everyone!" announced Trevor. "Look at this beautiful woman! Isn't she stunning? And do you know what? I've only just met her but I can tell she's as beautiful on the inside as she is on the outside! Come on everybody! Raise your glasses to beauty! Isn't it wonderful to behold?"

"To beauty!" everyone toasted.

Trevor gave Lucinda an excited hug. "You can start work when you're ready. You get to know everyone first. Sit yourself over there. Go on. If you're not laughing your head off by the time I bring out some food for this pair of reprobates then I'll eat your chair!"

Trevor assumed his position behind the bar presenting two menus to Hammer and Chisel. "Two beers gentleman?" He glanced over at Lucinda to make sure she was alright. A couple had given her a glass and were filling it up from a bottle. She'd be just fine.

"Just what the doctor ordered Trev'. It's been a funny few days," said Hammer slowly lowering himself onto a bar stool. "Come on Chisel sit down."

Chisel gave a wary look around the tavern although he felt a bit foolish for doing so then sat down on a stool next to Hammer.

Trevor put the two beers down. "After you tell me what you want to eat you can tell me all about it! If you like lamb then the stew today is to die for! Do you like lamb Chisel?"

"If you get a nice piece it's lovely. But it can be a bit fatty a lot of the time," replied Chisel looking at his pint appreciatively for a few seconds before he began drinking it.

"I completely agree! I've had lamb so bad you could make a string vest out of it! But not here. My lamb will melt in your mouth I promise! If it doesn't then I'll eat your stool!" said Trevor positively bouncing behind the bar.

"You can't argue with an endorsement like that Chisel," said Hammer, "shall we order two lamb stews?"

"Three!" corrected Chisel wiping the beer from his top lip with the back of his hand. "Let's get one for that new barmaid too."

"Don't worry! Don't worry!" said Trevor. "They'll order for her. And I bet it will be oysters. We're very lucky here. Just up 'coast they bring out some of the best oysters in England. She'll love 'em!"

"I'm not stretching to oysters," said Chisel. "We'll stick with the lamb stews if you say they're good."

Trevor made a big cross on his left breast. "Trust me darling! Let me give your order to the kitchen. Just a moment gentleman!" He disappeared through a door behind the bar.

"He seems nice," said Chisel about to take another gulp of his pint. "For an arse bandit."

Hammer looked around alarmed to see if anyone had heard. Fortunately no-one had. "Look Chisel. There's no need to point some things out. It's rude! And I'm not even sure he is. If your pint's bad or the food's bad then you can take the piss. But if it's not and we're well looked after why insult the man?"

"I was only saying," replied Chisel a little hurt.

"Well just think on. The world would be a much better place if more of us did."

Chisel knew Hammer was right. He chinked his glass against Hammer's glass. "Amen to that brother."

Hammer looked at Chisel glad he'd said what he'd said. Then they both raised their glasses and drank their pints down. When Trevor returned they were ready for another.

"Two more beers gentleman?" asked Trevor merrily.

"Don't mind if we do," said Chisel making sure Trevor had noticed him smiling broadly at him.

Hammer glanced at him wondering when did Chisel ever get it right? "Oh Trevor. Do you have a stablehand yet? Or have we got to sort out the horses ourselves? Because I'll do it now."

"All sorted my friend! That's where I've just been. Young John is seeing to them right now. You enjoy your beers." Trevor placed two more pints on the top. "And tell me what's been happening in your world lately!"

So they did. As much as they dared or could. Beers were gulped down. Delicious lamb stews arrived and eaten. Beers gulped down. More beers gulped down. And all the time Trevor had the remarkable ability to run his pub and listen to every word.

"So what doya think?" slurred Chisel a few hours later. "At the end of the day isn't it all bollocks? Talking of which. Where's the little boy's room?"

"Down there through the door on the right," said Trevor pointing helpfully.

"Thank you," said Chisel clumsily getting off his stool. He toddled off not feeling he had a care in the world. Very nice. He opened the door. The sun had just gone to bed and there was that wonderful smell of the summer night air. They had been very lucky with how warm and dry this summer had been. Very nice. He spotted the probable outbuilding happily toddling off towards it.

Inside there was a small lantern with a few moths buzzing around it. There was already a man in there.

"How do?" said Chisel entering.

"I've gotta see how you manage this with that bloody great thing round your front," replied the man.

"This?" asked Chisel reaching behind for the apron strings. "It's got to come off."

"Oooohhhh," said the man in an unfamiliar way to Chisel.

Chisel hung the heavy apron on a hook to begin fumbling with the buttons on his trousers.

"What a hand with those?" asked the man.

"No it's alright thank you. I've got it now." Chisel began urinating into the gulley.

"The Romans used to go to the toilet together and look how much they achieved!" said the man.

"I don't think that was the reason. Though I do wonder what have we lost from the Romans? How long will it take us to rediscover what they already knew?"

"Why waste time on your own?" asked the man. "Take someone with you and achieve two things instead of one!"

"Put it like that. It does sound productive," agreed Chisel.

"Rabbits!" said the man. "Do you think when they're out of sight they put on little trousers and smoke pipes at tiny hearths? Little jars of jam stacked on little welsh dressers behind them?"

Chisel thought about a question like that in the way you could think about things after six or seven pints. "No definitely not."

"Neither do I!" The man had finished but didn't seem inclined to leave.

Chisel put his hand on the wall to steady himself because of the time it was taking. Wasn't it quite remarkable just how much a drunken man could produce?

"I like you. You look like the sort of man who likes it straight," said the man.

"I like to think so," agreed Chisel finishing off. He gave his penis a few jiggles to dry it.

"I thought so. So you won't mind me saying it's a bit smaller than I like. But I'm up for a giggle if you are," said the man.

Chisel's brow involuntarily furrowed as he tried to work out what was going on. He knew something was going on. But what? And was there an insult in there somewhere too? "I'm sorry?" he asked taking down his apron off the hook.

"If you fancied a bit of a giggle I'm up for it," said the man.

"There you are!" said Hammer appearing suddenly. "I thought you'd fell in the river! Come on!"

"Sorry mate. Didn't know he was with you," said the man.

"It's not a problem honestly," said Hammer.

"Well you both seem very nice," said the man friendly enough.

"Thank you. You have a good evening." Hammer tied Chisel's apron strings for him then led him away.

"Is he coming out?" asked Chisel looking behind.

"They call him the spider. There are some of them you have to watch." He gave Chisel's bum a smack. "But he didn't get this little fly today did he?"

"Hey?" asked Chisel not understanding again.

Hammer said nothing just smiling holding the door open for him to go in.

"Do you think Trevor sells pork scratchings?" asked Chisel hopefully.

"I think it's time for the wooden hill. I've booked us some rooms. You wait there while I get the keys."

Hammer lent him up the wall so he wouldn't fall over. His eyes slowly closing his head lolling onto his chest muttering about pork scratchings. The classic sign that Chisel had had enough for one night.

# CHAPTER 32

## Bustle in your hedgerow

The next morning Hammer and Chisel were up early because although they'd had a lot to drink the night before they were disciplined. They'd had a good breakfast, settled up with Trevor, said a fond farewell and headed for the target house to await Nightnurse. Hidden in some bushes at the beginning of the huge front lawn they had emptied their aprons and spent most of the day leisurely cleaning their tools. Their horses were happy enough tied up with a long rein in a nearby lane. There was even a puddle if they needed a drink. Chisel had checked on them late in the afternoon when he'd gone for some provisions. They hadn't expected to see Nightnurse until nearly nightfall which it almost proved to be.

Nightnurse had gone back to Crow aka Catherine de Barnes not knowing what he would find out or consequently what he would do. She told him she hadn't sent any magpies as two of them had left and the third would only work for "silly money". But she'd found out one of the pair had gone "rogue" and warned someone on their list who had fled to his brothers – which was the place they intended to hit next! A daft bird had given them two birds at once! Then she told him about "the golden nugget". The target house had a lump of gold so big it had a name! It would pay for an island on its own! It was kept in a safe in the study with many other valuable gems the target had collected over the years. She suggested it would be a good tactic to threaten to kill the brother to get the target to open the safe. He was notoriously hard in business but would he willingly let his brother die to keep his safe shut? Nightnurse didn't need telling how to do his part but was excited to find out much he could "push" one brother against the other. He himself had no siblings. And if this "golden nugget" was all they needed why faff about with the other "chinless gits"? They had made love with the lost trust rekindled and he had left.

Nightnurse found them in the bushes. The first they knew he was there was when he spoke. "Good evening gentlemen."

Hammer and Chisel were getting better at hiding their surprise.

"Oh hello," said Hammer.

"Someone's doing alright for themselves," said Chisel nodding his head at the huge house.

Nightnurse crouched regarding the house. "It would have been better to get here after nightfall. There must be at least an hour of daylight left. Damn these long summer evenings." He looked at Chisel ominously. "You're a bit of a clown. A bit of a frustrated thespian?"

"I wouldn't have said..." Chisel began to protest.

"Shut up!" ordered Nightnurse. "You pretend to be an oddjob man looking for work. Find out what you can. Report back here when you have something."

Hammer reached into his apron pulling out an eyepatch. "This house looks strangely familiar but I can't be sure. Wear this as a disguise just in case. I forgot I had it."

Chisel put the eyepatch on.

Hammer reassured him. "Your own mother wouldn't recognise you!"

"Bastard!" replied Chisel. "You know I was an orphan."

"Oh yeah - sorry I forgot," said Hammer playfully.

"I want to know if he's there with his brother and where they are. And anything else I should know," said Nightnurse cutting out any creeping frivolity. "If you prove to be a useless saddlebag full of needless things I'll cut you around your seam with my knife. Do you understand?"

"That's a bit strong isn't it? He'll be alright," said Hammer defending Chisel as robustly as he dared.

"You Hammer creep round the back. See what's going on there," ordered Nightnurse.

All three of them understood clearly that there was no questioning him.

"Come on. Let's get this done," said Hammer helping Chisel up from his prone position. "And tone down the Brummie accent!"

Chisel broke cover making for the long drive whilst Hammer began working his way around the back remaining hidden in the plethora of rhododendron bushes.

As he got closer Chisel tried to work out the location of the tradesman entrance. There was surprisingly little going on. No gardeners sweeping the drive or pratting about in the borders. No grooms bringing out horses. No maids opening windows to shake out a rug or a sheet. The house seemed like a great whale just resting there with nothing to do. Then he reached the side of the house where an explanation was forthcoming in a most graphic manner.

About ten or so assorted servants were gathered around the crumpled remains of an old fella lying beneath a large horse. Both horse and old fella were quite still.

As Chisel got closer he could hear what someone was saying. "How dreadful! But if ever a full fare had been paid on life's coach George done it."

"How much better for us all if life's coach had been pulled by George. Not this invisible hand we never see. No one to tell us where we are going. Constantly getting lost on the way," said someone else.

"I'm in no hurry to join George just yet. Though my bones may be shaken over the cobbles and ruts I'm still of the opinion it is better to keep going than to actually arrive. But look! Today we can see that George has departed." The old servant looked up to the sky. "Somewhere up there George is resting having truly earned it. As long as we continue to speak of him fondly then he is remembered rightly. Dark cannot exist when light is allowed in! To George! The best shirehorse the estate ever had!"

"To George! The best shirehorse the estate ever had!" all of the assembled servants chorused together.

"The old git?" asked a young maid afterwards. "What's *he* doing under George?"

"Fancied himself as a vet I think," said one of the young grooms. "But no amount of tummy tickling was going to put George's heart right. Silly sod just wasn't quick enough to get out of the way when George keeled over. Anyway Nancy. Are you coming out with me on Friday night or what?"

"Whose that?" said Nancy pointing at Chisel.

Everyone stopped looking down at George turning to look at him.

"What do you want?" asked one of the older servant men.

Chisel spread out his hands inviting them to look upon his manner of dress. "I've come to deliver a baby! What do you think I want?"

"If I were having a baby I wouldn't want him anywhere near me! Not with the things he's got sticking out of him!" Nancy told everyone.

"You silly moo!" laughed the young groom at her. "He was being sarcastic!"

"Shut up you young fools!" said the old servant before turning to Chisel. "We may have had some work for you. A coffin for George for a start. But no one likes a cheeky chippie so sling your hook!"

Chisel was curious. "You'd put a horse in a coffin?"

The older servant pushed some of the others out of the way to get closer to Chisel. "And what's wrong with that? What do you do with dead horses where you come from? Well?"

"I think they use them for making glue."

The crowd of servants gasped in horror taking a step back in unison. Chisel felt to make sure his trousers hadn't fallen down. They hadn't. Amazingly they must have been shocked at what he'd just said.

"Thank God we work for a man who wouldn't countenance such a thing," said an old maid. "The old git -" she stopped to jab a finger at the prone figure under the horse, "because he's not from round 'ere will be fed to the pigs. Waste not want not and all that. But your kind who'd turn poor George into pots of glue - you deserve stoning!"

It was at this point Chisel looked down to take a bit more of an interest in the composition of the ground he was standing on. It was a gravel. Not pea shingle either. But great big chunks of Cotswold chippings. Now if this had been an attack mission rather than a reconnaissance one he would have popped a few arrows in the big servants bringing the rest of them into line. However, his bow was on his horse. No matter a couple of three-eighths chisels could do the same trick. But the eyepatch could affect his aim. He could take it off. But that risked being recognised. Now a reconnaissance mission could become an attack mission very easily but that was only because you'd failed in some way. And if he failed whose displeasure would he have to face? At that moment his over-riding consideration was not incurring Nightnurse's wrath. So that meant the correct course of action was to turn and run. So he did.

"You're all bloody wierd!" he shouted over his shoulder.

"You're a one-eyed Brummie git!" one of them shouted back.

"Are all Brummies so quick on the uptake?" someone shouted.

"I could have put three stones in his forehead whilst he stood working it out!" laughed another.

Little bits of the drive began to rain down on him but he was soon out of harm's way. He ran until he reached the safety of the bushes suddenly darting in. He'd wait a bit to let his breathing subside before reporting to Nightnurse he would have to try again later. What would he say about this time? The servants had had a bereavement and were all a bit raw. That would do.

He reached their hiding spot but Nightnurse was no longer there. He wasn't sure how long he waited watching the fading light letting the house slip away from its grasp.

"Find anything?" asked Hammer finally joining him.

"They're a crazy lot who think animals are more important than people!" replied Chisel.

"Hey?"

"Nothing. Did you find anything?"

"Nothing. There seemed to be a bit of a commotion at the side of the house earlier."

"Erh, that might have had something to do with me." Chisel briefly explained what had happened.

Hammer nodded not saying anything until he'd finished. "It's not important. What is - is where is he?"

"Nightnurse?" asked Chisel.

"No - The Tooth Fairy!" Hammer looked up at the sky turning inky. "It'll soon be his favourite time of the day."

"And somebody's worst," said Chisel darkly.

"Hold on! What's that? Chisel can you see something by that window?"

"What window? That house has got more windows than this apron's got pockets!"

"Ground floor. Start on the right. Fourth one in," said Hammer not taking his eyes from where he was looking.

"I just wish I could see better!" said Chisel.

"Take off my eyepatch then!" said Hammer.

"And risk being recognised?"

"It's dark now anyway. Take it off! I'll give it you back later if you need it," said Hammer.

Chisel took it off holding it out to his side for him to take. "It's a magpie! You can tell it by all that flashing white."

"Yes I know that!" said Hammer irritably. "But see how desperate he is to get in that room? Why?"

"Sin something shiny?" suggested Chisel. "They like shiny things don't they?"

"It's more than that! It's like that windowsill is red hot. That bird is frantic!" said Hammer risking standing up.

"It's just a pet that wants feeding. I've sin already just how much they love animals!"

"More of a reason to let it in then!" argued Hammer. "I think that magpie's trying to stop something!"

"Don't be ridiculous! It's a bloody magpie!" Chisel stopped himself as a terrible realisation made itself known to him. "You don't think it's one of ours do you?" he gasped.

"I'm going over there!" said Hammer looking down at him. "Are you coming?"

"Wait! Somebody's opened the window!" said Chisel pulling him down.

They both watched the magpie disappear through the open window.

"What do we do now?" asked Chisel

"Wait here for Nightnurse. This isn't our pigeon." said Hammer looking worried.

"Isn't our pigeon?" repeated Chisel looking at him disgusted. "What sort of expression is that? That reminds me of them Coventry twats that call a cob a "batch". And do you know why? Because us industrious Brummies made the effort to think of a proper name for it - a cob! Whereas those Coventry twats just say, "Oh we'll make a batch of those!" But you can make a *batch* of anything. You can make a *batch* of cannonballs. And are you gonna put a nice piece of ham and tomato on a cannonball? No! Lazy twats! In fact there's a better word for a Coventry twat and that's a Coventry Cu --"

Hammer hated that word and was about to put his hand over Chisel's mouth when he didn't need to. Chisel had stopped because of the unmistakeable sound escaping from the open window across the lawn.

"That was a gunshot," Chisel breathed out.

"I know," replied Hammer.

"Nightnurse doesn't use a gun," said Chisel.

"I know," replied Hammer.

"What do we do?" asked Chisel.

"I don't know," replied Hammer.

# CHAPTER 33

## What goes around comes around

In the study two brothers were talking in comfortable chairs. Henry whose study it was had that "quickness" about him that I think we all recognise as being able to turn his hand to anything. His brother who was called Ian was slightly older but more "delicate" looking. They weren't opposites but if you needed to borrow money from one of them you'd ask Ian first. Oh, and we already know Ian as Lord Ecin.

Henry was smiling fondly at his brother. "You inherited the title and the money but I don't begrudge you a thing. You were born to it in every sense of the word. I on the other hand - I think I would have been like a butterfly flitting from one flower to the next in the pursuit of pleasure wasting the family fortune!"

Lord Ecin shook his head smiling fondly back. As two brothers they were very close and always had been. "Nonsense! You have one of those great minds sweeping away the leaves from our roads of ignorance. Even when there's people like me stamping all over them again with our muddy boots you still carry on!"

"Ian you're my brother! Your muddy boots are always welcome on my drive! And to bring your new bear with you as well. He's been creating quite a stir with the staff it seems!"

"Well it's very good of you to stop what you were doing to look after me for a few days. I know time is precious to you. What was it you used to say when you'd refuse dessert?"

"Don't Ian you're going to embarrass me now," said Henry smiling in that way that had disarmed their mother so many times.

Lord Ecin wasn't going to be put off. "You'd get up from the table and say - "The hole in the wall to greatness is very slim. How can a man who has eaten too many desserts expect to pass through it?""

They both laughed fondly.

Henry confessed, "I don't think Cook was good with desserts!"

"You know brother," began Lord Ecin, "History gives out many brushes and paints but it's up to each of us in turn to make her happy with what we do with them. I think history will make you one of her favourites."

"You're so wrong. If you only knew the balls-up I made on the last deal!" said Henry. Something caught his attention. A slight rattle and movement of the door handle.

Lord Ecin noticed his brother distracted. "What is it Henry?"

"I think someone might be at the door. Could it be your diligent butler trying to get in with a tray of something?" replied Henry getting out of his chair. "You said he had been incapacitated recently. I'll give him a hand."

Henry was almost at the door when it opened precisely enough to let a dark figure slip in. The next he knew was pressure on his adam's apple perpetrated by the point of a fine sword.

"I don't imagine this is a social visit," he said calmly.

"Indeed not," replied Nightnurse looking very carefully at Henry and then at Lord Ecin. He quickly made up his mind who was the more dangerous of the two. "When I tell you you're going to sit back down and you," he pointed at Lord Ecin with his free hand, "are going to tie him to his chair with this." He stopped pointing to reach behind taking a length of thin rope from his hip which he threw perfectly into Lord Ecin's lap. "Now move!"

Henry instinctively reached out as he carefully sidled back to his chair whilst Nightnurse kept the sword point on his throat.

"Now sit down," said Nightnurse when they reached the chair. "You tie him in. If I think you're not doing it properly I will slice off your ears."

Lord Ecin was so scared he couldn't get up from his chair. "I wouldn't even know how to begin to do such a thing," he struggled to say.

"Don't worry Ian. Just round my front and round the back of the chair nice and tight. Just keep going until you run out of rope," encouraged Henry.

"Are you sure?" asked Lord Ecin shakily getting up.

"It's not up to him," warned Nightnurse coldly.

Henry coolly turned to Nightnurse. "Would you like my arms in or out? If they're in then I'm more likely to be able to wriggle free. If they're out wriggling free is nigh on impossible but you risk me taking a swing at you if you get too close."

Nightnurse regarded Henry knowing his initial impression had been correct. The slippery eel might have even practised extricating himself from such a predicament. Looking at the stout legs of the chair he decided to add some further insurance. "Leave his arms out," he ordered.

Henry's face was completely impassive. No-one would know if that's what he preferred.

Nightnurse watched intently as Lord Ecin tied his brother to the chair in hoops around the front and back whilst also surveying the room. Nightnurse could do that.

"Now tie his ankles to the chair legs," said Nightnurse.

"How's he supposed to do that?" asked Henry calmly.

Nightnurse bounded over to the window sliced the curtain tie backs free and bounded back with them. "These should do." He tossed them at Henry's feet.

"You move quickly," said Henry appreciatively.

Nightnurse regarded him silently deciding he really didn't like such calmness from a man in his situation.

Lord Ecin used the curtain tie backs to tie his brother's legs to the two front legs of the chair watched intently by Nightnurse.

"Now tie his hands behind the chair," said Nightnurse.

"May I suggest using the bell pull over there in the corner? It's long enough and should be quite soft on my wrists." suggested Henry helpfully.

Nightnurse bounded across slicing it cleanly in two where it appeared out of the ceiling. It fell onto the floor like a curled up snake. Nightnurse left it there. He bounded behind the chair taking out a set of handcuffs from his waistcoat he'd had made years ago but hardly used. He wasn't even sure he still had the key but as he had decided they would never be coming back off that didn't matter.

Henry had helpfully reached his hands behind the chair. "I hope you aren't going to be too long because this will start to hurt after a bit," he said.

Nightnurse could see the handcuffs wouldn't be long enough without even trying them. He had a better idea. He tossed them towards Lord Ecin.

"You put them on and sit down!" he ordered.

Lord Ecin regarded them like a kitchen implement that he knew did something but had no idea what.

Nightnurse was visibly irritated. "Don't pretend you don't know what to do!"

"I'm afraid he doesn't," said Henry bringing his arms back from behind his chair. "He doesn't believe in locking up his staff and there's not a kinky bone in his body. They could be something for stopping a bull's balls drag on the ground for all he knows."

Nightnurse was well aware that a lot of his success he couldn't explain. He took care of as many details as he could but lots of things he just seemed "to know". The reward for taking care of so many details he opined. It was his instinct that had found them in this room amongst the many in the house. He also generally knew when someone was telling the truth and this man was.

"Sit down!" he ordered.

Obediently Lord Ecin sat down. Nightnurse moved behind his chair reaching over him to place the handcuffs around his wrists. He then moved around so he was between the two brothers.

"Now gentlemen. Which one of you is Raven?" he asked pointing his sword first at Henry and then at Lord Ecin.

"I'm not Raven. And niether is this man," said Henry calmly. "I've never heard of a Raven. If you don't even know who we are how can we take anything you do or say seriously?"

"I don't like playing games. I'm not very good at losing. I have a tendency to lash out," said Nightnurse coldly.

It had had no effect on Henry but clearly Lord Ecin felt intimidated enough to please their dangerous intruder. "I don't know a Raven but

I do know a Lord that's always doodling them whenever he can. Do you think it might be him?"

"No Ian," admonished Henry, "you don't play the game like that! You don't say anything unless you really have to!"

Seeming quicker than a wingbeat Nightnurse slashed at the chair putting a six inch rip in the leather no more than two inches from the side of Henry's face.

"Impressive," said Henry carefully. "I can see you're very good."

"Please don't hurt my brother!" begged Lord Ecin.

"Brother?" laughed Henry. "Don't try to save your own skin by pretending we're related!" He looked at Nightnurse. "I've never seen this man before in my life! He's the new neighbour whose come round to borrow a few gardeners. That's all! If I think my life depends on it I'm not going to lie to you."

Nightnurse held up his hand for silence. This was proving to be the interesting conundrum he had hoped for. He had the time. He could play a little longer before they got down to business. He swung his sword to within a few inches of Henry's throat.

"Who is that?" he asked nodding very dangerously towards a visibly shaking Lord Ecin.

"I told you. The new neighbour. His name's Ian. He wants to borrow a few gardeners," said Henry clearly.

Nightnurse knew he was lying albeit very well. He swung his sword to within a few inches of Lord Ecin's throat. "Who are you?" he asked.

Lord Ecin looked desperately at his brother who was trying to shake his head without being seen to be doing so.

"My name is Ian. I am his new neighbour!" said Lord Ecin desperately lying. He shut his eyes.

"I told you!" said Henry. "Now what is it you want? And if you know what's good for you you'll be quick about it! My butler's due here at any minute with some guns!"

Nightnurse was disappointed. He admired Henry's gameplay so far but to make up such an outrageous lie seemed amateurish.

"Why would your butler be coming here with guns?" he asked.

"I like to fire a few off about this time. Look around. This study is peppered with holes from gunshot," said Henry.

It was true. There were holes in all the bookcases, in the floor, in the walls, there wasn't a picture in the room that still had a face on it.

"Your butler is not coming this evening. So whether he normally does with guns or not is irrelevant," said Nightnurse smiling coldly.

"It'll be your look out when he arrives," said Henry.

"He's not coming because I let it be known there is a mare trapped down a well a few miles off. All of your staff including your butler are on their way there now," said Nightnurse.

For the first time a flicker of doubt passed across Henry's face. "Why would you think such a thing would work? My staff are sneaking back this very second."

"No they're not. I saw how they reacted to George's death. Making them leave was as easy as kicking over a bucket," said Nightnurse watching Henry closely.

Henry's mouth fell open in profound shock. All pretence at playing any games leaving him. "George is dead?" he stammered. "The best shirehorse the estate ever had. This is dreadful!"

Nightnurse was intrigued to see so sudden a capitulation.

"Who is that?" he asked.

Henry's eyes were filling with tears the rims of his eyes turning red. "That is my brother Ian. And you should be more respectful for he is Lord Ecin." He barely had the strength to utter the words.

"Which one of you is Raven?" asked Nightnurse.

Henry's head fell into his chest. "Niether of us. Ian told you the truth although he didn't know it. Lord Tig prats around with all that kind of stuff."

With such a broken man Nightnurse realised he had the opportunity to find out an awful lot. "What happened about the man's after shave? Why was it cancelled?"

Henry looked up a man wracked with grief. "How did he die?"

"Heart attack probably," replied Nightnurse.

"There's some justice then. It would have been quick." Henry seemed to rally a little. "If I tell you you've got to promise me you won't harm my brother." He looked painfully across to Lord Ecin. "He was never involved in any of it. You promise me you'll let him go unharmed then I'll tell you anything you want."

Lord Ecin felt himself filling up. At such a time his brother's concern was for his safety.

"I make no promises but I see no reason for him to die," said Nightnurse.

"Fair enough," said Henry. He brought his hand up biting on his knuckles then dropped it pathetically. "With George gone our silly games are like petals on the breeze." He breathed out heavily. "What do you want to know?"

"Who decided to pull out?" asked Nightnurse.

"All of us. It was a unanimous decision – honestly."

"Why did you halt it?" asked Nightnurse.

"Several things. The man behind it turned out to be a crazy French doctor. Crow had exceeded her remit."

"What do you know about Crow?" demanded Nightnurse.

"He's really a very attractive woman. We all pretend she's a man but I think all of us have had a nibble since we began. But she's gone a little crazy so it seems. It is Crow who sent you isn't it?"

Nightnurse remained motionless.

Henry's eyes wet and red fixed Nightnurse. "I wouldn't get involved with her or any of it. There's something you don't know."

"Go on," said Nightnurse unmoved.

"Colonel Peru doesn't want to pull the plug. Keeping it secret from us he has already developed a lotion he calls "Toss Off". He wants to push ahead with a man's scent. But he'll make it a dirty business. The man's a blood thirsty brute. For years he's been making shedloads having men dressed as bears mauled to death by dogs for pity's sake! God knows how many dogs have died doing it!"

Henry had to stop at such a dreadful thing to utter. Then he composed himself. "Me and my investors aren't in to all that. Crow went too far with the bookkeepers we know. But whilst the sex was so good none of us wanted it to stop."

"Enough!" ordered Nightnurse.

"I'm sorry Ian," said Henry into his lap, "that you have to see your brother like this."

Lord Ecin shook his head. "You've done nothing wrong my brother. I know what Colonel Peru is like. He's a monster. He shot my butler in the bum!" He smacked his hands into his lap making the handcuffs jangle. "Don't you criminal masterminds always have something up your sleeve? Haven't you got some lever or button you can push to be rid of this intruder?"

"That's just it Ian. I'm not a criminal mastermind. I like to make money. It's strange people like Crow who take something exciting and make it dangerous. I don't understand it. I really don't. And without George what's the bloody point in it all anyway?" Henry's head fell into his chest again.

Lord Ecin looked intently at Nightnurse. "He can pay you. Whatever you expect this Crow will give you he can give you ten times that! That would be right wouldn't it Henry?"

Henry slowly raised his head. "I don't know how much he expects to make. I may have enough here."

"Let's keep this simple – You tell me where you keep the golden nugget and I'll decide if it's enough to let you live," said Nightnurse.

"Damn pillowtalk!" cursed Henry.

Nightnurse angrily bent down to him grabbing his collar. "Just tell me where the safe is mate!"

"Don't you want to see what that is first?" asked Lord Ecin raising his hands towards the window. "I think there's something trying to get in."

Nightnurse let go of Henry going over to the window. There was a magpie outside tapping on the glass. There would be no point in letting it in. He didn't know the magpie codes. Crow knew that which meant it was a magpie for the target. It could stay outside. The magpie wasn't important. He moved away from the window much to the magpie's annoyance.

Then there was a knock on the door. The voice of Resourceful muted and inaudible said something from the other side.

"So you were lying!" said Henry accusingly.

"I was not!" retorted Nightnurse. "That isn't your butler! I'll bloody show you looking at me like that!"

He bounded over to the door flinging it open for all to see. Resourceful looking a little shocked stood there holding a tray of guns.

"May I come in?" he asked Nightnurse politely.

Nightnurse nodded stepping aside to allow him in.

"I'm sorry to bother you my Lordship but I was asked to carry out a task on behalf of your brother's butler. All the staff had to leave on an urgent endeavour..."

At this point Nightnurse made himself visible to Henry from behind Resourceful. He was too mature to say anything but he'd made his point.

"...I can see now that my presence with these items might be fortuitous. I can see you are both incapacitated but would you like me to take a pot shot at this ruffian with one of these guns?"

Lord Ecin threw his hands up in alarm as best he could with them being handcuffed. "No! No! Don't do anything to danger yourself! Stand over there in the corner and just wait."

"Very good my Lordship," said Resourceful doing what he was told.

Nightnurse went over to him looking intently into his face. He glanced at the guns then back at Resourceful. "I see a rare intelligence in your eyes. Use it and don't do anything stupid," he warned.

Resourceful nodded in deference.

"Now where is the safe?" demanded Nightnurse walking into the centre of the room.

"Behind the Rembrandt over there," replied Henry secretly looking longingly at the tray of guns.

"I'm not really an art lover. Which one is the Rembrandt?" asked Nightnurse looking at the paintings around them.

"Over in the corner. The one with the man's face missing," said Henry pointing in the corner.

"Henry. They've all got their faces missing!" said Lord Ecin looking around the room.

"Shut up!" said Nightnurse.

"Pardon?" asked Lord Ecin. "I can't hear you with all that racket from the window."

Outside the magpie had decided it was going to be ignored no longer and was making a dreadful noise on the glass.

"I said shut up," said Nightnurse pulling on the edge of the painting so it hung away from the wall at ninety degrees. Behind it set into the wall was a metal safe door with a round wooden knob and a brass handle.

"What do I do?" Nightnurse asked.

"That noise is awful!" shouted Henry. "You've got to shut that up first! Isn't that bothering you?"

Nightnurse didn't think the noise was that bad but he was eager to have that golden nugget in his hands. The other gems made into rings for his lover's fingers. He readied his sword going over to the window. As he lifted the window he struck with is blade. But the magpie had cleverly waited a split second so he missed.

It fluttered into the room alighting on the top of a tall bookcase surveying the situation. An intelligent man bound in a chair. A good man sitting in handcuffs. An old man (he no longer recognised his old tutor) holding a tray of guns. And the person in charge - clearly extremely dangerous - reaching for a dagger. It seemed very odd to the magpie but these were people and they were odd. He hoped the silly amount of money he'd taken for this job was worth it because he sensed a powderkeg in there. He readied himself to move when the man let loose the dagger. The man was quick! He hadn't been hurt but the dagger now embedded in the wall had clipped his wing.

"Don't kill it! What's he ever done to you?" thundered Henry his passion returning.

The magpie's unwanted intrusion had annoyed Nightnurse. The target's dumb defence of it annoying him further. Something needed to die quickly. He bounded across the room snatching up a pistol from the tray pointing it at the bird. But just before he pulled the trigger when it was too late for him to re-aim the magpie had fluttered across to the table.

The loud bang of the gun made Lord Ecin and Resourceful recoil but not the other two.

Henry desperately shook in his chair trying to get out. "Leave the bloody thing alone!" he ordered.

Nightnurse flew across the room slamming the window and the bird's escape route shut.

"Calm down or I will kill the bird! Sooner or later it will die if you don't behave!" he said.

Henry stopped.

Nightnurse slinked over to the safe. "How do I open it?" he asked not looking away from it.

Henry looked to see the whereabouts of the magpie. It should be fine if it stayed where it was. "You pull on the wooden knob. It will come out about six inches," he said beginning to rock his chair. It looked like he was trying to turn his chair to get a better look at what Nightnurse was doing.

"Done that. What's that ticking?" asked Nightnurse taking a wary step back.

"Nothing to be alarmed about. It's the timer. You have a minute to turn the handle. If you don't turn the handle within that minute then you have to wait an hour before you can try again. It's a clever safe put in by a chap from Birmingham."

Nightnurse stepped back to the safe reaching out for the handle. He turned it but nothing happened.

Then everything happened at once!

Henry rocked his chair enough to tip it over sideways. As it went he shouted out, "Get down Ian!"

Lord Ecin threw himself to the floor.

Resourceful collapsed in an old creaky way with guns spilling off the tray with most of them going off.

The magpie shot up into the air from the table.

Nightnurse began jumping back from the safe.

But no man can move quicker than explosive. He might have time to jump out of the blast area if he's far enough away but not move quicker. It's impossible. Turning that brass handle was the last thing

Nightnurse ever did. His exact fate hidden in a great cloud of black and fiery smoke.

# CHAPTER 34

## Better late than never

There was a terrific ringing in Lord Ecin's ears. Above that the sound of an animal in distress. He opened his eyes but the acrid smoke burned them shut again. Then he heard his brother shouting.

"Ian? Ian? Are you alright?"

"Yes! I think so!" replied Lord Ecin coughing. "Resourceful are you alright?"

"I am here my Lordship," said a familiar voice. "Though I fear this smoke will be the death of us if I can't get rid of it soon."

Above the ringing he heard Resourceful stumbling about in the smoke. Then the sound of his brother alternately laughing and coughing.

"What are you laughing at? Your study's ruined!" asked Lord Ecin between coughs.

"It was the opposite of what I told him. You have to wait until the ticking stops!" replied Henry triumphantly. Then he began to bring up the world's biggest docker's oyster.

When he had finished Lord Ecin asked, "Why do they call it a safe? They don't seem very safe to me!"

"Stop it Ian! I can't afford to laugh again!" said Henry happily.

"Don't worry. Resourceful will soon have this smoke cleared for us."

"Don't get up stay underneath it," said Henry paternally.

He had barely finished saying it when they heard the scratchy sound of the window being opened. The smoke eagerly getting out of the room through it.

"Your butler really is very good," said Henry.

"He's the best," replied Lord Ecin.

"I'm afraid it wasn't me," replied Resourceful from the other side of the room. "I do believe I went in completely the wrong direction. I do apologise."

"Somebody's opened it!" coughed Lord Ecin.

Sitting underneath the window with grey smoke billowing out of it like a chimney Chisel and Hammer waited.

"I think there's someone still alive in there," said Chisel. "When I opened it I could hear voices."

"Just wait a bit longer until the smoke clears then we'll see what is what," replied Hammer.

The rate of smoke coming out of the window dramatically accelerated. Inside Resourceful had found the study door. The through draught's effect when he opened it had been quite amazing to watch.

With the last of the smoke leaving Hammer stood up to take a look inside. What he saw was like a punch to the stomach. In front of a great hole in the wall were lying a pair of legs wearing Nightnurse's boots. Where Nightnurse should have been was a great red and black gooey mess.

"Oh dear Chisel. What have you done?" he said rolling away from the window. "I know why I recognise this house now."

Chisel took a look inside but didn't roll away he just stared. "I don't know what to say. I mean it's worked a treat. But one of me safes has killed Nightnurse."

The magpie with a wing, a leg and half its beak missing struggled onto the windowsill with its last breath. Chisel gently picked it up feeling in his hands the life leave it. He held it out to Hammer. "I killed the magpie too. Not easy to kill a magpie." He wasn't pleased but shocked at his power.

"Look there's a note attached!" said Hammer.

Chisel placed the magpie on the windowsill gently removing the note. He smoothed it out.

"Oh the irony. The irony," whispered Chisel.

"What's it say?" asked Hammer.

"Make him open the safe. It's booby trapped! Love Crow Kiss" said Chisel slowly.

"Plato?" asked an old man's voice.

They both turned to the smoke damaged old man standing at the window looking down at the magpie. The magpie that had saved his life.

"What did you call it?" asked Chisel.

"His name's Plato. I trained him. I'm responsible for this. It was him pecking at my knees that saved me. He did that for me. But what have I done to him? Googlebum!"

Hammer suddenly looked at the smoke damaged old man intently. "What did you just say? Did you just say Googlebum?"

Resourceful looked up from Plato. "It means a lot of bad I'm afraid."

"I know what it means! My dad used to say it all the time. But I've never heard it since!" Hammer grabbed Resourceful's wrists as he leant on the windowsill. "Who are you?"

Resourceful didn't resist but looked intently back at Hammer. Chisel began to wonder how long two strangers could remain so without saying or doing anything. Finally Resourceful his voice thick with emotion spoke. "Is that you Little Hammer?"

"Dad?" stammered Hammer.

"His dad is dead! Stop messing with his mind! What are you a sick wizard?" said Chisel pulling on one of Hammer's arms. "Come away Hammer!"

They both turned to look at him and then Chisel saw. The eyes, the shape of their chins, the same ears that looked like onion rings. They could be related! But how?

He released his grip. "He watched you die on your deathbed!"

Resourceful gravely shook his head turning to Hammer. "I faked it to get away."

"Call yourself a father doing that!" spat Chisel.

Resourceful couldn't look at either of them. He looked at Plato instead. "We were young. We didn't know what we were doing. But when everyone knows your wife as the village taxi it's time to move on. I'm so sorry Little Hammer. I think I've tried so hard all these years to put that mistake right. I shouldn't have lied. I shouldn't have left you. I don't know what else to say."

Hammer slowly brought his hands away walking off a little.

"I'm glad I didn't have a dad rather than wun like you!" said Chisel.

It visibly wounded Resourceful. He began to teeter at the window.

Chisel wished he could take it back. "Sorry. But that's my friend over there," he mumbled.

"He's my son," whispered Resourceful, "and I didn't watch him grow up. What a fool I've been." He disappeared from the window.

Chisel wasn't sure if he'd feinted or what? He had a look inside to see Hammer's dad disappearing out of the study doorway. "Yeah not for the first time!" he shouted after him. Then he noticed a man in handcuffs struggling to untie another man from a chair. He glanced back at Hammer. He didn't know what to do with him but he could help the two gentlemen. He brushed Plato out the way and climbed in. Once inside he took out a sharp knife from his apron.

"What are you going to do?" asked a worried Lord Ecin.

"I'm going to cut through that rope for you," replied Chisel.

"My God it's you!" said Henry. "The chap who put the safe in. Have you seen how well it worked?"

Chisel took an uncomfortable glance at the gooey mess as he cut at the ropes.

"I'll be needing another one of course. And you Ian. You'll have a couple. Now we know they work so well with all the people I know there's a couple of year's work for you I should think."

Chisel looked at Lord Ecin. "Would you like to wear those permanently or shall I get them off for you?"

"Don't tell me you have a key for them! I thought the key had disappeared with him."

Chisel respected how the man had been unable to look at the gooey mess. Unlike the other one who was now positively poking at it.

Chisel took out a little bit of wire. "You don't need a key for ones like those. If you sneezed hard enough those would fall off. I don't know where he got them from but they're not from Birmingham." The handcuffs had fell away before he'd finished talking.

"That's very clever of you!" said Lord Ecin.

"Practical rather than clever I'd say," said Chisel looking around at the fantastic amount of mess his exploding safe had caused. Even the pictures that were still hanging had all their faces missing.

"Do you think my butler's son would like to come live with us? We've had quite a few new arrivals recently so it wouldn't be a problem," asked Lord Ecin in his friendly way.

"You heard then?" asked Chisel.

"Most of it not all of it. Quite a shock for both of them I should think."

"He's not interested in all that!" said Henry joining them. "I know talent when I see it! Have you thought about taking on a partner? One who can provide all the contacts and capital for expansion?"

"I already have a partner," said Chisel gently removing Henry's hand from where he'd placed it on his shoulder.

"It's been a long day. A lot's happened I can see that. We'll talk about it tomorrow. But you can put all this behind you. The double dealing and the deaths. I bet you like making things. That's what you really enjoy! Just think about the two of us or the three of us starting a firm making exploding safes! And nobody gets hurt who doesn't deserve it. What do you say? Go outside to talk it over with your partner!" said Henry bouncing with excited anticipation.

"He's still there?" asked Chisel.

"He's outside with my brother's butler. I just saw them through the window."

"Do you think now's an appropriate time Henry?" asked Lord Ecin.

"Of course it is! You don't move forward by standing still!" exalted Henry.

Chisel nodded seeing the sense of it. He started heading for the window then changed his mind heading for the study door. He would go the way Resourceful went to give them a little more time together alone. He might even decide to get a little lost on the way. He thought of Plato lying dead on the windowsill before he'd brushed him out of the way. He didn't want to end up like that. Life would be simpler if he just did things the best he could. Let all the others play the silly games.

# CHAPTER 35

## Whatever trouble there is will eventually blow over

As they drew closer to the mill Sam let Colin go on a little. They were there to buy horses and what Sam knew about horses you could write on the back of a stamp so it made sense for Colin to do the talking. But something was happening as he walked closer to the mill. It had been quite an emotional ride he had had that day already. It didn't appear to be over. Although he had never been to this place before he had a very strong sense of already knowing it. There was more. He felt almost as though he had gossamer wings like a fairy. They lifted him gently up above the level we normally know. He could see himself flitting delicately across a brook playing with the stones in its bed peeling back an otherwise white linen of silence. English hedgerows abounded no more than smoke in the mist. The trees like charcoal stitching to an enormous patchwork quilt laid over the bed of the land. Gentle with his breathing in case he clumsily blew it all away he slowly inhaled. The smell of rich dark earth filling his nostrils in a symphony of cyclic chaos laid bare. An understanding permeating through his skin and into his very bones – he was just a little bit of grit in some great cosmic mortar. Feeling at once so very small and yet strangely so very relevant. Knowing there would be a day when a great circle would be complete to bring rest for everyone and everything. Then poof! The little bit of strange reality he had just experienced was gone.

"Are you alright Sam?" asked Colin. "You looked very strange there for a moment."

"I felt very strange," replied Sam smiling weakly. "I'm not drinking again!"

"Ah we all say that! But you will." Colin looked up at the mill. They were standing at the front door. "Feels very "cosy" here. Do you get that feeling Sam?"

Sam wasn't about to attempt to explain what he had just felt but it was more than "cosy". He "knew" they'd be wasting their time knocking on this door. There was another one possibly green out of sight to the right. That was the door the miller used and would answer. He couldn't tell Colin this because it didn't make sense how he knew. He would either be right and frighten Colin or be wrong and look a bit of a prat.

"It's a very nice spot," he replied.

Colin knocked on the door. No-one answered. After a polite time he knocked again. Still no-one answered it.

"Shall we try around the side?" suggested Sam.

Colin nodded. The two of them began walking around to the side. The great vanes of the windmill were not moving above their heads. But still as Sam passed directly underneath one he looked up in awe.

He heard Colin say, "There's another likely looking door there."

"What colour is it?" asked Sam still looking up at the vane.

"Green. Why is it important?" asked Colin stopping.

Sam looked at him smiling. "I think it's going to be lucky."

They walked over to the door both of them knocking on it.

"Alright Sam alright. Remember I'm going to do the talking," said Colin.

Sam quickly sneaked in another knock making Colin smile.

They were both still smiling when the miller answered the door. He didn't look like his picture on the map. He was about fifty with thick white hair. A pair of spectacles stuck out of a top pocket of some kind of full length apron. Sam had not seen such a type of apron before. But he could see himself wearing one. The miller had very dark blue eyes and an obvious jovial demeanour. He immediately mirrored their smiles with an even bigger one.

"Good day gentlemen! My name is Burt. As I don't get any visitors. And you're not a customer. Can I assume you've come about the horse?" He sounded much better educated than Sam was expecting.

"Yes indeed sir," said Colin. "But did you say horse? We were told you had two."

"I'm sorry the other one went last week. News doesn't travel very fast in these parts," apologised Burt.

Colin turned to Sam. "One's not enough. We need two."

"There is Turnip Ted," suggested Burt. "He always has plenty of horses. But if he thinks you need them quickly he will charge you an arm and a leg."

"How far away is he?" asked Colin.

"If you're on foot you wouldn't get there before nightfall. That's if you didn't get lost - which people have a tendency to do in these parts. To be honest that's why I like it. If you don't want to be bothered you don't tend to be bothered."

"We're sorry for the intrusion," said Colin thinking about what to do.

"I didn't mean it like that of course! I can hardly expect to sell a horse without people being able to see it. Come on in fellas. You can have a drink whilst you decide what you want to do." Burt fully opened the door.

"Oh no thank you," said Sam. "I had enough to drink last night." Then he caught sight of what was behind Burt. The only way he would be able to describe it later was it was like what a peasant must have felt walking into a cathedral for the first time. It had been a barn of some sort but it had been converted into a workshop full of the most wonderful looking things.

"I can see you are a man who can appreciate what I'm trying to do here. Come in let me show you around," said Burt beckoning him in.

Sam stepped in and just "knew" he would be a part of this somehow. His father had told him when he began looking for his first house that you could look at many of them and be very logical in weighing up the pros and cons of each but he could guarantee it would come down to stepping into a place and just knowing that was the one. It was exactly the same feeling. For such a logical precise man as Sam it didn't make sense but there it was.

"Do all millers have such a place on the side of their mill?" he asked open mouthed looking at the benches and gadgets and bottles and tools and gears and beautifully fashioned things surrounding him.

Burt laughed warmly. "I'm not really a miller. But you need to earn a crust." He waited for Sam to laugh but he had missed the pun. Burt didn't mind he could see Sam was enthralled. "I'm more of an engineer."

"An engineer?" repeated Sam vaguely aware of the term.

"You see this is the trouble. Everyone's heard of a doctor or a lawyer or a merchant but not an engineer. And you should because being an engineer takes just as much brains." Burt clearly wasn't bitter or angry about the fact merely passing on his assessment. "It's Chaucer's fault."

"Chaucer?" asked Sam. "Canterbury tales and all that?"

"The very same," said Burt. "On the continent he had seen this new type of person respected and admired called ingenieurs because they were considered ingenious people. But when he came back he spelt the word with an "e" and the link with being ingenious was lost. Shame but it doesn't stop us."

"Stop you doing what?" asked Sam.

"Making the world a better place to live in!" said Burt very enthusiastically.

"The world's a big place," said Sam.

"That's what makes it so exciting! There is literally a world full of opportunities." Burt picked something off a bench handing it to Sam. "Whether it's a hairbrush that won't lose its bristles or a dam across a river to stop people getting flooded in the valley below. And absolutely anything in between you can think of! And it's all real! You can see what you've done! I love it!"

Colin had been watching the two of them from the doorway. He liked Burt. Passion was what made us human and not like the plants and animals. But they needed to find some horses. It wasn't ideal but one was probably better than none to begin with. He coughed loudly. "Burt may I take a look at your horse?"

Burt quickly came over picking up a bucket and handing it to him. "She's in the paddock out the back. Give that a shake and she'll soon come over."

Colin looked in the bucket. "What's this?"

"I call them pellets." He was clearly going to explain what they were when Sam shouted, "Burt you must tell me what this does!"

"Excuse me," said Burt eagerly hurrying over to Sam.

Colin left to find the horse. When he returned he'd probably been gone forty minutes or so. In that time the course of Sam's life had been changed forever. When Colin reappeared in the doorway Sam hurried over to him.

"I'm staying here with Burt. I'm going to ask Natalie if she wants to stay too. But of course it is up to her what she does. This is it Colin! This is what I want to do with my life!"

Colin was naturally taken aback at such startling news. Then he found his voice. "What about our problem? Do you think you'd be safe?"

"You saw how hard it was for us to find it! Burt says that's always the way. I've explained a bit of it and Burt says these people are like fat cats - if they don't get the mouse straightaway they can't be bothered to chase it."

"But what will you actually do here?" asked Colin. "Day to day?"

"Burt says engineering is lots of ideas and lots of numbers. I'm good with numbers Colin! I think we'd make a good team! It just seems so much more worthwhile than pushing bits of paper around!"

"You don't think you're still hungover?" asked Colin.

"I could be. But I don't think so." Sam put his arm around Colin's shoulder leading him outside so they could talk privately.

"I was a bit of flotsam washed up that you saved. Then we ran along the shore together. I will always be grateful for that. But I think I'll be more grateful that you brought us here." Sam looked up at the mill. "It's beautiful isn't it? I want to be a man like Burt that can make things like this happen."

"I'm pleased for you Sam," said Colin. "A bit worried for you too as well. But I am not your keeper. I couldn't stop you anyway. I only want to be sure you're doing the right thing."

"I've never been more sure of anything in my life! And it feels wonderful!" Sam made fists of his hands and shook them.

"But what about Natalie?" asked Colin.

Sam turned to him looking very fatherly. "I can see things today. I don't know why but I can. So I'll tell you I can see a future for you and Natalie here - at first. After that I can't see. But Burt has a small cottage he says the two of you could have. Natalie carries on working for me but helping us with numbers not skivvying. You could work for us too. We might all even be partners. Who knows? We might even make enough money for you to become the doctor you always wanted to be. Three bits of flotsam washed up on this shore to make good."

"Natalie's not interested in me like that. I don't believe she's interested in anyone like that," said Colin saying something he hoped wasn't true.

Sam put his hand on Colin's shoulder. "Take Burt's horse and find out. Go and fetch her now. Find out if this new shore we've found is one you want to explore together. If either of you don't then you're free to go with my blessings. But I think you might be pleasantly surprised."

"Put it like that Sam then I've got nothing to lose." Colin hugged him.

They released each other. Sam watched him hurry off towards the paddock.

"You know it's a new world every day for those brave enough to grasp it!" Sam shouted after him.

# THE END

Printed in Poland
by Amazon Fulfillment
Poland Sp. z o.o., Wrocław